BADLANDS

GARY KRUSE

Copyright © 2025 GARY KRUSE
All rights reserved.
No part of this book may be reproduced, or stored in a retrieval system, or transmitted in any form or by any means, electronic, mechanical, photocopying, recording, or otherwise, without express written permission of the publisher.
No AI Training: Without in any way limiting the author's exclusive rights under copyright, any use of this publication to "train" generative artificial intelligence (AI) technologies to generate text is expressly prohibited. The author reserves all rights to license uses of this work for generative AI training and development of machine learning language models.
Disclaimer:
This is a work of fiction. Names, characters, places, businesses, events and incidents are either the products of the author's imagination or are used in a fictitious manner. Any resemblance to actual persons, living or dead, or to actual events is purely coincidental.

ISBN-13: 9798309931255

To Nicole

Part One

1

Limbs sore, eyes gritty and dry, Willow stumbled along the deserted country lane, her hair a wild mess of red dreadlocks, black fire tattoos up her arms, an ear-spacer the size of a two pence piece stretching her left earlobe.

Her heavy Doc Martens scuffed the cracked and pitted tarmac, and every step was quiet agony, the straps of her rucksack scraping and digging into the raw skin on her shoulders. Her clothes – a black vest top and grey cargo shorts – were rumpled and covered with the grime of three days travel. So close now. So close. A warm breeze stirred the trees and bushes that lined the lane. The July air was full of the song of blackbirds and sparrows, robins and starlings, punctuated now and then by the screams of gulls.

Ahead, a raven swooped from the slate roof of an old chapel. It landed in the heat-haze shimmering over the bitumen, next to the gory mess of road-kill that had once been a fox. Screeching, it began to peck at the bloodied lump. Feeling like road-kill herself, Willow shambled to a stop.

She dropped her shoulders and let the rucksack fall to

the floor. Breathing deep, she pressed her hands into her lower back and jammed her hips forward. The muscles down her spine pulled tight. She winced, released and breathed again, wrinkling her nose against the tang of stale sweat and body odour, fingers gently probing the red skin on her shoulders. Crouching, she dug a metal flask from the side pocket of the rucksack, swigged stale water from the bitter-tasting rim and almost gagged as she swallowed.

Along the road, the raven flapped as it circled the corpse looking for fresh meat. Willow tucked the water bottle back into the rucksack, watching the great bird. Sliding the straps of her vest top back up her shoulders, she stood, reached into the pockets of her cargo shorts, and pulled out her phone. The home screen showed Willow before the dreadlocks and tattoos, before the spacers.

Chubby faced. Frizzy brown hair. Arms draped across the shoulders of the two girls on either side of her. On her left, Zoe, defiantly unsmiling, Goth-ed up, looking like doom and misery. On her right, Ellie, bright-eyed, braces, white hoodie and black leggings and flat-soled trainers. Sadness swelled in Willow's chest as she peered at the two girls in the picture. Both were dear to her, both estranged from her, one permanently, the other...

With a sigh, Willow unlocked the phone, checked the last text she'd received, the one that had sent her running home. There were no new messages from the anonymous sender. The calls she'd made to the number remained stubbornly unreturned.

Hearing the distant drone of an engine, Willow glanced up. The country lane ran straight for half a mile, and a

70s style VW camper-van in white and beige trundled towards her. Pocketing the phone, grabbing the rucksack by its top strap to spare her sore shoulders, Willow stood and jammed out her thumb. A longboard rattled on the top of the van. Shafts of sunlight sparkled on the windscreen.

Behind her, the raven screeched and flew across the chapel, over the long-abandoned graveyard towards the engine house of the old mine in the distance. Willow stepped back into the verge.

The van kept coming, no sign of slowing. Resigning herself to having to complete the journey on foot, she lowered her thumb, and went to turn away.

The van squealed to a halt, the longboard straining against the straps. The rear of the van lifted slightly, then settled on the clunky suspension. The driver, a young guy in wayfarers with a floppy black fringe, leaned over and wound down the passenger window. The smell of dope wafted out.

"Where are you heading sister?" He grinned, his teeth impossibly white.

"Aggie," she said.

He nodded, unlocked the door and pushed it open with his fingertips. "Hop in."

*

"You came running back from the other side of the world cos of one lousy message?"

The driver's name was Max. He was hunched over the steering wheel. He flicked a sidelong glance in Willow's direction. Outside, hedges flashed past, the air hissed and growled as it whipped by the open window. A blunt smouldered between the fingers of his right hand.

"It's not just a lousy message," Willow said. "It means more than that."

"It's a long way to come on a whim."

"It's not a whim. It means Ellie's in trouble."

"But you don't know what sort of trouble?"

"Well, no..."

"So surely there's easier ways of finding out."

"She's not answering her phone," Willow said. "Or replying to my messages."

She'd tried both the mystery number that had sent the text and the old number she had for Ellie but had got nowhere with either.

"She must have mates you can call. A boyfriend?"

Willow shook her head. Zoe would've known where Ellie was, the ghost of grief whispered. She blinked it away and reached into the side pocket of her rucksack. She pulled out a thick, loose hairband, gathered her dreadlocks behind her neck, and tied them back. Max braked, and the van slowed as they approached a sharp bend in the lane.

"I told you. We've been out of touch. I don't know her mates anymore, or if she's even got a boyfriend."

The van lurched as they turned.

"What about your parents?"

She rubbed the spacer in her ear. "What about them?"

"Have you spoken to them? I mean, they'll know if something is up." Max nudged the accelerator and the van lurched forward. The country lane gave way and opened to fields on one side and the first houses of St. Agnes on the other.

"No. I haven't."

"You think it may have been an idea to call them before you made a mad dash halfway across the world?"

"Can't."

Max blinked at her. "Can't?"

"I don't have their numbers anymore."

"What did you do, lose them or something?"

"Deleted them."

"Why'd you do that?"

Willow sighed and leant forward, jabbing the radio on. "You always this nosy Max?"

"Just curious is all." He shrugged and looked ahead.

An awkward silence stretched between them. Max dragged on the blunt and exhaled towards the open window, but the rush of air wafted the smoke back in. The van slowed to let a passing car through, then trundled forward. Ahead, the road dipped towards a roundabout.

"Look, I'm sorry yeah?" Willow said after the silence became unbearable.

Max half-turned and jerked a shoulder.

"I'm being an ungrateful cow."

"Yeah, you got that right." He half-smiled, and she smiled back.

She picked at a thumbnail and looked down at her lap. Max checked the mirrors and braked as they approached the roundabout.

"I don't like talking about it," she said.

"It?" Max extended the blunt to Willow. She took it with a smile of thanks, inhaled deep, relishing the scratch of smoke on the back of her throat and the herbal kick that came with it. She exhaled, and passed the blunt back.

"My past," she said. "My family."

"No worries. And you're right, I guess. It's not my business."

He spun the steering wheel hard, turned down Quay Road. Max negotiated the van through the oncoming traffic and the pedestrians clogging up the narrow lane. Tall trees cast long shadows across the tarmac. The side of the valley made an impenetrable wall to their right. Willow swallowed hard against the sudden rush of memories. Some came with the warmth of nostalgia. Others however… Maybe it was the memories, or the fact that Max didn't know her. Or maybe it was the dope loosening her tongue. Either way, Willow had a sudden urge to confess. "I did things," she said.

"Things?"

"I hurt people. I hurt Ellie."

"You mean physically?"

Willow shook her head. "The last time we spoke I told Ellie she was dead to me."

"Fuck."

"Yeah."

"When was that?"

"Three years ago."

"Three years!"

Willow nodded. "Yep."

"Damn."

"She was pregnant," Willow went on, peering out of the passenger window. A pack of surfers trudged past, wetsuits half unzipped, hair dripping seawater down their back, high on stoke, laughing amongst themselves. "The dad was my ex."

"Shit," Max said. He sucked on the joint, then handed

it to her. "You got any idea where she is now?"

She took it, dragged hard to kill the pain twisting inside her. Breathing out smoke, Willow shook her head. "No. All I've got is a couple of numbers." She passed the blunt back. "And my ex."

The thought of contacting Harrison made her stomach flip.

"Where you gonna stay?"

"I'm hoping they'll have a room at the Spars," she said.

Max nodded. "And if not?"

"Guess I'm bedding down in a shop doorway." She scrunched her nose up. "Wouldn't be the first time."

As they got closer to Trevaunance Cove, the valley opened up. Houses sat at its foot or nestled on its sides. They reached a complex of art studios, and Max turned into a gravel car park. As he braked, Willow lurched forward, seatbelt straining to hold her, then slumped back.

"Well, sister," Max said, sniffing and leaning on the wheel. "You're home."

He'd parked so they were overlooking the cove. The setting sun was lost behind the hills to her left, but it cast a warm yellow glow over the coarse grass and purple-brown heather on the hill across the valley. Rugged granite cliffs plunged almost vertically down into a triangular slither of turquoise ocean. Nestled at the foot of the hill, the walls of the Driftwood Spars glowed white. Disco lights flashed within, and the throb of music drifted up the valley on a summer breeze that carried the rich, pollen perfume of summer flowers. Despite the lingering heat of the day, a shudder ran through her body.

"Thanks for the lift." She unbuckled her belt. "What

do I owe you?" Max waved her away.

"It's on me," he said. "I was coming this way anyways."

"You sure?"

He nodded. "Just hope you find her."

"Yeah." Willow gazed hard at the cove, her mouth a grim line against the pain and anguish surging within her. "So do I."

She hefted the rucksack onto her shoulders, wincing as the straps buffed the sore skin. Smiled at Max and for a second the apprehension lifted.

"Thanks again."

She slid back the door. It gave a metallic shriek as it scraped along its runner. Willow hopped down, her boots crunching on the gravel, and slid the door shut again.

"Stay safe, sister!"

With a wave, Max gunned the engine. Willow stepped back. He reversed, braked, then clunked the gears, and gave a final wave goodbye as he drove back towards the exit, the longboard on top jolting and straining at the straps as the van trundled over the divots and potholes, then turned onto Quay Road.

As it vanished from sight, Willow turned back to the cove, shifting the rucksack to try and ease the pain in her shoulders. A heavy weariness burned her muscles. All she wanted right then was a soft bed and hot shower.

She peered at the coast path that wound up the steep sides of the valley opposite. At the top of the rise, the path carried on across the cliff top, but she remembered the second path, hidden from view, the one that doubled back towards the centre of St. Agnes.

It was the one that led home. There would be a hot

shower there and a bed; a bed in the room she'd shared with Ellie. But there wouldn't be a warm welcome.

Maybe Ellie was there right now, safe and sound and chuckling at the little game she'd played on Willow.

Unlikely.

She'd check, of course, to make sure. But not right away. Only as a last resort if she didn't turn anything else up.

She'd risk speaking to Harrison first. Maybe he could point her in the right direction, if he didn't scream in her face and tell her to go to hell. With luck, she'd find Ellie and get out of here again before her father ever knew she'd returned.

2

Willow squeezed through the crowds gathered outside the Driftwood Spars. She ducked into the main bar. It had a low ceiling crossed with dark wooden beams and old ship wheels above a stone fireplace. Behind the bar, a petite barmaid with an untidy bob of bleached blonde hair buzzed between the till and the pumps, taking orders with a smile, a look, a raise of the eyebrows. Beside her, a tall, ruddy-faced man with wiry grey hair belly-laughed at a customer's joke as he pulled a pint of blood-red ale. He wore a rumpled white shirt that pulled tight over his swollen stomach, straining the buttons. The gold lights on the wall and the thick red carpets made the room feel cosy yet claustrophobic.

Willow slipped her rucksack off her back and carried it by the top handle as she weaved through the crowd towards the bar. Harsh laughter, booming voices, and the smell of sweat and alcohol swamped her. From the adjacent room, the thud of drums and rumble of bass pulsed through her stomach. A gap opened up at the bar and Willow slipped through.

She rested an elbow on the sticky wooden worktop.

The old guy next to her did a double-take as he took in her dreadlocks, the dark spacers in her earlobes and the fire tattoos up her forearms.

In the other room, the music subsided, and cheers and applause spilled through the door.

Movement in the corner of her vision snagged Willow's attention.

A rakish man leant against the rough stone wall next to the fireplace. He had hollow pits around his eyes and an untidy beard the colour of wet sand, a long thin nose, and shoulder-length dirty blonde hair. As he sipped his ale, he peered over the rim of the glass and his gaze met hers.

Her heart jolted, and the breath caught In her throat.

Willow spun away. She glared at the dark oak bar.

Why him? Why here?

She glanced back.

He was frowning now. He had one hand in the pocket of his skinny jeans, the other cradling the ale glass. He wore a loose-fitting grey-black t-shirt and a Celtic cross on a long leather thong that hung around his neck.

"Help you, love?"

Willow turned back, and her heart jolted again. Her cheeks flushed. The barmaid stood before her, wiping her hands on a red and white tea towel. She had ice blue eyes and a barbed wire tattoo on her right bicep. A thin nose ring pierced her left nostril. Her cheeks glowed like she'd caught the sun.

Willow swallowed, and tried to smile. "I'm looking for a room for a couple of nights."

The barmaid frowned, cocked an ear to one side, and leant closer as the music kicked up again in the next room. She wore a black apron over a baggy grey

Metallica shirt and denim shorts.

"Sorry, what was that?"

Willow stood on tiptoe to lean across the bar. She caught a whiff of the barmaid's rich floral perfume and the hint of sweat.

"I need a room for a couple of nights."

The barmaid nodded, smiled, then turned to the tall, ruddy-faced guy behind the bar. "Pete!" He glanced over. She pointed at Willow. "She wants a room."

Pete nodded, muttered to the old guys in front of him, then finished pouring the ale. He plonked the pint glass down on the bar, tugged at the hem of his shirt, and sauntered over, looking Willow up and down, his gaze narrowing. "You not booked?"

Willow shook her head.

"You might be out of luck." He scratched the back of his head. "High season. Might be full."

"I'll take anything you've got," Willow said.

Pete reached behind him, still peering at Willow. He grabbed a book, lay it on the bar, and opened it up. "You on your own?"

Willow nodded.

He ran a stubby, nicotine-stained finger across a grid, chewing his tongue, and glancing from Willow to the page and back again. Another movement away to her right caught Willow's attention, and she turned.

The tall lean guy had shifted to the other side of the doorway and cocked his head, still frowning as he sipped his ale. Behind him, another song finished, and hands rose in the air applauding as raucous voices whooped and hollered for more.

"You're in luck."

Willow turned to Pete.

"Room twelve is free. No-one in there until Friday night."

Two days. More than enough time to find Ellie, she hoped.

"How much?"

"Fifty a night. B & B."

"I'll take it," Willow said.

"It's not grand, mind."

"So long as it's got a bed and a shower, it can be a stable for all I care."

"Bit better than a stable." Pete chewed the end of the pencil. "What's the name?"

"Willow." She kept her gaze fixed on him.

"Surname?"

She swallowed and the lie slipped easily off her tongue. "Keating."

He leant forward and scribbled her name down in his book. "How you paying?"

"Cash."

Pete's mouth folded into itself. His frown deepened.

"First night upfront," he said. "The rest on departure."

Willow shrugged and reached into the front pocket of her rucksack. She pulled out a fifty-pound note from the wodge of cash she'd exchanged at Heathrow and handed it over. Pete slipped it between his fingers, peered hard at Willow, then raised it to the light. Happy it wasn't a fake, he folded it into his palm and then turned to the till.

"Ruby," he barked as he punched up the sale.

The barmaid turned from the pint she was pulling and frowned.

"When you're done, can you take the lady to Room 12

please?"

Ruby glanced at Pete, then at Willow, and then back to Pete. "Sure."

She raised the pump and smoothed the head off the bitter, then passed it across the bar. In the backroom, the music began again in a blast of drums and distorted guitars. Ruby took payment for the bitter, gave change, then reached around the back of the bar, and snatched down a key. She opened the flap at the end of the bar. Dusting her hands on the apron, she smiled at Willow.

"Follow me, babe," she said, and headed towards the door to the street. Willow turned to follow her. When she got to the door she risked a final glance back. The tall, lean guy was still watching her from the doorway. He was smiling now, like he'd figured out who she was.

She flushed and scurried after Ruby.

*

The girl hurried out onto the street, leaning forward under the weight of her bulging rucksack, and the Reverend Richard Goddard watched her go, a smile twitching at the corner of his mouth. Once she'd vanished outside, he unpeeled from the wall and snaked through the crowds, exchanging nods, smiles, grins with the locals. He reached the bar and slipped into a space, rested his elbows on the sticky varnished wood, and gazed at Pete's back until the barman turned and came over.

"Same again, Pete," Goddard said, raising his empty.

"Coming up, Rev," Pete replied, taking the empty glass and replacing it with a fresh one.

As he pulled the pump and the ale spat and hissed out of the tap, Goddard nodded towards the door. "That girl," he said.

Pete glanced up at him.

"Who was she?"

"Reckoned her name was Willow."

Goddard frowned. "Willow?"

Pete shrugged. "That's what she said."

"Just Willow?"

"Willow Keating." Pete pushed the pump back upright and straightened the glass. "Why's that?"

"Keating?" Goddard peered at him. "You're sure that's what she said?"

Pete nodded. "Willow Keating." He grabbed the book from the shelf by the till, opened it, and turned it to Goddard, who peered at Pete's deft, neat scrawl. The name had been written against Room 12, in the annexe across the street.

"Funny," Goddard said, stroking his beard.

"What's funny?" Pete put the glass in front of him and took the fiver Goddard held out.

"Thought I recognised her is all," Goddard said, taking his change. He raised his glass, flashed a smile at Pete, then slipped through the crowd towards the table by the fireplace. More smiles, more nods of recognition. The people parted easily for him. He grabbed his leather jacket from the back of a chair, shared a joke with the group of surfers gathered around the table, and crossed to the front door.

He stepped out into the pastel blue light of dusk. Laughter drifted from a group gathered around the bench to his left as moths harassed the lights on the pub walls.

He swigged his ale, and peered across the street, to the small brewery that made a range of drinks for the Spars and the gift shop that stood next to it. The lights were off in both. The annexe lay around the back of them. No sign of Ruby or the mysterious Willow.

A gull screeched overhead. Goddard turned and walked towards the beach, then cut left and skipped up a set of stone steps that led to an ornamental garden area. Wooden benches overlooked Trevaunance Cove and an iron anchor sat in a bed of bright red flowers. He crossed to stand in front of the benches, peering out across the darkening ocean. A bee buzzed past his face as he dug out his phone, thumbed through his contacts and hit dial. He raised the phone to his ear and the beer to his lips. The sea breeze whipped at his hair. He smelled salt and the acrid tang of seaweed. The call connected.

"We may have a problem," Goddard said.

"What kind of problem?"

"The wrong person showing up at the wrong time sort of problem."

"Oh?"

"Someone's just checked into the Spars." Goddard turned and gazed back towards the pub. As the night crept in and the trees and valley sides became thick shadows, the lamps on the walls blazed brighter.

"Who?"

"She signed her name Willow Keating?"

"So?"

"So…" He turned back to the sea and sipped his beer. "She was lying. Her name's not Willow Keating."

"What is it then?"

"It's Megan Rae," he said.

Silence on the other end. And then…
"Shit."

*

From the narrow lane that wound down to Trevellas Cove, the stone and wood hut looked abandoned. The windows of the lower floor had been boarded up. Weeds grew from the foundations of the brickwork. Dandelions sprouted in the cracks between the flagstones of the steps that ran up the south side of the building to a locked and bolted door on the upper floor. The only evidence that anyone used the place was the lack of weeds beneath the arched doorway in the centre of the lower storey, and the motorbike tyre tracks carving through years of accumulated dirt.

Inside the hut, on the top floor, an electric lamp hung by its wire from the main beam that ran the length of the building. The lamp flickered and buzzed and cast dancing shadows across the wooden boards and the brick walls. A thick mattress had been butted up against the front wall. The coverless white duvet had been thrown back, and there was a head-shaped indent on the lumpy pillow.

The slight girl with the burn-scarred face sat on the end of the mattress. She had a phone to her ear, her knees drawn up to her chest. She wore grey knickers and a vest top that had turned from white to yellow over the years.

Across from her a leather trench coat hung from a nail in the frame of the boarded and locked door that led to the steps outside. Heavy black biker boots sat in the corner next to a red and black helmet, and an open suitcase stuffed with ten, twenty and fifty-pound notes. A black scarf with a death's head motif had been folded up and placed on top of the black leather trousers and bikers jacket piled beside the mattress. A six-inch-long serrated blade with an ivory hilt lay on the floor.

The girl swore.

"Why's she here?"

"Well that's the question isn't it?" Goddard said. "And we need to know the answer."

"You think she knows?"

The girl rose from the bed and crossed to the small square window opposite. She peered out at an overgrown field that rose gently to the distant cliff edge. A nest of rabbits grazed amongst the long grass. The trees around the field had become rustling silhouettes against the dying light of the day.

"I doubt that it's a coincidence," Goddard went on.

"Where the hell has she been?"

"I don't know."

Neither spoke for a long minute.

"So what do we do?" she said.

"She's staying at the annexe in the Spars. Put someone on her."

"I should do it."

"Not yet. Get one of the Chosen to do it."

"They won't know her if they see her."

"She's hard to miss," Goddard said. "She's got a head of bright red dreadlocks now."

"Shut up." The girl chuckled and turned her back on the window. "You're telling me the frumpy bitch has got hip?"

"Looks like it. Suits her too."

"Maybe you could put some moves on her. I'm sure she'll spill all on your pillows."

"Doubt it. She didn't seem too pleased to see me."

"So what do you want the Chosen to do? Scare her off? Threaten her?"

"Just get them to follow for now. Report back where she goes, who she sees. No contact."

"Still think I should do it."

"Too risky. If she recognises you..."

"How will she recognise me? I don't exactly look like myself anymore." Pain flashed across the warped and melted flesh that covered the right side of her face.

"Trust me."

The girl snorted. "Never."

"Raven." Goddard said and sighed, using the name the girl had taken two years earlier, after the fire, after the girl she was had been burnt away. "I'm serious. It's better this way."

"If you say so."

"Is everything set for tonight?"

"Yeah, we're all good."

"Pete will have the boat ready for you after closing. They'll be coming past the Bawden Rocks around 1 a.m. Two packages."

"Two packages. Understood."

"And you know what to do about our talkative little friend?"

"Wouldn't call him little, but yeah, I know. You've told me enough times."

"It's unfortunate," Goddard said. "But necessary. He says too much."

"Don't worry." Raven bent down, picked up the blade,

and peered into the cold steel. "He won't be saying anything much longer."

3

"This is it." Ruby slipped the key in the small gold lock and turned it. The latch clicked, and the clean white door swung back. Willow dragged her gaze from the tattoos on the back of Ruby's thighs that said 'Sweet' and 'Heart' and followed her into room twelve. The vague scent of furniture polish and freshly laundered sheets lingered in the air. The heavy white linen on the single bed looked thick and soft and practically invited Willow to slump down and sleep. Ruby opened the door at the far end of the room.

"Bathroom's in here."

Willow nodded and dumped her rucksack on the floor. She kicked off her boots and sat on the edge of the bed. The mattress felt thick and solid. Dragging off her socks, she scrunched her toes into the long pile of the cream carpet. Ruby closed the bathroom door and held out the key. Willow took it, smiling. "Thanks."

"Pleasure." Ruby leant against the chest of drawers and folded her arms. "You need anything else?"

Willow shook her head. "I'm good."

"Okay, well, I'll leave you to it." Ruby nodded, smiled again, and crossed to the door.

"Breakfast starts from seven thirty, up in the main dining room."

"Where's that?"

"Up the stairs by the main bar. Pete will point you in the right direction." Ruby flashed her a final smile, then reached for the handle and opened the door.

"That guy," Willow said.

Ruby glanced back. "Which one?"

"The tall guy by the fireplace. In the main bar." Willow rubbed her ankles and gazed up at Ruby through her dreadlocks.

"They're all taller than me, babe," Ruby said.

Willow felt the corner of her lips twitch. "I mean Richard Goddard."

Ruby grinned, edged the door closed and leant against it. "So you know our good Reverend then?"

"Used to."

"Want me to put a word in for you?"

Willow smiled. "Once upon a time maybe. But not now…"

"If you're interested, I'd move quick. He's Aggie's most eligible bachelor. Plenty of girls around here would lay an egg to get their claws into him."

"And you?"

Ruby winked. "Too much between the legs for me."

Willow smiled. "Listen, if he asks about me, just tell him my name's Willow, and I'm an Aussie visiting an old friend."

"You don't sound like an Aussie."

"Just tell him."

"You got a problem with him?"

Willow shook her head. "No. But let's just say that

there's... history between us."

"So, you and him were..." She cocked an eyebrow.

"No! God, no."

Oh, she'd fantasised about it though. At night. In the bath. Daydreams on the beach watching him surf. A silly crush, a teenage infatuation driven by raging hormones.

"Nothing like that. I'd rather not have him prying around right now."

"What about me? Can I pry around?" Ruby hooked her tongue over her top lip and winked. A strand of frizzy blonde hair fell across her face.

Willow blushed and lowered her gaze. "I'm not here for a relationship."

"Who mentioned a relationship? I'm just talking about dirty hard sex."

Her cheeks burning harder. Willow laughed, a short sharp bark, part shock, part humour. She shook her head. "Are you always this forward?"

"Don't ask, you don't get." Ruby winked, reaching for the door handle. "I'll let you get some rest. See you later."

She slipped open the door and edged outside. Willow stood and crossed to the bathroom. The door clicked shut. She could hear Ruby singing to herself, her voice receding as she got further away. Willow switched on the bathroom light and put her hands on the sink. In the mirror, her face looked gaunt and ashen. She swore.

She'd changed her whole appearance since she ran, hidden behind the dreadlocks, the ear spacers, the tattoos but she couldn't change her face, and she felt sure that Goddard had seen right through her image. If he told her old man...

She shook her head. Too late to worry about that now.

She undressed, showered, then dried herself and returned to the bedroom, dug out a baggy white t-shirt and cotton pyjama shorts, tugged them on, then ducked into her bag again. She pulled out her phone charger and the British plug adapter she'd got at Heathrow. She plugged them into the socket by the bed, and connected the phone.

She reached into the bag a third time, and rustled around in the wash bag she'd hastily packed on her mad dash from the crummy apartment in Sydney. Her fingers closed over a thin silver chain. She pulled it out, straightened it, and held the pendant in her palm.

It read, 'Sisters.' It was one half of a pair. When Willow found Ellie, the pair would be complete again.

Outside, night had fallen properly now, and the only light through the window came from the streetlamp in the car park. Willow sat on the bed, flicked into the messages, and found the text again. Just three words long. No name. No greeting.

"It's so dark."

Willow felt certain that the message was from Ellie. She'd replied, but her responses remained unanswered. She couldn't even tell if they had been read. Every time she tried to call the number, she got the voicemail. When she tried Ellie's old number, she got the same. If it was Ellie, she wasn't in the mood to talk. But why send the text?

Heart flickering, Willow dialled Ellie's old number again. After a long moment, an electronic female voice replied. "Sorry. The number you are calling is currently unavailable. Please try again later."

Sighing, Willow cut the call and opened the anonymous text. She thumbed the green telephone icon in the corner of the screen, then sat twiddling the 'Sisters' pendant with her free hand, and listened to the electronic beeps at the other end of the line throbbing through the handset.

*

On a marble island worktop in the centre of a clean, gleaming kitchen, a phone began to vibrate. The noise echoed off of the American-style fridge freezer and the glossy white cabinets, against the glass sliding doors that opened onto the decking and the view to the ocean beyond. It rattled the spoons and spatulas, the salad tongs and the sharpening steel in the metal jug on the island unit. The house had an open plan design, and the kitchen overlooked the living area.

There, on the cream leather corner sofa, a woman with thick auburn hair, clammy pale skin, and mascara tear tracks spilling down her cheeks turned and looked towards the phone. She stared at it for a long moment.

Then she sighed, huffed from the seat, and padded barefoot into the kitchen. She wore tight stonewashed Gucci jeans and a plain white Armani t-shirt. As she walked, she dragged her hair back from her forehead. She had a scattering of freckles across her nose and walked in a cloud of Dior perfume. When she reached the work surface, she stared down at the phone and jammed a hand on her hip.

That number again. Another call. She reached for the phone. Her fingers hovered over it. Maybe she should answer. But what to say? She'd done her bit, sent the message as the girl had asked. Okay so, she hadn't done everything she'd been asked to, but she had her daughter to think about now. If she answered, she'd be getting involved, and she knew where getting involved ended. She couldn't put her daughter at that kind of risk. Or herself.

The phone rang off. She breathed and felt a wave of relief sweep over her. But the call would come again, maybe more text messages. And with each call and text the pull to get involved would become stronger.

She grabbed the phone, switched it off, and threw it in the drawer next to the steel range oven. She stuffed it beneath envelopes containing bills, life insurance claim documents, and her husband's death certificate. She nudged the drawer with her hip and it glided closed, then she crossed back to the living room and tried to forget about it. She had a life to rebuild.

*

No answer.

Willow swore and slumped back onto the duvet, one hand thrown across her eyes, clutching the pendant, the other dangling off the edge of the bed and holding the phone. A hollow ache opened in her chest. She hadn't expected an answer, but every time she called she held on to the tiny glimmer of hope that she'd get one. Every time she didn't, that hope flickered out, and dark thoughts swept over her; thoughts of Ellie in a coma in a lonely, anonymous hospital bed where no one knew her name or who to call, of Ellie lying raped and murdered in a ditch, waiting to be found by some poor bastard walking their dog. Or worst of all, thoughts of Ellie sitting in safety, staring at the phone and laughing at Willow for flying halfway around the world on a wild goose chase, of Ellie not wanting anything to do with her, but wanting to show how much power she still had.

Willow screwed her eyes shut. *You wouldn't do that to me, Ellie. Would you?*

Tomorrow. Tomorrow she'd set out to find her. She'd apologise to Harrison. Convince him to help. He'd know where Ellie was.

Clinging to that hope, she swung her legs out of the bed, put the phone on the bedside cabinet with the pendant, padded across the carpet, and switched off the light. She kept the curtain open. The orange glow from the streetlamp spilt across the chest of drawers. She untucked the duvet, slipped inside, rolled to face the wall, then closed her eyes.

Tomorrow she'd start her search.

And when she found Ellie, she'd say sorry.

For everything.

4

Raven watched from the shadows of the car park opposite the Driftwood Spars as the last of the grizzled regulars staggered up Quay Road to their wives and their dogs and their miserable existences. The lights flicked off in the guest rooms until only one remained. Around the cove the night settled, a thick blackness broken only by the dazzling brilliance of the Spars, its white walls lit up still, even though the lights in the bar had been dimmed when the last of the regulars left.

Ruby came out of the main door after midnight, trudging up the hill towards the studio flat in Churchtown that she rented from Pete.

Pete's sudden venture into property rental had caused Raven a few problems the previous year.

She'd been squatting in the flat he bought since the harsh winds and the arctic cold of the Atlantic winter had driven her from the hut. She had also taken to stashing choice items of 'merchandise' in the loft. Ruby's unexpected arrival had brought her stay to a sharp end. Raven had beat a hasty retreat back to the hut, but had to pick the lock on the flat several times to retrieve said merchandise. Ruby never seemed to notice, just as she didn't notice Raven watching her disappear into the darkness now.

Minutes passed. Voices drifted on the breeze. The three Chosen emerged from the car park, trudging along the road that ran down from the hills past the brewery. They approached the door of the Spars, knocked, waited, then Pete opened up, and they stepped inside.

Silence settled again.

Raven checked her watch.

Almost time.

She'd been there since before closing, a shadow in the far corner of the car park, shrouded in the black leather trench coat, the hood, the face mask, hidden unless you got close enough to stare in her eyes. Not that anyone did. Like moths, they were attracted to the lights and noise of the Spars, shying away from the total darkness beyond its corona.

She checked her watch again. Half-past midnight. The boat was due in half an hour. She shifted the knife in the waistband of her leather trousers until it sat on her hip, then detached from the darkness, and swept towards the Spars. On cue, the wall lights switched off, and the cove plunged to black. She blinked, the lights now trails of green in her vision, and headed for the front door. With a final look around, she rapped her fingers on the dark oak. "Who is it?" a muffled voice said.

"Raven."

The door clicked open.

Raven slipped inside, peering at the Chosen who had opened the door.

He was known as Michael now, but that wasn't his real name. He'd given up his real name when he joined the

Chosen. They all had. It was part of their initiation, a sign of their dedication to Goddard's cause, a symbolic casting off of their old identity, their old ways and, in return, Goddard gave them new names.

All except her. She'd chosen her name. Goddard had resisted at first, but she was nothing if not tenacious and finally he relented. From that point on she became Raven.

In the moody gold lighting of the bar, Michael's face looked pitted and scarred with whiteheads ready to burst even as new acne began to flare angry red against his skin. He slipped back into his seat. Gabriel sat back next to Michael, arms folded across his scrawny chest, his fingers scratching at the backs of his elbow, his mouth twitching like a gagged Tourette's sufferer. Opposite him, the third male, Raphael, overweight and overawed, sat chewing his fingernails and staring at the table.

"It's time," Raven said.

Pete stepped from the alcove behind the bar. He nodded at Raven, moved out of the bar, and headed for the back room as Raphael, Michael and Gabriel scraped back their chairs and followed. The steps between the two rooms creaked underneath them as they crossed through.

Two hours earlier, the back room had been a mass of noise, sweat and beer, but the band had long since packed up and left, and the furniture - the dark oak tables, the half barrel chairs, the blonde wood benches - had been slipped back into place. The only evidence of the night before was a screwed up setlist in the far corner, a half-drunk glass of beer on the low stage, and a broken plectrum on the shelf above the stone fireplace where

Pete now crouched.

"Give him a hand," Raven muttered.

Gabriel and Michael scurried forward but Raphael lingered by the door, chewing his nails, working his tongue, his face bloodless, his forehead dotted with sweat. Raven peered at him. He couldn't meet her gaze.

Gabriel and Michael dragged a long rectangular flagstone forward and out onto the wood. Beneath the flagstone, the floor dropped away to darkness.

In centuries past, it had been a wreckers tunnel, a narrow, craggy passage running from a hidden spot up in the village, down to the cove and passing behind the fireplace. It had fallen into disuse and lay all but forgotten until Goddard heard about it and set about its reconstruction.

It had been a clandestine project, carried out in the small hours by out of work builders with empty pockets and the good sense to keep their mouths shut. Ignoring the tunnel up to the village, they'd expanded and shorn up the passage to the cove with lintels and beams making it possible for people to walk upright for most of its length.

Raven crossed to the fireplace and stared into its dark maw. A cool, damp breeze played across the skin around her eyes. Gabriel and Michael let the flagstone fall.

"Fuck me, that's heavy," Gabriel muttered, stretching his back.

Raven jerked her head to the tunnel. "Let's go."

Gabriel scurried forward, threw his legs over the edge, then swung down into the four-foot drop. He turned. Pete rolled him a torch. It stopped a yard from the edge. Gabriel snatched it up and switched it on, then turned immediately left and headed down the tunnel. Raphael went next, then Michael.

Pete passed Raven another torch.

"The boat ready?" Raven said.

"It'll be there," Pete said.

"Ok. We'll be back in an hour or so." Raven dropped down into the tunnel and followed the others.

Ahead, torchlight flashed on the square pillars and lintels of oak. Water trickled down the walls from the cliffs overhead, soaking the wood, making it stronger. The air felt cold and wet and smelt of damp rock. She saw the others as shimmering silhouettes in the dark. For the first dozen yards she had to crouch, but as the tunnel ploughed deeper beneath the cliffs, the space opened up, and she walked upright, quicker then, but always silent. Ahead, the men's feet scraped on the stone floor, and Raven heard their breath, harsh and rhythmic in the gloom. They walked for five minutes, the hiss and roar of the ocean getting ever louder.

The tunnel opened up into a dark cave. The torchlight flashed across wet rock walls, slick with slimy lichen. Water cascaded in a silver film from the rocks overhead. The cave narrowed to a split in the granite ahead of them. Eight foot high, three foot wide at the base, but tapering to a blunt point, six inches wide, and leaning to the left. They had to crawl or crouch through.

"Kill the torches," Raven said.

The light vanished and the cave plunged into darkness. The walls turned solid black and the night sky through the gap became a narrow wedge of midnight blue. Michael went through the gap first, then Gabriel and Raphael, with Raven bringing up the rear. The gap led onto a small ledge six feet from the base of the cliff, about fifty yards along from the beach huts and restaurant overlooking Trevaunance.

Tonight the tide was on the way in but still had a few hours to go before it reached its peak. They were a day past the new moon, and the world was a blend of shadows. Overhead, the clear sky blazed with stars. The ocean looked like oil as it lapped against the rocks. The breakers were a dark grey sludge oozing onto the slate beach. A small motorboat had been drawn up to the tideline. Pete's sons leant against it. They wore dark jumpers and oilskin waders.

Shouldering her way past Raphael, Raven dropped the six-foot down to the beach and crossed to the boat. The Chosen followed, grunting and breathing heavily as they went. As Raven approached, Pete's sons looked up. They looked grey in the feint light, tall and sturdy, like their father had been before the fags and the booze took their toll.

She nodded at the first, placed her hands on the wooden gunwale and swung aboard, landing in the centre of the keel. She moved to the bow seat as Gabriel and Michael leapt in. Michael moved to the single prop engine at the stern, while Gabriel slumped on the centre bench.

On the beach, Raphael stood wringing his hands and peering from the cave to cove and back to the boat.

"What's up with you, fatty?" Gabriel said.

"Don't like boats."

"Tart."

"I can't swim!"

"Don't fall out then," Gabriel chuckled, scratching his

arms and stomping his feet.

"Get in," Raven said.

Raphael pouted at her. She could see him thinking of running. She stood, glaring down at him, her hand slipping inside her coat to grasp the hilt of her knife. He lowered his gaze. Muttering self-pity, he trudged to the starboard side. Wheezing and spluttering, he dragged his backside halfway into the boat, then spilt over the gunwale and fell arse-first into the puddle of water at the bottom.

"Shit!" He leapt up and began slapping his backside.

"Idiot," Gabriel giggled.

"Me arse is soaked!"

"Shouldn't be such a fat fuck then should ya?"

Raven turned. "Enough."

Gabriel fell to silent chuckling. Raphael continued to grumble until he saw Raven watching him. Then he went quiet and sat on the centre bench with Gabriel, shoulders hunched, eyes downcast, looking thoroughly miserable.

On the beach, Pete's sons pushed against the bow. The keel scraped along the stones and the shards of granite, and the boat rocked backwards into the breakers. The boys kept pushing until they were waist-deep in the water, then gave a final, hard thrust and the boat drifted away. They stepped back to the beach as Michael gunned the engine. The roar filled the quiet night, startling a flock of roosting gulls who screamed into the darkness and over the clifftop. Michael steered a wide circle and then headed out to sea. Raven peered back across the water, saw Pete's son's climbing up the ledge, then looked forward.

Starlight winked on the crests of the waves as the boat

ploughed out towards the offshore stacks of granite known as Bawden Rocks. The land receded behind them. Lights from remote houses in the valley and along the cliff tops glimmered in the darkness. She could hear Raphael still grumbling to himself and Gabriel sniggering. Her hand moved to the hilt of her knife and shifted it on her hip, where it was easier to grab if needed, and she swallowed the urge to tell them to shut up.

She fixed her gaze on the Rocks as they loomed out of the night, stacks of dense blackness against the stars. Beyond them, Raven saw the running lights of another, larger motor cruiser. It came up from the south at a clip, the noise of its engine a doppler drone across the water that died as the boat slowed. As she watched, she saw two dense black shadows drop into the water, a flickering light on top of each.

"Over there," she said, pointing towards the cruiser. At the engine, Michael steered the boat on a line following her gloved hand.

Ahead, the motor cruiser had restarted its engine, spun away from land, and had already begun to power back out to sea, heading south. Ignoring the boat, Raven focused on the two flickering lights now bobbing in the water ahead of them.

They approached the closer of the two. Michael slowed the engine to a putter and eased the boat alongside. The package was a large flight case strapped to a circular inflatable tube of heavy-duty yellow rubber. The beacon on the top flashed across the water as Gabriel knelt on the centre bench, leaning over the side as they drifted closer.

Raven's hand closed on the hilt of the blade. She

dragged it from her waistband and stepped behind Gabriel, then held the blade out towards his back.

"Got it!" he gasped, grabbing the top strap. He heaved the case clear. Water splashed and dropped from the bottom into the dark ocean.

"Hold it," Raven said.

"Quickly!" Gabriel gasped. The case rocked in the strap. The weight of the case and its contents, as well as the inflatable and the water spilling from beneath, strained his shoulders. She stepped towards him with the knife, then raised the blade, and thrust it home.

Gabriel gasped as it pierced the circular tube of the inflatable, the pop echoing like a gunshot.

Raven reached out, grabbed another strap, and eased the flight case on board. She cut the straps away and threw the tube and the straps into the keel as Michael eased them towards the second package. It had drifted fifty yards astern. Like the first, it consisted of a flight case on an inflatable tube with a beacon on top.

"Think I wrenched me shoulder," Gabriel muttered.

Raven ignored him, focused only on the package as they eased towards it. Michael pulled alongside, the package on Gabriel's side of the boat again. Clutching his sore shoulder, he reached out to take it. Wrapped a hand around the hilt and went to lift it.

"Gah!" He spat. "No, sorry. I'll need a hand."

Raven flicked the blade at Raphael. "Make yourself useful and help him."

Raphael eyed the blade warily, then scampered across and leaned over. The boat rocked as he moved. Gabriel yelled and almost tumbled headfirst into the drink. Michael flew backwards, one leg jerking into the air, one hand thrown out behind him to steady himself. Raven clutched the gunwales to stop from spilling overboard. The water slapped against the sides.

"Jesus, lard-arse!" Michael cried.

Ignorant of the chaos he'd caused, Raphael reached out and grabbed the second strap. Raven hefted the blade again. She stepped behind Raphael and held it point down.

"Hold it still," she said.

She took another step forward. The tip of the blade glimmered in the starlight over the vast curve of Raphael's back. She could smell his stale, clammy stench, despite wearing the mask.

She raised the blade high.

Thrust it down.

The pop echoed through the dark again. The inflatable shrivelled with a loud hiss. Raphael and Gabriel lifted the package into the keel and shoved it next to the other one, the two cases practically filling the width of the boat. Gabriel slumped onto the seat still clutching his arm. Raphael plonked next to Gabriel, rocking the boat again, wheezing and oozing sweat like he'd run a marathon.

"Heading back, boss?" Michael said.

Raven didn't reply. She crouched down, leant over the gunwale and peered into the dark. She shifted the knife, laying the sharp edge flat against her inner forearm.

"Something wrong?"

"Think we may have a leak," Raven said.

"What!" Raphael leapt to his feet.

Raven spun. Flashed out the knife. The blade sliced through the flabby flesh around Raphael's throat. His face paled. His eyes went wide. His podgy hands flapped at the blood that pulsed down his neck and soaked his shirt. Raven stepped forward and lifted her boot, then planted it square in Raphael's chest. Still flailing at his throat, he tumbled into the cold sea. The splash rocked the boat.

"Christ!" Gabriel grabbed the sides again. Michael clung to the engine. Raven peered into the water.

Mouth flapping like a beached fish, Raphael dropped beneath the black waves. Raven waited, watching for him to surface. The sea settled, became like oil again. No bubbles. No flailing. The tide and the swell bumped the boat and the infinite night blazed overhead.

"Boss?" Michael said.

Still, Raven peered at the water.

She could feel every chamber of her heart pulsing, every blood cell oozing through her veins, every molecule of air in her lungs. The nausea blocking her throat tasted like black bitterness.

"Boss?"

Her skin tingled. The scars on her face and body throbbed. A dark heat swelled in her stomach, through her chest and down between her thighs. She closed her eyes and swallowed, breathing deep, knees trembling.

The sensation faded. The heat left her loins. The nausea dissipated. She opened her eyes and stared at the black water. Raphael was gone.

"Boss?"

Raven turned to Michael. He jerked at her gaze as if she'd struck him. She looked back to the water.

"Let's go," she said.

Michael and Gabriel stared at each other as she pushed

off the gunwale and crossed to the seat at the bow. She closed her eyes and breathed the salt air. The engine purred to life. She felt the boat move and rock with the swell, remembered the euphoria she'd felt when Raphael vanished from view...

... and smiled behind her mask.

5

The grey light of dawn spilt over Trevaunance Cove. Gun-metal waves lapped at the shingle. Overhead, a raven croaked on the clifftop. The girl emerged from the water, blonde hair tangled with sea-weed, salt-water dripping from the sleeves of her dress, her fingers, the tip of her nose, leaving a trail of splashes as she strode to the ramp leading up from the beach.

The cool morning breeze didn't touch her skin, didn't ruffle her hair, or tug at the hem of her dress. The mizzle was a veil she walked through untouched. Yet she left damp, bare footprints on the tarmac as she walked.

Those she passed - the early risers, swimmers, walkers, artists and dreamers - didn't see her, but they tugged jumpers tighter, hunched their shoulders, rubbed their hands as if winter brushed them. She moved on.

Up the road, past houses, the lifeboat station, a car park. She turned right, past the brewery, slipped around the back.

The light outside the annexe door glowed brightly in the slate morning. The shut door posed no obstacle to her. She slipped right through, leaving one bare, damp footprint on the step.

She drifted on, along the narrow corridor. Every step was silent, no breath or heartbeat to betray her presence. The room she wanted lay ahead.

So good to see her again. So long... so long...

She slipped through the door as if it were mist, emerged next to the sleeping girl. Her red dreadlocks spilt like blood across the crisp white pillows. She lay on her side, knees drawn up, hands clasping the duvet.

So different from when they'd last met. So broken now. But no more.

She was here for her. She'd always been here for her. The figure knelt by the bed, a warm smile spreading across her blue lips. And she reached out with cold, grey fingers, brushing a single red-dreadlock from the girls face.

She leant close. Close. Pressed cold lips against hot skin. And said...

"Flake."

"Bastard!"

Willow sat up. Heart hammering. Stomach wringing with nausea. A needle of cold pain lanced the back of her right eye. Grey light crept in through the open curtain and for one moment the girl from her dream remained, crouched and smiling sadly down at her. She blinked and the image of the girl slipped away. The needle of cold pain faded with it. Muffled voices erupted on the other side of the wall.

"You cheat! You dirty fucking cheat!" Willow turned and scowled at the plaster.

"I'm sorry, babe. I'm sorry. It didn't mean nothing."

The voices faded. Maybe they'd moved away from the wall. Maybe they'd fallen to whispering, mindful of the fact that it was barely dawn and they were having a blazing row. Willow didn't know, didn't care. It wasn't her fight. Wasn't her problem.

Her heart throbbed in her ears, her chest, her throat. The shock of being dragged awake? Or the fear of her dream?

If it was a dream. She shuddered. If it wasn't, if Ellie was a ghost then that meant—

More loud screaming cut off that train of thought and Willow was grateful. Ellie wasn't dead. It had been a dream. A dream broken by the idiots next door. Still arguing. Still muffled. A crash against a wall. Her head jolted towards the sound. The voices rose and fell but she couldn't make out words now. Only anger. And regret.

She slumped to her back, lay with her hand across her eyes. The room seemed to swirl and pitch around her. She felt sick as she remembered another night, another argument, thirteen years earlier.

*

Megan lay in her bed in the room she shared with Ellie, staring at the crack of light from the landing spilling through the gap at the foot of the door.

Her parents' screams had dragged her awake. Raised voices in the dark. Coming from their room next door. The vicious crack of an open palm striking a cheek, then shouting.

And one phrase in particular; her mother screaming, "You love them more than me!"

Protests. More accusations. More denials. She sat up. Hugged her shins and put her head on her knees. Tears burned her eyes, and she sniffed in the dark. Across the room, Ellie shifted in her bed. Her arm came up, pale and skinny and she threw back her covers.

"You okay Flake?" she'd said.

She raised her head and peered at Ellie. Sucked in a breath. A moment of silence.

A manic scream shattered the dark. A flurry of bangs like small explosions shook the frame of their door.

"I hate you, I hate you!" their mother screamed.

Ellie's eyes flared wide and white in the dark. As the screams and the concussive blows continued, Megan reached a small hand for her sister. "It's so dark," she muttered.

Ellie slipped across the room and into her bed, put her hand around Megan, pulled her head into the crook of her shoulder. Ellie smelt of strawberry shampoo and bubble bath. Her skin felt soft and warm in the dark.

"It'll get light soon," Ellie said. She kissed Megan's head. The wall shook under a heavy blow. Glass shattered.

"Stop it!" their father screamed.

Megan peered up at Ellie and saw the terror etched into Ellie's face. She squeezed her hard.

"You'll stay with me?" Megan said.

Ellie kept staring at the wall but kissed her sister's hair again. "I'm here for you, Flake. I'll always be here for you."

As the argument next door got louder, more violent, they burrowed under the covers, and put pillows over their ears. Megan wept, but Ellie set her face grim. She whispered songs and words of comfort, and after an age, Megan drifted into sleep.

The next day they woke together, climbed out of Megan's bed, and crept downstairs to find their father weeping in the kitchen, his face bruised, eyes bloodshot.
"Where's Mum?"
The tremor in Ellie's voice scared Megan more than anything she'd heard the night before and she glanced at her sister. Tears sparkled in Ellie's soft blue eyes.
"She left us," their father said. "She's gone!"
Ellie collapsed to the floor, head against the tiles screaming.
Megan felt her world flip. Shatter. Remake into something broken. Something unreal. And she hated it.
Grief and anguish churned inside her like a storm swell.
She ran away, from the pain, from the anguish, from the confusion. She fled to her room, slamming the door behind her, and burying herself in her bedsheet.

*

Quiet fell now in the room next door. The couple were talking, the boy pleading. The girl sobbing. Willow couldn't hear what was being said. A break-up? An apology? She didn't care. Her eyes felt gritty and dry, the jet lag gnawed at her skull, and all she wanted was another hour of sleep before she started the search for Ellie. But as she rolled onto her side and pulled the duvet to her chin, the headboard began knocking against the wall next door. The girl began to gasp and moan with pleasure now, not rage.

Willow threw herself out of bed and huffed into the bathroom. After a quick shower, she yanked on a pair of black leggings, a black vest and a three quarter length cream cardigan. She tugged on her boots, snatched up her rucksack and phone and was about to leave when she remembered the sister pendant. She grabbed it from the bedside cabinet, fastened it around her neck, then tucked it under her top. She left, slamming her door, and stomping hard down the corridor out of spite. Swinging her rucksack onto her back, the soreness on her shoulders from the previous day cushioned somewhat by the fabric of the cardigan, she stormed out of the annexe and onto Quay Road.

A dense Cornish mizzle had chased away the bright promise of dawn. She closed her eyes and breathed deep, tasting the rain. The smell of bacon cooking in a nearby house taunted her stomach. She exhaled long and loud, the last of the anger at the couple in the room next door ebbing away, and then opened her eyes again.

Opposite, the Spars stood silent, all the lights off except in the dining room. A solitary jogger clambered up the coast path, as seagulls cried and swooped over the cove. She could hear a radio playing in one of the houses behind her and a sleek grey Mercedes campervan turned into the car park opposite, wheel's hissing on the wet tarmac, wipers scraping across the windscreen.

Harrison wouldn't get to work for a good few hours yet. And there was at least an hour until breakfast in the Spars. Had the weather been better, she would've gone to the beach below, but a cold breeze swept off the sea and the mizzle fell heavier. She turned her back on the cove and trudged up Quay Road towards the village centre. At first, she had no destination in mind, but as she walked, the smells and sounds of the cove stirred in her memories of her youth. Back then Aggie had been a playground for her and her band of friends.

They'd spent whole summers running wild on the beaches, through the hills and the lanes, exploring the old engine houses and chimney stacks, kayaking along the coast, surfing at Porthtowan or Chapel Porth, swimming out to the granite stacks at the mouth of Trevellas, and clambering to the top, only to plunge into the ocean again once they got there. The days had been long and endless, filled with sunshine and laughter.

Completely the opposite of the nights at home.

Those golden days and terrible nights had gone. But as she trudged up Quay Road, with the brook burbling down the gully towards the sea, and the cool dawn breeze rustling the green ferns and the purple foxglove, the yellow laburnum and the hydrangea blossoming pink and blue and white on the roadside, she knew where she had to go.

She had a pilgrimage to make.

Two years too late.

6

The St. Agnes Museum was a twin-gabled stone building with arched windows and a grey slate roof, that sat at the end of a gated drive. The gate was open when Willow arrived. She walked up the drive and around the side of the building, trepidation fluttering in her chest.

The graveyard behind the museum was bordered by hedges and saplings with sparse foliage. The graves closest were older, the headstones weathered and cracked, some leaning forward or to the side as if disturbed from below. Willow made for the more recent graves at the far end of the yard. She walked along the rows of headstones, scanning the names on each until she found the one she was looking for.

It was a double memorial of white marble veined with grey lines. Yellow moss grew along the edges of the stone base. The lawn over the grave had been freshly cut, and the smell of wet grass hung in the air.

The headstone bore a simple inscription; the names of the family listed by age, with their dates of birth and death, and a single line tribute that read 'Never Forgotten'.

Their dates of birth were all different.

The dates of death, all the same.

Zoe's was the third name down, beneath her mother's and father's, but above her younger sister's. Seeing Zoe's name etched in stone bought a lump to Willow's throat. She sucked her top lip and sniffed.

"It was a tragedy."

Willow spun at the male voice, her heart jolting.

The Reverend Richard Goddard stood before her in tight denim jeans and a leather jacket. His thin nose looked ruddy in the chill air, and his hair hung mizzle-heavy and lank over his shoulders. He smelled of leather and rain. "Hello, Megan."

Willow flinched.

"How did you know?" she said.

"I never forget a face. Or…" He smiled and rubbed his jaw "…a right hook."

She flushed and lowered her gaze, tucked a damp dreadlock behind her ear and turned back to the gravestone. He stepped beside her.

"It was arson," he said.

"I know." She peered at Zoe's name. "They ever get who did it?"

"No." Goddard sighed. He buried his hands in his pockets, hunched his shoulders. "No, they never did."

Memories of fun-filled summer days raced like a sepia-toned film reel, bringing a lump to her throat. "I can't believe she's dead."

"Listen, Megan—"

"Willow," she said.

He gazed at her. "Willow?"

"That's my name now."

"Why not Megan?"

She jerked a shoulder in a half shrug.

"Megan's the name my mum gave me. I don't want anything from that bitch."

"Ok. Willow." Goddard smiled and shook his head. "Listen, I am sorry y'know?"

"For what?"

"For trying to stop you that day." He lowered his gaze and jammed his hands in his pockets. "If I'd have known what you were running from, I would've let you go. Both of you."

Ellie hung between them like a phantom.

"Have you seen her?" Willow said.

"Not for a couple of weeks or so." Goddard turned back to the grave.

"I think she's in trouble."

"Ellie?"

Willow nodded.

"What makes you think that?"

"I got a message."

"From Ellie?" He frowned.

"Think so."

"What kind of message?"

"A code we had. Wouldn't mean much to most people. But to me, it meant she was in trouble. It meant she needed me."

"What did it say?"

"It's so dark."

"Sorry?"

"That was the message. The code."

"And that's why you came back?"

Willow nodded again, hunching her shoulders against the cold mizzle trickling down her spine.

"When did you get this message?"

"Sunday morning. Oz time."

"You were in Australia?"

Willow nodded.

"You got back quick."

"She needs me." She glanced up at him. "If you've seen her..."

Goddard shook his head. "Sorry, Meg..."

She glared.

He caught himself, smiled. "...Willow. She's not been around as much recently."

"You said you saw her a couple of weeks ago?"

Goddard peered down at Zoe's gravestone. "She came to a prayer meeting. In the cove."

"A prayer meeting?"

"I run them," he said. "On the beach. For a few of my surfer friends."

"Didn't realise Ellie was into that?"

"She was a casual believer. Came occasionally, but not a regular."

"Since when?"

"Since the spring before you ran away."

Willow peered at the grave. A hollow emptiness opened in her chest.

"You didn't know?"

She shook her head. "She never told me."

Willow thought back to the weeks before she left. Ellie had spent more time out and about that spring. She'd never said where she was going and Willow had been too busy chasing boys and trying to keep tally with Zoe to ask.

"Was she ok?" She looked back at Goddard. "The

other week when you saw her?"

He raised a shoulder. "Seemed to be."

"She wasn't in any trouble at all?"

He pursed his lips, shook his head. "Not that she told me."

A breeze whipped through the yard, rustling the trees and bushes and sweeping a veil of mizzle across them.

"Have you seen your dad? He might know."

Willow stiffened. "He doesn't know I'm back."

"You didn't call him?"

"Can't."

"You can't?"

She shook her head.

"Why not?"

She gave a half shrug. "I deleted his number. Mum's too."

"You deleted your parents' numbers?" He dragged a hand through his hair.

"I've got nothing to say to them." She tilted her chin up, daring him to challenge her. He shook his head.

"You think maybe you should go and see him?" His voice was soft, gentle. She caught the hint of accusation there. "He was worried after you left."

Willow looked away. "Didn't care much when I was here."

"Ellie told me, y'know?" Goddard said.

Willow's heart jolted, and she peered up at him. He stood a good eight inches taller than her.

"Told you what?"

"Everything." He gave her a sad smile. "The fights. The messy divorce. What your stepmother did."

Willow swallowed, waiting for him to say more, but

he shrugged and lowered his gaze.

"And then I realised that I'd fucked up."

A guilty relief swept through Willow. Either he didn't know about that final argument, or he did and was keeping quiet. Either suited Willow.

"Your dad," he said. "He'd been frantic that morning you ran, woke up and found you gone. He called me."

"Why you? I mean, I never understood that," Willow said. "He could've called anyone. The police. Our mother. Even Zoe. But he called you."

"He knew that Ellie had been coming to my services. And he thought that maybe me and her were..." He shuffled his feet and looked to the ground, scratching his beard. "Well, he thought that we were sleeping together." He turned to face her. "But we weren't," he said. "I promise you that."

"Not my business." She tried to sound casual, but another wave of guilty relief swept over her.

"He thought she'd run to my place," he went on. "Only she hadn't. And I hadn't seen her. So naturally, I went looking. And I got lucky I guess. Cos you walked right into me."

"Always wondered how you found us," Willow said.

Goddard shrugged. "I put a few calls in. One of my regulars had seen you riding down to Trevellas, then walking up the far side. I figured you were walking the coastal path, so I headed to meet you."

"Not exactly luck then."

"Ok, more like prior knowledge and playing the odds."

"Do priests do that?"

"Do what?"

"Play the odds. I thought gambling was a sin."

"I'm a reverend, not a priest," he said. "And anyway, who said us Holy types don't know how to sin? Maybe we sin better than you normal folk cos we've got speed dial to God and can buy forgiveness in a flash."

He grinned and clicked his fingers. The sparkle in his eye and the smile on his face made him seem softer, warmer. An old feeling, a heat like molten gold blossomed in her chest, and she looked down, her cheeks warm and ruddy.

"She missed you," Goddard said.

The glow faded, and she thought of Ellie. She bit her lip.

"After you left, she talked a lot about you, told me you'd gone to London, that you were settling in ok. She seemed happy for you, but lonely."

Tears pricked Willow's eyes. She wiped them. "I missed her too."

"Go and see your dad." Goddard nudged her shoulder with his.

"Why?"

"Ellie might be there."

"Doubt it."

"Life's too short for anger, Willow," Goddard said. "And your dad *is* sorry."

She peered up at him. "Is he still with Connie?"

Goddard gave a tight smile.

"Not that sorry then is he?"

"He knows he's made mistakes. He'll want to see you."

"Maybe."

"If not for him then for you."

"Me?"

"The worst thing in the world is not taking the chance to make amends with your family," he said. "And then finding it's too late."

His gaze had fixed on a point in the distance, and Willow got the impression he was lost in memories.

"You talking about me or you?"

He turned and smiled at her. "I'm talking from experience."

"Wanna tell me?"

He shook his head. "Maybe another time. I've got to run. But go and see your dad. You'll feel better. And who knows, you might even find Ellie."

"Maybe."

He turned to go.

"Thanks," she said.

He turned back. "For what?"

She shrugged. "Listening."

He smiled, stepped in close and hugged her. The smell of his leather coat swamped her. His body felt strong and hard in her arms.

"It's my job."

He pulled away. Squeezed her shoulders, peered at her. She studied his lips, the pores of his skin, the flecks of grey in his beard. He looked tired. He smiled again.

"Let me know if you find Ellie," he said.

He let go of her arms, hunched his shoulders against the mizzle, and strode away, shoulders down, head bowed. He disappeared around the side of the museum building. Willow turned back to Zoe's grave.

Goddard was right. She knew that she needed to see her father. Not to apologise, or to ask for forgiveness but because it was the most obvious place to look. She was here for Ellie. Nothing else. She hefted her rucksack and stared at the grave again.

She wanted to say something to Zoe, even though Zoe was no longer around to hear it. They'd been best friends and the worst enemies. After all they had been through, walking away without a word seemed wrong, but she couldn't think of anything profound or noble to say, and everything she did think of sounded trite and meaningless.

Grief rising as a lump in her throat, Willow crouched down, kissed her fingertips, and touched Zoe's name on the headstone. An old memory stirred. A name from her youth. The name Zoe had called herself as a middle finger to her parents.

"See you around." She smiled through sudden tears. "Raven."

7

Raven closed the doors to the hut. Thin shafts of light pierced the darkness and lanced across the body of the red and black motorbike which stood in the far corner. She bolted the door, wincing as rusted metal scraped on rusted metal, then crossed to the stairs, her boots crunching on the dust and the hay and the shards of glass that littered the flagstone floor. The rickety wooden stairs creaked and groaned as she thudded up to the sleeping room above, legs burning with fatigue.

The air stank of damp wood and stale sweat. She crossed to the rear window and nudged it open, the cool morning air stirring motes of dust in the pale light, then moved to the mattress, untying the face mask as she walked. She pulled the mask away from her nose and mouth and threw it onto the floor. Her scarred skin tingled. She tugged off her leather gloves, tossed them beside the face mask, then untied her boots.

Her body ached. Her eyes itched. She kicked off the boots, clenched her toes, then pulled the knife from her waistband. She placed it gently, almost reverently, on the floor next to the mattress. Then she stripped down to her underwear. The exposed underwire of her bra dug into her ribs. She padded back to the stairs, snatching up the metal water bottle, picking her knickers out of her backside as she strode downstairs. She crossed to the tap behind the bike, flipped off the bottle lid, and turned the faucet.

Icy water splashed onto the flagstones with a wet slap. It sprayed her shins. She shivered and jerked backwards. After letting the water run for several seconds, she held the bottle under the tap, filled it, swigged down half of it, then filled it again. The bottle full, she switched off the tap, flipped the lid back on then padded back to the stairs.

As she reached the top step, she heard her phone start to buzz. She stopped, sighed, and shook her head. She stomped back to the mattress, snatched up her coat, and dug out the phone.

Goddard was calling. She answered.

"This better be important," she said, crossing to the rear window. "I need to sleep."

"Remember our little problem?" he said.

"What little problem?" she said.

"Megan."

"What about her?"

"She got a text."

"A text?"

"She thinks it's from Ellie."

Raven felt her stomach drop. "When?"

"Saturday night."

Raven shook her head. "Impossible."

"Is it?"

"You know it is."

"Do I? I've only got your word for it. How do I know

you didn't have a sudden attack of conscience?"

"Do I strike you as the kind of person who has a conscience?"

"Oh, you act tough, Raven. But who knows?" She heard his sigh down the line. "But if you are telling the truth…"

"If?" Raven snorted.

"Then someone else sent it," Goddard continued, ignoring her interruption.

Raven bristled, wanting to rise to the jibe, choosing not to. For now.

"What makes her think it's from Ellie?" she said.

"It was some sort of code they used to have. Meant one of them was in trouble."

"Let me find her," Raven said. "Let me stop her snooping."

"Unnecessary at the minute. She knows nothing. Have you put a Chosen on her yet?"

Raven blinked. Shifted the phone from one ear to the other. "No. I was gonna do it myself."

She screwed her eyes shut, gripped the phone hard, and waited for his outburst. It didn't come.

"Yeah, I think you're right. It should be you who follows her. One of the Chosen may be behind this."

She let out the breath she'd been holding.

"But it has to start now," he said.

"Now?"

"No time for sleep, Raven. This is too important. I've told her to go to her father's. If you hurry you'll catch her there. You can track her once she leaves."

"You want her… dealt with?"

"Not yet. She's more useful alive at the minute. Tell

me where she goes. Who she meets. My betting is, whoever called her back, they'll make contact. We need to know who that was."

"Killing her would make the problem go away," Raven said.

"It would make her go away, but the person who called her back would still be out there. And they could still cause us trouble even if she was dead. We have to find out who that is. Which means she lives."

"But—"

"I said she lives, Raven."

Not if I cut the bitch's throat. Raven swallowed the thought.

"Keep in touch," Goddard said. "And meet me tonight."

"Where?" She leant against the wood and gazed out across the fields to the cobalt sky where the last wisps of the dawn cloud stretched like skeletal fingers to the horizon. The mizzle had passed inland. The coming day looked fine and bright.

"There's a meeting tonight. Cornish First. At the Spars."

"Bit public ain't it?" She chewed a loose bit of skin on her thumb.

"Meet me after. In the hut overlooking Trevaunance. And Raven..."

"What?"

"I mean it. She stays alive."

Goddard killed the call. She glared at the phone.

"For now," Raven muttered.

She crossed to the bed, threw her phone on the mattress, and started dragging on her leathers. Once dressed, she tied the face mask around her nose and mouth. She tugged on her gloves, and then snatched up her helmet. Stuffing the phone into her pocket, she turned for the stairs. She took a step towards them, then stopped and looked back.

The blade still lay beside the mattress.

Goddard wanted her kept alive. Maybe his reasons were good. But he didn't know Megan the way she did. The girl had a talent for mayhem. And she wouldn't give up. She'd never give up. With Megan sniffing around anything could happen.

Raven stalked back around the mattress and snatched up the blade. Regardless of what Goddard wanted, if Raven got the chance, she wasn't going to waste it.

Tucking the blade into the waistband of her trousers, she stomped down the steps to the bike.

*

Willow's father's house had changed in the six years since she left, but she barely noticed the sterile chrome and glass and the smooth white walls. All she could focus on was the window to the room she'd shared with Ellie. No curtains. No ornaments on the windowsill.

When she'd left, there had been a drainpipe running down the side of the window. On the morning she ran, she and Ellie had clambered out of the window and down that drainpipe. They'd grabbed their bikes from the front yard and then pedalled hard along the track across the hills towards the coastal path. When they'd got a hundred yards away, Willow had looked back and seen the red light of dawn blazing on the window. Now, six years later, the drainpipe had gone, and the window was dark.

No movement. No noise from within. The place felt cold. Sterile. But someone had to be in because steam billowed from an extractor fan in the upstairs bathroom. She peered up and down the lane. No sign of anyone. The drone of a distant motorbike drifted on the breeze.

She could walk away, turn and head back to the Spars for breakfast, follow the path down to Trevellas, and set out for Perranporth early. No need to go in. No need to face him, or her, again. But she had to know if Ellie was in there, or if they'd seen her. The house loomed over her and she felt unseen eyes watching. Clear blue skies stretched overhead. Midges swarmed in the golden morning sun. The air had a damp, grassy smell to it. Willow gazed at the windows, saw a glimmer of movement behind one.

Her heart quickened. Was that Ellie? Too quick to tell.

She gripped the top of the white picket gate. Her gaze fixed on the front door, she eased the gate back. Nausea bubbled up her throat and burst on her tongue, filling her mouth with a bitter taste. She swallowed as she reached out for the door knocker.

Before she could grasp it, the latch clicked, and the door swung back.

Jonathan Rae squinted out of the shadows. Willow swallowed and stepped back. Six years had been kind to her father, she thought. He had a full head of thick black hair, flecked with the odd patch of grey around the temples. There were more lines around his eyes and his mouth, but his skin was still smooth and supple and tanned olive. He wore a blue and pink hooped polo shirt that was tucked into blue chinos. The smell of toast and coffee wafted from the open kitchen window.

"Megan?" His eyes widened.

She nodded. Her father's gaze flicked across her face, the spacer in her ear, the dreadlocks, the woollen coat, the heavy black boots. She caught a whiff of herself. She stank of stale rain and sweat. Embarrassed, she stepped back further.

"Who is it?" a female voice called out from within.

Bile stung the back of Willow's throat. She clenched her jaw and swallowed it back.

Constance Rae, or Connie as she liked to call herself, appeared behind Jonathan. One manicured claw with nails painted bright pink slithered over his shoulder. The other she slipped into the back pocket of her tight stonewashed jeans. The movement stretched her crisp white shirt tight across her plastic tits. In the years since Willow had left, her lips had ballooned, and her backside had vanished.

"Well, well." She looked Willow up and down, wrinkling her nose with disgust. "Look who's come crawling back."

"What do you want?" her father said.

Connie leaned her chin on Jonathan's shoulder. A smirk played across her bulbous lips. She blinked at Willow, her bulging goldfish eyes cold and harsh.

"Is Ellie here?" Willow said.

Jonathan frowned, but it was Connie that spoke.

"Ellie?" she snorted. "We kicked that little tramp out years ago."

Willow bristled and glared at Connie. She screwed up her fists. *Call my sister a tramp again and I'll pop your lips.*

She breathed deep then cocked an eyebrow at her father. "Is she here?"

"No," he said.

"You haven't seen her?"

"And neither have you obviously." Connie smirked. "By the way, which rock were you hiding under?"

Willow bit back the retort that tingled on the tip of her tongue.

"What do you want, Megan?" her father said.

"It's Willow now."

Jonathan frowned. "Sorry?"

"My name. It's Willow now."

Connie snorted and began to chuckle. Willow felt her face redden.

"Dad, can't you get rid of her?" She pointed at Connie.

"Oh I'm going nowhere sweetheart," Connie snorted. "What you've got to say to him, you say to me as well."

Willow glanced from her father to Connie and back to her father.

"Fuck this," she muttered. Then she turned her back and strode towards the gate. "I was stupid to think Ellie would ever come here." She got halfway down the path.

"Wait."

Her father's call stopped her short. She turned back. He had his back to her, bending low to talk to Connie, who sneered at Willow from over his shoulder.

"Five minutes," she heard him say. "Just five minutes."

A pause, then a nod from Connie. "Fine."

She looked down her nose at Willow, then turned and slithered inside. Jonathan stepped out onto the path and pulled the door forward until it stood ajar. Willow gazed back at him.

He sighed, put his hands on his hips, and looked to his feet.

"Six years." He shook his head. "Six bloody years, not a word, and now you just show up like nothing has happened."

"Where's Ellie?"

"That's all you've got to say?"

"What do you want me to say?"

"How about sorry for a start?"

Willow snorted and shook her head. She smiled sardonically.

"You're unbelievable."

"So you're not sorry for what you put us through?"

"What I put you through?"

"Do you realise how worried we were?"

"I doubt Connie even noticed." She buried her hands in the pockets and looked up the lane. A black and red motorbike cruised past. The noise receded behind Willow and the lane fell quiet except for the crows and the gulls and the buzz of bees in the lavender bush in next door's garden.

"Why did you do it?"

"Do what?"

"Run away."

"Seriously? You're asking me that now?"

"I deserve to know."

"You deserve to know." Willow gave a hollow chuckle. "If you gave the first fucking shit about us..."

She jabbed a finger at him, her face screwing up as long-buried feelings of betrayal stirred. Tears welled and stung. Her mouth seemed to glue itself shut as the words failed her. She swallowed and tried again.

"You're our dad," Willow said. "You were supposed to—"

Anger choked the words off. There were many things he was supposed to do. He'd done none of them. And the memory of what he had done, that last night before she ran, made her face throb.

"Forget it," she hissed. "I'm done." She stalked towards the gate.

"Running away again?" Jonathan said.

Willow had her hand on the top of the gate. She stopped. The anger and the bitterness she felt clouded her mind.

"You can't run forever, Megan," he said.

She felt her hackles rise at the use of her real name.

"I told you," she said. "My name's Willow."

"You're even running from your own name."

She yanked the gate open.

"You're right," Jonathan said.

For a second, she thought he was admitting he'd failed her, and turned to look at him.

"Ellie's not here. She hasn't been here for years."

"Ran out on you too did she?"

He shrugged. "No. We told her to go."

"Your own daughter?"

"She was out of control. We couldn't help her."

Willow bit her lip and shook her head. "I doubt you even tried." She opened the gate and stepped out onto the grass verge.

"If you find her," Jonathan said. "Tell her to turn herself in."

"What?"

"She'll understand."

"Dad, what? What?!"

Jonathan ignored her, turning and stepping inside. He glanced back as he closed the front door, but there was no compassion, no love in his face, only contempt. Then the lock clicked shut and Willow was left staring at the cold grey paintwork.

Swearing, Willow slammed the gate and stalked away along the lane, face burning, wild thoughts swirling through her brain. Turn herself in? What did he mean? What had Ellie done? Was it illegal, the trouble she was in? Was that why everything was so dark?

Lost in thoughts, Willow stalked past the gate of the field opposite. She didn't see the biker watching her from within.

8

As a kid, Harrison Gould had one dream. He didn't want to escape Cornwall and flee to London, didn't want to bum around chasing swell around the world, didn't want to go travelling like the rest of their peer group.

He wanted to go to college, become a mechanic, and work in his dad's garage in Perranporth.

Now, six years since she'd last seen him, Willow found him where he'd always wanted to be; underneath a car, elbow deep in grease and oil as music blared from the radio on the workbench at the back of the garage, and his workmates supplied a steady flow of tea, biscuits and crude banter.

"Bird to see you, Gouldy."

Al, a balding, pasty-skinned mechanic with a Scottish accent as thick as the copper moustache on his top lip, led Willow across the workshop and called out as they approached, wiping greasestained hands on his greasier overalls.

Harrison stood in the tyre pit, beneath a white Audi raised on hydraulic platforms, its tyres off and piled up beside it. He ran a mobile phone along the underside of the vehicle, talking as he filmed. He raised a thumb.

Al stopped and turned to Willow. "He won't be a minute."

Willow smiled.

"You say you're a friend?" Al said.

"An old friend," Willow said. "I've been away."

"Wanna brew?" he said.

Willow shook her head.

"Ok, well, give us a shout if you need anything." He smiled, then bustled back to the office.

The air smelt of rubber and oil. The gloom, the smells, the metallic clatter of dropped wrenches and bolts skipping across the floor seemed to press in on Willow. The rucksack dug into her shoulders again and she shifted it on her back. She'd taken off the cardigan, and carried it over her folded arms.

Harrison had moved to the front of the car, and other than a glance in her direction, didn't seem at all interested in who she was. Willow sighed. As a teenager, he'd been the same.

*

"What is it with you and machines?"

Megan sat on the workbench watching Harrison dismantle an outboard motor. The door to his father's workshop stood open, and bright sunlight spilt across the floor. The air smelt of oil and grease and sweat. The heat prickled Megan's back, dampened her armpits. She'd been there for hours now, moving only to get a drink from inside or take a pee.

"They're not like people," Harrison said, turning a wrench and peering hard into the network of wires and

machinery. "Everything has a purpose, and when it goes wrong, you can just fix the broken part. And they never let you down."

"I never let you down," she replied.

"That's why I like you." He glanced up from the motor, which she took as a small victory, then returned to working on the machine. She sat with her skirt up to her thighs, deliberately keeping her legs uncrossed hoping he'd sneak a peek at her knickers, and then maybe she could tempt him into showing her some real attention.

A week earlier, Zoe had told her, in giggling whispers as they sat on the bed in Zoe's room, music on loud to hide their conversation, about getting fingered by Freddie Hunt round the back of Chapel Rock at sunset.

Ever since, Zoe had been at her patronising worst, and Megan had been desperate to even the score, to prove to Zoe that she wasn't frigid, to shut the smug cow up for good. Had Harrison played his cards right, he may even have got a hand job out of it.

But he barely paid attention to her short skirt, her bare legs, her low cut top, or the garishly bright lipstick she'd plastered on. Time was ticking. Connie would be expecting her home for dinner and wouldn't hesitate to give her a clump if she was late. And the last time she'd tried to fight back, her old man had stepped in and given Connie free reign to get physical.

If she was going to even the score with Zoe, if she was going to prove she was no prude, she'd have to take matters into her own hands.

She peered through the grimy window, along the path, and towards the house. Deserted. Harrison's old man was at the garage, and his mother must've been somewhere else in the house.

A thrill of nervous energy tingled in Megan's tummy as she turned back to Harrison.

"Are machines more interesting than this?"

She lifted her top, flashed her bra.

Harrison turned. Eyes wide, he gasped. Already red-faced from the stuffy heat in the workshop, his skin went a deeper shade of purple. He looked away, fixing his gaze on the mess of wires and valves in front of him.

Megan held her top there for a long second. Harrison said nothing, didn't even look at her. Shame and embarrassment flushed through her like a red heat. She tugged her top down, and leapt off of the workbench.

"I've got to go," she muttered.

Tears trickled down her cheeks, and Megan scurried away.

*

Willow swallowed at the memory, the ghost of embarrassment stinging her cheeks. Would he remember that day?

Underneath the motor, Harrison finished the recording. He sauntered up the steps out of the pit, fiddled with the phone, then tucked it in the pockets of his overalls.

"You okay love?" he said.

He looked right through her, as if he'd never seen her before.

"Been a long time, Sparks," she said.

He frowned at the nickname she'd once given him, peered harder, looked beyond the dreadlocks and the spacers and the tattoos, and saw her.

"Megan?"

She shook her head. "It's Willow now."

"Willow?" His deep brow creased. His closely cropped dark hair had begun to recede at the temples. He smelled vaguely of sweat, of hard work and toil. "I'd forgot we used to call you that."

She smiled. "Everyone calls me that these days."

"You look..." he stepped back and peered at her. "...different."

She raised an eyebrow, smiling. "Different? That's the best you can do? The best compliment you can pay your ex?"

He flushed. "I'm sorry, I didn't mean to be rude, I just—"

"Sparks, I'm joking."

He flashed a nervous smile, narrowed his gaze, and studied her face for a long moment. Then he breathed out and his body loosened up. He smiled properly, and it made his eyes look brighter.

A pang of forgotten longing flared inside Willow, then faded. Those days had gone.

"So you're back for good then?" he said.

She shook her head. "Have you seen Ellie?"

He buried his hands in his pockets and looked to his feet, scuffing a boot on the chipped concrete. "Look, I'm sorry yeah, we never..."

Willow raised a hand. "I'm not talking about that."

She sighed and looked away, towards the racks of tyres in the cages. In another part of the garage, Al fired up a torque wrench, and its tortured howl drowned out the radio and the macho banter flying around the office. She turned back at Harrison. The screech of the wrench died. Harrison took a breath to speak.

"I think she sent me a message," she said, cutting him off. She didn't want to talk about the whole him and Ellie thing. Not then. She turned to face him. "And my old man said she should turn herself in. Sparks, I think Ellie is in trouble."

Harrison's gaze flicked across her face. He reached up and rubbed his head, looking for a second like the bashful schoolboy she'd once known.

"You don't know the half of it."

9

"You heard about Zoe?" Harrison said.

He had his legs crossed, his head bowed, drawing patterns in the fine white sand with his fingertips. Willow nodded.

"Bloody terrible that was." He shook his head like he still couldn't believe it had happened.

They'd left the garage and walked through town, barely speaking. The peak of the summer holiday season lay a few weeks away but the rush had already started. They hit the beach, trekked across the sand until they found a spot a little way from the crowds, in front of the Watering Hole beach bar, then sat down opposite each other, Willow with her back to the distant ocean.

"Did they have any idea who did it?" she said.

Harrison shrugged. "No. Police were bloody useless. They still ask for information every year.

Doesn't help though. No one seems to know anything."

"Come on, Sparks. Someone must know something."

"If they do, they're not saying anything."

"And Freddie?"

Harrison peered up at her, the ghost of an old hurt

flickering in his gaze.

"How did he take it?" she said.

Harrison shrugged and shifted on the sand.

"Badly," he said. "He was pretty cut up."

Willow kept her gaze lowered. She didn't want to meet Harrison's gaze. Freddie Hunt has been a sore point since...

"The police nicked him, y'know?"

Willow looked up. "What for?"

"They thought he started the fire."

"He wouldn't."

"Of course not. I told you, they were useless. Released without charge a few days later."

Willow traced a line in the sand, peered at Harrison. "You... ever see him?"

"Not since the funeral."

Willow nodded.

"Why'd you do it?" Harrison said into the silence. "And why with Freddie bloody Hunt?"

"Sparks, that was years ago." She peered towards Chapel Rock and twiddled the spacer in her left ear lobe.

"So? You never said sorry. I never saw you again. You bloody ran that night."

"It was a dumb mistake."

"Did you love him?"

"Sparks, seriously..."

"Don't call me that."

Willow peered at him.

"I hate you calling me that."

She shrugged. "You never complained before."

Harrison glared at her. "You hadn't slept with Freddie Hunt before."

Willow felt her face redden. She snorted and shook her head. "I'm not here for this." She put her hand out on the sand and made to rise.

"Not that bothered about Ellie then?"

"What?!"

"Still, nothing unusual there." She didn't miss the bitterness in his voice.

"How dare you."

"You ran out on her," Harrison snapped, cutting her off. "You left her alone to deal with all the shit you stirred up and then, when me and her were at our happiest, when we had so much to look forward to you—"

He clamped his mouth shut and glared across the beach towards the distant water. A tear ran down his cheek. He sniffed hard and cuffed it away. Willow sat staring at the fire tattoo on her right arm. The wind whipped sand into her face, her mouth.

"We lost the baby," he said.

"I know," she muttered.

"You did that." His face blazed with anger, with hate.

Willow looked up. "Me?"

"She went crazy. After you... what was it? Oh, yeah, you said she was dead to you."

Willow flinched and jerked away.

"Parties. Drink. Drugs." He sniffed again. "She miscarried. I thought that would change her. But it made her worse."

Willow shook her head. "So how is that my fault? I wasn't even here."

"You rejected her. When you said she was dead to you, you kicked her out of your life and it drove her crazy."

"I didn't make her do those things, Harrison." Willow touched her breastbone, the anger rising in her now. "She was a big girl. She had her own mind. And she never tried to make it up. She never said sorry."

"Why should she?"

"I LOVED YOU!" she cried, angry tears spilling down her cheeks. "And she knew that. But she fucking slept with you anyway."

"She was heartbroken, Megan."

"How d'you think I felt? I was alone on the other side of the world." She jabbed a hand vaguely towards the ocean.

"You chose that!" Harrison cried.

"And she calls up and tells me she's pregnant and, oh, by the way, the father is my ex fucking BOYFRIEND."

Harrison flinched as she shrieked. Like she'd struck him. He couldn't meet her gaze.

"She never even told me you two were a thing," Willow said. "And then she dumps that on me, and you wonder why I lost my shit?"

"You should've been happy for us."

"And she should've told me what was going on between you two before she was having your baby."

They glared at each other across the sand, the hurt they'd inflicted hanging between them. The sun slipped behind a bank of clouds, and the wind became chill on her bare shoulders. She unfolded her cardigan and slipped it on.

"Fuck it," Willow said. "I'm not here for a history lesson, or a lecture. If you don't know where she is…"

"You're right," Harrison said. "She is in trouble."

Willow froze and peered at him. Every fibre in her

body screamed at her to leap up and walk away and to hell with Harrison bloody Gould. But she was there to find Ellie. To make amends.

"What kind of trouble?"

"You ever heard of Eric Steinberg?"

Willow shook her head, confused by the sudden change of topic. "Who?"

"He's some big wig local property developer. His firm was behind that." He jerked his head towards a hotel development behind the Watering Hole. There'd been an old family pub when Willow left, but that had gone and been replaced by a towering building of glass and steel and white walls. "The development in the hills. A couple of resorts up in Newquay, Padstow, new housing estates in Redruth, Truro, Penzance."

"The guy's loaded. A multi-billionaire," Harrison continued. "At least he was."

"Was?"

"He jumped off the cliffs at Droskyn about a month ago. Low tide. Middle of the night. Straight onto the rocks. Some poor kayaker found him there the following morning."

Willow peered at the Droskyn Point cliffs at the south of the beach. Sunlight glimmered on the windscreens of the cars on the cliff top, and beyond the cars she could see the stately facade of the Droskyn Castle. A solitary figure stood against the railing along the clifftop peering out across the sand.

"What's this got to do with Ellie?" Willow turned back to Harrison.

He peered at the sand, his index finger tapping a half-buried grey stone.

"Everything apparently," he said. "Cos the way the papers tell it, Ellie was blackmailing Steinberg when he jumped."

10

On the clifftop, the breeze howling in off the ocean stung Raven's eyes as she peered out across Perranporth beach. The Cornish flag rippled on top of Chapel Rock, an island of granite in the middle of the sand. The ocean glowed turquoise. White-crested waves rolled into shore. A gull settled briefly on the wooden fence a few yards away from her, then squawked, and flew into the sky as she reached under her face mask to scratch an itch on her scars. She'd parked the bike on the road that ran alongside the Droskyn Car Park.

Far below on the beach, Megan was little more than a dot of flaming red hair in a vast expanse of dull wet sand. She sat halfway between the Surf Lifesavers Club and the Watering Hole, with Harrison a dumpy shadow next to her.

Raven dialled Goddard and put the phone to her ear.
"Well?" Goddard answered.
"Think I've found who called her back."
"And?"
"Harrison Gould."
Goddard went silent. The wind roared in the handset. A red setter bounded towards her, all floppy ears and

sloppy tongue. She held her palm out. It snuffled her glove.

"Scout!" The owner, a harried-looking guy with wild grey hair and ruddy cheeks, wheezed after him. "Leave the lady alone! I'm sorry miss, he..."

Raven turned towards him. He met her gaze, and his face paled. Maybe it was the mask, maybe the scars that ran up the side of her eyes. Or maybe it was her gaze, granite-hard and ice glass blue.

He swallowed. "Here, Scout," he said, softer now. "Come on, boy."

Scout licked her glove once more, then bounded across the grass, weaving in and out of the sundial and up onto the steep bank. The owner gave Raven one last look, then hurried away. She smiled behind the mask.

"Well..." Goddard said. "That's... surprising."

"Is it?" Raven turned back to the beach. "He was always a puppy dog around her. And Ellie."

"How does he know though?" Goddard said.

"Maybe they were closer than Ellie made out?"

"Possible. But then, why call Megan back? If he's worried about Ellie, why not call the police?"

Raven traced a crack in the wooden fence with a gloved finger.

"S'pose I better ask him," Raven said.

"Yes, I suppose you had."

She peered down at Megan and Harrison on the sand. A couple of surfers strolled past them, heading to the water with boards under their arms. A kid flew a kite that swooped and lunged over their heads. A group of teenagers had scaled Chapel Rock and were taking selfies by the flagpole.

"I should deal with Megan too."

"No, I've got a better idea."

"Such as?"

"Call your copper friend."

"Wilkes? Why?"

"Because I want some dirt on Megan Rae. She's been running for six years. She said she was in Australia, but where else has she been? What's she been doing? I want something we can use against her."

"Killing her would be easier."

"And more likely to draw unnecessary attention. Remember, knowledge is power."

"So's a knife in the back."

"We haven't got this far by killing all of our problems, Raven. If we can control her, we can neutralise her. And you never know... we may even be able to convince her to join the Chosen."

"Unlikely," Raven said. "So what do you want Wilkes to do?"

"Just some basic police work. Run her name through the PNC database. Europol. Interpol. Find out if she's got a record anywhere. Run the alias she used at the Spars too. Willow Keating."

"And if he draws a blank?"

"Then we'll find something else. In the meantime, speak to Gould. And Raven..."

"What?"

"Take it out of town. We don't need the police snooping around right now."

"Don't worry," she said, peering down at Harrison on the beach with Willow and smiling behind the mask. "I know just the place."

*

"According to the press," Harrison said. "Ellie and Steinberg had been having an affair for a year or so. Meeting at weekends. During lunch breaks. Evenings. There were like a dozen pictures of him and Ellie coming out of some hotel or other, or in some bar touching hands. They even had a picture of him coming out of her flat."

"Her flat? Ellie owns a flat?"

"No, it's a rental."

"In St. Agnes?"

"No." He pointed towards the town. "Just behind my old man's garage. On Wheal Leisure." "Here, in Perranporth?"

"Right here. Apparently some Vicar friend helped her get it after the..." He faltered. Willow looked at him. He couldn't hold her gaze.

"Well, after the whole miscarriage thing." His voice went low and tapered away. The miscarriage and their recent argument hung like a cloud of mizzle between them.

"You mean Goddard?" Willow said, breaking the tension.

"Yeah... yeah think that was it."

"Richard Goddard helped her get this flat?"

He shrugged. "It was something like that anyway."

Willow peered towards the town, fiddling with her 'Sisters' pendant.

"He never mentioned it," she muttered and began to wonder what else he'd failed to mention. Before she could wonder too hard, Harrison had started speaking again.

"Anyway, the picture shows Steinberg walking out of her front lobby at about 2 a.m. There ain't too many innocent reasons why he'd be there at that time of night."

Willow's thoughts swirled with Harrison's words. Ellie had a flat. Ellie had a lover. Goddard helped her get the flat. But Goddard hadn't mentioned anything to her. Willow shook her head, blinking.

"Sorry, but this is ridiculous," she said. "Ellie wouldn't do this."

Harrison sighed. "I didn't believe it. Not at first. But the pictures... it's her, and it's Steinberg, and he's coming out of her flat."

"Doesn't mean they were having an affair."

"I'm just telling you what I read."

Willow glared at the dunes. The anger at his words, his accusations burned within her.

"And what else did you... read?"

"Some reports reckon that she'd got pregnant again."

Willow flinched like she'd been slapped. She turned her glare on Harrison. He looked sheepish, downcast, his eyes hooded, the sun casting long shadows across his face.

"Others say she'd found out something about him that would've brought him down. Either way, they reckon she was demanding cash from him, substantial amounts, and was going to go to the press if he didn't pay up. The theory is he couldn't pay up, couldn't bear the shame, so he jumped."

"You said he was loaded?"

"Yeah, was. But he laid off half his workforce last

winter, and now they reckon his business isn't exactly flush with cash."

"Who's they?"

"The press. Social media."

Willow snorted. "Like they ever get anything right. Anyway if this is true, why is she in trouble? If she was pregnant, maybe he was threatening to walk away and leave her with nothing? Maybe she's the victim in this?"

"She was blackmailing him."

"So the papers say."

"The police said it too."

"The police?"

She saw his shoulders slump, and he exhaled loud and hard. A pained look crossed his face. His voice became a low murmur.

"A few days later, they issued a warrant for her arrest."

"For getting pregnant?"

"For blackmail." He sighed, chest heaving. "And for stealing confidential council papers."

"Woah, Harrison. Slow down." Willow waved her hands and shifted backwards on her hips. "You're losing me. What are you talking about?"

"She worked in the County Planning Office in Truro. That's where she met Steinberg, if you believe the press."

"Which I don't," Willow said.

Harrison shrugged. "Her boss caught her copying documents. Council documents, minutes from meetings, planning applications, financial reports, internal emails, basically anything and everything she could find that mentioned Steinberg. She copied them onto a USB stick. He walked in on her, and before he could stop her, she'd fled, took the stick with her. That was about a month ago. No one has seen her since."

"Goddard's seen her."

Harrison frowned. "That reverend bloke?"

Willow nodded. "Reckons he's saw her a couple of weeks back."

"Did he go to the police?"

"No idea," Willow said. "What about you? When did you last see her?"

"She was at the beach festival back at the end of May. I saw her there. Didn't speak to her."

"And she was okay?"

"Looked it. But Steinberg died that weekend and then the whole storm blew up that week."

Willow peered hard at Harrison. The wind howled along the beach, whipping dry sand across her face. It stung her cheeks. She screwed her eyes shut. Turned her head away. When the howling died and the sand settled, she looked at Harrison again.

"This doesn't make sense," she said.

He shrugged. "Doesn't mean it's not true."

"You know her. You know she wouldn't do this."

"I thought I did, but Steinberg is dead. There's pictures of her with Steinberg. She was caught copying council files about him and now there's a warrant out for her arrest, and there's no sign of her anywhere."

Willow stared at him. "You believe this?"

Harrison looked away.

"You do, don't you?" Willow said.

"I don't know what to believe."

Rage fogged her thoughts. She jabbed him with her finger.

"You know HER."

The jab rocked him back. He gave Willow a sulky look, then lowered his head again.

"I did, once. But that Ellie... she's gone."

Willow shook her head. "You're wrong about her."

Harrison gave a half shrug. "I'd love to be wrong. I really would. But where is she?"

Willow glared at him, hating the sorrow and the pity that drooped his hangdog face. "I thought you'd know." She spat the words. "I thought you cared about her."

"I haven't seen her. Not since the whole Steinberg thing blew up."

Gritting her teeth, Willow hunched forward and dug her fingers into the sand. She looked towards the town. A sparse crowd dotted the benches beneath the green and white canopies outside the Watering Hole. A class from the surf school trudged back up the beach towards their base on the sand, carrying large foam boards two by two. Grey and white clouds scudded over the houses banked up on the sides of the Perranporth valley, and a steady flow of water glistened in the sun where the Perrancombe and Bolingey streams met on the sand, and ran off towards the sea.

"Where's this flat?"

"Told you. On Wheal Leisure."

"Where on Wheal Leisure?"

"First building on the right past the garage. She lives in Flat D."

Willow stood and threw the rucksack over her shoulders.

"Where are you going?" He looked up shielding his eyes from the sun.

"To find my sister," she said.

11

Life had always been simple for Police Constable Tom Wilkes. Policing was all he wanted to do. Policing and having a family with Ann. The job gave him adventure, excitement, the thrill of making a difference. And life with Ann gave him comfort and security, a sense of stability. They lived in a new-build house, on the outskirts of Perranporth, off the main road to St. Agnes. Three bedrooms. No kids yet. But they'd been trying. And no plans for anything more exciting than holidays to the south of France in the summer.

Until one mistake.

A moment of weakness.

He couldn't remember her name. He could remember her body. Lithe. Slender. Tits to die for. And the tattoos beneath them…he'd kissed those tattoo's long and hard that night.

His best mate's stag weekend. Five guys. A weekend away in Ibiza last summer. The last night. He'd been good the rest of the time. Not got too drunk. Stayed away from the recreational drugs that had been readily available and as readily consumed by the rest of the party. But that night, his resolve caved in. He wanted one night, just one night of wild debauchery to remember when he was old and dead from the dick down.

He hadn't planned on getting laid. But the drink and the pills took him over, and he ended up with his hands all over her. And she'd whispered in his ear, and they'd staggered out of the club, back to his apartment.

The sex had been wild. Much wilder than anything he and Ann had ever done. And when it was over, he'd crashed out on the bed, and she'd vanished the next morning.

He felt guilty, of course. But the others had done far worse that weekend. And it was a one-off, a moment of regret. But a weight off his shoulders too. He'd always have the memories. And Ann would never know.

Then a message with a video attached dropped into his personal email about six weeks later.

Do what we want and Ann never sees this.

The video showed him and the girl screwing. Someone had snuck back in while he was distracted and recorded the whole thing. He never found out who.

He deleted the email, pretended it hadn't happened. Then came the phone calls, always when Ann had gone out, or when he was on duty. And always the person on the other end would mention a small, specific detail that told him they were watching.

Then they found him.

He'd finished his shift, slipped into his car. Glanced in the rear-view mirror as he was about to pull away and saw a shadow in his back seat, their eyes visible beneath a heavy black hood, and a black mask styled with a skeletal lower jaw over their nose and mouth. He'd gone to turn, but the blade touched his throat and he froze.

"You're ignoring us." The voice was female. She sounded young but there was steel in her tone.

"I can't help you!"

"You've got no choice."

"Please. My career."

"Your career will be fine if you play ball. You might even find yourself on a fast track to the top. But if you don't, well, I'm sure Ann will enjoy the movie."

A phone landed on the front seat then, with the video playing.

"What do you want?"

"Nothing. Yet. But we'll have little jobs for you. Do them well, you'll be rewarded. Don't and…"

The blade nicked his throat. He gasped. Then the pressure vanished. The door opened and the shadow vanished into the night before he could respond.

When he got home that night, he lied to Ann about cutting himself shaving when she asked about the small wound on his neck, and had lain awake all night wondering what to do.

The following day, the first instruction had come. Nothing major. Find a piece of info and pass it on. It didn't seem like much. A home postcode. Not even the full address. Just a postcode.

Telling himself it would do no harm, he gave it to them. Afterwards, he heard nothing for a month. He almost convinced himself it was over. Then he got another phone call asking him to run a PNC check on a prominent local businessman and pass on what he found. He'd hesitated. Almost refused.

Then Ann mentioned a figure lurking outside their house that afternoon, in a leather coat, hood up, a mask over their nose and mouth. By lunchtime the next day the check had been done and passed over.

More requests. Lose a charge sheet. Forge a signature. Track a phone number. They came by phone, from an anonymous number that changed every time. Recently, however, the calls had stopped and once again he had started to hope it was over.

That hope had just died.

He stood naked in his bedroom, halfway to the en-suite shower, his phone ringing on the bedside table. The house was empty. Ann had left for work in Padstow. Heart fluttering, his tongue flicking over his lips, cold sweat beading on his forehead, he considered not answering.

The phone kept ringing. His resolve failed and he snatched up the phone.

"Haven't I done enough for you?" he said.

"Not yet." The voice was female and cold.

"What do you want?"

"I want you to run two names through a PNC check, Interpol, Europol."

"I'm a bobby, not the Head of Scotland Yard! I can't do that!"

"We can always arrange a private cinema viewing for Ann."

He sighed, grit his teeth, longed to tell the shadow to get lost, but the thought of Ann being made to watch what he'd done...

"What names?"

"Megan Rae."

"Rae? As in Ellie Rae?"

"Yes, Constable."

"Is this connected to the Steinberg thing?"

"Not your business."

"But..."

"Not your business."

He sighed. "And the other name?"

"The other name is Willow Keating." He scribbled the names down. "Check the last one with Aussie police too."

"Aussie police?"

"She was in Australia until recently. They may have something. Call me on this number when it's done."

"And is that it then?" he said. "Am I square?"

The voice chuckled. "You'll never be square, Tom. Never."

12

As apartment blocks went, Ellie's didn't look too bad from the outside. It was in better condition than the one Willow had called home in Sydney. Hell. It was better than most of the digs Willow had crashed in these last six years.

Ellie's had a triple gabled facade and stood three storeys tall. Copper watermarks streaked the grey and cream paintwork beneath the plastic overflow pipes and the window ledges, but at least the windows closed and the lock on the red security door worked. Plant pots with white and blue flowers sat on either side of the step, and three of the four parking bays outside were taken up with new-ish cars. Willow gazed up at the middle flat on the right of the building.

Ellie's flat.

The windows had a blank, abandoned feel. Willow gazed around. The Catholic church across the road looked shut up. A low, red-bricked building, it looked more like a community hall than a church, and only the placard on the gabled porch and the cross on the peak of the porch revealed its true purpose. The car park up the bank behind the church was almost full. A steady flow of pedestrians passed in and out, heading for the beach or the shops, or coming back laden with bags and beach furniture.

She turned back to the apartment, found the buzzer for Flat D on the metal call panel by the door, and pressed it. The button felt greasy beneath her fingertip. An electric crackle, followed by a crude pulse, rang out from the speaker grill at the bottom of the panel. Willow stepped back and looked up at the window to Ellie's flat. Nothing seemed to move within.

The crackle died. The door remained locked. Willow kept peering at the window, hoping, but not expecting, to see Ellie sneaking a peek down at her. Nothing happened. With a deep sigh, she turned away. Another dead end.

Then the door behind her buzzed, and the latch clicked open.

Willow turned and peered up. She couldn't see anyone in Ellie's window, but the door had been opened from inside. Someone was watching her. She turned to the door again. If it was Ellie...

Hope fluttering, Willow reached for the handle, pulled the door open, and stepped inside. Concrete stairs zigzagged up the centre of the building. An antiseptic smell lingered in the brightly lit stairwell. The walls looked clean and recently plastered. Willow peered up.

A face peered back over the bannisters on the top floors.

Not Ellie. The fluttering hope faded. The face staring back was male, balding, with long hair around the sides and back, like a monk. Narrow rimmed specs, and a grey cardigan over a large beer belly.

"You okay, love?"

"Yeah, I'm…" Dare she mention her relationship to Ellie? If people thought she was the wicked witch who had bought down Steinberg, maybe mentioning they were related would be a bad idea. She decided to play it safe. "I'm looking for Eloise Rae. I heard she lived here."

"Press?"

Willow shook her head. "No."

"Police?"

"Do I look like police?"

"Who are you then?"

Willow frowned. "Why's it important?"

"Because…" The guy put his hands in his pockets and sauntered down the stairs. "I'm her landlord, and she owes me a couple of months' rent."

Willow began to climb the stairs and met him on the second-floor landing.

"So, she does live here then?"

The door to Flat D stood closed. No lights on inside.

"She did. Haven't seen her in about a month." The landlord looked Willow up and down, then stepped in close, lowered his spectacles to the end of his ruddy bulbous nose, and squinted at her face. "You look a lot like her. Except the hair. Family?"

Willow nodded. "I'm her sister."

"Don't suppose she gave you the back rent then."

"Sorry. I haven't seen her in..." she hesitated, settled for a white lie, "..a while."

"Two bleeding months she owes me now. Taken the bloody keys with her as well. Good job I've got a master set."

"Can I go in?" Willow said, pointing at the door.

The landlord peered at her, tilting his head back until he looked down his nose. "You sure you're family? Only we've had some funny sorts knocking on this door?"

"Oh?" Willow's pulse quickened.

"Yeah." He sniffed and burrowed his hands in his pockets again. "Some weirdo in biker gear. Couple of dodgy looking blokes. One of 'em had terrible acne. Knocking at all hours they were. Had to threaten to call the police a week back. The biker had got in the block and was trying to kick the door down."

"And did you?"

"What?"

"Call the police?"

He shrugged. "They went away. I didn't bother. But I reckon she's in trouble."

Willow gazed at the door. Now that he'd mentioned it, she could see the boot mark on the green paintwork.

"Course, I thought it was all to do with that business bloke she was knocking off."

Willow's head snapped round to face him. "Steinberg?"

"Yeah, funny old business." He scratched his head like a plumber examining a particularly troubling leak. "But it explains a lot. I mean, for a tenant she didn't spend much time here. The odd week, maybe a weekend. It's not the first time she's disappeared for a month. But she's always paid her rent before now. And..."

"So can I go in?" Willow said, growing bored of his rant.

He blinked. "Sorry?"

"Please? I want to check. Make sure she's not in

there."

He shrugged. "If you must. Just wait a second, I'll get the spare key."

He turned and huffed back up the stairs. Willow watched him go, then turned to the door. She bent forward and studied the frame closer. She could see a chip of the wood missing and a gap where the lock had lifted from the frame. She nudged the door but it didn't budge. The landlord huffed back down.

"Don't know why you're bothering," he said. "She weren't there last time I went in. Hadn't been there for a while."

"You've gone in?"

"Course." He sniffed and dug a key out of his pocket, bent and put the key in the lock. "After those blokes were round I wanted to make sure they hadn't got in and done any damage."

"And had they?"

He turned the lock. "Place was deserted. Looked fine though. There you go." He smiled, nudged the door open and stepped back.

Willow peered inside. A rhombus of daylight spilt across the blonde wood laminate floor from an open door at the end of the hall. A stale, musty smell drifted from within. Like the windows hadn't been opened for a long time.

"Take your time," he said, passing her the key. "I'm in the flat above. Just drop the key back when you're done."

She pocketed the key and smiled. The landlord wheezed away. Willow watched him until he got halfway up the stairs, then turned back to the flat. Ellie wasn't in there, that much was clear straight away, but with luck, she may find something, anything, that would tell her where Ellie was.

She stepped into the hallway and closed the door behind her.

*

Raven pulled into the small patch of concrete outside the Catholic church opposite. The bike spat and growled beneath her. She killed the engine and the bike settled. She could see Megan's flame-red hair as she walked up the stairwell inside. Kicking the bike stand down, she swung her leg off and retreated into the shadows of the awning over the church door. Less visible there.

Raven looked up at Ellie's flat. No sign of life.

What are you here for, Megan? The USB? The docs? You won't find them. And you won't find Ellie either. There's nothing here for you. Unless...

She swore, her stomach cold.

Unless Goddard had been right. Unless that bitch had lied. Unless she had made copies.

Raven clenched her jaw. Her scars throbbed. She should've come back, kicked down the door, knocked out the fat-fuck landlord, and ransacked the place. But she hadn't and if there were copies, Megan would have them now.

Anger rose as a ball in Raven's throat. She swallowed it down, clenching her fists. If Megan did have them, Raven had to get them back.

Because if she didn't, she'd end up going the same way as Raphael.

GARY KRUSE

13

The door thunked shut behind her and Willow stood with her back against it, listening hard. She heard a few footsteps on the floor above and the muted growl of a car passing on the road outside. Inside, the silence felt thick and heavy. She stepped forward, her boots loud on the laminate. She traced a hand along the cream walls until she reached the open door. It led into the lounge. She touched the glossy white frame and peered in.

Dust motes swirled in the bright light spilling in through the two windows opposite. A rumpled leather sofa sat against the wall to her left, beneath a mirrored clock. A nest of MDF coffee tables, painted white, stood between the windows. An empty metallic-purple vase stood on top of them. Willow stepped into the room.

She glanced at the electric fire on the wall by the TV, at the thick grey rug on the floor. She could see gaps in the floor where the laminate had shifted and in places the beading had snapped loose. Behind her, a small U-shaped kitchen area with cheap laminate cabinets and worktops ran off of the main lounge. The dust itched her nose. She crossed to the left window and opened it. The rush of fresh air stirred the dust motes and rattled the frame of the picture hanging on the wall between the windows. Willow half-glanced at it and went to move to the next window. Then she realised what she'd seen and stopped to look again.

The picture showed her and Ellie as teenagers clowning around on the stone bridge at the foot of Trevellas. It had been taken facing up the valley, a colour shot showing most of their group trekking down towards the shingle beach. Behind them, the brick engine houses rose into a dazzling blue sky. Willow peered hard at her thirteen-year-old self.

The Megan she had once been.

Short and stocky, she wore a frumpy purple jumper and black leggings. She'd jumped on Ellie's back the instant the picture had been taken. She had her arms wrapped around Ellie's neck, squinting, beaming, her mouth full of braces. Her mousy brown hair fell in dull curls about her ruddy face. She looked how she had felt then, how being Megan always felt. An awkward mess.

Ellie, on the other hand...

She was sixteen, and her smile gleamed in her dazzling eyes. Her hair fell blonde and silky smooth around her flawless oval face. She wore green Wellington boots and a three-quarter length blue duffel coat with wooden horns for buttons.

In the background, coming down the path, she could see Freddie Hunt, thick-lipped and broody, with his mop of blonde hair falling around his face. Harrison was there as well, clutching a car magazine under his arm, keeping his head down and his hands jammed in his pockets. And behind Harrison, two younger girls; Freddie and Zoe's sisters.

The only one missing was Zoe herself. She had taken the picture. It had been the October half term, and they'd been running amok in the coves and the caves, on the beaches and the clifftop paths of the Badlands all week. Ellie had been sent as a chaperone after a run-in with a local bobby the day before.

Smiling at the memories - Ellie's perfume, the scream she'd given as Willow leapt on her, the salt wind blowing in her face off of the ocean as she clung to Ellie's back - Willow placed her fingertips on her sister's cheek. A bittersweet sadness swelled inside her.

Good times, long gone.

"Where are you?" she muttered.

She sighed, let her hand drop to her side, and peered around.

She saw an iPhone charger plugged into one of the sockets in the kitchen, the cable dragging across the worktop, the wall switch off. Probably Ellie's. No phone though. She crossed to the kitchen and opened the cupboards, saw tins of beans, tomatoes, vegetable soups, packs of sugar, flour, Taco's, rice in one. In another she found sauces - tomato, soy, Worcester - and oils. A fridge stood beneath the worktop next to the sink, humming. She opened it.

Empty.

She opened the freezer compartment at the top, the flap rattling in the hinges. Empty as well.

She closed the fridge, rummaged through a few drawers, cupboards, found washing powder, cleaning detergents, bleaches, plates, cups, cutlery, tea bags, coffee, saucepans... the menial products of everyday life. Anything perishable seemed to have gone. She closed the drawers, squatted on her haunches and gazed around. If it hadn't been for the photo, it would have been hard to tell that Ellie had lived there at all.

It was the same in the rest of the flat. Oh, Ellie had left wardrobes full of clothes and boxes full of trinkets and trophies and soft toys from her childhood, but there was absolutely no clue as to where Ellie had gone. Or why people had been so desperate to break in here. There was no laptop. No USB stick, no sign of the council documents that Harrison had mentioned. No cryptic messages scrawled on notes for Willow to decipher. No signs of struggle. No signs of a fight.

But at the same time, it didn't feel like Ellie was coming back anytime soon.

Willow recognised the signs, having fled her own digs more than once in the last six years, normally when she couldn't pay the rent and things got heavy with the landlord, or when one of her roommates wouldn't take no for an answer. You took everything important and fled, leaving the rest of your life behind.

Like Ellie had done here.

The knocker banged on the front door, shattering the silence.

She stalked down the hall, heart punching up her throat. The landlord peered in, his pale, podgy features distorted by the frosted glass. "You okay in there?"

Willow threw open the door. "Where is everything?" she said.

He blinked up at her. "Sorry?"

"It's like a show home. No post. No bills scattered around. No mess. The fridge is empty. And the freezer. Where is it all?"

He shrugged. "That's how I found it. Post goes in the box on the wall outside. I've emptied hers a couple of times and got the pile in my flat, but everything else..."

"So there was no laptop? No papers left lying around? A USB stick?"

"Not that I saw." He shook his head.

"You're sure?"

"That was how I found it. Haven't touched a thing."

Willow peered back into the flat.

"You want the post?" he said.

Willow nodded still staring. She stepped into the hallway again, turned the corner into the lounge and looked around.

Willow chewed her lip. "When did you say you last saw her?"

"Told you. About a month ago."

"No, when exactly did you last see her?"

He puffed out his cheeks and rubbed the back of his head. "Christ, I don't know. I didn't pay much attention to it."

"Tell me about it," Willow said.

"About what?"

"The last time you saw her. How was she? Happy? Sad? Angry? Worried?"

He shrugged. "I couldn't say. She just seemed like herself. I mean, she'd been a bit quiet for a while."

"You spoke to her a lot then?"

"Don't mean that. She liked a party, did Ellie. But they stopped about six months back. Had her fancy fella round a few times."

"How'd you know?"

He flushed and rubbed the back of his head again.

"Well… I'd just… hear them…"

"Doing what?"

His face went beetroot, and Willow realised what he meant.

"I weren't perving!" he pleaded, but Willow turned away. "And like I say, other than that, she'd been quiet. And a month ago I stopped seeing her. Took me a week or so to realise she weren't there."

Willow looked around the bare living room barely hearing him now, her thoughts on Ellie.

Harrison and the landlord hadn't seen her for a month, and the Steinberg story had broken a month ago. And when it had, Ellie had upped and run.

Goddard though. He'd seen her two weeks back. So, she *was* still around. The question was, where the hell was she?

"Hang on though," the landlord said, running his chin, his brow furrowed. "Thinking about it, the last time I recall seeing her she was on the phone. Late at night and pretty upset."

"Upset?"

"Well, agitated really. She was pacing outside in the car park. I'd been round a mate's for a few drinks and came past her, and she was talking to someone, asking them if they'd met up with someone or other."

Excitement flickered in Willow's chest. "You know who she was talking to?"

The landlord shrugged. "No idea. But she kept asking them if this… this… Ryan or Royston had shown up?"

"Ryan?"

The landlord scrubbed his forehead with the pads of his fingertips, frowning hard as if thinking was a task.

"Something like that." Realisation sparked in his gaze and he clicked his fingers. "No. That was it. Raven."

Willow's blood went cold. "You what?"

"That was it. Raven. I remember cos it was about three in the morning and I remember thinking why's she looking for birds at 3 a.m.?"

"You're sure she said Raven?"

"One hundred per cent."

It couldn't be. Zoe was dead. She'd visited Zoe's grave that morning. She'd seen the outpouring of grief on Facebook at the time. It couldn't be her?

Could it?

"When was this?"

The landlord shrugged. "About a month ago. Why?"

"You ever see her again?"

He frowned, rubbed his head again.

"No," he said. "No. That was definitely the last time. You think it's important?"

Willow shook her head, her thoughts spinning with ideas, possibilities, wild dreams or terrible nightmares. Was it important? Maybe. Or maybe it was just a wild coincidence.

Ellie could answer that. But from what Willow could see, Ellie wasn't coming back here anytime soon.

14

Willow stuffed the picture from the wall into her bag and followed the landlord out into the stairwell, then locked the door and handed him the key.

"I'll get the post," he said, scurrying up the stairs as Willow stared at the faded boot print on the front door. The biker had wanted to get in there pretty bad. Hadn't, of course, thanks to the landlord. She heard his footsteps on the stairwell, his breath loud and chesty, a plastic bag rustling in his hands.

"Just junk mainly," he said, handing it over.

Willow peered in the bag. Circulars, white envelopes with franked or pre-paid postage from a bank, a mobile company, a broadband supplier, then enough glossy flyers to cover a good-sized wall, a few take away menus. No council papers. No USB. She closed the bag.

"You can check the box on the way out too," he said, smiling.

"Cheers." She turned and headed for the steps.

He cleared his throat. She glanced back.

"The rent?" he said.

Willow frowned and shook her head. "What about it?"

"Well, she's your sister. And she owes twelve fifty."

Willow blinked. "One thousand two hundred and fifty pounds?"

He gave a sheepish smile. "I know you're not to blame, but I've got overheads to cover, and I ain't got that sort of money to cover it."

Willow shook her head. "Neither have I."

"So what do I do? Who do I contact to get the money back?"

"You got a number for Ellie?"

"Tried that. No answer."

Willow nodded. Hadn't expected anything else. "Look, I can't pay you now. But give me your number. I'll see if I can sort something."

"It's pretty urgent," he said.

"Appreciate that," Willow replied. "But there is literally nothing more I can do right now."

He sighed, stuffed his hands in his pockets, and gave her a number. She copied it into her phone and made a mental note to tell her old man all about it when, if, she next saw him, then headed for the front door. She stepped outside, blinking in the afternoon sunlight. The door clicked and thunked shut behind her. She walked to the letterboxes on the wall and lifted the flap on Ellie's box with the crook of her forefinger. She slipped her hands inside. Empty. Or else whatever was in there was too close to the bottom for her to reach.

She withdrew her fingers, dropped her shoulder, and swung her rucksack down to the floor. She unzipped it and pushed the bag of letters inside before zipping it up, then hefting it onto her back again. With a final glance at Ellie's windows, she turned and walked through the cars in the car park, her thoughts on Ellie, on council papers and USB sticks…

On Raven…

As she turned towards the Co-op, a flicker of movement in the corner of her vision made her turn. A figure in biker's leathers and a black and red helmet stepped back into the shadows of the porch of the Catholic church. She almost ignored them, but then she remembered what the landlord had said, about the biker who had tried to kick Ellie's door in. Heart jolting, mind whirring with possibilities, Willow spun.

"Hey!" she cried.

The biker flinched, then ran for the bike parked in front of the church. Willow bolted after them, straight into the road. A horn blared, Willow turned and saw a car screaming towards her. She yelped, heart jackhammering, and leapt back onto the pavement. The car roared past. Across the road, the biker had leapt onto the bike.

"Hey!" Willow sprinted across the road. "Stop!"

She leapt the wall as the biker tried to kickstart the engine. Boots scuffing the tarmac, concrete jarring her knees, Willow sprung for the biker and grabbed their wrists. The bike howled to life. The biker wrenched the wheel left. Willow staggered, boots scraping on the floor. The biker hauled the wheel right, and Willow clung on.

"Where's Ellie?" she screamed into the blank visor. "Where is she?"

The biker twisted the bars. Wheels screaming, the bike skidded forward. The biker jerked from Willow's grip. She stumbled, and her knees scuffed the gravel. The rucksack fell to her elbow, the strap bending her arm. She grabbed the strap, and swung the bag at the biker's back.

It struck, but the blow was weak, ineffective. Instead of speeding off, the biker turned and snatched the other strap, tugged the bag away. Willow, still gripping her strap, yanked it back. The biker slipped from the seat. The wheels crunched into the gravel as the bike skidded. Willow yanked again, and the biker tugged back. The straps stretched taut between them. Willow pulled, and the biker pulled harder. Seams began to pop. A thread burst loose.

"Get off!" she screamed.

"Hey!" a male voice cried out.

Willow turned.

Harrison was sprinting towards them. Others from the garage followed.

The biker looked towards his voice. Willow felt the grip slacken. She sprung forward and pushed the biker back.

A cry from within the mask. Willow and the biker clattered to the floor together, the bike falling with them. Willow rolled away, and rose to her knees. The biker kicked her hard in the gut. The toe of the boot felt like a rock. The air whooshed out of her lungs. She gasped, and fell backwards.

"Get off her!" Harrison said, and leapt the wall.

Willow heard the scream of an engine. She looked up through breathless tears. The biker had leapt back onto the seat and was now speeding from the car park and out onto Wheal Leisure. Strong hands wrapped around her shoulders.

"Are you ok?"

She looked up at Harrison, frowning, concern on his

face. She nodded, then stared after the bike, her shoulders sore, leggings ripped at the knees, blood welling from the grazes beneath, lungs burning to breathe. Her bag lay a few feet away, the seams of its straps frayed. The bike vanished around the bend, leaving Willow and a band of bemused mechanics in its wake.

15

Raven hit the roundabout without stopping, skidding through in a cacophony of squealing brakes and bellowed curses. She sped across, out of Perranporth, towards Newquay. She bent low over the handlebars, and gunned the engine. The bike roared around the curve and up the hill, the wind howling around her visor. She swung past the holiday park and the golf course into Goonhavern. At the roundabout, she threw a right to take the road back to St. Agnes, then braked in a gravel bay outside the gate to a field. The wheels kicked up loose stones and dirt. Gripping the handlebars, she skidded to a halt and kicked down the stand.

With the bike upright, she slapped the handlebars. "Shit!"

The shout was muffled by her visor. Her pulse roared in her ears. She breathed hard. A steady flow of traffic thrummed past. A few drinkers sat at the benches outside the New Inn, and a people-carrier pulled up in the car park outside. She swung off the bike, crossed to the gate, and put a gloved hand on top, then leapt over and into the field. Slipping behind the hedge, she cast her gaze around, making sure the field was empty. Then she unclipped her helmet and tugged down her mask. The air felt cool on her burn scars. She rubbed her jaw.

She'd blown it. Megan almost had her. Grabbing the bag had been an instinct. She'd seen the girl come out with the bag, and a dozen thoughts had crashed through her mind. Had there been another USB after all? Was it in the bag? Or had Ellie copied the papers and left them for Megan to collect? Was that why Harrison had called her back? The opportunity had been too good, and if she'd managed to grab the bag, if she'd got hold of the contents, all her problems would be over now, she realised.

But she hadn't. And worse, she'd almost been caught.

She screwed her eyes shut. "Shit!"

Free of the mask and the helmet, her voice echoed across the plough marks, startling a blackbird that had been pecking at the broken, sun-baked earth. It screeched skyward. Raven watched it go, then glared at the field. Wilted leaves protruded from the dirt. Wire netting ran around the inside of the perimeter, covering a two-foot wide furrow all around the circumference.

The fields belonged to Duchy Farms, which in turn belonged to Goddard. Duchy Farms produced and supplied organic and ethically farmed veg to restaurants, shops and local businesses across Cornwall. From time to time, the vans also transported some choice extras from Goddard's side business too.

Her temper faded. She breathed deep, sucking in the smell of the soil beneath her feet. She closed her eyes and let the breeze play across her ruined skin. She'd got away, unidentified and without blowing their cover. But it had been close.

If Goddard found out...

She swallowed hard. He'd understand. She'd seen an opportunity. Tried to take it. Failed, yes, but...

Who was she kidding? He wouldn't understand. He'd warned her to keep her distance. Follow and observe. She'd been reckless. And others had suffered for less. At least he didn't know. Yet. But he would. He seemed to know everything. And he'd be pissed if he found out. Super-pissed. And if she still had nothing to show for it, then who knew what he'd do.

She swallowed again.

She had to make amends.

Her first thought was to kill the girl. But no... he'd distinctly told her not to. And maybe he was right. Harrison, her father...people knew Megan was back, that she was looking for Ellie. If she went missing as well, it would be one coincidence too many.

Goddard valued information. What exactly did Harrison Gould know? He'd called Megan back. He'd sent her to Ellie's flat. Why? In all of her hours tailing Ellie, in all the days and nights and weeks she'd spent watching or waiting for those who were watching to report in, she hadn't seen, and no one had mentioned, Harrison. As far as she was aware, Ellie and Harrison hadn't met, hadn't spoken since the miscarriage and the break-up three years earlier. And they'd been watching Ellie and Steinberg a long time. Far longer than either of them had known.

And yet...

Raven deals with the Ellie problem and five days later Megan's back and snooping, and all because of Harrison Gould.

Which meant she'd missed it. They'd all missed it. Harrison knew something, maybe everything. Maybe he'd had a copy of the USB. Maybe he'd taken copies of the papers. Maybe that was what Megan had found in the flat.

She had to find out and there was only one way to do that now. She dug the phone from her pocket and paced into the centre of the field.

Time to call in a debt.

Time to get reacquainted with Harrison Gould.

She hit dial and waited for the call to connect.

*

Legs shaking, nausea filling her gut, Willow leant forward on the plastic seat and clutched her temples between her palms. She sucked in a deep, trembling breath, and then exhaled, the air whistling through pursed lips. The movement of her ribs made her bruised stomach muscles throb with the memory of the biker's kick.

"You okay?"

She looked up. Harrison stood in the office doorway, clutching a mug of tea. The radio blared in the garage outside. Then it cut off and the silence seemed deafening. Chains rattled as shutters were pulled down and cages locked up. Laughter echoed from the walls.

"Been better." She lowered her gaze and studied a crack in the vinyl tiling on the floor.

"Made you tea," Harrison said.

She heard his footsteps on the floor as he crossed and put the tea next to her.

"Still take two sugars, right?"

She nodded. "Thanks."

She glanced at the dark hair on his arms as he put the mug on the desk behind her, then turned back to the floor. She pressed her heels down to try and stop her feet from shaking, but it made her knees jerk instead. She closed her eyes and leant back, peering up at the fluorescent tube lighting overhead. Outside, the lights began to click off.

"Want me to clean those?" he said, pointing at the grazes on her knees. The blood had dried black.

She shook her head. "It's fine."

"They'll get infected."

"It's ok."

"Seriously, I don't mind."

"I said it's FINE." She turned on him, her voice shrill and harsh. Outside, the laughter and the banter faltered. After a few seconds of awkward silence, it flared up again, louder now, more exuberant. Fake.

"Well, I... guess I'll just leave you to it then."

He stood. Guilt flushed through her. She reached out and grabbed his wrist.

"Harrison."

He turned and peered down at her.

"I'm sorry." She tried to smile, but her lips wouldn't work properly. "It's just..."

The tears came fast and unexpected, and before she realised it, he was hugging her, and she was burying her face in his shoulder and crying hard. She could smell his aftershave. Joop. The same he'd worn since he was a teenager. He held her until the tears stopped. When she sat back, smiling sheepishly and flushed with embarrassment and guilt, the garage was empty and they were alone.

"I'm sorry," she said again.

Kneeling in front of her, he shook his head. "Stop apologising."

She wiped her eyes with the tips of her fingers. Shook her dreadlocks behind her shoulders. "Think I've got a fair few things to apologise for."

"Haven't we all?"

He had his gaze cast down, his hands in his lap. The past, and their argument that afternoon, hung between them, but as she peered at him she saw the boy she'd met in primary school and feeling angry seemed to her like a waste of all those years. She went to speak as he looked up and started talking at the same time.

"I never meant-"

"Me and Ellie-"

Willow lowered her gaze, face flushing. When she looked up, he was frowning. Overhead, the fluorescent strip light fizzed and flickered. The clock on the wall ticked away the seconds. His gaze flicked across her face. He reached out and put his palm against her cheek. She closed her eyes, breathed in through her nose, touched the back of his hand.

"I'd forgot how pretty you were," he said.

She snorted and opened her eyes. "Harrison, please..."

"I mean it." He leant closer. She held her breath, her gaze locked with his.

He moved his lips to hers.

She turned her cheek. "I can't..."

He stopped. Let his hand fall from her cheek onto his lap. Nodded. "I'm sorry. I shouldn't have done that."

"It's ok."

"No, you're here looking for Ellie. You've just been in a fight and now I'm trying to..." He sighed, his face red. He stood and crossed to the door to the office, and unhooked his jacket. "Where are you staying?" he asked her, digging his car keys out of his pocket.

"The Driftwood Spars."

"I can drop you back, if you want."

She shook her head. "You don't have to."

"I'd like to. For... everything."

She peered at his back as he busied himself with his keys, the ring binders on the shelf above the PC, the invoices in the plastic yellow out tray.

"Ok," she said.

"I won't be a minute." He hustled out of the office and into the toilet without looking at her. She sat forward, knitted her fingers, and let her arms hang between her knees. Her eyes felt dry and gritty, and the jetlag gnawed at her. It took all her effort to stay awake, despite the sting of the grazes on her knees and the throb of the bruise in her chest.

She stood and stretched, then paced around the office. The nausea had settled now, and her limbs had stopped shaking. She sat again, wincing as the grazes split with the bend of her knees. She leant forward, opened her bag, and dug out the picture from Ellie's flat. The glass had split in the corner, but the picture was undamaged. She stared at her sister, at the life she'd run away from.

"What's that?"

She gasped, looked up. Harrison had come back into the room and was staring at the picture.

"I found it in Ellie's flat."

She held it up to him. He crossed the floor, reached out, and took it. As he peered at it, a dopey smile spread across his lips.

"I remember that day," he said.

"You do?"

He sat in the seat beside hers.

"Yeah, we trekked down to Trevellas. Ellie had been sent to keep an eye on us cos Freddie has smashed someone's window and we got a talking to from the police. She was being a right mizzly cow, and then Zoe called you a name, and it made Ellie laugh, so you jumped on her back, and you both ended cackling like witches."

"Willow," she said, peering at the picture. "She called me Willow."

"Yes!" Harrison chuckled. "And Ellie asked why and Zoe said..."

"Cos she's got legs like tree trunks and hair like a willow tree." Willow smiled and shook her head.

"That was the day we first kissed," he said.

She peered at him, remembering the game of hide and seek, the cave, the dark, the taste of mint on his breath as his lips brushed hers.

Ellie had stumbled in on them.

"Looks like you two are cosy," she'd said. They'd pulled apart fast, faces burning and didn't speak to each other for the rest of the day. It had been another year or two, spent bickering and outwardly hating each other, before they'd kiss again as boyfriend and girlfriend.

"What will you do?" Harrison said, glancing at her. "When you find Ellie."

Willow sucked in a breath. Her stomach spasmed from

the kick, and she winced again.

"Slap the shit out of her for scaring me." She peered at Ellie in the picture. "Then hug her to death."

"I mean after."

She looked up at him.

"After?"

"Will you stay in Cornwall?" She peered back at the picture.

"There's nothing for me here now."

"I'm here."

She could feel him staring at her, but couldn't look at him.

"You and me," she said. "That was a long time ago. I'm different now."

"You're still Megan to me."

She took the picture from his fingers, gave Ellie one last look, then slipped it in the bag.

"I need to get back," she said, standing and throwing the rucksack over her shoulders. "I'm tired, sore. It's been a long day."

She crossed to the door, moved out into the garage. A rectangle of light spilled under the gap at the bottom of the shutters. She heard him switch the light off and close the door to the office. She couldn't look at him.

"Look, Megan."

"It's Willow," she said.

He sighed.

"Ok. Willow. I know there's... history between us. And we've both done things that have hurt one another, but it's been good to see you today."

Willow turned to face him, and folded the cardigan over her hands.

"And I just want you to know that... if you ever want me... just to talk even... I am here for you."

He stepped towards her.

"I'll always be here for you."

She nodded. "I'm tired, Sparks. I need to sleep."

He looked crestfallen. But he gave a grim smile and strode to the shutters. He pushed them up. They screeched and rattled on their runners. Light spilt in. He stood beneath them, flourishing his arm towards the car park outside.

"Your chariot awaits, fair maiden." He grinned, but she could see the hurt in his eyes.

She ducked under the shutters, reached out, and ran her fingers along his arm. She flashed him a sad smile, then crossed to his car as he locked the garage behind her.

16

"So it's my day off tomorrow…"

Willow looked up from the news report she'd been reading on her phone. Ruby dropped onto the barstool opposite her, tucked a loose strand of sandy blonde hair behind her ear, and leaned her elbows on the dark oak table between them. The main bar of the Driftwood Spars was busy with the early evening trade. Locals and tourists alike propped up the bar or gathered around the tables or in the booths, eating or settling for a liquid dinner of the best ales from the Driftwood Brewery opposite.

"… and I was thinking," Ruby went on, "that I'd like to spend the day with a gorgeously rad hippy chick with red dreadlocks, y'know, tatts and spacers, the whole works, but then I'm thinking, where am I gonna find a girl like that around here?" She cocked her head and smiled.

"Any suggestions?"

Willow looked back at the report on her screen again.

"I told you I'm not here for a relationship."

"And I told you I'm talking about dirty hard sex." Ruby hooked her tongue over her teeth and winked. Willow chuckled in spite of herself.

"You're a nightmare."

"So you up for it?"

Willow glanced at Ruby over the top of her phone. She could still see the headline of the article she had been reading.

REVEALED: THE SECRET MISTRESS WHO BROUGHT DOWN PROPERTY TYCOON ERIC STEINBERG.

After Harrison had dropped her off at the Spars she'd gone to her room and crashed out, only to wake when the couple next door started screwing again. She'd retreated to the bar to get dinner, ordered fish and chips and a vodka and coke, and then retreated to one of the tables at the side of the bar, beneath black and white pictures of old St. Agnes.

She'd spent a few minutes watching the regulars at the bar and the group of officious, politically woke types setting up a public meeting in the side room, then, when her meal arrived, she'd dug out her phone and searched for Eric Steinberg as she ate.

She'd hoped that Harrison had got it wrong, but he hadn't. He'd got everything spot-on except for the venom with which the press attacked Ellie. Even as she peered at Ruby over the top of the phone, she could see the picture of Steinberg coming out of Ellie's flat. And it definitely was Ellie's flat in the picture.

"Seriously," Ruby pressed. "What else are you gonna do?"

Willow sighed, locked the phone, and put it face-down on the table next to her empty plate. She leaned forward, pinched the rim of her half-empty glass, and swirled the vodka and coke around inside, making the ice rattle in the bottom. In the side-room, rows of chairs had been laid out facing the low stage at the far end. An eclectic mix of surfers, intellectuals, fishermen, and middle management types milled around the aisles and on the stage, or else gathered around the small bar inside the doorway by the step. Willow sipped her drink, the vodka numbing her lip.

"I'm not here for a holiday," she said, placing the glass back down.

"Ok." Ruby shrugged. "Why are you here?"

Willow stared at the ice as she considered how much to tell her.

"I'm trying to find my sister," she said.

"Trying to find her? Meaning you don't know where she is?"

Willow shook her head.

"I'm presuming there's some big family drama behind this," Ruby said.

"What makes you say that?"

Ruby shrugged. "There normally is when... family lose touch."

Willow noticed the pause, but it was the quick look away and Ruby clenching her jaw that she noticed more.

"You talking from experience?"

"So this sister..." Ruby stared at her. A wall had gone up within, and Willow couldn't help but wonder why.

"Ellie," Willow said finally. Ruby didn't react.

"Ellie? When did you last see her?"

"Six years ago. I ran away."

Ruby cocked an eyebrow. "Wow. Some drama."

Willow gave a wry half-smile. "You have no idea."

"So why are you back now?"

Willow rattled the glass again, and lowered her gaze. She had a choice now: go all in, or keep it vague. Five minutes earlier she would've kept it vague, but she had an inkling that Ruby had a history with her own family. And maybe it was sympathy or the hope that Ruby would help her to understand, or maybe it was the fact that Ruby had stunning eyes and smelled good, but whatever it was, Willow decided to go all in.

"She's in trouble," she said.

"For what?"

She reached down and unlocked her phone, opened up the news reports, and passed the phone to Ruby.

"For this."

Ruby frowned, took the phone, read the article.

"Holy fuck." She looked up at Willow. "You're Ellie Rae's sister?"

Willow nodded.

"They talked about you."

"Who did?"

"The press. The T.V. I remember. They were doing this big piece on the South West news, and they were going on about it not being the first drama for your family, how you ran away, and hadn't been found."

Willow swallowed and lowered her gaze. It hadn't been forgotten. "Holy fuck. You're Megan Rae?"

"Willow now." She met Ruby's gaze.

"Do they know you're back? Your family, I mean."

"My old man does."

"That must be a relief for him."

Willow snorted. "Hardly. He was always more interested in keeping his new wife sweet than me and Ellie."

"My sister and me," Ruby went on. "We used to talk about you."

"Me?"

"When it happened. Back then, I couldn't believe you could run out on your sister like that." She twisted her lips. "Bit different now of course."

"Meaning?"

"Doesn't matter." Ruby shook her head. "So why did you run out on her?"

Willow peered at Ruby, wondering again what she was hiding, then figuring that it didn't matter. She was here for Ellie. Nothing else.

"I wasn't meant to. Ellie was supposed to go with me."

"Why didn't she?"

The tall lean figure of Richard Goddard stepped through the main entrance to the Spars, deep in conversation with a prissy looking woman in a skirt suit with a plain bob of blonde hair and thin framed glasses balanced on a pinched nose. Goddard wore a leather jacket and drainpipe jeans. He'd tied his hair behind his head and his wet-sand beard looked combed and groomed.

Questions ran through Willow's mind. About him and Ellie. About Zoe. About Raven.

"Because of him." Willow nodded in Goddard's direction.

He moved through the bar without looking her way, trudged up the steps, and was accosted by a painfully thin man with glasses, sharp cheeks and a shaved head.

"Goddard?" Ruby said. "What did he do?"

"Tried to stop us."

"And Ellie stayed because of him?"

"She stayed cos I knocked him out."

Ruby's head snapped around. Her eyes went wide. "You what?!" she barked a quick laugh.

"He tried to grab me." Willow half shrugged. "I lashed out and clocked him right on the chin. He just crumpled."

"Shit!"

"I started running, but Ellie wouldn't leave him. She told me to go, told me she'd follow, that she'd meet me in London. We'd arranged to stay with a friend of hers from Uni." Willow peered at the ice in the bottom of the glass again. "She never showed."

"Damn." Ruby looked over her shoulder at Goddard who was now weaving through the crowds, smiling, shaking hands, schmoozing like a politician. "Did he know where you'd gone?"

"Apparently so."

"And he never told the police?"

"He's good at secrets, Goddard."

Ruby turned back to her. "Oh?"

"I found out today that he put Ellie up, helped her out a few years back when she went off the rails. He forgot to tell me that." Willow lifted the glass and drained the rest of the vodka and coke. "Which makes me wonder what else he's forgotten to tell me."

Goddard moved around the back of the table on the stage and was about to take the centre seat when he looked up and met Willow's gaze across the two rooms. He stopped in mid-crouch, his eyes impenetrable pits beneath his brow. Then he smiled, raised a hand, and took his seat.

"You gonna ask him?" Ruby said.

Willow shook her head. "Too many people right now."

"He'll be here a while. These Cornish First meetings last a couple of hours."

Willow frowned. "Cornish First?"

"It's some local pressure group Goddard runs. All about Cornish rights or something."

For the first time, Willow noticed the pop-up banner at the end of the table. The words 'Cornish First' were written in white military font over a black and white Cornish flag background.

"Bit radical for a vicar, ain't it?"

"Told you," Ruby said. "He's our resident hipster reverend now. Surf and Salvation."

"You sound like a convert."

"Not likely. It'll take more than a few prayers to save my twisted soul." Ruby picked up a beer mat and began tapping it on the wood. "You could stick around, have a chat with him later."

"I'm knackered," Willow said. "I need to sleep."

"How about I call you then, when he's done here?"

Willow peered at Goddard again. He was shuffling papers on the desk as the crowds began to take their seats. Chairs scraped back, and laughter drifted over the raucous buzz of chatter. The prissy looking woman sat next to him, laid a hand on his arm, and leaned in close.

"Yeah," Willow said. "Sounds good."

*

Doug 'Dog' Hughes had lived in St. Agnes all his life, surfing the breaks at Trevaunance and Chapel Porth since the heyday of the Badlands when he and the boys had done everything in their power to promote the idea that outsiders weren't welcome.

Now in his early sixties, his thick, muscular arms and vast chest still bore the scars from the early days. Some of the scars, the jagged patch on his right thigh, the thin pink strip up his left arm, he wore proudly, testaments of his nerve, relics of the epic wipeouts he'd suffered to prove himself.

Other's hurt more. The small oval scar in his trapezoid, the thin slash across his cheek, the deep groove in his right pec. Those had cost him blood, the odd night in the cells, and one, the scar in his trapezoid, had cost him his best mate.

He'd got it trying to help him after a frenzied attack one night in Newquay. Five blokes had jumped them as they walked through the backstreets after a few post-surf bevvies. Dog had been hit over the head, then they set on his mate.

He always maintained that the first blow had meant to kill him. But they'd failed, and he recovered to chase them off with the same baseball bat they'd used on him. He knocked one down, the others fled, and he knelt by his mate trying to staunch the wounds. He didn't see the guy he'd knocked down get up again, and all he remembered was a heavy blow on his back. It was only later when he'd chased the bastard away, that he'd realised he had blood on his chest, and that it was his blood from a stab wound in his shoulder. A couple of ambulances arrived a minute later. They managed to patch him up, but his mate was dead. They never found the attackers.

There were other scars too, but these he wore on the inside: the girl who'd ditched him for a wealthier man, the dog that had been his constant companion in the Badlands days (and the reason for his nickname) who had succumbed to cancer and had to be destroyed, the stillborn son, and the subsequent break up of his only marriage.

He'd lived alone since, in a two-bedroom cottage on the edge of the village, and up until a couple of years ago had still been a regular in the surf breaks, the last of the old crew, a local legend who had no time for the newcomers, especially the surf and salvation lot. Goddard had tried to recruit him. And had been told exactly where to stick his God.

They'd left him alone.

Then came the final wipeout: surfing the Cribbar, two winters back. He'd overcooked it, gone down hard, smashed his hip, got winched from the water. Surgery...a replacement hip... rehab...

The doctor has advised against surfing again, but he couldn't stay away from the water. He bought a paddleboard, mastered it in a single session, and then set about his new hobby; exploring and photographing the hidden coves of the North Cornwall coast.

It wasn't surfing, but it was the next best thing, and on one of his early trips he'd met Lisa, a divorcee with no kids, soft curves, and pixie blonde hair. Between Lisa and the ocean, he felt a sense of peace.

Now, as he paddled into a secluded rock arch half a mile south of Hanover Cove, shifting his weight with the swell to keep the board steady, a black rucksack strapped to his back, he found himself in the odd position of looking forward to heading home and showing her his pictures when he was done. He'd never shared the ocean with anyone before, but he shared it with her.

He let the swell carry him into the arch, paddling towards the patch of sand at the back of the cave. The world around him went dark. Daylight rippled silver on the black water. He breathed the sharp, salty smell of the seaweed. The nose of the board scraped the sand, and he stepped off into the shallows. His legs felt stiff, his shoulders and back sore. He dragged the board clear, lay the paddle on top, and closed his eyes.

He sucked in a deep breath. He smelled his sweat, the tang of seawater, the taste of it on his lips. He dropped the bag to the sand, dug out a black metal water bottle, and took a deep swig. The freshwater tasted cool and clean against the salt on his mouth, and it dribbled down his lips into his grey goatee beard. He glanced back to the cave mouth, a wedge of pale light at the end of a dark tunnel of rock. He finished drinking, put the bottle on the sand, then dragged the board and his rucksack up until the bow sat on the ledge of rocks behind the sand. He turned and waded back into the water.

Wild swimming in secluded spots had become his favourite part of these trips. Often, he found himself alone with the gulls, the odd seal if he got lucky. The icy water eased his stiff legs. He went in up to his thighs, then dived under. The water rushed past, burbling in his ears. He surfaced, then swam a lazy front crawl out of the cave and into the fading daylight.

A salmon-pink sky stretched across the gaps between the stacks of granite on either side of him. To his right, part of one of the stacks had long since collapsed, and he swam for the rocks piled up there, clambering out and over them. He looked north to the golden, sun-kissed cliffs of Cligga Head and Hanover Cove. The rocks there looked almost red, like blood; a trick of the sun or the iron within maybe. Far out beyond the rocks, in the open ocean, he saw seagulls diving in a wild pack, hitting the water then rising straight up as if panicked. He clambered up the rocks, shielded his eyes, and peered out.

He could make out the ocean writhing, and the odd flash of grey; a pod of dolphins heading up the coast, he figured, hunting a bait-ball of herring, maybe mackerel or cod. He watched until they had vanished from sight, then he clambered back down and cannonballed into the sea from the rocks. The clear water rushed over him, and he pushed up, burst out of the water and, shaking his head, relished the salty coolness that ran down his face.

One more swim, maybe, he thought. Across to the cove opposite, to see if any seals were lurking within. Doubtful, especially now the pupping season was almost over, but he was enjoying the tranquillity, the feel of the ocean lifting and dropping him, the cry of the gulls overhead, the splash of water on the rocks. He'd take pictures after. For Lisa.

He surface-dived and came up a dozen yards further on, then swam into the cave.

The darkness swallowed him.

He swam until his knees buffed the sand, then stood and staggered from the water with a glance back. Bright daylight spilled in through the cave mouth. He turned his back to the light, cupped seawater in his hands and splashed it over his face. He stumbled on a submerged rock, regained his footing, then looked up.

He saw a shape in the darkness; a patch of deeper

black. He swayed forward, water sloshing around his legs. The ocean bellowed against the walls behind him. He placed his hand on a rock to get his balance, narrowed his gaze, and leaned forward.

The shape looked bloated and watery, like a barrel jellyfish. He'd seen one at Trevellas once; a jelly-like mound the size of a car tyre. This looked the same, only bigger; about three times the size.

He edged forward. A sickly odour hit the back of his throat. He wrinkled his nose, crouched low, reached out. As his fingers touched it, a swarm of shadows buzzed up at him. He screamed, fell back, and roaring filled his ears. He felt flies, small, hard flies, up his nose, in his ears, in his mouth. He scrambled into the water, ducked under, came up, and spat hard.

He crept forward, swatting at the few remaining flies as he approached the pale mass. He frowned into the gloom.

Realisation struck. His guts clenched. He fell to his knees and spewed. The vomit hit the beach with a wet slap. The yeasty stench made him gag again. He threw up, twice, three times more, his stomach clenching like a tightly-cinched belt beneath his ribs. The nausea faded.

He sat back, spitting bile, and peering into the cave. He could see the flies swarming in the dark again.

Swarming and settling on a swollen, waterlogged corpse.

17

The phone rang, dragging Willow up from sleep. She blinked and gazed around. Took in the white walls, the window, the clothes strewn across the floor of the room. On the soft carpet, the phone kept ringing. She snatched it up.

"You decent?" Ruby said. "Only, our reverend friend is finished." Willow swung her legs out of bed and massaged her temples.

"Sorry, I crashed out," she said. "Who's where?"

"Goddard's here. In the bar. You wanted to talk to him."

Willow yawned. Her breath tasted stale. "Give me five minutes," she said, "I'll be over."

She rung off, and checked the time. Quarter to ten. She'd got back from the talk with Ruby about half-past seven, stripped to her underwear, and lay on the bed intending to rest her eyes before having a shower, but crashing out instead, the jet lag taking hold. Now as she woke, her stomach growled, even though she'd already had dinner. She crossed to the walk-in shower, stepped under the head, and turned the water on.

She showered, dried herself, then threw on a peach

summer dress with a white tie-dyed pattern, a clean pair of knickers, and her sandals. She grabbed her phone and her key, and headed out of the room, leaving the bag on the floor. She left the annexe and crossed the road. Dusk had settled in pastel blue hues over the cove and the lights glowed on the outside of the Spars. When Willow stepped into the main bar, Ruby glanced up, smiled, and nodded to the fireplace.

Goddard sat behind a single dark oak table facing her, a pint of ale in front of him, his hair tied back. He smiled, showing brilliant white teeth through his sandy beard, and gestured towards the empty seat opposite.

Willow nodded, mimed a drink, and crossed to the bar.

"You scrub up well," Ruby said, grinning as she fixed Willow a vodka and coke. "Reckon the good reverend could be on if he plays his cards right."

Willow rolled her eyes as she took the glass. "Do you ever think of anything else?"

"Not when I look at you." Ruby flicked her brow and crossed to a waiting customer at the other end of the bar. Willow wove back to the table, keeping her glass high, sliding through the crowds, the loud voices, the raucous laughs, the lustful stares, her gaze fixed on Goddard, now leaning back, his feet crossed beneath the table. He stood as she approached, leaned forward, and gave her a quick hug, then sat back down as Willow perched on the cushioned stool opposite.

She sipped her drink, the vodka sharp and chemical in her throat.

"So how'd it go?" Goddard said. "With the old man."

Willow snorted and looked to the fireplace. "About as well as expected."

She ran through the day, from meeting her father, to Harrison's revelations. Goddard peered down at his glass.

"So you heard about the whole Steinberg thing then?" Willow nodded.

"It was a shock, I'll be honest," Goddard said. "I mean, she'd had a rough couple of years, lost her way a bit. But I was so surprised when it came out because she'd got herself straight again. And she'd always been so against that. She always said that people who cheated were bastards."

"Do you believe it?" Willow said.

Goddard sipped his drink. "You don't?"

"Ellie... my Ellie... she wouldn't do that."

"Maybe she wasn't your Ellie anymore."

"Maybe." Willow shrugged.

She peered at him, at the shadows beneath his brow, the loose strand of hair that had slipped out of the band and hung down his sharp cheek. The question she wanted to ask hung on the tip of her tongue, held back only by doubt, and the fear that she might not like the answer she'd hear. After all, her father had thought Ellie and Goddard had been sleeping together. And though Goddard had denied it, maybe he hadn't been telling the truth.

"Why didn't you tell me?"

"About Ellie and Steinberg? Look, it's only paper rumours and I'm not one for spreading gossip about people. I'm a reverend, remember? I keep people's secrets close to my chest." He smiled and saluted with his pint glass.

Willow lowered her gaze and traced a swirl in the dark

wood with her fingernail. "You put Ellie up after the miscarriage. Harrison reckons you got her clean." She looked up at him.

Goddard nodded. Sipped his ale.

"She needed help." He shrugged. "I helped her."

"But when we spoke this morning, you never said anything."

"It didn't come up."

Willow lowered her gaze again. "Did she stay with you?"

"No," Goddard said.

That uncomfortable relief swept through her again. Ellie getting with Harrison had been hard. If she'd slept with Goddard too, knowing he'd been Willow's teenage crush, well, that would've felt like spite.

"Where did she stay then?"

Goddard leant forward. "There's a youth hostel in Perranporth, around the headland from the Droskyn Castle. I know the owner. I do the odd service there, Christmas and Easter. It's popular with backpackers. I got Ellie a bed there, and in return, she did a bit of work for Sheila."

"Sheila?"

"The owner."

"How long was she there?"

"About six months, I think. 'Til she got clean. Then she got the job in the planning office and moved into someplace round the back of the seafront." "Yeah, I found that," Willow said.

"Any sign of her?"

"Looks like she's been gone about a month," Willow said. "But you said you saw her a couple of weeks back."

Goddard nodded. "Yeah. She came to a prayer meeting at the cove." Willow sighed and looked to the fireplace.

"So she's got to be close then." She sipped her drink and rolled it around her mouth. "I just hope I find her before the biker does."

"Biker?"

Willow told him about running into the biker outside the flat, how the biker, amongst others, had tried to break in before. When she mentioned the scuffle, he clenched his jaw, his face flushed red, his eyes widening. Was he angry she'd been attacked? For a second she dared to hope that he cared for her.

"Are you ok?" he asked when she finished. His face had gone smooth and tanned again, his jaw unclenched. She wondered if she'd imagined it, but then she saw that his eyes were still wider, wilder, than normal.

"I'm fine." Willow waved the question away. "Couple of grazed knees is all. Just wish I knew what this biker has to do with Ellie and Steinberg."

She leaned forward, a red dreadlock falling over her shoulder.

"And what this all has to do with Zoe?"

"Zoe? As in your friend Zoe?"

Willow nodded. "Ellie was looking for her. Or at least, for someone using her name."

"Ellie knows Zoe is dead," Goddard said. "She was at her funeral."

"Is she though?" Willow looked at him, wondering if he thought she was crazy, not particularly bothered if he did.

"Is she what?"

"Zoe," Willow said. "Is she dead?"

"I buried her, Megan—" She scowled at him.

"Sorry. Willow. Believe me, as much as I would love it to be otherwise, Zoe is dead."

"So, someone's using her name then."

"Zoe's name?"

Willow shook her head. "Not her real name. The name she gave herself. Raven."

Did his nostrils flare as she spoke? Did a blush of heat rise in his cheeks? If so, they were gone as soon as Willow doubted she'd seen them.

"You're making no sense."

"The last time the landlord saw Ellie she was on the phone, asking about someone called Raven."

"And that was Zoe's nickname?"

Willow nodded. "Which is quite a coincidence, don't you think; Ellie looking for someone who just happened to share the same nickname as my dead best friend?"

Goddard reached out and placed a hand on the back of hers. His fingers felt warm. Smooth.

"Willow," he sighed, lowered his gaze. "I know how much you'd love to believe Zoe is still alive. But I buried her. I buried the whole family. If Ellie was searching for someone called Raven, that person is not Zoe."

Willow glanced at him, then looked away.

"Just wish I knew where Ellie was," she muttered.

"I'm sure she's ok," Goddard said.

Willow gave him a tight smile. "So what's this Cornish First thing?"

"It's just a little project I've been working on for a few years now. Cornish homes for Cornish people mainly. But we also look at employment, social benefits, ensuring government grants and subsidies are benefiting

Cornish businesses. That sort of stuff."

"What started that?"

"You grew up here. You know what this place is like. There's wealth here, and plenty of housing, but a lot of it is tied up in London bank accounts, or owned by London people who leave the home here empty nine months of the year, or else rent it to tourists and cream out all the profit. And meanwhile, you take a walk through Truro, Newquay, Redruth," he counted the towns off on his fingers, "and all you see are homeless people living in shop doorways, begging for change, and hoping to make it through to summer, or kids popping laughing gas, or worse, then ending up dead on a slab because some London dealer has been pushing bad shit."

His eyes blazed as he spoke. He poked the dark lacquered wood hard and leant forward, his face flushed behind his sandy beard.

"So what's the big plan then?" Willow said. "Ban Londoners from buying property?"

Goddard shook his head. "Not entirely. But we want a commitment from the County Council that at least fifty per cent of all new builds reserve property for local people. And all repos are offered to the local community for the first six months of listing."

"You think that'll make a difference?"

He sighed and sat back. "It's a start at least."

Willow drained her drink and slid her chair back. "Well, good luck with it, yeah?"

"There's a vote next Monday," Goddard said, rising as well. "I've got a petition online. More signatures we get, the more chance we've got of getting the policy through the Council. Wanna sign?"

"You think it'll make a difference?"

"Every signature counts."

Willow shrugged. "Ok, why not. Might as well do some good while I'm here."

He dug a notebook out of his leather coat, tore out a page, pulled out a pen, and scribbled on the paper.

"This is the website," he said, handing the page to Willow. "And this is the address of the hostel. Ask for Sheila."

He tapped the note. Willow read it, then gazed up at him.

"You think Ellie's gone back there?"

He shrugged. "Worth a shot, isn't it? She knows she'd be safe there. Any journo or paparazzi sniffing around would have a hard time getting past Sheila." Willow gave him a tight smile.

"Thanks."

She folded the paper in her hand. Goddard hugged her again. She tried not to notice how good he smelled.

"Let me know what Sheila says." He smiled, then slipped around the table, and crossed to the main door, waving at Pete as he went, who returned the gesture with a nod. Willow watched until he'd gone outside, then looked around for Ruby. She was gathering glasses from an empty table and making her way back to the bar as Willow approached.

"Well," she said. "Any luck?"

"He put her up in some hostel in Perranporth a few years back. Reckons she might have gone back there."

"So you going to look?"

"Tomorrow," Willow said.

"I can drive you if you want," Ruby said.

"It's your day off."

"Yes, well remembered."

"Why?"

"Why what?"

"You don't know me," Willow said. "Why would you want to run me around Cornwall?"

"Told you." Ruby slipped behind the bar, put the empties on a shelf out the back, then grabbed a towel from one of the pumps and wiped her hands. "I was planning to spend the day with a gorgeous hippie with red dreadlocks anyway. Guess my luck is in."

"You sure you don't mind?"

"It'll be my pleasure." Ruby tilted an empty glass towards her. "You want another drink?"

"I'm done," Willow said. She smiled then turned to go.

"You might need this," Ruby said, scribbling on a beer mat. She slapped the pen down and held out the mat.

Willow frowned. "What is it?"

"My address, dummy."

Willow smiled, taking the beer mat. "Thanks." The address was on Churchtown, in the village centre.

"9 o'clock. Door is to the right of the supermarket."

Ruby slipped out the bar, slid past, squeezing Willow's hand as she went.

*

Goddard passed the brewery, turned right up the path towards the clifftop, then glanced back. Satisfied he was alone, he dug the mobile out of his pocket, opened the contacts, found the one he was looking for, and hit dial. In the distance, the ocean looked like liquid silver as it lapped against the dark jagged cliffs in the falling dusk.

"Perranporth YHA hostel. How can I help?" The female voice on the other end sounded bright and friendly.

"Sheila, it's me," he said.

A pause. Then… "You can't call me here."

"Listen," Goddard went on. "You're gonna get a call. Or a visit."

"From who?"

"She'll call herself Willow. But that's not her name."

"And what is her name?"

"Megan," Goddard said. "Megan Rae."

Silence. Then…

"I told you that girl was trouble."

"Look, it will be fine. This Willow, she knows nothing. She's come back on a whim, and she's looking for Ellie. All you've got to do is convince her that Ellie's run off to London."

"And how do I do that?"

"Up to you," Goddard said. "But she has to think that Ellie's gone and not coming back."

"What if I'm not around when she comes?"

"I've told her to ask for you."

"I'm not here twenty-four seven you know."

"Fucking hell, Sheila," Goddard grit his teeth and huffed. "Tell your bloody staff that if anyone asks for you then they have to speak to you and you alone."

"I don't like this," Sheila said. "I should never have let her stay here again. She was enough trouble the first time."

"It's not like you had a choice, is it?" Goddard's voice went cold and hard. "How is your son?

Still leeching off his constituents and living the high life in Westminster, is he?"

"He's a good boy…"

"Who just happens to enjoy inviting pretty and dangerously young Eastern European girls to his Thames-side penthouse while his wife and kids play happy families in Truro."

"Please…"

"Do as I say, and your boy can carry on living his life of sin and dubious morals."

"Like you're one to talk."

"God moves in mysterious ways." Goddard turned back and peered up Quay Road. Homely lights glowed in the cliffs and wooded hills around the cove. "Just do what I ask."

"Fine," Sheila hissed.

"And call me when it's done."

"Where is the girl?" Sheila said.

"That's not a question you need to be asking," Goddard said.

He rang off. One problem dealt with.

Sheila would do as she was told. She was too terrified of her boy getting found out to do anything else. Now for Raven.

Willow had said too much, although she didn't know it. Raven had gone for her. He'd told her to keep her distance. She'd disobeyed. He needed to make sure she didn't make a habit of it.

And her name was known now, to Willow at least.

Wondering if she was becoming more of a risk than an asset, Goddard hunched his shoulders in his jacket and set off up the path towards the hut, and to the rendezvous with his rebellious little enforcer.

18

Total darkness had fallen over Trevaunance by the time Goddard trudged up the steps towards the shelter overlooking the cove. Light from the Schooners restaurant cast a pale glow across the receding waters and the wet sand. A couple strolled towards the surf, a pair of silhouettes walking hand in hand on the beach. The cliffs around the cove were visible only as walls of solid blackness against the inky night sky. Ahead, the shelter – a solid wooden structure hunkering into the shoulders of the valley side – looked empty.

He knew Raven was there though, even as he stepped inside. He could smell her, a primal musk of leather and sweat. Then he saw her, a shadow in the corner, betrayed by the pale strip of flesh visible around her eyes, the only part of her face not hidden by her heavy hood or the black mask over her nose and mouth. She stepped forward.

"Well?" she muttered. "Any thoughts on what to do about Megan?"

He nodded. "A few."

He leapt forward, grabbed her shoulders, and threw her back against the wall hard.

"What the fuck!?" She tried to push back.

He backhand-slapped her around the face. She gasped, then her voice vanished as his hand clamped across her mouth, forcing her back against the wooden wall.

"You're not untouchable, Raven," he hissed in her ear. "I told you not to touch her."

She went still as his free hand closed around her throat. He pressed her windpipe, but she didn't panic, didn't start to struggle. She just glared at him from beneath the hood.

Then he felt a sharp pain in his groin.

He looked down.

The knife seemed dull in the gloom, but the blade, six inches long and serrated, pointed right into his leg. One move and she could slit his balls off and leave him to bleed out.

He chuckled, let go of her throat, raised his hands, and backed away.

"Ok," he said. "Ok. Stalemate."

She peered hard at him, lifted the blade, and pointed it at his face.

"Step outside," she hissed, her voice muffled by the mask, but not enough to hide the anger in it.

"You can put the knife down," he said. "I've proved my point."

"I'll put the knife down when you step outside."

He sighed, stepped back outside the hut. Raven followed him out, then motioned for him to go back in.

"You don't have to worry," he said, moving past her.

"Don't have to trust you either," she said. "Get against the far wall. Keep your hands up."

He backed up. "You always this touchy?"

"I am when someone tries to choke me." She stepped

back inside, a short slender shadow in the doorway.

"I had to prove a point," he said. "You were reckless today."

"You told me to follow her."

"Follow. Not attack."

"She went for me," Raven said. "I was just watching."

"Why would she do that?"

"Someone's been talking."

"I know that. She knows your name. She knows Ellie was looking for you."

She went still. "How? Gould again?"

"The landlord."

"Saying what?"

"Stuff." Goddard shrugged. "Enough for her to put two and two together."

Raven had gone completely still now.

"This…altercation," Goddard said. "Did she recognise you?"

"I was in my leathers. She didn't see my face."

Goddard sighed. "Well, that's one bit of good news."

"There's more bad news yet," she said.

"More?"

"She had a bag when she came out. Looked like it had papers in."

"The council stuff Ellie nicked?"

Raven shook her head. "No. The originals are gone. But copies maybe. Maybe even the USB."

"How'd she get that?"

"I think Gould stashed them with the landlord, told him to give it to Megan when she showed."

Goddard massaged his forehead and screwed his eyes shut.

"We need to get it back though," Raven said.

"You told me all the leads had been tied up."

"And you told me the sister wouldn't be a problem."

"She won't be much longer." Goddard breathed out through his nose. "I've set something up. This time tomorrow, she'll be heading to London. I doubt we'll see her again after that."

"Still need those papers though. I think we should head down to her room, take her out, take the papers too."

"Yeah, because that'll work won't it? Bloody murder in the annexe; not even God could get us off then."

"We have to do something."

"We haven't got this far by taking risks."

"This whole business is a risk," Raven said. "You're relying on people staying silent, on doing what you want."

"I'm trusting the selfish instincts of sinners," he said. "They don't want their dirty little secrets aired in public. And this is costing them nothing except their integrity. And given what I've got on them all, they haven't got much of that to start with."

"Steinberg got suspicious though."

"So what do you want us to do? Quit?"

"I want Megan-fucking-Rae out of the picture."

"I told you. I've arranged something to take care of that." He sighed. "You go and speak to Gould. Find out what he knows. But do it quietly."

"What about the girl? The papers? The USB?"

"Let me deal with that," Goddard said. "She trusts me. I can get them from her, without killing her."

"Best way to silence her."

"Best way to have half of Devon and Cornwall police

swarming around turning this into a bloody circus. We stay quiet. We stay low key. We don't take stupid risks."

"Letting her live is a stupid risk," Raven spat.

She turned to walk away. He peered at the silhouette of her back.

"Raven," he said.

She stopped. Didn't turn.

"You fucked up today." He saw her head twitch towards him. "It doesn't happen again."

"That a threat?" She stood still, a shadow in the night.

"You're not untouchable."

Still, she didn't move. After a few seconds, her voice drifted back to him. "Neither are you."

Then she strode away.

*

The pale blue light of dawn seeped through the window at the end of the room. Along the annexe a door slammed, and Willow heard footsteps stomping up the hall. She sat on the bed with her back to the headboard, her knees drawn up, and the phone in her hands. The screen glowed blue-white. She had the thin silver chain in the corners of her mouth and the 'Sisters' pendant swung against her chin. Letters from Ellie's flat lay scattered across the floor.

She'd slept for a few hours before jet lag had dragged her awake again, tossed and turned for an hour, then gave sleep up as a bad job. She'd made herself a cup of tea with the last tea bag and pot of UHT milk, and then went through the post. She'd found nothing but circulars; no council papers, no USB carefully stashed in an envelope, just junk mail. She left it scattered across the carpet and retreated to the bed, then started flicking through her phone.

At first, she'd been looking for nothing in particular, the news on the BBC app, the Australian Herald website, Facebook. Then, remembering what Ruby had said about her name cropping up in the reports about Ellie, she typed 'Megan Rae' into Google. The search returned millions of hits, none of them relevant. She added 'Cornwall' and struck gold.

The first hit was a headline from BBC South West that read TRAGIC PAST OF STEINBERG'S MISTRESS REVEALED.

Willow opened the story. It talked about Steinberg's suicide, the revelation that he'd been having an affair with Ellie, and the police warrant for her arrest on charges of theft and blackmail. Then the tone changed, and Willow bristled with anger as she read on.

For the parents of Ellie Rae, this tragedy and its aftermath must stir up painful memories of the disappearance of their younger daughter Megan, who ran away six years earlier and has never been found. According to one source, who requested to remain anonymous, the disappearance of Megan had a profound effect on Ellie.

'Ellie had always looked out for Megan, so when Megan left she kind of went crazy. Started partying hard. Got into trouble with drinks and drugs. She lost a baby because of it,' the source said.

As Willow scrolled, a picture came into view; she and Ellie in wetsuits on the sand at Porthtown, the cliffs rising craggy and stern behind them. They were holding large foam surfboards, and the sun made Willow shield her gaze. The sea wind had whipped her frizzy brown bob across her face, but she was grinning. Her teeth were full of metal. She had her free arm draped over Ellie's shoulder. The picture bought a twinge of sorrow. Willow went to close the article, but a link, underlined in bold type, caught her eye.

LOCAL GIRL MISSING POLICE SEARCH UNDERWAY.

She clicked the link and cringed as she saw her own face smiling up at her. It was the school photo she'd hated the most, taken when she was fourteen. She had been desperate to look hot, but always feeling like a frump next to Ellie. And Zoe for that matter. In the picture, she had puppy fat cheeks, deep dimples, and her hair fell in a tangled mess of copper brown curls. She had the braces on her teeth here, and her eyes looked half-closed.

Blotting the picture out, she read about her disappearance. Amidst the wild speculation about moors murderers and the possibility that she'd fallen down an old mine shaft, the facts were pretty much accurate.

Goddard was in a second picture halfway down the page, his arm around Ellie, a bruise below his eye, probably from where Willow had clumped him the day she ran. Another picture showed her father and Connie at a press conference, both looking grim. Her mother appeared threequarters of the way down the page, severe and aloof, looking down her nose, as she strode into a police station.

There was a final picture at the bottom of the article; a group shot of Ellie, Willow, Zoe, Harrison, Freddie, his sister, Zoe's sister and parents, all in kayak gear, standing at the top of the slipway in Trevaunance, a fleet of yellow kayaks amongst the reddish-brown seaweed on the sand behind them. It had been taken a year and a bit before Willow had run away, after the school photo, before the picture on Porthtowan. The kayak trip up the coast had been Zoe's birthday treat, paid for by her parents.

Willow peered at her old friend. Her jet black hair fell around her pale, serious face. Zoe never smiled in pictures. Instead, she settled for a severe stare. She wore black lipstick and nail varnish. Her hair had been naturally blonde, but when she hit thirteen, she went Goth; dyed her hair, and began wearing pentagrams and inverted crosses around her neck which sent the headmistress of their Church of England school apoplectic every time she saw it and resulted in her parents calling in Goddard.

To his credit, Goddard had seen it for what it was: teenage rebellion. But her parents had been less than pleased and, because Zoe loved nothing better than sending her parents loopy with rage, she insisted they called her Raven, the name taken from the hair dye she'd used. Raven Black. Her parents had refused, but Willow and the gang had all played along.

A few weeks later, on that trip to Trevellas, Zoe had given Willow her nickname too. Willow hadn't liked it at first, thinking it more of an insult, but the more she tried to stop her friends calling her Willow, the more they did it. She gave up and, over time, she accepted the nickname. After running away, she owned it.

Now, sitting in the room as the light paled and the day

came on, she looked at the Megan in the picture, standing between Ellie and Zoe. Taller than the school picture, not as round-faced, but still stocky, still frumpy. She looked happy, her eyes bright, her smile wide, braces gleaming (she cringed inside). Her arms were over the shoulders of her best friend and her sister.

A pang of grief twisted in her chest. Zoe dead. Ellie missing.

And Megan...

Megan hadn't come back from Australia. She was Willow now. And she had to find her sister. She let the chain drop from her mouth.

Ellie had the other half. Willow had bought it for her as a gift for Ellie's sixteenth birthday. All she wanted right then was to make the two halves whole again.

19

Goddard left his house a few minutes after 6 a.m. He'd forgone his usual jeans and t-shirt look for a Ravenesque black hooded top, black trainers and jogging pants. The hoody had a built-in snood that could cover his mouth and nose.

Hood up, he slipped into his car and turned the key. He flicked the wipers to clear the morning damp from the windscreen. He put down the visor to block out the gleam from the low morning sun, then pulled away and drove towards the Penwinnick Road, where he threw a right and headed down towards Trevaunance. At the bottom of Quay Road he turned into the car park of the Driftwood Spars. He parked the car in such a way that had a clear view of the entrance to the annexe. He grabbed his phone from the pocket in the car door, fired off a quick text, then hunkered down.

A few minutes later, Pete shambled across the car park in his slippers, drying his hands on his blue chef's apron. It had grease stains down the front, and frayed edges along the bottom. He reached behind his ear as he walked, and tugged out a cigarette. He put the fag between his lips, rummaged in his pocket, then pulled out a lighter. Stopping, he turned his back to the wind and cupped his hand around the fag. When he turned back, the fag tip glowed orange. He puffed out a cloud of smoke, put the lighter back in his pocket, and pulled out a set of keys. Reaching Goddard's car, he bent low to rap on the window.

Goddard lowered his hood and leant across, winding the window down.

"Up early, rev?"

The smell of cigarettes and cooking oil wafted in through the window.

"Mind you don't set yourself alight with that thing." Goddard nodded to the cigarette. "There's enough oil on you to keep you burning for days."

Pete grinned, which meant the corners of his mouth dropped, and he dragged his top lip up over crooked yellow teeth.

"Master keys," he said, reaching in and dangling the keys over Goddard's hand.

"Good man."

He dropped the keys. Goddard caught them.

"Drop 'em back to the bar when you're done."

Goddard went to wind the window up, but Pete kept leaning inside.

"Don't suppose your gonna tell me why you need them, are you?"

Goddard shook his head and smiled. "Best you don't know that, Pete."

"This something to do with that Willow creature?"

"Maybe."

"What's she done? Did she steal sommat of yours?"

Goddard let his gaze rove towards the annexe. Was the

USB in there? The council documents? Would he finally find out what Ellie had on him? "You could say that."

"Well." Pete slipped out of the window and stretched. "If you get caught in there, you didn't get those keys from me."

"Cheers for the vote of confidence."

Pete sucked on the fag and trudged away. Goddard wound the window up then settled back to wait.

He'd decided to come here after meeting Raven the night before. If she was right, if Megan did have the papers and the USB, getting them back was almost as important as throwing Willow off the hunt for Ellie. Finding out meant trying to get into her room, but breaking and entering wasn't a speciality of his. Persuasion and manipulation were. After leaving the hut the night before, he'd gone back to the Spars, spoke to Pete about getting the master key, then headed home, the arrangements made. He'd slept for five hours, and now here he was, staking out the annexe, waiting for Willow. With no idea of her routine, her plans, he had to watch and hope that he got lucky.

It took a while. Time crept by. Early morning runners jogged past. A few cars headed down towards the cove. An old guy walking two grey-white Yorkshire Terriers stopped and looked in the window of the closed brewery, lighting his pipe as the Terriers yapped and scampered around him, then headed up to the coastal path.

After an hour, he saw a flash of red slip past the window of the annexe, and then she was there, hunkered beneath her bag, dreadlocks falling around her face. She wore the same dress from the night before: peach with white tie-dye patterns, and heavy Doc Martens. He admired the flame tattoos up her folded arms, idly wondered where else she had tattoos. She kept her head down, crossed the road towards the Spars and slipped inside the dining room.

Goddard checked his watch. Just gone 7.30. As soon as she was out of sight, he stepped out of the car. He threw his hood up, pulled the inner snood over his nose and nudged the driver's door shut with his hip. Hands jammed in the pouch of his hoodie, he hurried across the road and into the annexe.

He walked with his head bowed, his face almost hidden until he came to the door of Room 12. He dug the master key out of his pocket and slipped it into the lock, looking back along the corridor to make sure he was alone. Then he opened the door, stepped inside, and closed the door behind him.

A glance around the room told him he was wasting his time. There were no papers here, no USB, just clothes strewn around the floor; a pair of leggings, a vest and a black sports bra. A white porcelain mug stained with dribbles of tea stood on a wicker coaster on the bedside table amongst a scattering of biscuit crumbs. The empty plastic biscuit packet had been stuffed inside the mug. The duvet had been tucked up at the end of the bed. He crossed to the bathroom door and peered in.

A few toiletries, deodorant, perfume, shower gel, stood on the vanity shelf above the sink. Wet towels lay in the bottom of the shower. A single sheet of unused toilet paper sat on its lonesome on the tiled floor by the toilet.

For the sake of being thorough, he went back into the bedroom and checked the drawers of the bedside table. They scraped back on their runners, then thunked when they couldn't open any further. He found only the Gideons Bible in the top drawer. He peered in the small metal bin beside the table. It contained squeezed tea bags, empty milk pots, used wooden stirrers. He rocked back to his haunches. The smell of her perfume lingered in the air, but couldn't mask the musky smell of her body that rose from the bed.

She didn't smell like Ellie. He remembered Ellie smelling clean and fresh, floral, like she never broke a sweat. Willow smelt hormonal. Fertile.

He took one final look around the room, then swore. The papers or the USB or whatever she had must be in her bag. And her bag was with her up in the dining room. Of course she'd keep them with her, they were valuable, maybe she didn't even realise how valuable, but he had to get hold of them.

The question was how?

He stood then opened the door again, his hood and mask still in place. He stepped into the hallway and the door clicked shut behind him. He heard the lock on the door to Room 11 clunk open. Before it could open fully, he buried his hands in his pockets and stalked along the corridor. Whispers and laughter rippled towards him, but he barely heard the sounds. By the time they were halfway along the corridor he was outside and stalking back to his car, frustration bubbling within him.

*

"You're sure there's no more rooms available tonight?"

Willow stood by the till in the dining room, the salty, dehydrating taste of bacon and sausage thick in her mouth as she put her purse back into her rucksack. Across the counter, Pete took the fifty-pound note she'd given him in payment for her room and slipped it into the till drawer.

"Sorry, miss," he said. "We've got a wedding in over the weekend. All the rooms are booked."

"Know anywhere else I can try?"

"There's some B&Bs in town. They might have space."

"Any recommendations?"

He gave half a shrug. "I run me own. I ain't about to give out the names of me competition." He slammed the drawer shut and shambled out from behind the bar.

"Drop the key back at the bar when you go," he called back to her.

With a sigh and a roll of the eyes she pushed the heavy oak door open, threw her rucksack on her back, and trudged downstairs and out through the main bar. It had gone half eight now. Time to crack on finding Ellie.

She'd head back to her room, grab the last of her clothes and her shower things, and then head to Ruby's. With luck, Ruby would know of a decent place to stay.

She squinted against the sunlight as she left the pub and stepped onto Quay Road. Raucous laughter echoed up from the cove. She turned and saw the couple from the room next door staggering up the road clinging to each other. The guy had dark wiry hair and broad shoulders. The girl was slim and blonde with teeth too big for her mouth. Irritation rising, Willow hunched her shoulders. She was about to stalk off when the girl called her.

"Hey, neighbour."

Willow sighed. Turned.

"You did well for yourself."

"What?" Willow stared from one to the other and back again. They were grinning stupidly, clinging to each other like mussels on rocks, and the guy was bending to kiss the girls neck even as she spoke. It took all of Willow's restraint not to kick him in the balls for being a sleaze. "Your fella. He looked pretty hot."

"What fella?"

The girl rolled her eyes, like Willow was being deliberately coy. "The fella you had in your room."

It occurred to Willow that they'd been on the wacky backy. "What are you chatting about?"

The couple were almost next to her now. The smell of vodka wafted from them like a chemical cloud.

"Come on." The girl nudged Willow, who had to close her eyes and breath deeply to stop herself from slamming the girl's head into a wall in response. "No need to be coy. We're all grown adults here."

"Sorry," Willow said. "What the actual fuck are you talking about?" "You had a guy in your room last night," the boy said.

"No, I didn't."

He frowned. "Course you did. He left as we came out."

Willow peered from one to the other, her blood freezing, her stomach dropping to the floor. "What did he look like?"

"Pretty hot!" The girl giggled.

Temper breaking, Willow grabbed her by the jumper and pulled her close.

"Tell me!"

The girl screeched.

"Get off her!" The boyfriend lunged for Willow's wrists.

She slapped him away, and dropped the girl, shooting them both a withering glare. Then she spun and sprinted across the road.

"Fuck is wrong with you?" the girl screeched after her.

She ran for the annexe, burst inside, barging through two of the guests. She half-stumbled, then righted herself. They screeched protests at her.

"Sorry!" she yelled back, then sprinted for her room. When she reached the door, she slammed her hands against the wood. It didn't budge. She tried the handle. It moved, but didn't catch. Locked. She stepped back, examined the wood, and remembered the boot print on Ellie's door.

Her breath came in heavy gasps. Her pulse throbbed in her temple. The door looked fine. No boot marks. No sign of a forced entry.

She dug out her key, and slipped it in the lock. She went to turn it, but a warning flickered in the back of her mind, sense finally breaking through.

What if he was still in there?

She pressed her ear to the door, then the palms of her hands. She listened, but all she could hear was her breath and her heartbeat whomping in her ear against the wood. The room seemed quiet.

She stepped away. Her fingers pinched the brass key. She eased it left. The latch moved, creaking. She winced at the sound. The lock slipped free and she nudged the door open. It swung back with a faint squeal. She peered around the edge.

The room looked the same as when she had left it:

clothes on the floor, the unmade bed, the dirty teacup on the bedside table. There was no sign of anyone in the bedroom. She pushed the door open fully and stole a proper glance behind it.

No-one.

She crept inside and stepped towards the bathroom, listening hard for any whisper of movement, any hint of breathing. She stopped by the door frame. From where she was, she could see the toilet, the sink, and the mirror above the sink. No sign of anyone lurking.

She edged forward, fingers gripping the frame. A moments pause, then she swung into the doorway.

The bathroom was empty.

Relief swept through her. She looked around the room. Nothing had moved, nothing had changed. The room looked exactly as it had when she'd left an hour earlier.

The neighbours, in their drunk or doped up state, had got it wrong. No one had come in here. She felt the panic start to recede. She dumped the bag on the bed, unzipped it, and began to throw her clothes inside. She gathered her toiletries from the bathroom and stuffed them in her bag as well. She left the towels in the shower, and the bedclothes unmade, and took a final look around. Satisfied she hadn't left anything, she turned to leave.

Then she saw it.

A large boot-shaped smudge of dirt behind the door. It was coming into the room.

Her thoughts flicked to the boot print on Ellie's door, to the altercation with the biker, to what the landlord had said.

"We've had some funny sorts knocking at this door."

She crouched down, throat dry, palms damp, fear

fluttering in her stomach. She swore. Closed her eyes. The people hunting Ellie had found her too.

20

"It wasn't your footprint?" Ruby said.

The clock in the car read eighteen minutes past nine. Willow slumped in the passenger seat of Ruby's white Fiat 500. A bunch of ceramic blue and purple flowers hung from the rear-view mirror, clanking together as they swayed and shimmied with every turn in the road. Sunlight glimmered on the diamanté studded steering wheel cover.

"No, it was way too big. This was a man's trainer."

Ruby peered at Willow through tortoiseshell Wayfarers. She wore a lime green summer dress with white ankle socks and pumps, and her hair hung loose and frizzy around her face.

"Did they take anything?"

"Not that I could see. But then, there wasn't much to take. Anything of value was in my bag. Not that there's much in there."

They were driving along the road from St. Agnes to Perranporth. High hedges whipped past the passenger window, obscuring all but the briefest glimpse of the fields beyond. Through the driver's window, the land dipped into a steep valley of fields and remote farmhouses. The shadow of clouds scudded across the landscape as the wind howled through the gap in the passenger window. Across the valley, she could see the blocky shapes of lorries trundling along the A30.

"And the room was empty when you got there?"

Willow sighed, leant her elbow against the glass, and brushed her fingers along the handle above the side window.

"Yep. Empty. No sign of anyone. I wouldn't even have noticed the print if it hadn't been for those idiots next door telling me they saw someone coming out."

"You're sure the print hadn't always been there?"

They passed a boutique cafe on the roadside, and the road began to plunge and wind down to Perranporth.

"No," Willow said. "But given they reckon the guy came out of my room, it had to be his."

"And the door hadn't been damaged?"

"Nope." Willow glanced in the wing mirror. Nothing behind them. No one tracking them out of St. Agnes.

"So whoever he was, he must have had a key."

Willow gave a half shrug. "Or picked the lock."

"You want me to tell Pete?"

"Why Pete?"

"Well someone could be walking around with a key to the rooms. I think he'd want to know."

Willow shook her head. "Doesn't matter. I'm not staying there now, am I?"

"But the other guests…"

"I think this is to do with my sister."

"What makes you say that?"

"I know people were following her, watching her. They tried to get in her flat."

Willow glanced in the wing mirror again. A bike crested the hill behind them. Her heart clenched as she recalled her fight the previous day, but the bike was a black Harley, and the rider was a large guy with tattoos up his meaty forearms.

"I think they're watching me now." She looked at Ruby.

"But... why?"

Why indeed? In the mad dash from the room, she hadn't thought about it, but the question had occurred to her as she'd trudged up Quay Road towards Ruby's flat, constantly checking around her in case she was being followed, and half expecting to get thrown into the back of a van at any minute. Having mulled it over for a while now, she thought she had the answer.

"The Steinberg thing."

"But he's dead."

"His business isn't though. And my guess is that whatever Ellie had on him, it was big enough to bring the whole business down. Which is why people are so desperate to get it back."

"What did Ellie have on him?"

"Dammed if I know," Willow said. "There was nothing at her flat."

"And they think you've got it now?"

"Or they think I'll lead them to Ellie."

Silence fell. Willow kept one eye on the road behind, looking for any hint, any sign that she was being followed. Other than the Harley, the road was quiet.

"What's the plan today then?"

Willow stirred and looked to the driver's seat. A lock of sandy blonde hair had fallen over Ruby's eye and she flicked her head to get it out of the way.

"Well." Willow shifted her backside in the seat. "With luck, I'll find Ellie at this hostel and then we can both get the hell out of here."

Ruby threw the car left towards the clifftop car park. She edged down a narrow road lined with cars on one side so she had to drive on the wrong side of the road. She reached the end and threw another left down Tregundy Road.

"You say Goddard's put her up here before," Ruby said.

"Apparently." Willow shifted in her seat. The sun felt warm on her scabbed knees through the car window. "Might be staying here myself if I don't find Ellie today."

"Told you," Ruby said. "You can stay at mine."

"You barely know me."

"So? There's always room in my bed for hotties like you." Ruby grinned and winked.

Willow chuckled and shook her head. "Not exactly shy, are you?"

Ruby stared forward, her face serious. "I learnt long ago that shy doesn't get you what you want."

Willow peered at her, sensing that sorrow bubbling beneath the surface again, a bitterness that she couldn't keep from leaking out.

"Is this about your sister?"

Ruby shook her head. "Forget it. You've got your own problems."

Willow kept staring at Ruby. Did she see a touch of defiance in the upward tilt of Ruby's chin? Of wounded pride in her pursed lips? Of heartbreak in the damp sparkle in the corner of her eye? Then Ruby sniffed and blinked. Her face settled and Willow wondered if she'd imagined it all.

"Tell me," Willow said.

"Why?"

Willow shrugged. "I'm interested."

"It's nothing really. I just spent a lot of years pining for someone who I thought I couldn't have. Then it turned out I could've had her cos she felt the same way, but by the time I found out, it was too late. She was with someone else."

"What's that got to do with your sister?"

"Who said it had anything to do with her?"

Willow shrugged. "No one. But just from a few things you've said it sounds like there's some drama with your sister. Or your family."

"Isn't there a drama in every family?"

Willow nodded. "Guess so. But if you want to talk about it…"

"I'm fine," Ruby said, smiling. "Just don't forget the offer for the room is there."

The road passed between the Droskyn Castle holiday apartments, and a block of houses, and headed out onto the clifftop, ending in a sharp left that brought the car right outside the hostel. Beyond the hostel stood a padlocked double gate. Opposite the gate, the grass verge plunged away to the rocks and the ocean below.

"Looks lovely," Ruby sniffed.

Willow peered at the long, single-storey cream building. It had a corrugated roof and wooden picket fencing around its front. The sky behind it blazed brilliant blue. Willow nudged her sunglasses up her nose.

"You think Ellie would hide out somewhere like this?"

"Maybe," Willow said. "I've stayed in worse places."

She saw water stains running down from the corners of the guttering, the edges of the window frames. A wired window in one of the gables had been smashed. Several of the slats on the picket fence around the side had been broken.

"It looks like a dive."

"Yeah," Willow said, unlocking the door. "It does."

"You want me to come with you?" Ruby said as Willow grabbed her bag from the back seat.

"Honestly?" Willow said. "Yeah, I do. But if Ellie is here, then I should go alone."

Ruby nodded. "Well, give me a call if you need me."

Willow smiled. "I will."

She stood and closed the car door. Ruby reversed to park up, the engine growling, the tyres hissing on the tarmac. Willow strode towards the front door.

*

Harrison Gould screamed as Raven ground salt into the three-inch gash in his shoulder. She stepped back from the bed, sweating in her biker's leathers, her nose and mouth covered by the black skull mask, and watched him writhe, his body jerking, his lips drawn back, teeth-gnashing, hands twisting and turning in the handcuffs that bound his wrists and feet to the bars on the head and footboard. Blood oozed down his shoulder and joined the copper blood and urine stains on the mattress. Raven cocked her head and peered at him.

"Why d'you call her back?" Raven said.

"Please!" Gould screamed. "Please! I didn't."
"Liar!"
"I DON'T KNOW. IT WASN'T ME."
"Who was it then?"
"I don't know!"

Raven stalked across to him and slapped him hard across the face. The sound echoed around the abandoned room.

"LIAR! You brought her back here. You've been working with Ellie. What do you know? Why is she here?"

"Please…" Harrison gasped through the tears. "I don't know anything."

"Fine." She shrugged and dropped her gloved hand into the bag of swimming pool salt at her feet, the tails of her leather coat spreading across the floor as she crouched. "You asked for it."

"No! NO! Please!"
"TELL ME!" Raven roared.
"Willow…"
"What about her?"

"She thinks Ellie called her back." Harrison began to jerk and twist again as Raven stepped towards him, salt dropping from the sides of her hands and hitting the carpet. "It must be her. IT MUST BE ELLIE."

"Sure it wasn't you?"
"It was Ellie. IT HAD TO BE ELLIE."

Raven stood over him. Fear flickered in his gaze. Sweat beaded on his top lip and forehead. He stared at the salt like it was anthrax.

"Liar," she said.

Then she drove the salt into his wounds and his

screams echoed through the deserted corridors of the abandoned hotel. She got up. Dusted her hands off and look towards the doorway.

Outside of the room, in the gloom of the corridor, backlit by the weak sunlight struggling to burn through the dirt of the windows, Al looked pale and queasy in his mechanics overalls. He chewed his oil-stained fingernails, his mouth working silently as if he were praying. He saw Raven watching and looked away, grimacing. She turned back and gazed down at Harrison. Blood oozed from where he'd bit his lips.

Behind the scarf, her scars stung as they scraped against the thin cotton, the sting a ghost of the burning agony that had once torn through her body. The pain that made Harrison jerk and struggle in the restraints was nothing compared to what she'd suffered.

Grabbing another handful of salt, she knelt on the end of the bed and began to crawl up his body like a twisted lover. He shook his head, eyes bulging as she put one hand by his cheek, the other holding the salt above him. He couldn't tear his gaze from it. She put her face close to his as if leaning into a kiss.

"No, please, no. I don't…"

"What was in the flat?"

He stammered, head jerking, eyes flicking from Raven, to Al, to the salt.

"I don't know. Please. Don't. Please!"

"Don't know much." She slammed her hand into the wound, twisted it, tearing the flesh, grinding the salt deep into the damaged tissue. "Do you?"

His anguished howl filled the room. The chains clanked and rattled as he spasmed. As he writhed, his face moved through the shafts of light piercing the heavy gloom. She rolled off him again and wiped his spit from her face.

They were in an abandoned hotel, built in the early 1900s. It had become a wartime convalescent hospital in the forties, and a hotel again after. But through bad luck or bad management, the place had gone out of business in 2006 and hadn't been re-opened since.

Some of the rooms looked as though the occupants had just stepped out. The room they occupied for example. The bed had been made. An old make-up bag sat amongst the dust and cobwebs on the dresser. The phone had been left off the hook as if the speaker had gone to get someone else and never came back. But the moth-eaten curtains, the grime on the windows and the thick funk of dead mice and putrefied bird shit, told the true tale of neglect and abandonment. The salt had been used to generate chlorine for the old swimming pool and been left there when the last owners locked up and gone. Raven had found it in the old stockroom back when she'd spent a night exploring.

Getting in had always been easy. The fence around the place had been an afterthought, a flimsy ring of metal fencing, easily breached. Squatters came in and out as regularly as the hotel guests of old. Or at least they had until Goddard had arranged for its purchase, and Raven had chased them off.

The deal had gone through, then 'stalled' as elaborate plans went before the council only to fall at the first hurdle. And in the meantime, the town's coke heads came at irregular intervals, always under the cover of darkness, and always in the early hours to get their latest stash of top quality gear, fresh off the boat and straight out of the Duchy Farms warehouse on the outskirts of Redruth.

For the most part, the public avoided the place, the kids scared away by the rumours of a bloodthirsty ghost of a nineteen twenties murderer haunting the rooms, waiting for unsuspecting innocents to stumble into his lair and then cut their throats, the adults by the strung-out wasters who hung around and by the screams and lights in the dark.

Gould's screams died away. He slumped in the shackles, gasping and crying.

"I swear," he said, shaking his head. "I don't know anything. Please…"

Raven stepped closer and pinched his jaw. "What was in the flat?"

He began to whimper. She heard running water dripping under the bed. Looked down and saw a dark stain spreading across his overalls from his crotch and trickling down into the mattress.

She wrinkled her nose against the stench of piss.

"You disgusting…" She put her wrist to her mouth and stepped away.

"He's telling the truth!" Al stepped forward, covering his mouth, looking sick.

Raven sneered at him.

"I swear," Al said. "He didn't recognise her."

"Still could have called her back though,"

"Enough! Look at him. Look at him!"

Raven wrinkled her nose in disgust and sneered at the teary, piss-stained, snotty mess on the bed. "I'd rather not."

"Does he look like he's got the balls to lie to you?"

Raven didn't reply.

"For pity's sake, let the boy go. He knows nothing."

Harrison had closed his eyes and was weeping freely, heavy racking sobs filling the room, the chains rattling as he writhed.

"Who told you I have any pity?" Raven said.

"Look, I get it ok You're a twisted, vicious bitch. But show some decency for once. Let him go."

"What's the matter, Al? All a bit too real for you."

"I made a mistake ok?" Al stepped into the room and held his hands out. "I got greedy, took what wasn't mine. And I appreciate Goddard's silence, I truly do." He looked Raven up and down.

"But I cannae be part of this."

Raven peered from him to Harrison and back again.

"Please," Al said. "Let him go"

"He knows something. And he's going to tell me if I have to cut his balls off to make him talk." She turned to the bed, drawing the knife from the pocket of her leather coat.

"No more!" Al grabbed her shoulders. Dragged her back. Threw her towards the dresser. She stumbled across the room, rolled and crashed into it. The wooden drawers shattered. The glass splintered. Shards flew up around her. Her shoulder struck the wall. She cried out. Fell to her knees. The knife skittered across the floor.

She tried to rise, but Al grabbed her, threw her again. She landed face down on the floor. Dust erupted from the carpet. She spluttered, then gasped as Al fell on her. He wrapped his hands around her neck. Squeezed. She bucked. Jerked. He wouldn't let go. Just squeezed tighter. She slammed her head back. Hit thin air. Clawed at the carpet. It disintegrated in her fingers. Spots began to pop in her vision. She gasped. Bucked and writhed. She couldn't shake him. And she was running out of air.

She gave a final gasp, flailed and flapped, then went limp, became a dead weight.

He let go. She felt the pressure ease from her windpipe. Amateur.

"Is she..." she heard Harrison say. Then Al got off of her.

She spun and surged up, grabbed Al by the head, drove him back to the wall. He howled and clawed at her face. She felt his nails rip her mask down, carve into her scars. White pain flared across her face. An old agony rekindled. She howled rage and hate. Slammed him into the wall.

The plaster cracked as his skull struck home.

He gasped.

She gripped his skull, squeezed it between her palms, and spun his head hard. The crack of his neck breaking echoed around the room. Harrison screeched. Al's body crumbled to the floor.

Raven stepped back sucking air. She could smell shit rising from the corpse at her feet. She kicked and spat on it for good measure.

"Idiot," she muttered.

"You?"

She turned.

Saw Harrison gaping at her, his mouth slack with recognition. She turned to the dresser.

In the last shard of glass hanging in the mirror frame on the dresser, she saw the scarf had been ripped off. She flinched, not from the half of her face covered by pink and white swirls and pits where her skin had been burned and melted away. Not from the blood oozing over her scars from the three long gashes there.

But from the other half.

The half where her hair grew in a short blonde stubble, where she could see the ghost of the girl she'd once been in the soft tilt of her eye, the smoothness of her cheek, the thick pinkness of her lips. The anger rose like a coiled snake inside her. She glared at her reflection, at the monster she was and the beauty she'd once been.

"You!" Harrison began to buck and writhe. "But you're-" In two steps, she was on him.

"De-"

She grabbed his throat and squeezed it hard pouring the rage and the agony and the hate into her grip. His eyes bulged. His face burned red. Then purple. He bucked and writhed, the chains rattling. Mouth wide. Air squeaking out. He pulled at the cuffs, twisted, pushed his hips up. Raven's hand slipped. She lost her balance. Harrison sucked air.

"Zo-"

She grabbed his throat. Tighter now. The name died on his lips. She jammed her knees on his elbows. His face turned purple again. Tongue flapped in his mouth. Then he bit down hard.

Blood burst from his tongue as the tip rolled away. It seeped from his closed lips, down onto the mattress. He jerked, bucked, twisted, thrust. The blood pooled in the back of his throat. His eyes flicked around the room.

She squeezed harder, put all of her pain, her hate, her rage into her hands.

His face went a dark puce. His movements became weaker. The last of his breath rasped from his bloody mouth. His eyes rolled back.

He lay still.

Raven squeezed harder, squeezed until she heard his bowels empty, smelled his death stench fill the room.

Then she let go, gasping, her arms sore, her wrists throbbing.

The blood spilling from his mouth made her gloves slick. She jabbed them on the mattress, wiping the gore off. Then she stepped away from the corpse. The rage, the hate, the agony faded.

Seconds passed. Her heart rate settled, the nausea bubbling in her gut faded, the adrenaline rush seeping away

She stared at the two corpses, covering her nose against the rising stench. She grabbed her mask from the floor where it had fallen.

Goddard wouldn't like this, but Al had gone for her. And Harrison…he'd seen her face. He'd blow her cover. All their cover. He had to die too. She'd had no choice and Goddard could accept that or not. She couldn't control what he thought.

She could control what happened next though. The bodies could lay here till nightfall. No one would find them. She'd come back with Gabriel and Michael, and take the bodies out into the Atlantic and ditch them in the sea.

In the meantime, she still had no idea if Harrison had sent the text or what exactly Willow had taken from the flat. And now, with Harrison dead, the only person who knew was Willow herself.

And Goddard had said to let him handle her.

Which meant Raven had a choice.

Obey Goddard and hope he got to her before the troublesome bitch wrecked everything.

Or take matters into her own hands and take whatever consequences Goddard threw her way after.

With a final glance at the bodies, Raven snatched up the knife, tucked it into the waistband of her leathers. She fixed her mask around her face, and stalked out of the room.

21

As Willow approached the hostel, the door opened and a large woman stepped out. She had bulldog jowls, spiked grey-blonde hair, and a shapeless black cardigan over dirty blue jeans that bulged beneath the tightly synched waistband.

"Help you, love?" She wiped her hands on the tea towel she was carrying.

Willow smiled and lifted her sunglasses into her dreadlocks.

"Are you Sheila?"

"Yeah. Why?" Sheila's gaze narrowed.

"I'm looking for someone," Willow said. "And a friend of mine reckoned they might be staying here. They said to ask for you."

"Oh aye. Who you looking for then?"

"My sister."

"Name?"

"Ellie," Willow said. "Eloise Rae."

Sheila's eyes flared then narrowed again. She threw the tea towel over her shoulder.

"No-one by that name 'ere."

Willow put her hands on her hips and looked to the

cliff edge. The disappointment tasted bitter. Goddard's lead had felt like a lifeline, a hope to cling to, the best chance to find Ellie. Now that chance seemed to slip away. At the cliff edge, a gull soared up into view, drifting on a thermal. It cawed and dived towards the hidden sea. Willow turned back to the woman.

"Well, has she stayed here recently?"

"I'd have to check." The woman didn't move.

"Well, can you then?"

"Who told you she'd be here?"

"Goddard," she said. "Richard Goddard."

The woman's face remained impassive but her jaw muscles clenched.

"You better come in."

Willow followed her into a reception area with white walls, and shabby vinyl tiling on the floor. The fluorescent lighting gave the place a sterile, clinical feel. A hatch had been built into the wall facing the door, and she could see beyond it, into a small office with folders and files piled randomly on the shelves above a flat-screen PC. Outside the office, a price list had been clipped into a silver plastic frame that hung on a wall dotted with badly filled Rawlplug holes. Two doors led out of the reception.

The one to the left led into a large communal dining area. She could hear voices and laughter. The smell of coffee and burnt toast made her mouth water. The other door led into a long corridor with doors on either side.

"Wait 'ere." Sheila pointed to the counter, then disappeared through the right-hand door.

Willow heard a door in the office open and then Sheila stepped in, scratching her inner thigh and sighing as she crossed to the files on the back shelf. She tapped her fingers along the edges, then hooked her thumb into a metal hole in the side of one and dragged it out. It scrapped free, its green cover bent and frayed. Sheila turned and waddled to the desk, dragged back a plastic chair and opened the folder.

Willow rose on tiptoe to peer over the counter as Sheila flicked through the pages, her thumb swollen and red.

"Here you are," Sheila said, flipping the folder around and passing it up onto the counter. "That's last time she stayed 'ere."

Willow scanned the page. It had a list of names, room numbers, dates, prices, then a column to indicate whether they'd paid or not. There were also columns for mobile phone numbers and home addresses, with a final box for signatures.

Ellie's name appeared halfway down the page. Willow recognised her graceful, slanted script, with its elegant loops on the double l and the capital E, immediately.

"That were about a month back," Sheila said. "Reckoned she may go to London after."

"London?"

"'Ent seen her since Thursday last."

Willow gazed back at the page. Ellie had checked in on Tuesday, June 4th, and stayed for over three weeks, then checked out again on the 27th; two days – give or take the time difference – before Willow got the text.

Digging out her phone, Willow checked the mobile number for Ellie on the page against the one in her phone. It matched the old number she had for Ellie, but not the number that had sent the text. She checked the home address. She recognised it straight away.

Only it wasn't the address of Ellie's flat. She tapped the page with her finger and peered at Sheila.

"What's this, the address of a next of kin?" Willow said.

"Home address," Sheila said.

"That's not Ellie's address."

"It's what she put. It's where she said she was living."

"It can't be."

Sheila shrugged. "It's what she wrote."

Willow peered at the address again. It didn't make sense. That wasn't where Ellie was living, she knew that, and even in her most desperate hours, Ellie would never have gone there. Yet there it was, staring up at her.

It was the place both of them had vowed never to set foot in again.

*

"You're sure she said London?"

Willow stepped out onto the road then turned back to Sheila who had stepped out behind her. The sun felt hot on her shoulders and arms. Squinting, she dropped the sunglasses over her eyes.

"It's what she said." Sheila threw the tea towel over her shoulder. "Just 'fore she left, she thanked me, then said she's heading to London and letting things blow over."

"Was she going right away?"

Sheila shrugged. "Di'nt say. I'm presuming so, but can't swear to it."

"And she didn't give you a forwarding address. In case anyone came asking?"

"I'm a landlady, not a bleeding secretary."

Willow stepped forward.

"Please," she said. "It's important. I'm her sister. If she told you anything at all, she'd want you to tell me."

"She told me nothing and I 'ent one for askin' either."

Willow sighed. There was a nervousness about Sheila, about the way she couldn't meet Willow's gaze, the way she kept pawing at the towel as she spoke, that made Willow think that she wasn't telling her everything. But she didn't seem ready to break down and confess all.

"Ok, well, thanks for your help."

Flashing what she hoped was a grateful smile, Willow turned and headed back towards the car. Ruby had her eyes closed and the driver's seat lowered flat, her arms folded across her chest, her feet on the dashboard. As Willow approached, she opened an eye and sat up. Reaching down she began to wind the seat back up, and as Willow reached the passenger door, she leaned across and unlocked it.

"Any joy?"

Willow shook her head. "She was there, but she left last Thursday."

Ruby turned the key as Willow clunked on her seat belt. As the engine rattled to life, Willow glanced back at the hostel. Sheila stood at the gate with her arms folded, her eyes narrowed with suspicion.

"I think that cow knows more than she's letting on," Willow said. "But she's not telling me anything."

"She don't look the most friendly."

The car rolled forward and the hostel swung out of view as Ruby headed back up Tregundy Lane.

"So where d'you think she is now?"

"London," Willow said. "Apparently."

"London?"

"It's what Ellie told that battle-axe."

"You think she's heading to that Uni mate who put you up?"

"Maybe," Willow said. "But I already called her when I landed. She hadn't seen Ellie but she said she'd call me if Ellie turned up, so if she is heading that way, she's not got there yet."

"Does she know anyone else in London?"

"Maybe. But even if she didn't, it's a great place to get lost in. Trust me, I've done it."

They passed the Droskyn car park. It had begun to fill up as the temperature rose and the sun blazed overhead, drawing more people to the town and its long stretch of white-gold sand, but with the school holidays a few weeks away, there was still plenty of space within.

"So what are you going to do now?"

Willow shrugged. "Not sure. But there was something odd. At the hostel."

"Odd?"

"Well, the battle-axe was acting weird. Couldn't meet my gaze. Seemed in a rush to get rid of me."

"You think she was lying to you?"

"Don't know about lying, but I'm sure she knew more than she let on. But it wasn't just that."

Ruby threw a right then another right and hit the road back to St. Agnes. "What was it then?" she said.

"Ellie put my mum's place down as her home address. Not the Perranporth flat."

"Maybe she knew she wasn't going back to Perranporth. Or she was trying to throw off those people following her?"

"Possibly," Willow said. "But why say she was living at our mum's? She hates our mum. She'd put Dad's address before she'd Mum's"

"Unless that's where she's gone," Ruby said.

Willow's instinct was to protest, but the instinct died in her throat. Could it be? The mystery phone number... possibly her mother's... maybe Ellie had already been thinking about sending the message... but she didn't want to say where she was or use her own phone because maybe Ruby was right, maybe she was trying to hide from the people after her.

Is that where you are Ellie? With her?

Hope flickered in Willow's heart. She turned to Ruby. "D'you mind driving me to Helford?" she said.

*

Goddard paced across the furrowed field, glancing left and right at the leaves poking through the dried, crumbling earth. Despite the constant heat and lack of rain, the crop had grown well. Another good harvest beckoned, another profitable year for Duchy Farms.

He and his older brother, Matthew, had inherited the business when their father died eight years earlier, when the business had been failing and Goddard's first instinct had been to sell up and get back to Morocco as soon as possible. But Matthew had thrown himself into managing it, and Goddard had been persuaded to keep it running, partly out of respect for his dead father, but mainly because it seemed to drag Matthew away from the drugs that had been playing an ever-increasing part in his life since their father's diagnosis with lung cancer.

Goddard left him to it, went back to Morocco, ran his surf and prayer camps, then came back after a frantic call from his mother. Matthew had OD'd, and this time Goddard returned for good.

He took over the business, set up his surf and prayer camps in St. Agnes and then set about trying to get his brother clean. He kept the business going in the hope that it would give Matthew purpose, a reason to get clean and stay clean.

It worked.

For a while.

But Matthew had never been up to running the business full time again and still relapsed regularly.

The second OD, caused by snorting coke mixed with drain cleaner, had changed Goddard forever. He realised now that his brother was lost to drugs. Matthew was, and always would be, an addict. Nothing Goddard could do could change that.

But he could manage the risks. The time spent in Morocco had put him in touch with any number of surfers who liked to indulge in the white stuff and some of those had a direct dial to a supply line of the purest coke available. If the risk to his brother was bad coke, he'd have to manage that risk by supplying good coke.

It began with small quantities at first. Enough for personal use. But Matt started waxing lyrical about the gear to his addict mates, and Goddard, by now ordained and running the Methodist church in St. Agnes, was burying too many young kids who'd OD'd on the bad gear flooding the market from London on the County Lines routes. He upscaled, got a few of the kids clean, kept them as Chosen, runners.

The purpose was simple. If kids were going to take drugs, he couldn't stop them. But he could make it as safe as possible. He took no profit from it. Didn't need to. Duchy Farm's gave him the cash he needed, and the preaching topped that up. His prices were low, his gear was good, and he profited from the trade in other ways.

He learned things; the sins and vices of those in power. Cornish First was already up and running. And now, with the knowledge he gained, where before it had found its campaigns falling on deaf ears with the councils and its petitions being at best ignored and at worst outright rejected, suddenly it was able to make real headway. And the best part was, while he was already well known as the face of Cornish First, none of the users, those whose habits made them open to blackmail and extortion, none of them ever knew who was behind the drugs operations.

That's what he had Raven for.

She stood in the shadows of the trees that ran around the perimeter, hooded, masked and shrouded in her leather coat, watching the group of Chosen walking around the field, pulling up wire mesh from around the perimeter and rolling it up.

Goddard checked his watch. The Duchy Farms truck would be here any second. When it arrived, two of the Chosen would load the bundles of wire into the back of the truck, while the third would distribute the truck's cargo into the open boots of their waiting cars, now parked inside the main gate.

For anyone watching from the road or the distant houses, it was just another day on the farm. And yeah, there was a risk if the Duchy Farms truck got stopped on the way, before the switch, but the warehouse was only a few miles away so the risk was low.

It was made even lower because the truck had Duchy Farms on the side. The reputation of the firm as an outstanding purveyor of ethically sourced produce was an effective cover.

Goddard's only regret was that despite the success of his projects, and for all the wealth and power it had given him, its first objective had failed.

Matthew had fatally overdosed eighteen months back. The shock of losing her first son had taken his mother too, a month later. He'd thought about backing out then, letting it go. But it had become bigger than his brother by that point. It gave him real power, and the ability to make a proper difference in people's lives.

And if a few had to die to make it happen?

He flinched, and his mood darkened as the old guilt squirmed in his gut. And the old justifications. Those who died had made their choice. They didn't have to stand against him. But they had. And they had to be removed. A means to an end.

The end being tipping the balance of power away from the corrupt local politicians and the London elite who bled the county dry and giving it back to the people who were born and bred in the Duchy.

He reached the end of the furrow, nodded at Raven, then stood next to her, facing into the field. The lorry was approaching up the country lane. They stood in silence but he could feel the nervous energy rippling off of her. She kept shifting her weight from foot to foot and rubbing her scars beneath her scarf. As she went to speak, the phone buzzed in his pocket. Raising a finger to silence her, he took out the phone and looked at the screen.

Sheila.

He answered.

"Well?"

"She came 'ere," Sheila said. "Looking for her sister."

"And?"

"I did as you said. I told her she went to London."

"You think she believed you?"

"Had no reason not to."

Goddard smiled down at Raven.

"You did well, Sheila," Goddard said. "You're son's lucky his mother's not as thick as he is."

"Now-"

Goddard cut the call, no longer interested in what Sheila had to say. "You look happy," Raven said. "Should I be worried?"

Goddard grinned wider. "The Willow problem is solved," he said. "She's on her way to London as we speak."

"Doubt that."

"She took the bait." He turned to face Raven. "She's out of our hair. And no one had to die this time." He cocked an eyebrow, like a schoolteacher proving a point to a stubborn student.

"Happy days," Raven said, turning back to the truck. The sarcasm in her voice cut through his good mood.

"You think Sheila's lying?"

"No," Raven said. "But I know Willow better than you do. She may believe Sheila. And she may run to London now. But as soon as she hits a dead end there, she'll come scurrying back, causing trouble again."

"She's gone, Raven. Gone. She won't come back," Goddard said. "Have a little faith, will you?"

Raven snorted.

"That's your gig," she said. "I'd feel a damn sight better if I knew that bitch was as dead as her sister."

She flashed him a dark glare, then stalked towards the truck, which had pulled into the field and stopped a dozen paces away, its engine growling and rattling, sending the crows and the starlings scurrying from the trees and into the summer sky.

Goddard watched her go. She carried hate within her and a lust for death. Not for the first time, he wondered if he'd made the monster, or if the monster had always been there, lying dormant, waiting for someone to unchain it.

Whichever it was, as he watched the Chosen back away as she approached, as he saw the nervous glances they exchanged, it struck him that right now, she was useful. But she was starting to become a risk.

She'd gone against him fighting Willow. And as good as she was at terrifying the Chosen into silence, their loyalty was built on knowing Goddard would look after them. The death of Raphael, as necessary as it had been, had scared them. The more violent she became, the more she intimidated and bullied them, the more chance there was that one of them would decide their loyalties would be better rewarded elsewhere.

He couldn't allow that to happen.

She couldn't compromise the network he'd spent years building. They were close now. Close to making a real change.

For now, she was useful. One day that would change.

All he had to decide was when.
And how he'd dispose of her.

22

"When did you last see her?" Ruby asked.

They were on the main road into Helford. Trees whipped past outside, and Willow glimpsed the odd house hidden amongst them, or a patchwork of fields when the foliage thinned. She felt nauseous, her throat dry, a bitter taste on her tongue.

"Ellie?"

"Your mother," Ruby said.

"About ten years ago. I came down here to visit. It didn't end pleasantly." Willow blinked, remembering the argument that had led to her storming out and waiting in the rain for her father to pick her up again.

"Was Ellie with you then?"

Willow shook her head. "As far as I know, Ellie hasn't seen Mum since the bitch walked out on us."

"So why would she come here now?"

"Desperation maybe." Willow shrugged. "Or maybe she had nowhere else to run."

The road branched right, leading into the village. The sat nav kept them going straight, onto the next turn, then a left turn a little way further on. The foliage closed in around them again, and the road ended at a large black gate with brick pillars topped with giant stone orbs. Beyond the gate she could see her mother's house; a faux-Georgian red brick detached property with white framed windows and a double front door, painted black, at the top of a grand semi-circle of blonde stone steps. A chimney rose from the gables at each end.

"She's done well for herself," Ruby said.

"Yeah," Willow replied, bitterness stinging her tongue. "Hasn't she just?"

Ruby pulled up close to the gates and jammed on the handbrake. She turned and gazed at Willow.

"You look pale," Ruby said.

"I hate the bitch." Willow peered down at the loose thread spiralling from her bag strap. The tug of war with the biker the day before had loosened the stitching and Willow wound it around her fingertip, making her skin flush angry red.

"You want me to come with you?"

Willow shook her head. "Thanks, but I've got to do this alone."

She reached for the handle, nudged the door open, and stepped out into the cool shade of the foliage. The house ahead loomed over the gate, silent, the windows dark. Birds trilled and whistled through the trees, the branches whispering and rustling with the breeze and the flapping of wings.

Willow's footsteps crunched on the bracken and twigs covering the cracked tarmac. She could smell the earth and bark and sun-baked leaves. Ahead, the house seemed to peer down at her like an imperious patriarch. She stopped by the left pillar where she saw a metal panel with a plastic button beneath a speaker grill. She reached out, pressed the bell, then stepped back.

"Hello?"

She recognised the voice, electric and static-filled as it was.

"Heelllooo!" the voice came again, impatient and sardonic.

"It's..."

The words died in her throat. She couldn't say it. She couldn't say her own name. "I'm looking for Ellie Rae," she said instead.

"Are you press?"

"No." Willow peered back at Ruby. "Mum, it's me. It's Megan."

*

"You're not scared, are you?" the boy said as he shoved back the fencing, creating a gap for the girl to slip through.

They were seventeen, in the first throes of young love, and desperate for a place for her to take his virginity. They'd gotten randy in the dunes at Fistral, only to get interrupted by an overfriendly border collie. They'd tried his place, then hers, but their parents were home and privacy was at a premium. Then he suggested the old hotel on the south end of Fistral Beach.

"It's supposed to be haunted," he'd said, hoping to impress her.

"Don't worry, princess," she'd replied. "I'll be there to fight the ghosts off for you."

Now, as he pushed back the fence, and peered at the dirt-darkened windows, the scummy grey walls, the abandoned shopping trolleys, beer cans and bullet-shaped cases of nitrous oxide scattered across what had once been a loading bay, he could feel fear flickering in his stomach.

"Told you, princess," the girl said, striding past him. "I'll look after you."

He slipped through the fence and followed her towards the broken fire escape, watching her arse sway in her tight pink shorts. He could see the line of her knickers through the sheer fabric. She wore a white vest with no bra that cut low down her slender, lithe back. He loved the scattering of moles across her fair skin, and the way her blonde hair fell in glossy strands across her shoulders. And as he stepped next to her, he particularly liked the side view of her boobs, and the point of her nipples sticking through the fabric.

He slipped his arm around her waist. She turned, and they kissed. Her lips tasted of berry balm. She stumbled on a laughing gas canister and pulled away. He stared at the building. The fear wormed its way into his chest now, fluttering like arrhythmia.

"You sure you want to do this?" he said. "I mean, I understand if you're scared."

She rolled her eyes. "Please," she said. "There's no such thing as ghosts."

As they reached the fire escape, she scampered up ahead of him, her feet ringing on the rusted iron steps. He followed, reaching the top of the stairs as she pushed the door back and vanished inside, heading right.

"Hey, wait!"

He quickened his pace, reached the door, and lurched into the gloomy interior. The smell of mould and dampness and dust swamped his throat. He raised his hands to cover his mouth and nose and squinted down the corridor, through shafts of grey-white light. He saw doorways - several open, most closed - lining the left-hand side, peeling wallpaper, frayed carpets and shards of broken glass across the floor.

But no sign of her.

"Lucy!" he called out.

No reply. The fear flickering in his stomach began to grow. He looked back to the fire escape and wondered if he should get out now. Then he shook his head. He was being daft. The rooms were empty. Nothing here could hurt him. His imagination liked playing tricks on him. He hadn't heard a footstep on the carpet behind him, or on the floorboard overhead.

Then he felt a breath on his neck.

He whipped around, heart hammering.

Deserted. A net curtain swayed in the breeze coming through a broken window next to him.

"Lucy!" His voice quivered.

Still nothing. He glanced towards the fire escape. The urge to run grew stronger. It took all of his willpower to ignore it. Running would ruin any chance he had with her.

He sucked in a breath and then set along the corridor. He peeped into rooms in various states of disrepair. Some were practically ruined. Others still almost immaculate. He saw no sign of Lucy.

He passed the last room on the left. Empty.

Figuring she'd gone up to the next level, he reached to push the door back. He heard a whisper of noise behind him again. Spun.

The corridor stood empty. He sighed. Smiled. Turned back to the door.

Screamed. His legs collapsed. He sprawled on the floor.

Lucy had her face pressed to the glass, her nose upturned, with crossed eyes and her tongue lolling out. As he fell she collapsed into fits of giggles and staggered into the corridor.

"What a hero!" She laughed.

"You cow!" He leapt up, and she screeched and fled through the door, her laughter echoing up the footwell, her footsteps booming on each step as she ran and he chased her.

They spilt out onto the second floor, her first, stumbling through the door, then him, charging after her, his fear gone, laughing crazily. They passed more open doors, more broken glass, a partially collapsed wall. The floor seemed to shake and creak with every step.

She swung on a door jam and disappeared inside a room. He followed, and she leapt on his back.

"Gotcha!" she cried, giggling, her hair swinging into his face.

They stumbled onto a dusty yet immaculately made bed. He rolled onto his back, and she fell on him, kissing him hard. He grabbed her chest.

"Ow!" she cried. "Easy. That bloody hurt."

"I'll kiss 'em better." He grinned, rolling on top of her, and trying to lift her shirt. She squeezed his sides. He collapsed into a hysterical shriek. She rolled him off and tugged her shirt down.

"I need to pee first," she said.

She sloped off the bed and scurried into the bathroom,

flashing her tits at him at the doorway. Then, with a wink, she kicked the door shut. He laughed, then gazed around the room. Pale light fought its way through the dirt-covered windows. The smell of damp still lingered. And something worse. Like burst sewer pipes. He'd kind of hoped for somewhere more romantic for his first time.

His hard-on pressed against his jeans. He wondered whether he should take his clothes off. Decided against it. It would look too forward. He slipped the rubber out of his pocket though, put it on the bedside table, sweeping off a thick layer of dust first. The smell had grown stronger. He wondered if it would put her off. It wasn't exactly stoking the mood.

He swung his legs off of the bed then crossed to the window. Dead flies dotted the ledge. Wrinkling his nose, he fiddled with the jammed lock. He hit the glass with the palm of his wrist but got nothing for his trouble except a sore hand. Behind him, the bathroom latch clicked. He turned. Lucy stepped out wearing nothing but a pink cotton thong.

His mouth went dry. His cock throbbed. He couldn't breathe.

"Ready now." She smiled.

He swallowed. Now that she stood almost naked before him, he didn't know what to do. He felt unprepared. She smiled, lowered her gaze and tucked her hair behind her ears. She looked beautiful, vulnerable, and he stepped towards her.

Then the world roared beneath him, and the ground lurched away.

He fell in a cloud of broken floorboards, ripped carpet, and shattered plaster. He crashed to the floor, his left leg folding under him. It snapped at the shin. He screamed, then clenched his teeth to cut it off. Dust and smoke swirled around him. He looked up. The smell of sewers seemed stronger here.

"Zack!" Lucy cried out from the room above.

Pain burned up his body, through his legs, bringing nausea and dizziness with it. He squinted up at the hole in the ceiling. Lucy peeked over the side.

"Are you okay?"

"My leg. I think it's broken."

"I'll come down."

She disappeared from view. He heard her feet pounding overhead, getting fainter. The smell seemed to waft over him again. He looked around the room he'd landed in.

He saw the bodies and the flies swirling around them. And screamed.

23

Willow stared at the dead intercom.

Her mother hadn't replied, and the gate stayed resolutely shut. She looked to Ruby, thought about retreating to the car, then heard a whirring behind her. She turned back and saw a CCTV camera spinning to examine her.

It stopped, whirred as if focusing, then went still. Several long seconds passed. A jay erupted in a burst of blue from the trees that lined the wide gravel drive. Beyond the house, the sail of a yacht glided along the hidden river. Tiring of waiting, Willow reached for the buzzer again, but before her finger could press the metal button, the gate clunked, unlocked and swung back on its hinges. With a final glance at Ruby, who waved her forwards with both hands, Willow trudged up the path, her boots crunching on the gravel.

As she reached the wide steps the front door opened and her mother stepped out, cold faced, thin-lipped, arms jammed across her chest.

"It's you," Fiona Rae said.

"It's me," Willow replied. "Why did you think I was the press?"

"Those parasites have been plaguing me ever since that bloody story broke."

Fiona stood on the top step, slim and elegant, with glossy black hair and a sharp face. She wore a thin white gold chain around her neck, and a narrow band set with crystals on her ring finger, with tight white jeans and a black Armani t-shirt. Aside from the ghosts of crow's feet in the corners of her eyes, and the odd strand of grey in her black bob, she'd hardly changed in the last six years. She still looked more like Ellie's sister than Willow ever had. Her gaze flicked over Willow's face, her clothes, her hair. She wrinkled her nose in disgust.

"So what's brought you crawling back?" Fiona said.

"You gonna invite me in?"

"Do I have to?"

"Well, I am your daughter."

Fiona's thin lips went bloodless. "You were always more his daughter than mine."

"And you were always quick to blame me for that." Willow cocked an eyebrow.

"What do you want?"

"Is Ellie here?"

"No. Why would she be?"

"She gave your address as a next of kin in a hostel she stayed in."

"And?"

"And I'm wondering why she would do that?"

"No idea."

"You haven't seen her?"

Fiona stepped out of the front door and eased it shut behind her.

"No," she said, her head half-turned to the door. Like

she was looking towards someone inside. Willow narrowed her gaze. A flush of anger swept through her.

"You're lying." She stalked up the steps, barged past her mother and into the hallway, a cavernous room bigger than any house Willow had ever lived in, with marble floors, white walls and a large ocean oil painting on one wall.

"What are you doing?" Fiona cried, grabbing her arm.

Willow caught the fragrant, floral scent of her mother's perfume, and flushed as she caught a whiff of her own dry, sandy smell. Her mother seemed to smell it too because she flinched.

"I haven't said you can come in, Megan," she told her.

"It's Willow." She shook off Fiona's hand and strode into a large, open plan lounge and kitchen. The front windows overlooked the drive. Through the back windows Willow saw an immaculate garden that ran down to the banks of the Helford River. No sign of Ellie there.

"What?" Fiona said.

"My name's Willow now."

"Willow?" Fiona snorted. "What kind of ridiculous name is that?"

"Ellie!" Willow called. "It's me."

"What are you doing?"

Willow spun. "She's here," she said. "Ellie. I know she's here" She stalked back out into the hallway.

"Ellie!" Her voice echoed up the stairs.

"You're crazy," Fiona said. "Bloody crazy."

"She put down your address. In a hostel in Perranporth. Said it was her home address about a month ago. Why would she do that?"

"I don't know. She wasn't here."

Willow glared at her mother. "We'll see."

She ran for the stairs, but Fiona moved faster and slipped in front of her. She thrust her hands out and jammed them between the cream wall and the dark wood handrail.

"Get out!" Fiona hissed.

"Where is she?" Willow screamed. Her voice echoed shrill and harsh up the staircase. Spittle flecked out of her mouth.

"I said get out!"

Willow glared at her mother. She tried to push past, but Fiona grabbed her shoulders and pushed against her.

"You take one more step and I'll call the bloody police on you."

"What are you hiding up there?"

"I mean it."

"Ellie!" Willow tried to push past, but Fiona pushed back again.

"I'll call them. I'll call the police!"

"On your own daughter?"

"If I have to."

Willow glared at Fiona, who glared right back.

"You've always been trouble, Megan."

"And you've always been a selfish bitch, Fiona."

She saw her mother's eyes widen, her lips thin. Her hand swung out, struck Willow's cheek. Willow stumbled back, grabbed the bannister for balance. Anger burned in her gut. She breathed deep, swallowed down the urge to hit back. She glared at her mother.

"Feel better?" Willow said.

"Get out of my house," Fiona hissed.

"Where's Ellie?"

"Get out!"

"Where's my sister?"

"I don't know!"

"You're lying."

"Fine." Fiona dropped her hands. "Bloody fine. Go up. Search. Knock yourself out. You won't bloody find her, because she's not bloody here!"

Willow stalked past, stomping up the stairs, onto an airy landing, with two doors on either side and one in front.

"Ellie!"

The lock on one of the bedroom doors clicked. The door squealed as it swung open. For one glorious moment, she thought she'd found Ellie. Her heart swelled. Then she saw who it was and her heart shrivelled.

"Dad?" she said. "What the hell are you doing here?"

Jonathan Rae emerged from the bedroom, shirtless, a towel wrapped around his waist, his grey chest hair damp. He lowered his gaze.

"The same thing as you," he muttered. "Looking for Ellie."

"Where? In the shower?"

Footsteps padded up the stairs. Willow looked to her mother, standing with her elbow on the bannister, her throat and cheeks flushed red, then back to her father. He couldn't meet Willow's gaze. Looked guilty. Sheepish.

Like he'd been caught red-handed doing something he shouldn't.

Willow looked from one to the other.

"Were you two fucking?" she said, unable to keep the

disgust from her voice.

"Watch your mouth!" Fiona said.

"Ellie's missing and you two are fucking?"

Fiona gazed away. Jonathan sighed. "Megan..."

"It's Willow."

"I'm not calling you that," he said.

"Like I care." Willow turned and stalked towards the stairs. "You two are sick."

"Megan!"

She thundered down the stairs, her heart spasming, her brain spinning, trying to take in what had happened, what she'd seen. She saw the door open in front of her and wanted nothing more than to run out into the heat and the sunshine and burn. She heard footsteps hammering down the steps behind her.

"Megan!"

She leapt the last three steps and ran for the door.

"Willow!" Jonathan said.

The name stopped her short. She had her hand on the door handle. She could step outside. Walk away from her parents forever. But seeing them, knowing what they had been doing, it stung too much. She spun. Tears spilt down her cheeks.

"How could you!?" Her voice sounded brittle and shrill. "You two ruined our lives. You ruined everything. And now you're doing this?"

"We couldn't help it," he said.

Fiona appeared at the top of the step, her face cold and impassive as she stared at Willow. The flush in her throat had gone.

"We didn't mean it to happen," Jonathan went on. "It just did. You...you should be pleased!"

"Pleased!" Willow laughed, a cackle that sounded insane and inhuman. "Pleased that you two are getting your fucking kicks while Ellie's nowhere to be found? After all these years? All the pain, all the shit you put us through, and now you want me to be happy because you two are shagging again?"

She snorted and shook her head.

"It's not like that."

Willow looked up at Fiona, who had folded her arms now, and taken a couple of steps down the stairs.

"Tell it to someone who gives a shit," Willow said.

She turned to the door.

"Willow," Fiona said.

Willow stopped and peered into the daylight.

"You're going to run again?" Fiona ran her fingers along the banister as she glided down and into the hallway. "Is that your answer to everything?"

"I won't get any answers here." Willow turned.

"You can't run forever," Fiona said. "And where are you going to go? Have you got any idea where Ellie is?"

Willow peered at Ruby in the Fiat at the end of the drive. She should keep on walking. Out of that door and out of their lives. She wasn't here for them. She was here for Ellie. Trouble was Fiona was right. She still had no idea where Ellie was.

"And you do?" Willow glared back.

Fiona shook her head. "No, we don't."

"So give me one reason why I should stay?"

"Because you owe us," Jonathan said.

Willow snorted. "I owe you?"

"You disappeared, Willow." Fiona spat the name. "Vanished without a trace. Not a word from you for six years. And now you're back and acting like you're the only one who cares about Ellie."

"You two never have."

"We do care," Jonathan said.

"Not exactly breaking your necks looking for her, are you?"

"Because we know what she's like," Fiona said. "She's done this before. Just vanished into thin air for months at a time."

"Unfortunately," Jonathan said, "these disappearing acts are pretty regular."

Willow peered from one parent to the other. "So what, every time she goes missing you two get together for a bit of fun for old times' sake while you tell each other how worried you are about her?"

"We hadn't seen each other since the divorce," Fiona replied. "But Jonathan was worried this time."

"This time?" Willow said. "If Ellie does this so often, why are you worried this time?"

Fiona and Jonathan shared a look, a raised eyebrow from Fiona and then Jonathan nodded. Fiona sighed and turned to her.

"Because this time she called you back," she said.

Willow glared at her mother, then at her father. His eyes were downcast, furtive. He kept glancing at Fiona, who kept her cold gaze fixed on Willow.

"Look," Jonathan said, "let me get changed. Then we can talk."

Willow snorted. "I've got nothing to say to you two," she said.

"Still running," Fiona muttered.

"Fine!" Willow said. "Let's talk." She folded her arms

across her chest.

"You might as well invite your friend in," Fiona said. "I'll go and put the kettle on." She glanced at Jonathan then slipped into the kitchen.

An awkward silence filled the hallway as Jonathan stared at Willow. In the kitchen, Fiona ran a tap, filled the kettle then flicked it on. As the kettle began to hiss and rattle, Jonathan went to speak. Maybe he wanted to apologise, or explain, but then he must have decided against it because he closed his mouth, shook his head and trudged upstairs.

"I'll be down in a minute."

Willow glared at her father's back. Every instinct was screaming at her to get out, to run back to Ruby and drive off. But, as much as it pained Willow to admit it, Fiona was right. She didn't have a clue where Ellie was. Maybe the three of them could work out a plan to find Ellie. Or maybe they'd reveal a lead that would show Willow the way. Dropping her bag at the foot of the stairs to show she was coming back, she stepped outside and waved Ruby in.

*

"It's not Ellie's number." Willow passed her phone over to Fiona.

They were sat around the gleaming white table in a kitchen so dazzling that Willow half thought about slipping on her sunglasses. Fiona sat opposite, Jonathan next to her, with Ruby taking up the fourth seat. Fiona glanced at the phone, then passed it to Jonathan. He'd put on a dark blue shirt, tucked into stonewashed Levi's with a brown leather belt, and smelled of Armani.

"What does it mean?" he asked, glancing at Willow.

"It's a code we used to have?" Willow said.

"Code for what?"

"That's between me and Ellie."

Jonathan went to retort, but Fiona cut across him.

"But she didn't send this?" Fiona said.

Willow shrugged. "I don't know. It's not her number, but no one else knows about our code, so it has to be her."

"Unless she told someone," Jonathan said.

"Who though?" Willow asked.

"A boyfriend, maybe?"

"I showed Harrison," Willow said. "He didn't know."

"She had other boyfriends," Jonathan said. "And she wasn't short of friends either."

"Really?" Willow said. "Damned if I can find them."

"Has Goddard seen her?"

"Who's Goddard?" Fiona frowned from Jonathan to Willow and back again.

"Some priest up in St. Agnes," Jonathan said. "Used to be in a church, but he's freelance now. He runs these surf and prayer sessions at Trevaunance. Ellie used to go a lot, after the whole wild child phase."

"He hasn't seen her for a fortnight or so," Willow said. "Harrison for a month."

"You tried her flat?" Fiona said.

"Empty," Willow said, ignoring the look Ruby gave her. No need to mention the biker unless she had to.

"What a mess," Jonathan said.

"Yeah," Willow replied.

She peered from Jonathan to Fiona, then to Ruby, who

shrugged and gave her a tight smile. She looked back at her parents. The past hung between them, silent and oppressive.

Willow had a thousand things she wanted to scream; accusations, blame, insults. Between them, Fiona and Jonathan had ruined the happy childhood she'd once shared with Ellie.

Fiona, jealous of the attention and affection Jonathan showed to his daughters, had walked out on them, breaking all their hearts. Then Jonathan, scared of another failed marriage, had turned a blind eye to the emotional abuse that Connie, his second wife, had inflicted on his daughters and refused to even listen when they both said that the emotional abuse had turned into physical violence. And in the years since, neither one of them had searched that hard for her, or thought to keep close to Ellie. Neither one had even known she was missing until Willow had returned. And when they found out, they jumped into bed with each other. The disgust tasted bitter in her throat and it was all she could do to stay sitting at the table. But Ellie wasn't here and three heads had a better chance of finding her than one.

"So, what do we do?" Willow said.

"Well." Jonathan looked at Fiona. "I guess I better come clean to Connie."

"I meant about Ellie." Willow gave him a withering stare.

"Oh." He flushed and looked at the table.

Ruby shifted in her seat.

"You could try that number again," she said. "Both of them."

Willow nodded, grateful for Ruby for making the

suggestion. She doubted Ellie would answer, but it at least allowed her to get out of the room and away from her parents. She scraped the chair back and felt a thrill of malicious pleasure at the flaring of her mother's nostrils and the thinning of her lips at the sound. Willow rose and made for the patio doors.

Then the shrill ring of her father's phone pierced the kitchen. Willow stopped and looked back.

His face grew visibly white and his thumb was trembling.

"It's Connie." He frowned at Fiona, who shrugged and looked away. "I, er... I better get this."

As he stood up he put the phone to his ear. "You okay, love?"

Willow stared at her mother, who stayed seated, not looking at Jonathan, apparently not interested that his wife was on the phone.

"The police?" Jonathan said.

The word grabbed Willow's attention. Jonathan spun. His face was pale. A sick feeling gathered in Willow's stomach. Her heart began to pound. Her mouth went dry.

"What do they want?"

A loud electronic chime filled the kitchen. Fiona frowned at her phone on the table. Willow could see a picture moving on the screen. Too distant, the angle too awkward to get a good look.

Ruby however stood and crossed to the front window. "Looks like they're here too." She turned to Willow.

Willow felt her stomach plunge. The silence in the room thickened. Fiona's front door rang again. She stood and hurried from the room. Ruby crossed back and stood next to Willow, frowning.

"Connie, honey," Jonathan said. "I'll..." His voice broke, and Willow could see the fear in his paling face, his widening pupils. "I'll call you back."

He killed the call and peered at Willow across the white island unit.

"Dad?" Willow said. "Dad, what's going on?"

"I don't know." He leant on his knuckles, his brows furrowed. "The police came to my place. Looking for me."

"For you?" Willow said. "Why?"

The kitchen door opened. Fiona came back in, followed by a tall man, immaculately turned out in a three-piece suit, with closely cropped, wiry black hair and smooth dark skin, and a shorter woman, wearing smart jeans and a black leather jacket, her bob of black hair tied into a rushed ponytail. They wore grim expressions.

Willow felt her knees buckle. "Dad!"

She slumped into a seat and reached out for Jonathan, but he ignored her. Instead, he slipped around the island to stand next to Fiona, taking her hand as they swapped a dark look.

Ruby moved to stand behind Willow and put a hand on her shoulder. Willow clutched it, her heart juddering as she struggled to control the cold, hard fear rising from her gut.

"I'm Detective Inspector Pierce." The woman's voice was thick and sombre.

She gestured to the man next to her.

"This is D.C.I. Harry. Are you Eloise Rae's parents?" Jonathan nodded.

"Yes," Fiona said.

"And you two?"

"This is Ellie's sister," Jonathan said. "Megan, and her friend, Ruby."

"Megan Rae?" D.C.I. Harry asked.

Willow nodded. Harry cocked a brow at Pierce. Pierce looked at Willow as if she was the missing piece of a puzzle which, in a way, she guessed she was.

"Mr & Mrs Rae, please take a seat," Pierce said.

"What is it?" Jonathan said.

"Please?" Pierce pointed to the chair.

"Just tell us," Fiona said.

Pierce glanced at Harry again. He nodded. Pierce sucked in a lungful of air. Turned to face Jonathan and Fiona.

"We've got some bad news," she said. "About Eloise."

"She's missing," Fiona said. "We know."

Pierce shook her head. "I'm sorry, Mrs Rae," Pierce said. "Sir."

Willow couldn't breathe. It felt like she had concrete in her lungs.

"But we need you to come with us."

Fiona gripped Jonathan's arm. She looked ghost pale, like every ounce of blood had been leeched from her body. Ruby squeezed Willow's shoulder, her nails digging into Willow's skin. Willow barely felt it.

"Why?" Jonathan said.

"We've found a body, and we've reason to believe..." Pierce glanced at Harry, then back at Jonathan and Fiona. "We've reason to believe that it's Eloise."

Silence.

Then a howl, tortured, inhuman, like a soul in agony, filled the room. It was Willow.

Screaming.

24

Dusk had fallen by the time the van pulled into the petrol garage on the main road into Newquay. Raven sat astride her bike, shrouded in the shadows in the far corner of the forecourt, her lights off. She was watching every vehicle that came in. She saw Michael at the wheel and Gabriel next to him, his gaze flicking agitatedly around at the cars at the pumps. They pulled up in a parking space at the far end of the garage, away from the lights spilling out from the shop. The van's brake lights flared red, then went out.

Raven swung off of her bike, threw a quick look at the drivers filling up and their passengers, then strolled towards the van. It had Duchy Farms on the back and across one side. As she approached, the driver's door popped open and Michael jumped to the tarmac. She flicked up the visor on her helmet.

"So what's this job?" Michael said, his face an angry riot of spots and pits and pustules.

"Removals." Raven gripped the handle of the side door. Michael thumbed a button on the van's key fob. The lock gave a metallic clunk as it opened and Raven slid the door back. It rattled on its runners then clanked into place. She peered inside.

Two rolls of carpet and a length of blue nylon rope, frayed at the ends, lay on the wooden floor. Otherwise, the back was empty. She could smell old mud and dampness inside.

"What are we removing?"

"You'll find out."

She slid the door shut again and turned to Michael.

"When I leave here you follow me. We're heading to the old Fistral Hotel. We'll park up in the loading bay. The... packages are in a room on the ground floor. Two in total. Bit of heavy lifting. Might be messy."

"How messy?"

"Burn-your-clothes-when-you're-done messy."

"Pay?"

"When we're done."

"Better be worth it."

Raven ignored him, turned, and headed for her bike.

"Does Goddard know about this?"

Raven didn't answer. She dodged around the cars at the pumps and headed for her bike. Flicked the visor back down. Adjusted her gloves. She swung one leg over the bike seat, fired the engine, and grabbed the handlebars. The engine roared and rattled, then puttered as she put it into gear and eased out onto the main road. Glancing in her wing mirror, she saw Michael and Gabriel following.

Most of the traffic was heading out of Newquay and she rode in unhindered. Orange streetlights flicked past. The Gannel lay in darkness to her left. The traffic slowed as she approached a roundabout, and she looked back.

Michael and Gabriel were two cars back.

At the roundabout, she threw a left. The ruined hotel sat at the end of a promenade of Victorian terraced houses, on the corner of a bend in the road. She'd ridden fifty yards along the road when she saw the first glimmer of blue flashing lights ahead. A warning flickered in her mind. She felt the close-cropped hairs on the back of her neck prickle.

She cruised on another twenty yards, then braked and steered into the kerb. Behind her, the van squealed to a stop. She peered at the scene ahead.

Police tape had been stretched across the road and tied off on opposite lampposts. It flapped and rippled in the warm breeze. Two coppers in high vis jackets stood behind the tape. Half a dozen police cars and a couple of ambulances had parked across the street behind them, blue lights strobing across the houses on either side. Aside from the two coppers by the tape, she couldn't see any other activity. No forensics tent, no one in boiler suits combing the scene for clues. She had a good idea where they would be though. It gave her a sick feeling in her stomach. Resisting the urge to cut and run, she swung her leg off the bike and strolled towards the van.

She tried to walk casual, but she felt as though she was walking through quicksand.

As she approached, Gabriel wound down the passenger window and Michael leant across.

"Trouble?" he said.

Raven nodded towards the group of local gossips huddled at one end of the police tape, puffing on fags, their shapeless bodies wrapped in cardigans and oversized pyjamas, standing in fluffy slippers or tatty looking sandals.

"Go and ask," she said.

"I ain't talking to them! I'll be fucked if they ID me!" Michael said.

Raven turned to him. "That wasn't a request."

"Why don't you do it?"

Ignoring the queasy feeling in her gut, and the trembling in her knees, she forced herself to glare at him through her visor. He glanced at Gabriel, who was scratching the back of his hands, then sighed.

"Fuck's sake," she heard him mutter as he unlocked the door and jumped out. He nudged the door shut and then, with a final glare at Raven, he tucked his hands in the pockets of his skinny jeans. It made the shoulders of his red puffer jacket swell up.

"So what you thinking boss?" Gabriel said as Michael stalked away. "Someone got done?"

She didn't reply. The gossips turned as Michael got close, then clamoured to tell the story. From behind the tape, one of the police officers watched Michael carefully until a van with a satellite dish on the top braked to a halt and a T.V. crew leapt down. Seeing the reporters, Michael had the good sense to extricate himself from the rabble and trudge back, keeping well away from the press van. As he approached, Raven backed along the side of the van, out of view of the cameras.

"Well?" she said.

"Apparently a pair of horny teenagers stumbled across two bodies this afternoon."

Raven looked beyond him. Beneath the helmet, she clenched her jaw. Panic coursed through her. What would Goddard say? What would he do to her?

"I take it those were our packages," Michael went on.

Raven didn't reply. She tried to think, to plan, but the panic fogged her mind, and all she could see was the blue lights flashing over her. Clenching her fists, she swore.

"So what now?" Michael asked.

Goddard... he'd have to be told. He'd need to prepare for any chaos that would follow when the press made the connection between Harrison and Ellie. And they couldn't hang around here. Already the press were doing their pieces to camera. If they panned around, if they caught a Duchy Farms van on film, Goddard would be doubly pissed off. The police were already starting to look their way again.

"Get out of here," she said.

Michael was back in the van before she got on her bike. He started the engine, threw a U-turn, and drove away casual, not too fast, not too slow. Just a delivery driver trying to find an alternative route.

She gunned her engine and followed him out, not looking at the camera crew or the police cordon. She followed him back to the roundabout. Once there, Michael threw a right, while she threw a left and headed towards Fistral. She weaved in and out of the parked cars and the intermittent flow of traffic, riding on auto-pilot, numb, her thoughts confused. She pulled into the car park behind the golf course, drove to the far end, in the darkness, and killed the engine.

The bike settled and ticked over, but her hands and legs kept quivering. Nausea bloated her stomach. The helmet seemed to choke her. Oblivious to her surroundings, she tugged it off and sucked in lungfuls of air. Her breath tremored as she exhaled. She closed her eyes and rested her head on the handlebars.

She should run, hit the road, and get out now before Goddard found her, before he knew what had happened. But where would she go? She had money, more than enough, stashed back at the hut. But all her connections, her life, such as it was, that was all here. She wasn't exactly in a position to go straight again. According to the authorities, she was dead already. Wherever she went, she'd have to start again and start alone. Trouble was, she didn't have the first clue how.

"Shit!" she spat.

Voices drifted from the path behind the car park. It ran through the golf course to the beach. She heard laughter, a girl's screech, fast footsteps. Couldn't see who it was through the bushes. She looked around. A few cars were still dotted around the car park. Music throbbed and the smell of Mexican food wafted from Gilmore's at the entrance to the car park. No one looked her way. Still, she tugged the scarf that had hung around her neck up over her mouth. Better safe than sorry.

She grabbed her phone from the pocket of her jacket and stared hard at the screen. She had to make that call. Better it came from her than the others. She could explain. Maybe she wouldn't have to run.

She sucked in a deep breath and exhaled low, with her eyes closed, gripped the phone tight to stop her hands from shaking. Then, opening her eyes, she unlocked the phone, found Goddard's number, and hit dial. He answered before the first ring had even finished.

"I wondered when you'd call," he said.

"Listen, there's something I've got to tell you."

"They've found the body. I know."

Her stomach plunged. "How?"

"It was on the news. All over the news, I should say."

"Look, I'm sorry, yeah, but it wasn't my... they..." She was babbling, the words tumbling out in an effort to get them across before he lost it. "Al, he went for me and they saw my face and I had no choice. I had to do it. To protect us all."

"Al?"

"I was going back for the bodies tonight, but the police... some horny couple found 'em... I was gonna put it right."

"Raven, calm down. What's Al got to do with this?"

"The news... the bodies..."

"Bodies? There's only one body?"

"What?"

"Who are you talking about?" Goddard said.

"Harrison. Alan McCallister," she said.

"What about them?"

"You said you knew?"

"Raven... don't try my patience cos it's a bit bloody thin already. What have you done?"

"I killed them," she said. "They're dead. I was trying to get Harrison to talk and Al... he bottled it, he attacked me. Ripped off my mask. I broke his neck. Then Harrison saw me and I..." She remembered Harrison's eyes bulging as she throttled him.

The line went silent. She could hear him breathing hard at the other end. He hadn't known. A bitter taste filled her mouth. Her stomach flipped.

"Where are the bodies now?" His voice sounded low, dangerous.

"The police have them. Some randy couple stumbled over them."

"Why the fuck didn't you get rid of them?"

"I didn't have time. It was broad daylight. I went back there with Michael and Gabriel tonight and the place was crawling with police and ambulances."

"Fucking hell, Raven. First Ellie, and now this..."

"Ellie?" Her stomach spasmed again. "What about Ellie?"

"They fished a body out of a cave near Cligga Head last night," he said.

Raven's blood ran cold. The hairs on her neck prickled. Fear wriggled down her spine.

"They think it's Ellie."

The world dropped away. Everything went dark. The shadows seemed to swell and engulf her. She felt sick. She'd made sure. Taken Ellie far out into the channel. Dumped her over the side. Watched her sink to the bottom. How had she come back?

"It's a mess, Raven," Goddard said. "A big fucking mess. And there'll be consequences. Big ones."

"Goddard, please. I didn't-"

The phone went dead. Trembling, tears spilling down her ruined cheeks, she stared at the handset. Then nausea struck her like a fist.

She fell to her knees and threw up on the tarmac.

Part Two

25

Willow put her toes over the edge of the cliff, scrunching them against the jagged rock. She peered down, straight down to the rocks and the swirling, foaming tumult of turquoise and midnight blue. Sharp rain lashed against her bare calves and pattered against the rucksack on her back. Gulls swooped around her, their screeching cries like mocking laughter. The wind stung her eyes and whipped through her sodden red dreadlocks, dragging her peach dress tight around her body. She had her sandals in one hand, a bottle of vodka, half-empty, in the other.

All she had to do to join Ellie was to lean forward. Just a foot. Maybe less. Maybe only an inch. She could already feel herself teetering. Swaying. It wouldn't take much to send her completely over the edge. She closed her eyes.

Gravity seemed to drag her forward and pull her back all at once, as though she stood on a tipping point, perfectly balanced between life and oblivion.

She'd been drinking for forty-eight hours. Ever since the hospital.

The coppers, Pierce and Harry, had taken her parents in their car. They'd offered to take her too, but she'd chosen to follow with Ruby instead. With her world plummeting off-kilter, she needed a friendly face with her, not the awkward silence of being wedged in the backseat with her parents.

When they parked up, for a long minute, Willow found she couldn't move. She stared ahead, seeing nothing, her stomach in turmoil, her mind recoiling from what awaited.

"Hey."

Ruby's soft words sounded like a scream in the void. Willow turned. She felt Ruby's hand slide around hers.

"I'm here with you," Ruby said.

Willow nodded.

"Shall we?"

Willow nodded again. Ruby stepped out of the car, Willow stayed seated. The passenger door opened. Willow turned to Ruby.

"I won't say it'll be ok," Ruby said. "But we have to do this. Together."

Willow let Ruby reach in, unclasp the seatbelt, then Ruby took her hand and coaxed her out. Willow felt woozy. Numb. She heard the door clunk shut behind her, then Ruby guided her into the atrium, through a maze of sterile, clinical corridors, into a metal lift and then out, along a deserted corridor, until they reached the double doors outside the mortuary.

Fiona and Jonathan were already inside. Willow could hear her mother screaming. There was only one reason her mother would scream like that. The realisation that Ellie lay dead within stole the strength in Willow's legs, and the resolve in her heart. She slumped into the plastic seat and put her head in her hands. She wanted to weep, but shock stole her tears. She stared at the wall opposite with its dents and its scuff marks, and its posters advertising bereavement counselling and local funeral parlours.

After several minutes the double doors leading into the mortuary opened, and Pierce, the female copper, emerged. She asked if they were ok. Willow didn't respond, but she heard Ruby mutter a reply. Then the copper had crouched to her haunches in front of Willow.

"You can go in if you want," Pierce said.

Willow stared at the doors. Ellie lay dead in there. Walk in, and she'd see her sister, cold and pale, lying on a slab. She shook her head.

Pierce closed her eyes and nodded, then sucked in a deep breath, and let it out as a sigh.

"Look, maybe this isn't the right time, given..." She glanced back at the steely grey doors behind them. "...but then, maybe there's never a right time."

Willow turned to her.

"Your sister dated Harrison Gould for a while?" Pierce said.

"You know that?" Willow replied.

"I looked back through her file. Did you know him?"

"Yeah, I know him."

Pierce nodded again, and her face became grave.

"What's happened?" Willow whispered.

Pierce blinked. "It can wait."

"No. Tell me."

Pierce looked from Willow to Ruby, then back to Willow.

"I shouldn't..."

"Tell. Me." The words came out like a low growl, as the grief and the fear gave way to anger. Pierce swallowed. Lowered her gaze.

"We found him."

"Found him? He wasn't missing."

"I'm sorry. But Harrison is dead too."

Willow had collapsed but she couldn't remember it. All she could remember was Ruby crouching next to her, holding her head to her shoulder and kissing her scalp as Willow sprawled on the floor weeping and Pierce stood to one side looking for all the world like hell had opened up inside her. That was when her parents had come out.

Willow looked up from Ruby's shoulder. Her mother wailed into Jonathan's shirt as he guided her outside. Her hands trembled as she clutched at thin air, and her teeth were bared. Jonathan had bloodshot eyes and his face looked gaunt and chalk pale.

"Megan..." he muttered, holding an arm out towards her, inviting her in.

She glared at him. She slipped out of Ruby's grip and stood.

"Is it her?" She knew already, but she needed her Dad to say it. "Is it her?"

Jonathan guided Fiona into the seat next to Ruby. She clung to his shirt like she couldn't let go. He crouched before her.

"Answer me," Willow said.

Jonathan put his head on Fiona's forehead. He sucked in a breath, and as he exhaled, he fell into a racking sob.

"My god..." he muttered. "My god..."

"Answer me!"

But her father had dissolved into tears and he and Fiona clung to each other, oblivious to Willow staring down at them. Willow spun and stormed into the mortuary, ignoring Ruby and Pierce screaming after her to wait. She burst past stunned porters, her heart kicking in her throat, her mind fogged with just one purpose.

Find Ellie. It's what she had come back for. Find Ellie.

Then she saw her, lying on the steel slab. Pale and waxy, her body bloated, her lips purple-blue, a white sheet pulled up over her shoulders, revealing the bruising around the jagged gash in her throat.

She stared at the wound. She wanted nothing more than to look away but she couldn't tear her gaze off it. She was fixated on it. Like it was the only thing in the world she could see. Her body shook. Her breath became ragged gasps. The room spun. Tunnelled away until the slab seemed ten times bigger. The cold white lights swirled above Ellie.

Willow sucked in a deep breath. Then screamed. Cried. Roared denial. Hands grabbed her.

Ruby. Pierce. The male copper. But Willow shook them off.

And ran.

Ruby gave chase, screaming for her to come back. She didn't stop. She ran straight out of the mortuary. Up the stairs. Out of the hospital. Through the car park. She could hear Ruby screaming her name. Chasing her. But she kept on running.

She outran Ruby. She outran them all. But she couldn't outrun grief.

On an anonymous residential street in the heart of Truro, she fell to her knees and threw up. Threw up until she had nothing left inside, until it felt as though her stomach was trying to eject itself through her mouth. Then she burst into tears and the tears brought the pain of Ellie and Harrison's deaths, and all she wanted was oblivion. She'd found an off licence. Grabbed two bottles of vodka. A six-pack of beers. And a bottle of Jack Daniels.

"Having a party?" the guy behind the counter said.

Willow glared at him, paid, then stalked out, walked the dark, pre-dawn streets of Truro, avoiding everyone, conscious only of the pain burning in her stomach and the need to quench it with the drink. As the sun rose that morning, she walked out of the city and began to cut across country. That day she trudged through fields and forests, over streams and rocky hillocks, vaguely heading northwest like St. Agnes was a homing beacon pulling her in. She crashed in a disused barn, finished the beers, finished the whiskey, wept silently not only for Ellie but for Harrison too.

When she woke in the barn the next morning, on Saturday, she didn't move, just drank vodka and wept until she heard footsteps outside, and laughter. She grabbed the last bottle of vodka, her bag, her phone, and ran again, and spent the day staggering back towards the coast, not knowing, not caring, where she was. She walked in a daze, her mind lost in memories of Ellie and Harrison. Dusk fell. Then night. She drunk her way through most of the alcohol and reached St. Agnes in the early hours.

Walked through the village. Past her Dad's house. The lights were on but she kept on walking. Across the old mining works north of the town and then up onto the coastal path. And then up to the cliffs. Dawn had broken behind her, bringing with it a storm sweeping in off of the Atlantic.

Now, footsore, soul-sore, all she wanted to do was to plummet over the cliff edge and into oblivion.

She grit her teeth. Tried to lean forward but her body seemed to tilt backwards. She screwed her eyes shut. Tried to make herself jump. To force her knees to bend, but it felt like they had become locked.

She wanted to die. But she couldn't take that step.

Just lean, she told herself. Lean forward. Tilt her head. She could barely stand anyway. Lean forward and let gravity do the rest.

She remembered Ellie, that last morning when Willow ran, fearful, always looking back, even as they cycled away, biting her lip, terrified, but not of getting caught.

Of leaving.

Of the world beyond.

Willow had always been the adventurous one, the one who saw no fear. Ellie had liked the familiar, the comfort of home, even when home was hell. She couldn't leave any more than Willow could stay.

But Willow should've stayed. Because if she'd stayed, Ellie would be alive now. Not dead on a mortuary slab with a gash in her throat. She'd be alive. And Willow...

Wouldn't exist. She'd still be Megan. But Megan was dead.

And maybe it was time for Willow to die too. To join Ellie. Because all she wanted to do right then was see her sister, talk to her, hug her, kiss her one last time and tell her she loved her.

Tell her she was sorry for the cruel words she'd

spoken.

But she couldn't. She'd never get to say sorry.

She'd never see Ellie again. There would be no reconciliation. Ellie was dead. And anything and everything she could have been, the life she could have had, her hopes, her dreams, they were dead too.

But Willow...

Willow was still here. Still breathing. She could feel her heart punching her ribs.

She wanted her heart to stop. It hurt too much. Every beat felt like cold agony in her chest. And she wanted to tear it out.

She wanted it over.

All she had to do was lean.

She opened her eyes.

Looked down.

The tumult roared below. It swirled and roiled and smashed against the rocks, spitting spray at her. She wanted that oblivion. The wind howled at her and the rain stung her legs. She couldn't move. She threw her head back and screamed to the sky.

"Willow!"

She looked over her shoulder.

Goddard. He ran towards her. Panic on his face. She blinked. Frowned. Why the hell did he always show up?

"Come away!"

She shifted her feet to see him better.

Then she felt the earth slip beneath her. Her stomach plunged. She gasped. Looked down. Saw the grass and rock splitting, small pieces tumbling away. Spitting into the sea. The ground growled and roared as it detached from the cliff. There was a second of weightlessness when she and the rock seemed to hang in mid-air. Then the chunk of rock fell. And she fell with it.

She lunged for the cliff edge. The vodka bottle and the sandals spilt from her grip. She groped at thin air. Her eyes went wide as Goddard got closer. She saw the terror on his face. Felt it in her stomach. The vodka bottle smashed onto the rocks.

"Willow!" Goddard leapt.

As she plunged he grabbed her wrist. Her shoulder jolted as he caught her. The rucksack slammed into her back.

She swung from his grip. Her mouth felt dry. Terror and panic swept through her. Her bare feet clawed at the rocks. The jagged granite tore her toenails. Goddard winced, eyes bulging from the strain. "Grab my elbow."

She reached up. Her fingers slipped off his bare skin.

"Grab!" he roared.

She threw her hand up. Clasped his forearm. He began to pull. She didn't move. Her feet scrabbled at the rocks, tearing her toes, her soles. He lifted her a foot. Her toes gripped rock. She stared down. The ocean smashed against the rocks and the foam seemed to reach for her ankles. She looked back up.

"Push!" Goddard cried.

She grit her teeth. Dug her toes in. Pushed. She rose. A foot. Two. Then more of the rock crumbled. She fell. Goddard lost his grip. Weightless again she hung, eyes widening.

She was going to die.

She started to fall. Goddard threw out at arm. Grabbed the only thing he could. Her bag. It jerked her shoulders. She gasped.

She swung there, suspended above the tumult, the ocean roaring like a beast denied beneath her, peering hard into Goddard's eyes. She could hear the seams on her bag, already weakened in the fight with the biker, starting to pop.

Any second they would split.

She would fall.

Then Goddard roared and yanked her up. The straps dug in, burning. Her feet found a rock. She pushed with her toes. He pulled again and they tumbled up together, spilling backwards onto the grass. They scrambled away. Five feet. Ten.

A bigger chunk of rock, three feet wide, cracked and plunged to the ocean below. They lay on the grass, Willow on top of Goddard, her face buried in his chest, her heart still hammering, her fingers and toes starting to burn and sting.

"I've got you," he said, holding her in his arms. He kissed her scalp. "I've got you. You're safe."

She lay in his arms, bleeding, her soul torn, and wept.

26

Stay or go? The question had been spinning through Raven's mind since the phone call with Goddard on Friday evening and got more pressing with each passing day. She'd heard nothing from Goddard or the Chosen but she knew that wouldn't last. Retribution would be coming. It was just a question of when and how. She'd stayed in the hut, half expecting them to burst in and finish her off at any minute. The knife never left her side now, and she slept in twenty-minute bursts every couple of hours. When she was awake, the questions began again.

If she ran, where would she run too? She was dead. Officially. She couldn't start over again, reappear alive and well in another place and pick up like nothing had happened. Wherever she went, she'd have to spend her life in the shadows. Not that she cared. The shadows suited her. She was a ruin, a monster made flesh, her body warped and scarred by the fire that had claimed her parents and sister. No one wanted to look at her corruption. Living in the shadows meant she spared them the disgust, and she spared herself from their ogling, their jeers and their pity.

But it left her with few options.

London appealed. The city was big enough to hide in but she had no contacts. No way into the underbelly. She could make contacts. She knew where they lived. Where they operated. Goddard had gotten her to track enough of them.

But making contact, gaining their trust, that would take time. The name Raven was already one the London dealers knew and loathed. She'd broken up enough County Lines, cut off enough cocaine supply chains to earn their enmity and that of their jailed brethren. They'd likely kill her on sight, rather than give her somewhere to hide, or a chance to start again.

She could head south. Did Goddard's reach cover the Isles of Scilly? She didn't think so. But they were small, with no major population centres. Not a great place to hide. And sooner or later, someone would find her.

She could stay. Wait it out. The one thing she did know was Goddard wouldn't act himself. He'd get one of the Chosen to do it. Incompetent idiots. She'd see them coming a mile off, and they'd die trying to kill her. But once Goddard made his move, she'd have to run.

Which brought the problem of where again.

She sighed, swung her legs off the mattress and stood. Shafts of sunlight pierced the cracks in the roof tiles, catching dust motes swirling, disturbed by her steps. The boards creaked under her bare feet. She unlatched the window, peered over the fields. The sky burned blue overhead, the morning storm had moved inland.

Stay or go? Who knew? But she had to decide. She turned from the window, and as she crossed to the steps, her phone began to buzz on the floor by the mattress.

She froze. Stared at the phone, willing it to stop. She could feel its vibrations throbbing along the floorboards and up into her bare feet. The phone spun and slid as it rang. She crept up on it and peered down. She expected to see Goddard's number but it wasn't. She picked up the phone and answered.

"Police Constable Tom Wilkes," she said. "How's the lovely Ann?"

"I've got news," he said.

"About?"

"Those names you gave me."

"And?"

"According to the PNC, a Megan Rae went missing from St. Agnes six years ago. They knew she went to London but from there the trail went cold."

"Ok."

A pause on the line.

"Thing is... she's back. She's Ellie Rae's sister. The Steinberg girl. This Megan just turned up out of the blue."

"What did you find on Willow Keating?" Raven said.

"Did you hear me?"

"It's irrelevant."

"But..."

"Willow Keating?"

She heard him sigh. But he didn't push it.

"No record of a Willow Keating in the PNC database. Or in Europol or Interpol."

"Pity."

"But I did put a call into the New South Wales police."

"And?"

"And... they were tailing a Willow Keating for about a month."

"Were?"

"She vanished. They haven't seen her since the weekend."

Raven sat on the mattress and leant forward. "Why were they tailing her?"

"They think she's running drugs for some local dealer."

Her breath caught in her throat. "You're sure?"

"That's what they said. Apparently, there was a fight at some party on Bondi beach. She was arrested but released without charge. But the police linked the address she gave with this local dealer. And they started trailing her. Turns out, she's been running packages all over Sydney."

A smile played across Raven's lips.

"They stopped her once," Wilkes continued. "Searched her, but she was clean. They were building evidence for a raid, but now she's gone they're struggling to find the runners."

Raven didn't speak. Megan Rae... a mule... no different to Michael or Gabriel...

"Anything else?"

"There's one thing."

"Which is?"

"This... Willow Keating? The NSW boys gave me a description."

"And?"

"Red dreadlocks. Tattoos. So I spoke to Pierce."

"Who?"

"The detective in charge of the Ellie Rae case."

Raven didn't reply. She let the silence linger.

"They're the same person aren't they?" Wilkes said.

"Did the Australian's have anything on Megan?"

"Answer me! Megan is Willow isn't she?"

"Did they have anything on Megan?"

"Look if they're the same person I have to tell the NSW boys."

"You just have to keep your mouth shut."

"But..."

"Tomsannie77@gmail.com," she said.

He fell silent.

"You know what I'm saying don't you, Police Constable?"

"Yes."

"Good. Now, did the Aussie police have anything on Megan?"

"No. Nothing."

"Fine," Raven said.

"So is that it? Are we square?"

"Told you, Tom." Raven stood and headed for the window. "You'll never be square."

She hung up the phone and stared out the window. Megan Rae... a drugs runner... and more than that... she was Raven's way out of the mess she was in, the path to Raven's redemption. She found Goddard's number and hit dial. Her breath caught in her throat as she waited for him to answer. The electronic pulse at the other end of the line throbbed in her ear. Then it connected.

"I've got nothing to say to you," he said.

"I've got something for you. About Megan."

There was silence on the other end. She could almost hear his brain working. His inclination to hang up would be fighting his desire for knowledge. Knowledge, he'd always said, was power. After what felt like forever, his desire for knowledge won.

"Go on."

"She was a mule. A runner. In Sydney."

"For who?"

"Some local dope dealer the Sydney cops were after. They've been tailing her for a month before she came home."

More silence. Voices drifted up from the front of the hut, people traipsing up the lane from Trevellas.

"How'd you find out?" he said.

"The copper contact I've got."

"Is it legit?"

"Think so."

"Interesting..."

She held her breath. Waited for him to speak again. Had that been enough to earn forgiveness? Or would she still have to face the consequences for her mistakes?

"I've got a job for you," he said.

"Oh?" She felt a flicker of hope. Was she forgiven? Redeemed?

"She's here."

"Who?"

"Megan. Or Willow as she now calls herself."

Raven frowned. "At your place?"

"Yeah."

"Dead?"

"No. Unlike you, I can be around people for more than ten minutes without snapping their necks or throttling them."

Her breath caught in her throat.

"Look, I had no choice. Gould saw my face. And Al..."

"Save it," he said. "It's done."

She swallowed. She wouldn't apologise. She'd done that once. She wouldn't do it again. But she wanted to. She could feel it bubbling in her throat. She clenched her jaw to bite back the words.

"I've got her phone," Goddard went on. "I've got the text that brought her home. And the number that it came from."

"Recognise it?"

"No," he said. "But I'm sending it to you. See if you do. And if you don't, I want you to find out who's number it is."

"And if I do?"

"Find out what they know. And... convince them they're better off keeping it to themselves. Got that?"

"Yeah." She turned to face the darkness in the hut again. "Look, if the police tie the Gould thing on me, I won't rat you out."

"Just get the name."

He rang off before she had a chance to answer. She peered at the phone. It pinged. Just the number as promised. Didn't recognise it. No other message either.

She wasn't forgiven or redeemed. Fine. But she had a task at least. She wasn't condemned yet. For the first time in two days, she stopped thinking about whether to stay or go and began to plan how she'd find who sent that text.

And when she did, how she'd silence them.

*

Goddard killed the call. Text the number to Raven, then crept back into the bedroom. Willow lay asleep on the bed, knees bloodied, face pale, shins and arms bruised. Her right hand still lay upturned on the duvet from where he'd used her thumb to open her phone. The dressing gown he'd helped her into when he'd got her back had ridden up her thighs. She had grass stains on the backside of her white cotton knickers. Heat gathered in his lower stomach as he peered at her thick legs and the curve of her buttocks. She had more meat on her than Ellie had.

He studied the bag by the bed. After she'd crashed out he'd searched that too, hoping he'd find the USB or the missing docs. His luck hadn't stretched that far. No USB. No missing docs. Where the hell were they? He stroked his beard and kept watching her.

Was it true? Had she been a runner, like one of his Chosen, running gear around Sydney for a supplier like him? Was she a user herself? What other secrets did she hide? What other kinks and dark habits? How could he find out? And how could he use them? If asked, would she run gear for him? Would she buy his produce? Raven had said she ran dope. Maybe she'd used the harder stuff too.

With a final glance at her grass-stained backside, he put Willow's phone on the bedside table, turned his back on her and walked out onto the hallway. He eased the door closed then, putting the questions of Willow past to one side, he went downstairs and into the kitchen.

He made the second phone call. Michael answered.

"What's up boss?"

"I need you to do a job for me," he said.

"Shoot."

"Raven has a lead she's chasing."

"You want me to help her?"

"Not exactly." Goddard peered out of the backdoor, twitching the net curtain with the tip of his finger. The grass out back still looked yellow from the heat of summer despite the morning rain. Damp patches lingered on the yellow stone paving slabs around the edge. Beyond the gate at the back, he could see a man changing the linen in the bedroom of the house behind. "I want you to follow her."

"Okay..."

"Tell me where she goes. Who she meets. Who she speaks to." Goddard let the curtain drop and crossed to the kettle. He picked it up and ran it under the cold tap. The water burbled into the bottom. "And keep me posted. I want to know every move she makes."

"What's up? You don't trust her?"

"That's between me and her. Just do what I've asked."

"Sure."

"And take Gabriel with you." He turned the tap off, clicked the lid of the kettle down.

"Gabriel? Why?"

Goddard paused. Considered once more as he put the kettle on its base and switched on the electricity. It began to rattle and hiss. Raven had been a good ally. And as good as Michael was, he didn't have her particular set of skills. But come Monday night when the vote was won, he'd be needing her particular skill set less and less. She was becoming a liability. Reckless. Sloppy.

And her handiwork was starting to draw attention to itself.

As good as she was, her time was almost up.

"Because when I give the word, when I've got what I need from her," Goddard said. "You two are going to kill Raven."

Silence. Goddard peered at the steam starting to coil from the kettle spout.

"Okay," Michael said.

"And Michael..."

"What?"

"She doesn't walk away this time."

27

The land slipped away from her and her feet scrabbled in thin air. She spun and grabbed for his hands. But the rock tumbled and though their fingers brushed, she couldn't grab him. He screamed her name as she plunged, down, down, falling forever, into oblivion.

She twisted in mid-air.

Saw the rocks approaching. Sharp and jagged. The ocean roiling around it. And on the sand... a corpse... Ellie's corpse... bloated and pale... her throat scarred. As Willow fell, Ellie's eyes snapped open.

"Megan," Ellie said.

Willow screamed.

And woke.

She bolted up. Heart punching against her ribs. Breath roaring in her ears. The world swaying and pitching around her. Cold sweat prickled her skin.

She wasn't in the ocean. She hadn't been dashed to pieces on the rocks.

She was alive. Wearing a thick white dressing gown in a strange bed in a strange bedroom. Panic flickered through her.

She looked around. Grey walls... a sleek charcoal black

wardrobe... a large square mirror on one wall, framed with tangled roots...dark oak floors...a small collection of multicoloured Moroccan bowls strewn randomly across a grey oak shelf beneath the mirror. Not a room she recognised.

Shafts of bright sunlight felt warm on her bare legs as they lanced through the narrow window. She looked around, took in more details; a black silk dressing gown with a golden dragon motif on the lapels, hanging on the back of a white door, the smell of her sweat, the sour taste of her breath, the crisp edge of the fresh bedsheets... and a monumental hangover kicking at her forehead. She lay back and pinched her nose, closing her eyes.

Goddard's place. It had to be his place.

He'd caught her. Dragged her back from the cliff edge. She'd fallen into his arms and wept. After that things got blurry. She remembered his arms around her shoulders...tentative steps in barefoot. And tears. Lots of tears.

For Harrison.

For Ellie.

She felt a dull pain under her ribs, like a stitch, from where she'd wept. She could feel the tears burning at the back of her eyes, in her throat. She'd sobbed for them both. Didn't think she had any tears left.

Even so, she felt a tear trickle down her cheek as she eased herself into a sitting position against the white wood headboard. The movement, slow and steady though it was, brought waves of nausea rolling through her. She breathed deeply until it passed then saw a cup of water and a pack of ibuprofen on the oak top of a white bedside cabinet, next to her phone. A note had been propped against the glass.

"Guessing you'll need these when you wake. :-). Richard."

A smile teased the corner of her lips. It was Goddard's place. The last of the panic dissipated. Tentatively, she reached for the pills, popped two out and put the rest back on the side, then she shifted her backside around and reached for the glass. Threw a pill into her mouth, took a swig of water and swallowed.

She gagged.

For one terrible second, she thought she was going to spew it all back up. But she clenched her jaw and breathed hard, and the feeling passed. She forced the water down, taking the pill with it.

She took the second pill, sipping the water, but still had to fight against nausea to get it down. The water tasted lukewarm like it had been sitting on the side for a while, but it still felt like liquid silver in her alcohol dried throat.

The glass empty, she slipped back under the covers, intending to close her eyes for twenty minutes and then find Goddard. But she crashed out and when she woke again, the sunlight had moved and was slanting along the back of the door. She guessed a couple of hours had passed.

Her head felt better. Still tender, but she didn't feel the waves of nausea when she sat up. On the bedside table, she saw a fresh glass of water and a pack of paracetamol with another note.

"Just in case, :-)."

She smiled, necked a couple of paracetamol, then finished the glass. Dizziness touched her when she swung her legs out of bed, but she breathed deep, eased herself upright then crept across the room. The wood felt rough underfoot. Straightening the dressing gown, she opened the door.

She stepped out into the dimly lit landing and saw two doors, both white, one closed to her left, the other, ahead across the landing, open. She saw grey ceramic tiles, figured that was the bathroom and crossed the landing. The bathroom was fully tiled, grey on the floor, white on the walls, with a walk-in shower, a floating toilet and sink on a pedestal, and silver taps. She closed and locked the door, pissed, then washed her hands. Contemplated having a shower, but thought she'd better find Goddard first. She left the bathroom and padded down the bare wood stairs.

Goddard was in the kitchen. Bare-chested, wearing olive green board shorts, his long hair hanging damp down his back, his unkempt beard soft and shaggy. He stood over the cooker stirring a bubbling pot of what smelled like pasta. Steam coiled from the pan, and the light from the window in the back door shimmered in the heat from the hob. He looked lean and strong, and as Willow padded up the narrow hall, he turned and smiled. His teeth looked dazzling white, his eyes dark and heavy. A warm fuzziness spread in her chest.

"Feel better?" he said.

"I can walk at least," Willow said, smiling weakly.

He nodded to the wooden table behind him. "Take a seat."

She dragged the chair back, slumped down. She studied his wide shoulders, narrow waist, taut, hard calves.

"Thank you," she said.

He smiled. "Not a problem. Seems my purpose in life is to help the Rae family."

Willow thought of Ellie and a ball of grief blocked her throat. She looked to the knots and swirls of the tabletop.

"Sorry," he muttered. "That was...insensitive."

"It's not your fault," Willow said. "Ellie..."

She couldn't finish the sentence, because she wasn't entirely sure what she wanted to say. Ellie brought it on herself? Ellie didn't deserve that? Ellie was a diamond who'd been let down by her selfish bitch of a sister? Or did she want to say her name in the hope that it might make the fact that she had died...no she had been killed...less real. Or maybe in the hope that, if she spoke her name, it might bring Ellie's spirit back, give Willow the chance to say goodbye.

"I told your father you were here," Goddard said. "Hope that's okay."

"Yeah." Willow nodded.

"Want a drink?" He glanced up from stirring the pot.

She nodded. "Just water."

"Can't tempt you with a vodka and coke?" He grinned.

The taste of stale vodka rose in her throat and she put her hands to her lips and shook her head. "I'm never touching that stuff again."

Goddard chuckled. "You must have put a fair amount away."

Willow flushed and looked to the table. "Ruby..."

"Who?"

"The barmaid. From the Spars."

"What about her?"

"Does she know I'm here?"

"Don't think so." Goddard shook his head.

"Guess I should call her."

"Friend?" Goddard said.

Willow twisted her lips. "Probably the only one I've got around here. Although maybe not now I've run out on her too." A pang of guilt stabbed her chest.

Goddard crossed to the sink, picked up a glass from the cupboard underneath and rinsed it out. He filled it and placed it on the table in front of Willow. She peered at the water. Explaining to Ruby how she had ended up in Goddard's bed might lead to awkward conversations that she didn't want right now. Conversations about why she'd been dangling from a clifftop at dawn, apparently intent on destroying herself.

"How'd you find me?"

"Your dad," Goddard said, turning back to the hob. "He called me after the hospital. Told me you'd run off. I said I'd keep an eye out for you."

"Déjà vu," Willow said, lifting the glass to her lips. The water tasted cool and clean.

"And it's a bloody good job I found you again. A few minutes more and..." He left the thought hanging. And for the first time realisation struck.

She could've died. Were it not for Goddard, she would've.

The water turned to cement in her throat. She forced it down but then dissolved into tears. She buried her face in her hands, felt her shoulders and diaphragm spasm, each one feeling like a stab to her heart. Other thoughts crashed through her mind; if she hadn't been wearing the bag, if the seams had split... she heard again that terrible popping as they broke. How had she not fallen?

How was she still alive?

She saw the dream... Ellie's dead eyes staring up as she fell...

Willow had failed her. Again. As she always had... when Willow ran...when Willow told Ellie she was dead to her...when she never called Ellie back... when she hadn't found her in time...

And now Ellie was dead. She'd come close to joining her. The tears burned as they fell. She wanted oblivion again. Instead, she felt strong, warm hands on her shoulders, and let herself be guided into a hug. She squeezed against Goddard until the waves of emotion sweeping through her died away.

"The pasta..." she said.

Goddard chuckled.

"Don't worry, it's done," he said. "I took it off the hob. Not exactly important right now though."

"God I'm a mess," she muttered.

"Understandable," Goddard said. "What's happened to Ellie... it's horrifying."

Willow looked at the swirls on the tabletop again.

"Who would do that?" she said into his chest. "Who would do that to someone? Why? What did she ever do?"

She felt him shake his head. "I wish I knew. Ellie... she was a sweet girl. A little bit messed up maybe, but then who isn't? And she always had a knack for trouble. But this..." Another shake of his head, felt rather than seen.

"...maybe she just upset the wrong person at the wrong time."

"But who though?" Willow said. "Is it this Steinberg thing again? Or this bloody Raven character?"

"You don't have to figure this out."

"If not me then who?"

"The police? I mean it's their job after all."

"Fat lot of good they are," Willow sniffed. "They didn't break their backs to find me."

"Look, have some food," Goddard said, slipping his hands out from around her, leaning back and holding her shoulders, his dark eyes flicking across her face. "Then you can take a shower. Your bag is in the bedroom. Have you got fresh clothes at all? Shoes?"

"My boots are in the bag. And my clothes." She shook her head. "But they're all worn."

"I can wash them for you. I've got some old t-shirts and shorts you can wear in the meantime."

She smiled her thanks. Then the heat of guilt spread across her chest, and she felt her face crumple into tears again.

"I'm such a fucking nuisance." She wiped her eyes with the heels of her hands.

"Hey," Goddard reached out and stroked her shoulder. "You're fine. Okay? I understand? And I'll help you get through this."

Willow turned to him. Up close, she could see flecks of gold in his brown pupils. His eyes didn't look dark here. Just soft and warm.

"Thank you," she muttered.

"Come on," he said, smiling. "Let's eat."

He squeezed her shoulder, then crossed back to the hob. She watched him walk, took in the easy roll of his shoulders, the stretch of the tendons and muscles in his brown calves, the way his board shorts sat on his hips, the band of his underwear visible over the top, and tried to tell herself it was gratitude and the comfort of the familiar that kindled the small warm glow in her chest.

*

The Duchy Farms warehouse sat around the back of an industrial estate a few miles outside of Redruth, a mile and half off of the A30. It had good road links to the rest of the county and beyond but was far enough away from civilisation to avoid prying eyes. On a late Sunday afternoon in early July, the few businesses that had opened - a garage, a wholesale surf shop, a clothing warehouse - had closed their doors for the day and traffic, both on foot and by vehicle, was all but non-existent.

The metal shutter to the Duchy Farms warehouse stood half-open. Inside, two of the dozen rows of fluorescent strip lights were on, their pale, sickly glow barely penetrating the darkness. Half a dozen trucks and a single black and red motorbike sat parked up in the loading bay and the sickly sweet smell of rotting fruit and veg drifted from the skip by the shutters.

Raven sat in a chair in the main office, her feet up on the chipped and faded wooden worktop, the soles of her heavy leather boots spilling grit and dirt onto the surface. She peered hard at the soft white glow of the computer screen in front of her.

The number that Goddard had given her sat in the search engine box on the screen. Below it, a few random hits had come up, but the numbers they showed meant nothing to her. She'd been hoping for a business page, or maybe a social media site, a link to the number that could give her an instant ID, but all she'd got back was nonsense, only showing portions of the number she'd put in, as code, or as data from academic papers, showing a maximum of three numbers at a time. Sighing, she closed the search engine and spun on the chair, swinging her feet off of the bench.

It had been a long shot. And it had failed. Still, she had other methods. She stood and crossed to the door to the office, stepped outside and checked the clock on the wall over the main storage area. The first van would arrive soon. She needed to go. Goddard hadn't exactly showered her with forgiveness and if he caught her here, the little credit she'd regained may vanish altogether. She logged out of the PC, killed the lights in the office and crossed towards the shutters, dialling the mysterious number again. She'd called it twice that day, and both times it had rung out. She expected it to do the same this time.

This time, however, the call connected and a female voice answered.

"Hello?"

Raven stopped. She turned her back on the daylight spilling through the open door by the side of the shutters. The voice at the other end sounded young. Not childlike though.

"Hello," Raven said. "Who is this?"

A pause.

"Who's this?" the girl said.

Smart then. At least, smart enough not to give herself away. A teen then. Raven thought fast. The number belonged to someone who'd text Megan. Who'd known Ellie. Maybe they knew Ellie was dead. Maybe they didn't.

"I'm a friend of Eloise Rae's," Raven said.

"Are you the police?"

The corner of Raven's mouth twitched. "No, I'm not the police. I'm..."

"What are you doing!?" A voice in the background. Adult. Female. Frantic. Raven listened hard.

"Mum?!"

"Put it down! Put it..."

Muffled voices, an adult voice, female, raised. But Raven couldn't make out the words. Then the line cleared.

"It's ok, missy, don't worry. It's fine."

Another pause. Then the mother came on the line.

"Who is this?"

"Hi." Raven kept her voice light and airy. "I'm an old friend of Ellie's. I..." She sniffed like she was crying. "I just heard..." She faked a sob.

"We don't know anyone called Ellie." The call cut off.

In the silence of the warehouse, Raven blinked at the phone. Who had she been talking to?

The mother hadn't sounded panicked. Just terse. Abrupt. What did it mean? Who were they? Had the mum sent the text? The teenage girl? How did they know Ellie? Too many questions. Needing someone who could get her answers, she scrolled through her phone, found the number for Wilkes again and hit dial.

"Haven't I done enough?" Wilkes hissed as he answered.

"I need you to track a number."

"I can't! I barely got away with tracking the names. My sergeant wanted to know why I'd been calling the New South Wales police!"

"I'll send Ann the video then, shall I?"

"You don't understand..." he said.

"You don't understand," Raven replied. "I'm not asking you to do this. You're doing it or I ruin your marriage. Actually, I'm pretty sure your parents would be interested to know what their son got up to abroad. And speaking of your sergeant, I'm sure he'd enjoy the film too."

"Jesus..."

"This is the number." She read it out.

"Hang on." He sighed. She heard him scrabbling for a pen at the other end of the phone. "Go again."

She read it once more.

"I want to know where it's based. And a name. I called them less than ten minutes ago. And it's been sending texts. One late on the 29th of June. Maybe more."

"I can't do it now," he said. "No one will be around at this time on a Sunday."

"Tomorrow then," Raven said. "You call me by six pm."

"That's not enough time."

"You call me by six pm or Ann gets the video. Clear?"

She heard him sigh. "When will this be over..."

"Clear?" she said again.

"Clear."

She killed the call. Pocketed the phone, and crossed to the bike. She wheeled it outside, then closed and locked the shutters and stepped out through the side door. She clasped the padlock around the latch, then threw her leg over the bike, and rode away, her thoughts occupied by the voices on the phone. Specifically, the voice of the older woman.

GARY KRUSE

She'd heard it before.
She just couldn't remember where.

28

Willow shut the shower down then stood under the last jets of water. Her stomach felt settled, and the water had washed away the sweat and stink of booze. The water ran cold. She let it trickle down her face. The shower clunked off and she opened her eyes, stepped out and grabbed a towel from the chrome rail on the wall.

She'd already squeezed most of the water out of her dreads in the shower and now wrapped them in a towel to help drain out the rest. She grabbed a second towel, dried herself, then wrapped it around her body.

She caught a glimpse of her face in the mirror, but looked away quickly, unwilling to look herself in the eye. She picked up the Sisters pendant from the windowsill, went to put it on then hesitated.

A lump rose in her throat. She still didn't know where the other half of the pendant was. Hadn't been found with Ellie's body. Would she ever find it? Would the two halves ever be reunited? No. Because Willow and Ellie would never—

Closing her eyes against her grief, Willow squeezed the pendant in her palm. A tear trickled down her cheek. She breathed deep, exhaled through her nose. A sharp pain stabbed her temple. She opened her eyes.

Saw the face in the mirror. Not her face now.

Ellie's face.

Blonde hair. Grey-blue eyes. Sharp chin.

A jagged gash in her throat.

One hand reaching for Willow.

She yelped. Jumped back. Her ankles bumped against the plastic bin beside her. It clattered over. She yelped again. Spun. Saw it lying on its side, dirty face wipes and cotton buds spilling across the grey tiles.

"You okay?" Goddard's voice drifted from outside.

Willow's gaze snapped back to the mirror. Saw her face. Not Ellie's. Hers. She blinked. Looked away. Looked back. Blinked again. Still her face. The sharp pain had faded.

"Willow?"

"Yeah." She swallowed, crouched, and stuffed rubbish back into the bin. Slipped on the pendant. Unlatched the door and stepped out, all the while avoiding looking at the mirror.

"Feel better?" Goddard said, emerging from his room.

"Yeah," she said, pulling the bathroom door shut behind her.

"I've left some clothes on the bed." He nodded to the room Willow had woken up in. "And I've put your stuff in to wash. Should be done in twenty minutes or so."

"Thanks." She smiled. "And thanks for looking after me. You didn't have to."

"Course I did," he said. "I mean, Christian charity and all. What sort of Reverend would I be if I didn't offer shelter to the needy?"

"I wasn't exactly needy," Willow said. "Just selfish."

Goddard's face went sad and he reached out. His fingers closed around her hand and he squeezed.

"It's not selfish to grieve."

"No, but it is selfish to drink yourself into oblivion because your sister's died and you can't cope."

"Think you'll find that's called grief too." He gave a soft smile.

"Thanks anyway," Willow said.

"As I said, it seems I was put here to help the Rae's in their hours of need." He let go of Willow's hand. Turned to the stairs and went to head down. She could still feel the shape of his fingers on her palm.

"Oh, while I remember." He stopped at the top of the stairs and smiled back at Willow. "We're holding a service. For Ellie."

"For Ellie?"

"In an hour or so. On the beach at Porthtowan. Nothing major. Just a few people who knew her.

Some of my surf and prayer group. You want to come?"

"I'm not exactly religious," Willow said.

"You don't have to be. But I think it will do you good to see what people thought of her."

"How many people?"

"Half a dozen?" He shrugged. "Maybe more."

"I need to find a place to stay tonight," she said.

"You can crash here for a couple of days."

She gazed into the bedroom. A service for Ellie. On a beach. Not a church, all stuffy and heavy with fake rituals. Amongst nature. By the ocean where they'd grown up, played together, laughed, ran, swam, surfed.

She nodded.

"Ok," she said. "Sounds good."

He smiled. "Give me a shout when you're ready." She smiled back.

"Thanks again," she said.

"No problem." He turned and trudged down the stairs. Willow watched him go, drinking in his silhouette. He disappeared from view, but she heard him whistling into the kitchen. Alone now on the landing, she glanced back at the handle to the bathroom.

Her mouth went dry. Cold fingers seemed to stroke her heart. Had she really seen Ellie?

Ignoring the prickling sensation running up her neck, Willow crossed to the spare room to dress. She avoided looking in any more mirrors.

*

"Our father, who art in Heaven..."

Willow sat on the rocks, a dozen yards back from the circle of mourners gathered around Goddard. She had her arms wrapped around her legs, hugging her woollen cardigan over them. Underneath, she wore the black combat shorts and the baggy white t-shirt that Goddard had left on the bed for her. Beyond the circle, the ocean reared in glassy green-blue peaks and crashed onto the sand in a cascade of foam. The late afternoon sun threw golden light across the beach. A few kids clambered over the rocks, and a young couple walked a dog in the surf. Otherwise, the beach was deserted. Her throat felt thick and gummy and she could feel the tears pricking her eyes.

The service had been short but sincere. Of the people

around her, she only knew Goddard. He'd introduced her to his flock; to Jacinda and Kate and Benjamin and the others, but their names meant nothing to Willow. They were strangers to her. And yet they spoke eloquently, sincerely, of Ellie's vivacity, her laughter, her spirit and energy. They talked of her kindness, her compassion, her desire to help. And they remembered her beauty, the spark in her eyes, the way she smiled, the way she moved, danced, ran.

They captured Ellie with their words and it was like she stood next to Willow, her breath on Willow's neck, her fingers in Willow's hands. At one point Willow half-turned, the memory of the face in the mirror still fresh, half expecting to see Ellie behind her, torn between relief and disappointment when she wasn't.

Lowering her head, Willow walked around the prayer circle, padding barefoot around their boards and their bags, scattered in a rough pile on the beach. She walked towards the surf until the long foam run-off caressed her toes. Then she folded her arms and stared to the horizon. They had set up around the headland, away from the main beach and the crowds. For privacy Goddard had said. Suited Willow.

She watched the gulls and the distant peaks of breaking waves and her thoughts drifted to another time, another sunset on the beach, not here, but at Trevaunance. Two days after their parents had split.

Willow had run out of the house in tears. There'd been an argument; Willow kicking off about a trivial problem but in truth kicking off because the safe, comfortable world she'd known had fallen apart. She'd fled to the beach in tears and had sat on the rocks, weeping, wailing, despairing. Eventually, she'd heard footsteps behind her and when she turned her head, she saw Ellie standing a dozen feet away.

"Everyone's worried," Ellie said, the setting sun making her blonde hair gleam.

"Good," Willow replied.

The waves lapped around the rock on which Willow sat. It was autumn. The summer tourists gone. The beach all but deserted. She stared at the horizon, where the cloudless sky burned orange. She cuffed tears from her cheeks. Felt movement beside her and then Ellie's arm slipped around her shoulders.

"You okay?"

"Fine."

Willow put her head on Ellie's shoulders.

"No you're not, Flake," Ellie said. "How could you be?"

"Everything's fucked."

"Yeah, you're right."

She sat for a while with her head on Ellie's shoulder, listening to the waves on the rocks and the seagulls screaming, the smell of salt and sand drifting on a warm breeze that made Ellie's hair tickle her cheeks.

"Why can't she just say sorry!" Willow said. "Why does she have to leave?"

She felt Ellie shake her head. "I don't think she is sorry."

"She's a bitch."

"She's still our mum."

"I hate her."

"Yeah..." Ellie's voice had gone distant...sad. "So do I."

Along the beach, a solitary surfer ran into the breakers, throwing herself flat on the board and paddling hard through the white water.

"Was Dad mad?" Willow said.

"He was. But he's worried now. He wants you to come home."

"Do we even have a home anymore?"

"It'll always be our home, Flake."

Flake. Ellie's nickname for her. Short for Corn Flake. It began as an insult. Willow had thrown a strop because Ellie had spilt the last of the breakfast cereal over the kitchen floor and Willow had accused her of doing it deliberately because she knew how much Willow loved Corn Flakes. Ellie had teased her by singing 'Corn Flake' at her. A silly argument. They'd only been three and six at the time. But Ellie had called her Flake for days afterwards, and it stuck. Stopped being an insult. Became a term of endearment.

"It won't be the same."

"No, it won't," Ellie said.

On the clifftops above a dog barked. As the rolling peaks of the ocean crashed in, Willow had caught a glimpse of the surfer paddling parallel to the shore. The fire overhead died and the sky became a soft pastel blue.

"Things will get better though," Ellie said, squeezing her shoulder.

"You promise?"

Ellie smiled. She had dazzling white teeth and eyes that sparkled. Willow had always wished she had Ellie's looks instead of her frumpy, freckle-filled mug.

"Course I do."

Willow had touched her forehead to Ellie's shoulder,

then peered at the water. As the light faded, it looked like oil lapping around them.

"It's so dark," Willow said.

Ellie took her hand. "Don't worry. I'm here for you."

Willow gazed at her sisters long lean fingers, at the glossy nails, the soft skin. "I'll always be here for you," Ellie said.

Except she wasn't.

Not anymore. Willow's thoughts recoiled from the past, and as she tumbled back to the present and a world without Ellie, a bank of glowering clouds rolled across the distant horizon.

"You okay?"

Willow cuffed at the tears on her cheeks and turned. Goddard stood before her. He had a triple fin swallow tail surfboard under one arm, and he wore his wetsuit unzipped to his waist. He had a faint tan line, plunging in a V beneath his neck. His eyes looked like black holes in his face and she had to peer hard to see the whites and the soft brown pupils. The kids on the rocks had gone.

The couple with the dog had moved further along the beach now, towards Chapel Porth. She and Goddard were alone.

"Not really," she said.

He nodded, understanding.

"We're all finished here," he said.

Willow peered over his shoulder. The rest of the group were already trailing seawater up the beach. They'd hit the waves before the memorial, and now, with the memorial done, they were heading back to their homes, their lives, their loved ones. They had places to go. People to get back to. Who did she have?

"I'm gonna stay for a bit," she said. "I..."

Words failed her. She sucked in a breath, let it out in a long, low whistle. Her lips trembled. The grief seemed to fill her chest.

"Are you ok?"

Willow nodded. Then crumpled. Her face screwed up. Tears spilt down her cheeks. She choked back a sob, put her fingers to her lips. Her shoulders spasmed as she tried to hold back the emotion, but she couldn't do it.

Her knees buckled and she fell to the sand.

"I let her down." She sobbed. "She needed me. I wasn't there."

Strong arms enfolded her. She could smell surf wax, sea salt and sweat. She buried her head in his chest.

"It's ok," he said. "You've done nothing wrong."

"I should never have left!"

"It's not your fault."

"She hated me. I said she was dead to me! And now she is."

"You didn't do this."

"We never..." The words failed as a sob caught in her throat. "...I never had a chance..." she sobbed again, "...to say I'm sorry."

She dissolved into tears. Cried until her throat hurt. Until her eyes burned. Until a sharp hard pain stabbed beneath her ribs. Goddard held her. He squeezed her shoulders, whispered comfort. Eventually she fell silent. She sniffed and wiped her eyes.

"I'm sorry," she said.

Pulled away. Gazed up at him.

Tears trailed down his face. His eyes were red-rimmed and wet. Her gaze flicked over his. She could feel his pulse through his chest. Or maybe it was hers. She could smell him. Feel him. His lips looked soft and warm and his arms felt strong and steady. Her breath caught. Then she couldn't help herself. She leant forward.

Her lips brushed his.

A molten heat flared in her chest.

She pulled away. He peered hard at her.

Then he slipped his hand around the back of her neck and pulled her mouth to his. They kissed hard and furious. She held his face. Felt his hand slip under her cardigan. Squeeze her thigh. Her bum.

She slipped her tongue in his mouth. Pulled him down on top of her.

They fell back into the sand. Didn't speak. Didn't need to. Everything she had to say to him, she said with her hands, her mouth, her body. She tugged down his wetsuit as he unbuttoned her shorts. She kicked them down to her ankles and reached between his legs. He paused. Lifted his body and peered down at her. He felt hard and hot in her fingers.

"Are you sure?"

She bit her lip and nodded. He peered at her. She craned her neck. Kissed him again. Pulled him down. Onto her. Into her. She gasped as he slipped in. Gripped his back. Sucked his lips. Licked his neck. He bit her shoulder. Squeezed her backside, her breasts under the shirt.

They screwed quick, hard, him coming first, her holding him inside her, bringing herself off on him.

Afterwards, he peered down at her.

"Are you ok?"

She felt tears pricking her eyes and now the desire had

passed, all she could feel was guilt like nausea inside her. She slipped out from beneath him, tugged her shorts up, straightened her shirt.

"I shouldn't have done that." She sat up, wrapped her arms around her knees. "I'm sorry."

He shook his head. Pulled up the wetsuit. Smiled. "You did nothing wrong."

"Ellie..." Willow said.

He took her hand and squeezed it.

"What about her?"

"What would she think? I mean, she's dead and here I am screwing on a beach." Goddard sighed.

"I'm sure Ellie would understand."

Willow shook her head. "What sort of bitch am I?"

"You're human," Goddard said. "It's not wrong to want physical comfort. When we're all alone, when things are at their worst... that physical contact... it reminds us that we're *not* alone."

Willow frowned at him. "Aren't you supposed to like... condemn me for sinning or something?"

He smiled. "I can if you want. But I'm not that kind of priest." He sighed and stood. "I am the kind of priest," he said, "who could do with a nice soft bed right now."

Willow peered at him. She didn't miss the glint in his eye.

"Yeah," she said, feeling guilty and elated and wondering if she was just going mad all at once. "Me too."

29

They drove back in his black Ford Focus, made it into his kitchen before they tore at each other's clothes, throwing them aside, then collapsing to the kitchen floor, Willow on top, Goddard underneath. She came hard and fast, then let him take her upstairs where he made love to her, slow and hard, teasing her body with his fingers, his tongue, his sex.

After, they shared a bath and a bottle of wine.

"I've got a question," Willow said as they sat in the bath, her at one end, him at the other. Her legs were bent over his thighs, and she leant forward and kissed the side of his face, his neck. "What sort of question?"

"The religious sort."

"What, now?"

"Yeah."

"You think this is the right time for a theological debate?"

"Absolutely." She cupped water in her hands and let it fall over his chest, then traced the lean muscles with her fingertips.

"Is it serious?"

"Depends."

"On what?"

"Well, you know what we've just done?"

"What about it?" He said.

"Do you think it's a sin?"

"Didn't we cover that on the beach?"

"I don't mean that." She shook her head. "I don't mean what we did. I mean like…you... well, you're a Reverend. I mean, a fucking hot one, but still, you're one of God's chosen..."

Goddard chuckled at that. "Never been called that before."

Willow smiled, traced a finger through the water. "And well, we're having... y'know... sex outside of marriage and all that. And I'm curious. Do you think we're sinning?"

Goddard blinked. "Why'd you ask?"

"Just thinking," she said. "I mean, I guess if you pushed me I'd say I believed in God or …. something. But I'm not devout."

"More a pick n' mix believer?" He grinned.

"Guess so," she said. "But you... you're a priest..."

"Reverend." He raised a finger to point out.

"Well, a reverend then. But you're like... a true believer. Does it bother you that you may have committed some sort of... mortal sin." Goddard shook his head.

"You ever read the Bible?"

"Can't say it's ever been high on my reading list."

"I did." He scratched an itch under his arm. "I mean, not every page, but enough to make me realise that God, whatever that is, it isn't what's in the Bible."

"But you're a reverend. Aren't you supposed to like...

follow it verbatim."

"I'm not a reverend anymore. I gave up the church. Had my own flock to guide."

"But you believe in the Bible?"

"I believe in the Divine. But the Bible?" He smiled and shook his head. "It's more about...interpretation."

"Interpretation?"

"Look, most of what's in the bible, it's myth. Metaphor. It's not the actual word of God. It was written by men. And to be honest, some of the stuff in there is just plain evil."

"But you believe in God though?"

"Of course." Goddard shrugged. "But not because of the Bible."

"Then why?"

Goddard gazed at her. In the warm light of the bathroom, he had honey-brown eyes. "You surfed right?"

"As a grom, yeah. Not for a while now though."

"Ok, so when you're surfing, you're waiting yeah? Floating on the water, feeling the swell and it's eternal yeah? Like the heartbeat of the Earth. And it lifts you and drops you but it never throws you too high or drops you too low. You're just there. In the ocean's grip. Until you challenge it at least. And when you see that wave and you paddle for it, there's this moment, when the wave hits you and takes you and you feel its power and you realise that power..." he shook his head. Closed his eyes. His face went serene, smooth and she could see him remembering that feeling. She remembered it too.

"That power," he said. "It's been here forever, before you and me, before our parents and their parents and all the parents that there's ever been, and it'll still be here long after we're dead and gone, and when you feel that power, for that moment, that second, you're part of the wave, and you feel how small you are, but you also realise that you're part of that power too. That's God to me."

"So, what about the Bible?" Willow said.

He shrugged. "Just words. God... it's so much bigger than that."

"So you don't think what we're doing is a sin?"

"What is sin?"

Willow shrugged. "You're the reverend, you tell me."

"You enjoyed it, didn't you?"

"Well," she smiled and lowered her gaze. "Could be better."

He grabbed her sides, squeezed. She squealed with laughter, her backside slid out from under her and her legs flew up. The water splashed up the sides of the bath. She grabbed the roll top to stop herself from falling. "Better, eh?"

He kissed her hard. She put her hands around his face and held his mouth to hers. When they broke apart, she smiled at him.

"You talk like a poet," she said. "Not a priest."

"You didn't answer my question."

She kissed him. "Do I need to?"

He shook his head. "Then how can it be a sin. We're not hurting anyone. Are we?"

"No."

They kissed again.

"People are doing a lot worse to each other," Goddard said.

Willow's mood darkened as her thoughts turned to Ellie, dead on a slab in the morgue, her throat cut. Imagined the terror she must've felt. The pain. The fear. Willow could feel it too. She slipped close to Goddard. Put her arms around his neck and rest her head on his shoulder.

"Hold me," she said.

"You okay?"

"Ellie," she replied.

He squeezed her tight, and in his arms and his words, she found a crumb of comfort in the hell of her grief.

30

A telephone pierced the quiet darkness. Willow jolted awake with a gasp. From the bed beside her, Goddard reached up and touched her arm.

"It's ok," he said. "It's just one of my flock."

Groaning, he swung his legs out of bed then leaned back and kissed her forehead. She smiled.

"I'll be back in a bit."

He snatched his phone from the bedside table and padded naked from the room. Willow stared after him, the guilt and the desire still warring inside her. He smiled back at her as he stepped out onto the landing and closed the door behind him. The landing light clicked on and a strip of gold spread across the carpet through the gap at the foot of the door. In the inky blue darkness she lay back on the pillow and stared around the room; at the Moroccan pottery on the shelves above the radiator, the wax stained empty wine bottle with the stub of a candle in its neck on the bedside table, the coffee table book of surf shots leaning against the cream wallpaper behind an oak jewellery tree laden with chains and thongs that hung from the forked and varnished branch. Her bag sat on the floor next to the bed, her clothes drying on the radiators and on the airer on the landing. As Goddard's voice drifted away, she reached down into her bag and pulled out her phone. She hadn't looked at it since the hospital and had turned it off before the memorial service without checking the notifications, the grief still too raw, the hangover still too fierce to face the barrage of messages and missed calls.

She had butterflies now as she turned it back on. The screen glared bright in the dark, and as the phone finished its start-up, it began to vibrate.

Willow swore.

Half a dozen missed calls, three voicemails, and a text from Ruby, plus another text from a number she recognised but couldn't place.

She opened the first of Ruby's voicemails. Ruby's voice played husky and thick through the phone speaker. The guilt squirmed through her gut as she listened.

"Hey, it's me. I'm so sorry about your sister, hun. I hope you're ok. Call me."

Next message. Sent in the evening after two missed calls. "Hey, babe. I'm getting worried. Please, I know this is a shit time, but please, just call me or text to say you're ok."

Willow swallowed as the guilt grew inside her. She played the final message. It had come through that morning.

"Willow, it's me." Her voice sounded edgy, angry now. "Have I done something to piss you off? Why are you ignoring me? Just call. Please." Then the text.

"I no we're not a couple, but I thought we wz frnds!!! Some frnd u r."

She signed off with three angry face emoji's. Willow

put the phone to her head and closed her eyes. Another friendship ruined. Another person she'd pissed off. She sighed, opened her eyes and opened the contacts. She scrolled to Ruby's number, went to hit call but hesitated, her thumb hanging over the green button.

She couldn't make that call. Not then. Ruby was bound to ask where she was and how could she tell her that she was in Goddard's bed. From the calls and the texts it was obvious that Ruby had been worried about her and all the time, Willow had been here, getting laid and not even thinking to call or text Ruby to let her know where she was, that she was safe.

She locked the phone screen, ignoring the other message from the vaguely familiar number. Instead, she tossed the phone on the edge of the bed next to her, reached out and lifted the surf book from the side and began flicking through the pages.

It featured waves, ocean shots, line up shots and close-ups of surfers charging down barrels, the waves curling and spitting foam overhead. The water in the pictures looked deep blue, icy glass, turquoise green or in one stunning picture, backlit sunset red. The places were tropical, exotic, otherworldly, and she longed to be in those places, away from the hell and the chaos she found herself living through. She closed the book, shook her head.

Too much unfinished business here to go right now. But she wanted to. God, she wanted to.

With a sigh, she turned to put the book back. As she shifted, her thigh knocked her phone. It slid off the side of the bed and plunged to the floor. Instinctively, Willow snaked out a hand and grabbed it. The book swung loosely in her other hand. Its corner caught the edge of the jewellery tree. The tree teetered, rocked.

Then it plunged to the floor, striking the carpet with a heavy thunk.

*

Goddard stepped into the kitchen and flicked the lights. The fluorescent strip buzzed to life and chased away the shadows. The blinds were open and the world outside looked black. He nudged the door shut and cut the inane chatter he'd been spouting just in case Willow had been listening.

"Got a bird there boss?" Michael said.

"What you got on Raven?" Goddard said, ignoring the question. He crossed to the blinds and yanked them down.

"Not much. She went to the warehouse."

"She do anything?" He dragged a chair out from under the table, the legs scraping on the floor tiles, and sat down. The wooden seat felt hard on his naked backside.

"Couldn't tell. We couldn't get too close cos she had the shutters half up and she'd have heard us driving in. So we waited down the road and followed her when she left."

Goddard frowned, pinched his nose. He could smell Willow's sex on his fingers; musky and rich. "How long was she in there?"

"Twenty minutes... maybe a bit more."

"Where'd she go after?"

"Nowhere. She's back at her hut now."

Goddard rapped the tabletop with his fingertips.

"What do you want us to do?"

"Nothing. Just keep tabs on her. Let me know when she moves."

Goddard cut the call. Laid the phone on the table and stared at the range oven opposite. What had Raven been doing in the warehouse? Sabotage? Stealing gear? Maybe just using the computer to search for the number he'd given her, but he'd have to check. Not now though. He had other priorities.

His gaze settled on the knife block. Remembered Raven's warnings. About how much trouble Willow was. And Raven had been right about one thing; Willow hadn't followed the bait to London. And now she knew Ellie was dead, there's no way she would. So maybe Raven was right about this as well. Maybe it would be best.

No. No. Whatever he wasn't, he wasn't a killer. That was Raven's speciality.

Besides, Willow was in his bed, in his thrall now. If he could keep her there, he could control what she discovered. Where she went. Maybe he'd be able to dig out her dirty little secrets too. A sure-fire way to buy her silence. Much more his style.

Ignoring the knives, he slid back the chair, tucked it in, then killed the lights, and padded back upstairs.

31

"Shit," Willow said, peering down at the fallen jewellery tree and the tangle of chains, leather thongs and pendants beneath it. She put the book back, put her phone on the side, then swung her legs out of bed. She could hear Goddard coming back, the stairs creaking beneath his feet. Naked, she crouched on the floor and picked up the tree.

It was undamaged, no new splits or cracks. She breathed out, relieved and placed it on the side in front of the book. Then she reached down and grabbed a leather thong that had gotten tangled with a silver necklace with thick links. She untangled them, hung them back, then grabbed another three chains. They came apart easily and she hung them back on.

Goddard was on the landing now. She doubted he'd get mad if he saw it, but she still wanted to make it right before he did. She was a guest after all and trashing his room wasn't exactly polite. She heard the bathroom light click on, then the steady flow of urine as he peed.

She grabbed another necklace; a delicate, thin cord of silver links, different from the rest, more feminine.

And familiar.

In the bathroom, the toilet flushed and water gushed from the sink taps.

She saw the pendant swinging from the chain as she went to hang it back on the tree. She felt her heart jolt, stopped halfway through hanging it and peered harder at the pendant. The bathroom light clicked off. The floorboards creaked as Goddard padded back towards the room.

Still staring at the pendant, Willow frowned.

The pendant said 'Forever'.

She reached for her own pendant, still around her neck, and put it against the one from Goddard's tree.

It matched perfectly.

The completed locket read 'Sisters Forever'. Her stomach churned. Anger sparked hot in her chest.

The door opened. Willow looked up. Goddard, a naked silhouette against the light on the landing, stood with one hand on the door, the phone in the other, a puzzled look on his face.

"Are you okay?"

Willow stood and backed away from him. She felt sick. Tears stung her eyes.

"Willow?" He took a step towards her.

"Don't!" Willow raised a hand. He stopped.

"What's wrong?"

She held up the pendant. He frowned.

"Ellie had a chain like this," she said.

She saw his lips pale. He swallowed.

"Is this hers?"

"Willow..."

"ANSWER ME!"

Goddard jumped, and she saw his face darken, but she

didn't care about being rude now.

"Is it hers?" she hissed, and jabbed the chain towards him. It swung in her fingers, the light from the hallway catching on its edges.

Goddard's gaze flicked from her to the pendant and back again. The silence stretched between them. She could hear her heart pounding, feel it throbbing in her ears.

"Is. It. Hers?" she said, punctuating each word with a jab of the fist holding the chain.

"Yes!" He nodded. "But listen..."

"Did you kill her?" The words were out before Willow could stop them. They sounded crazy but to hell with crazy. She could feel her body trembling, a deep ache in the back of her legs threatening to steal the strength from her. She was seconds from collapsing on the floor and only the anger raging through her kept her upright.

"Willow, please, calm down." He had his hands open, held up, palms towards her. He stepped closer, she stepped to one side. His voice sounded clear and calm.

"Calm down?" Her face screwed up. "My dead sister's necklace is in your fucking bedroom, Richard!"

"Please." He kept his voice low, calm. "I get you're upset. I get it. But please."

"Why is it here?"

He sighed, closed his eyes, hands held out in supplication, pleading.

"She stayed here," he said, opening his eyes again. "After the miscarriage. After her life fell apart. She stayed here."

"What's this..." Willow jabbed the necklace at him, "...doing in your room?"

He peered at her, and his eyes looked sad, weary. "Please don't do this..."

"Did you fuck her?"

He lowered his gaze and shuffled back from her. The body language told her everything she needed to know, but she wanted to hear him say it.

No. She needed to hear him say it. She needed his confession.

"DID YOU!"

"Yes..." his voice sounded small like a naughty schoolboy caught out. He shook his head.

Willow gasped. Chuckled madly. Bit her lip, looked around the room. She could feel her emotions, swirling, raging, crashing inside her, like the ocean against the rocks, a tumult of rage and grief and jealousy and bitterness, smashing and rolling and swirling together, till she felt like she would explode.

"So what?" she said, the bitterness spilling out with every word. "You fucked me to get the full set did you?"

He closed his eyes. "Willow, please..."

"YOU LIED!" she screamed, and saw him flinch. "You told me nothing happened between you and Ellie. You said it wasn't like that."

"I'm not proud of what happened." He slumped on the bed, put his head in his hands. "She was staying here. I was trying to get her clean. We got talking one night. She started crying. I held her. We kissed. We..."

"Fucked like rabbits?" Willow spat, arching an eyebrow, sneering down at him.

"Willow..."

"Fuck you, Richard." She jabbed a finger at him. "Just... fuck you."

She glared at him. He looked small, shrunken, folded in silhouette on the edge of the bed. She snorted, then turned and snatched her peach dress from the radiator.

"I'm done," she said, dragging the dress over her head. She grabbed her bag from the floor, moved around the room, tugging her clothes from the radiator and shoving them into her bag. She didn't look at him as she stalked onto the landing and started taking her stuff from the airer. She could feel her face burning with guilt and embarrassment. Grabbing her last pair of knickers and shoving them in the bag, she swept back into the room.

Goddard hadn't moved. She grabbed her boots, sat on the bed and pushed her feet inside. Then she wrapped Ellie's chain in her hands and went to put it in the side pocket of her bag.

"You keeping that?" Goddard said.

"It's Ellie's." She closed her hand around it. Stood, threw the bag on her back, tucked her phone inside and stalked to the door.

"She gave it to me," he said.

"Bullshit." She yanked the door open.

"She said she couldn't wear it anymore."

Willow stopped. Every instinct was screaming at her to go, but his words brought her up short. She stared out onto the landing. She wouldn't look at him. She never wanted to see his face again.

"She said she'd betrayed you. She said she wasn't a good sister. And she needed to find herself again."

"Liar," Willow spat.

"I'm not lying. She said she'd be back for it when she felt she deserved to wear it again. When she'd made it up to you."

Willow blinked back the sudden tears. She heard movement behind her. Could feel him stepping closer. The hairs on the nape of her neck prickled. Her shoulders tensed. Her breath had caught in her throat.

"She said she knew," Goddard went on. "How much she'd hurt you. How much she'd let you down. I told her she was wrong. She'd been a good sister. She'd looked out for you."

A floorboard creaked behind Willow. She stiffened.

"But you," Goddard said. "You ran out on her. You abandoned her. And when she got lonely and took comfort in the arms of a man she grew to love, a man who felt just as lost and empty as she did when you left, you rejected her. And you didn't just reject her. "You said she was dead to you."

Willow flinched.

"And now," Goddard continued. "You run back, and storm around demanding answers, acting like you're the only one who cares, and when it all goes to hell, when you realise you've failed, you jump into my bed, looking for comfort, for shelter, and then you lose it when you realise your sister did the same, all those years back. And it makes you so jealous."

"I'm not jealous," Willow hissed.

"Could've fooled me."

He was standing right behind her. As the tears spilt hot down her cheeks, as his cold, cruel words - words she'd spoken to herself in the depths of long lonely nights on the other side of the world - pierced her soul, she could feel his breath, warm and hot on her skin. And she hated him and wanted him and hated herself more for wanting him.

"Ellie was wrong." His voice went low. She felt his breath on her ear. "She always deserved to wear that necklace. She was always your sister. But you..." Willow closed her eyes.

"You're just a selfish little cunt."

Her eyes flared open. She snarled. Spun in a tight circle. Threw her right fist out. And for the second time in her life, her knuckles crashed into his jaw. Pain burst up her arm. Goddard's head snapped back. He fell to the floor with a thud and a grunt. She glared down at him.

"Fuck you, Richard."

As he groaned and rolled on the carpet, clutching his face, she stormed downstairs, the steps thundering underfoot. She swung open the front door, stalked out, then spun and slammed it shut. She glared at the white plastic, breathing hard. The anger, the humiliation of his words stung her. She punched the door.

"Bastard!"

She spat at the window. The hallway light flicked on. Panic flared in her breast.

She spun and ran hard. Tears spilling. Ribs burning. Fist throbbing. Out of his street. Out onto the main road to Aggie. Stars gleamed bright and furious overhead, the night sky, cloudless. Air roared in her ears. Her feet pounded the tarmac.

Not looking, she fled into the road. Headlights pierced the dark. The horn of an approaching car screamed out. She didn't stop. Let it hit her. Let it end this.

It didn't hit her. She cleared the road. The car howled past. Willow spun, watched the taillights recede into the dark.

She began to breathe, heavy and deep. Glanced across

the road. Goddard hadn't followed her. She tugged her hair back, swore and then swore more, harder, louder, until she screeched into the night.

In one of the houses along the roadside a light came on and a window screeched open. Her heart jolted. Not wanting another fight, she scurried away, head down, shoulders hunched. Ran until she reached the museum.

Then, with no better place to go, she clambered over the gates and hustled along the drive, around the back into the graveyard where she slumped onto an iron bench.

Her feet hurt. Her body ached. She could smell Goddard, taste him on her lips. She swore again. Shafts of moonlight picked out the gravestones, made them look hard and grey and eerie. Alone with the dead. She snorted. Where she deserved to be.

Her best friend was lying in a forever sleep not a hundred yards from where she was. And Ellie…Harrison… would they be buried here? Were they with Zoe now? Or had Ellie lingered here? Was Willow really seeing her sister in mirrors and in dreams? Or was she just going nuts?

Guilt and shame pricked her conscience. How could she have slept with Goddard when her sister and her childhood sweetheart were dead? She felt something in her fist. Opened it and saw the other half of the 'Sisters' necklace laying in her palm. The chain spilt over the edge of her hand and swung silently.

She clenched her fist around it. Held it to her lips and screwed her eyes shut. She heard a low, keening noise, like an animal in pain and realised that she was making it. She gasped and leant forward, weeping again. Would she ever stop crying for Ellie? She buried her head in her hands, waiting for the storm of emotions to pass.

When it did, after seconds or minutes or hours she couldn't recall, she sniffed and sat back. Blinked up at the stars. Was she up there? Ellie. Was she watching her now, looking down with Zoe on one side, Harrison on the other?

Was she here? Now? Watching Willow grieving?

Or was it all bullshit? Was she truly alone?

"I'm sorry," she whispered to the stars.

A noise in the dark, an animal screech - half banshee, half angry child - made her head snap around to the shadows under the hedges and the trees. She couldn't stay here.

But where to go? She fastened the second necklace around her throat, kissed the pendant then tucked it under her dress. As she stood, her phone vibrated in her bag.

She dragged it out and checked the display. Just a spam text, selling minutes or data or some shit. She went to tuck her phone away, but then she saw the other text, the one from earlier, the one she hadn't read because Ruby's words, the bitter loathing in her messages had stung her too hard. She recognised the number but with no contact assigned she couldn't tell who it was from. She could only see the first line.

"Sorry for your loss. But you're..."

She opened the message and as she read it, her body tingled with excitement and fear in equal measure.

"Sorry for your loss. But you're in danger now. We need to meet. The car park at Trevellas. Six am tomorrow. If you're not there, I'm not waiting. If you don't come, or can't come, then do yourself a favour. Get out. Go back to Australia. And stay there."

She stared at the number, then at the message, then at the message before that.

"It's so dark."

The message that had brought her home.

The sender had been silent for almost ten days now since they had sent the first text. And now they had decided to break their silence and do...

...what?

Warn her? Threaten her? Tease her?

She read the message again. Her brain whirring. They knew about Ellie, that Ellie was dead, that Willow had been in Australia. They knew the code... and only Ellie could've told them. They must have known Ellie personally. And then they had called her back.

They had sent the first text.

Not Ellie.

She felt sadness swell like a cold balloon inside her. Even at the end... even when she'd been in trouble, Ellie still hadn't called her back.

She sniffed, blinked back tears and cuffed her eyes. For one second it crossed her mind that maybe she should go. Jump on a bus to Newquay. Fly to Heathrow. Then on to Singapore, or Dubai, or China and then back to Sydney, where she could be Willow again, and no-one had ever heard of Megan-bloody-Rae. But there were people there looking for Willow in Sydney now, since the fight on Bondi. She'd get no peace in Oz.

She thought of Ruby currently pissed off with her, lying alone and angry not more than a mile away. She thought of Ellie, now dead but never able to forgive Willow for what she'd said. She thought of Harrison and

Zoe. She thought of all the times she'd run away from the things that hurt her, that scared her.

When she'd seen Ellie's body, she'd fled until she ran out of land and then she'd run straight into Goddard's bed, looking for comfort, for someone to hold her the way Ellie had when they were kids. But no one ever could and now she was running again. From Goddard. From the lies he'd told her, and the truth he'd spat that had hurt her more.

Where had running got her?

Haunting a graveyard in the middle of the night.

Fear had driven her away from everyone she loved. And fear for Ellie had driven her back. She couldn't run again. She'd failed Ellie in life. And now Ellie was gone, she owed it to her memory to stop running.

She had to face the person who sent the message.

She had to find out what they knew.

But first, she had a bridge to build with yet another person she'd let down.

32

In the bright, harsh light of the bathroom, Goddard glared at the vivid mess of purple skin running deeper black around his eyes, at the broken red veins and the yellowing flesh around the edge of the bruise. His lower eyelid had swollen. He pressed his fingers to his sharp cheekbones and pain lanced up into his scalp. He screwed his eyes shut, lights popping behind his eyelids, and grit his teeth. Gave a long breath that came out like a low hiss.

"Bitch."

He sucked in a lungful of air and opened his eyes.

She'd marked him twice now. There wouldn't be a third time. He'd make sure of that.

"Fucking bitch."

He gripped the edge of the sink to stop himself from trembling.

He should've destroyed that bastard necklace. Given it to Raven to throw into the ocean after Ellie's body. Or he should've never accepted it in the first place.

Ellie had held it out to him, a few weeks back, the night he'd sent her back to the hostel, after sharing his bed one more time. She made him promise that whatever happened to her, somehow, someday he'd get it back to Megan.

And he had.

Not intentionally of course. He'd never intended on her getting it. He had intended on binning it the minute the door had closed, but a slither of guilt, that old weakness, had stopped him from doing it. But Willow had it now. And whatever slim chance he'd had of getting her on board had gone.

Why had he kept it? For the memories? He had a few. Ellie had been a good fuck. Better than Willow at least. But it wasn't that.

His conscience had got the better of him. He'd laboured in the years since his brother and mother died to beat his conscience down, to focus on the outcomes, on what he had to do to make the world a better place. For the most part, he could keep a lid on it, stop it from getting the better of him.

But on that day it had snuck up on him, unawares. It had felt wrong, getting rid of something precious to Ellie. He hadn't known that she had to die then. And he'd still held out hope that he could turn her. He'd put it on the jewellery tree and forgot about it.

Never thought about it again until Willow had it in her hands tonight.

"Shit." He pushed off of the sink and yanked the light off. Cheek throbbing, he stalked onto the landing and back to the bedroom.

The only saving grace was that he'd managed to think fast enough to convince Willow the chain had been left years ago, that she still had no idea how closely involved in Ellie's death he was. Now he needed to act before she made that link.

Going for Willow now, after her sister and Harrison had been found murdered, would be too reckless. It would pose too many questions in the press and with the police and it would attract altogether too much attention.

There was only one way now for him to cut off that link.

Only one person knew everything. Only one person knew what he'd ordered and why. She'd been useful for a time. The best even. But she'd outlived her usefulness now.

He snatched up his phone.

It was time for Raven to die.

*

It took less than twenty minutes to cover the distance between the museum and Ruby's flat.

Churchtown was deserted. A solitary light glowed in a room above the pub.

There was a second light in the apartment above the supermarket.

Willow stopped in the shadows opposite and gazed up. She saw Ruby rise from the bed wearing silk black pyjamas, her mop of sandy hair hanging wet around her jaw. Guilt twisted inside Willow. She crossed the road and stepped up to the front door.

As she reached for the doorbell, she paused. She remembered coming here, two or was it three days back now? The morning she went to the hostel. The morning she thought she'd find Ellie. The morning she still had hope.

She swallowed the sudden lump in her throat. The urge to run swelled inside her again. This was madness. She didn't have to ring the doorbell. Ruby didn't know she was there. What good would coming back here do? What did she owe Ruby, except thanks for driving her around? They weren't a couple. They hardly knew each other. Willow could go anywhere she wanted, vanish into thin air, this time for good. She lowered her finger, went to turn away.

"So, you've come crawling back, have you?"

Willow gasped and looked up. Ruby had slid up the window, bent underneath it and now stood with half her body outside, her hands on the sill. Below the window, the shop shutters had been bolted and padlocked up for the night. Lurid graffiti tags covered the rusting sheet of hinged metal.

"You scared me," Willow said.

"I scared you? I've been worried bloody sick about you for the last forty-eight hours. Where were you?"

Willow stepped back so she could look up. "Can I come in?"

Ruby peered hard at her. "That depends."

"On what?"

"What you're here for."

Ruby's skin glowed orange in the streetlamp, and it cast dark shadows across her face. The tilt of her nose, the glimmer of light on her piercing, the black silk clinging to the slender curves of her body, made Willow's heart spasm.

"To explain."

Ruby shrugged. "What's to explain? I don't own you. You can do what you like. But I'm not a fool. I thought we were friends. But I guess I was wrong."

"We are..."

"Friends don't leave each other hanging with no contact for forty-eight hours when one of them is worried fucking sick!"

Willow lowered her gaze.

"And if you're just here to make yourself feel better," Ruby went on, "do me a favour and just keeping walking." She went to slip inside.

"I'm sorry," Willow said.

Ruby hesitated. "I can see that. But why should I care?"

"I've been a bitch."

"Agreed. But again, why should I care? You're cute, but I can get cute in a thousand places." She ducked her head inside. Slammed the window shut. The glass rattled.

Willow stepped back. "Ruby!" The light went off.

"Fuck," Willow muttered. She dropped her rucksack on the pavement, slumped against the panelled wood of the door and slid to the step. She put her head in her hands and dragged them back through her dreadlocks. A couple of late-night dog walkers strolled past. She wondered what they made of her sitting in the doorway with her head in her hands. A small part of her felt conspicuous. The larger part couldn't have given less of fuck if she tried.

The urge to run grew stronger. She could feel it whispering in her ear, coaxing her with the promise of freedom. All she had to do was stand, walk away. She could walk to Trevellas. Bed down in one of the old engine houses then set out at first light to meet whoever was waiting for her. She'd find out what they wanted and then...

What? Run forever? What good would that do? If she ran, who'd stay and find out what happened to Ellie? And if Ruby was nothing but a passing acquaintance, why did Ruby's anger hurt? She closed her eyes and put her head back against the door.

Heard the voice of her mother, the voice of her father... *"Running away again?"*... *"You're even running from your own name."*... *"You're going to run again?"*... *"Is that your answer to everything?"*...

Then she heard another voice. Ellie's. Or maybe her own. She was too tired to tell.

"You run, you prove them right."

Ellie's voice or her own, it sent a flash of defiance through her. She wasn't going to run. She was going to meet the person who'd sent the text. She was going to find out what they knew.

And if she could she was going to find out who killed Ellie. And why.

Before all that, she had amends to make with Ruby.

She dug out her phone, unlocked it and clicked into the messages. She opened a new text message and went to type, but her fingers hesitated above the keypad. What to say? How to start?

"I told you I'm sorry. You asked why you should care?" she began. *"It's a good question. And I can't answer that. Truth is, you don't have to care. But I do have to explain why I ran out on you when all you've done since I've got back is help me. I owe you that."*

She hit send.

The message flagged up as delivered. Then as read.

She looked up. The light in the room stayed off but she could see a dark shadow in the window and felt Ruby peering down.

She started a new message.

"I've been scared, Ruby. Scared for so long. Scared that everything will fall apart again. Scared because every time I get close to someone they leave." She hit send again. Delivered. Read.

"Every person I've ever cared about has broken my heart." Send. Delivered. Read.

"My mum. My dad. They both left me. In their own way. Mum actually did leave and my dad may as well have done. So I ran. Halfway around the world. And lost Ellie but I always hoped we could find each other again. But now she's been taken from me. And she'll never come back."

A tear she didn't know she was crying splashed on the screen. Willow jabbed at her eyes with the balls of her hands. Crushed the tears away.

"The other night, when I found out Ellie was dead, I wanted to run right off the edge of the world. I almost did. But I couldn't take that step. Goddard saved me. Pulled me back from the edge and took me home. I slept with him, Ruby. I did what I always do when bad stuff happens to me. I ran. Straight into his arms. Straight into his bed. I know we're not a couple and maybe you won't care what I've done. But I do care. Because I'm tired of running. The last time I ran, Ellie died. And I never got to see her again. Or say sorry. So I've got to do all I can to make it up to her. I'm meeting the person who sent the text that bought me home. Tomorrow at 6 am. At Trevellas. I'm not a strong person. I want someone with

me. I'd love that person to be you. But I understand if you're not interested. Either way, I need you to know that I know I let you down."

"And I am sorry."

She leant her head against the door. Waited. The messages had been read. Minutes passed. Was Ruby replying? Sitting in the dark constructing her response. Or had she thrown the phone away in disgust?

Willow leant forward. It looked as though Ruby was still watching her in the dark. She leant back. Waited another minute.

Then sighed and put her phone in her bag. No reply. It was all she deserved. She hauled herself up. Dusted off her backside. Threw the rucksack over her shoulders and caught a whiff of her own sweat. She'd need a shower before she met whoever it was she was meeting.

With a final, regretful glance at Ruby's window, she set off. She could take the coast path, stop in at the hostel where Ellie had stayed. It would be fitting. Like she was following in her sister's footsteps.

She could shower. Catch a couple of hours sleep then get up with the dawn to hike back to Trevellas.

She'd gone two doors down when she heard the latch click behind her. She stopped and looked back. Ruby stood in the doorway, a slender silhouette in black pyjamas framed by the light of the staircase behind her.

"I must be fucking mental," she said. "But get your sorry arse up here."

Willow smiled, turned and walked back.

"Thank you," she said as she slipped past Ruby, who kept her face stone-like and impassive. She smelt clean and fresh. Like she'd just stepped out of the shower.

"Just get up there before I change my mind."

Willow trudged up the stairs. Her legs ached, her eyes felt gritty and the grief felt like a cold ball in her chest.

"And just to make it clear," Ruby said. "You're sleeping on the floor."

Willow reached the top step and turned into the studio apartment.

"You're a bitch y'know?" Ruby stormed up after her.

"I know."

"I was so worried about you I've barely slept and there you are, jumping into bed with the Right Reverend Richard fucking Goddard."

"I'm sorry."

"Are you though?" Ruby's face blazed with anger. Her eyes smouldered and her throat had gone red. "I mean, you can fuck who you like."

"I..." Willow went to speak.

"Don't lie," Ruby said. "Don't fucking lie."

Willow lowered her gaze. Shook her head. "No. I guess I'm not. At least, not about the sex part."

"Jesus fucking Christ." Ruby turned and stalked to the window. She jammed her hands on her hips and stared out into the dark, looked over her shoulder, and glared at Willow. Turned on the spot, first right, then left, then stalked to the corner of the room.

"So why aren't you with him? Why are you here?"

"He lied to me."

"He's a bloke, it's what they do."

A smile twitched the corner of Willow's lips. "He said he never slept with Ellie. But then I found this."

She reached under her dress, pulled out Ellie's half of the pendant and held it out to Ruby.

"What is it?"

"It belonged to Ellie."

Ruby stepped forward, took the pendant in her fingers. Her grey-blue eyes flicked up and met Willow's gaze. Held it for a long moment then peered at the necklace.

"It was on his bedside table. It'd been there for years."

"You're sure it's hers?"

Willow nodded. "He told me. Then called me selfish."

"Got that right didn't he?" Ruby let the chain drop.

Willow didn't say anything. She gave a soft, apologetic smile.

"I need a drink." Ruby leapt up and stormed towards the kitchenette. As she passed Willow grabbed her wrist.

"Hey," she said. "Thanks for-"

Ruby spun back. In one stride, she grabbed Willow's face and kissed her hard. The backpack fell from Willow's shoulders. A delicious heat erupted in her chest.

Ruby pulled away, still holding Willow's cheeks.

"I fucking hate you," she said and kissed Willow again. "But I'm glad you're ok."

Ruby stepped back. Bit her lip and cocked her head. She clasped her hands in front of her, fiddling with her fingers.

"You stink. Take a shower." Ruby nodded towards the bathroom door. "Then you can tell me about this mystery person you're meeting tomorrow."

Ruby stalked into the kitchenette as Willow turned and headed for the bathroom, a small smile on her lips.

33

They walk, hand in hand, their footsteps silent as they glide through the night. They pass through halos of orange from the streetlights but cast no shadow. Ahead, a fox scampers from a side alley, sending bins tumbling in a clattering of metal.

It stops in the middle of the road. Turns golden eyes on them. Its lips curl back in a snarl. Spittle drips from the tips of its canines. Its head dips low, its claws splayed on the tarmac. The fur along its back rises. It yelps and snaps at them.

Still, they walk on.

The fox shuffles back, snarls, then whimpers and bounds away. Ahead, a drunk slumbers in the doorway of the butchers. He stirs as they pass, but does not wake.

They walk on. Reach the door next to the supermarket. They don't need to knock.

Drifting through the wood, they glide up the stairs, their legs echoing the movement of climbing even though their feet leave no trace on the carpet. Darkness around them, but they need no light.

They know where she is.

At the top of the stairs, they stop. Share a glance. A

smile. A squeeze of hands that no longer feel.

They slip through the door, into the studio flat.

She's asleep, dreadlocks splayed around her head, her back to Ruby, who lies facing the window.

Another glance. A nod. She must be warned.

They creep forward. The temperature in the room drops. Breath frosts in front of the sleeping women. Ice gathers on the inside of the window. Skin pimpling, Ruby turns and tugs up the duvet, leaving Willow exposed.

She shifts on the bed.

They edge closer, closer. Hands extended, they reach for her.

She must know. She must know.

They bend and reach and dead-cold fingers brush warm skin and they squeeze and press and lean close and—

*

Screaming, Willow jerked awake and sat bolt upright.

"Whassup, whassup, whassup, whassup!" Ruby sat up, clutching the duvet.

Blinking, Willow stared at the side of the bed, at the doorway. Sweat dampened her skin and the sheet beneath her. A needle of cold pain pricked the back of her eye, then flashed out of existence. She scanned around the room. No frost on the window. Her breath didn't cloud before her. And the figures who'd reached for her…

She closed her eyes and swallowed deep.

"Are you okay?"

Ruby touched her shoulder and Willow jerked, her

eyes snapping open. She turned. Flashed Ruby a weak smile.

"Fine," she said. "Bad dream is all."

Ruby frowned, studying her face. "You're sure?"

Willow nodded.

Ruby sighed and shook her head, letting her fingers slip from Willow's shoulder onto the duvet.

"You scared the shit out of me." She slumped back on the bed.

Willow snuggled into her, keeping her back to Ruby. "Sorry. I didn't mean to wake you."

"It's okay." Ruby shifted to her side and slipped a hand over Willow's waist, crushed her chest against Willow's back. "It's fine." Her kiss brushed the back of Willow's neck then burrowed down into the covers.

After a few minutes, her breathing settled into the deep rhythm of sleep.

Willow kept her eyes open, her gaze fixed on the wall.

Because every time she closed her eyes, she saw them again.

Ellie and Harrison. Reaching for her.

And she wasn't entirely sure she'd been asleep when they had.

34

The sound of an engine jolted Raven from sleep. Heart hammering, she snatched the knife up and leapt to all fours, back arched, teeth bared, blade held high, coiled and ready to pounce. Shadows clung to the walls of the hut around her. Thin shafts of light pierced the gaps in the wood and brickwork. The air smelled stale and felt cold on her bare legs and arms.

Nothing moved around her. The only sound was the steady drip of water coming from the tap below her, no one breathing, no footsteps scuffing on the flagstones.

Satisfied that no one was waiting to pounce, yet silently cursing herself for falling asleep all the same, she uncoiled and stretched. Her breath tasted stale, and her throat felt dry. The sound of the engine grew louder. Resisting the urge to snatch a drink from the tap downstairs, she crossed to one of the cracks in the brickwork and peered out.

It wasn't a great view, but she could see the narrow lane outside, and that had been enough to watch Gabriel standing in the sloping drive opposite the night before. Though it had been dark, the smell of his joint had given him away even before he started fiddling with his lighter.

Now though, he was gone.

Her first thought was that the engine was Michael or one of the other Chosen coming to pick him up or raid the hut. But the car that approached, delicately negotiating the narrow gap between the high hedges and the trees, was a small Fiat. She almost dismissed it, but then saw the flash of flame-red dreadlocks in the passenger's seat. She recognised the face a second later.

Megan.

And in the driver's seat... Ruby? Raven frowned. Since when had those two been buddies?

The car passed. Raven ran to the pile of clothes on the floor by the mattress. She dragged on a pair of black jeans, a hoody, wrapped the mask around her face, then threw on the trench coat. Pulling up the hood, she crossed to the bolted door at the top of the steps leading up from below.

She listened for any movement from the basement, then unlatched it, nudged it open, and stepped out into the daylight.

She stood beside a low stone wall, at the top of a set of steps that ran down the side of the building to the road. She ignored the steps and leapt the wall, then ran across the wild field.

*

"You think they'll show?" Ruby said.

Willow sat in the passenger seat of her Fiat 500, gazing at the blue and purple ceramic cups that hung from the rear-view mirror. Ruby sat in the driver's seat, picking at the diamantés on the steering wheel cover. The sky behind the ridge at the top of the Trevellas valley was washed pale with the dawn, and golden light spilt over the foliage, the pathways, and the abandoned engine houses with their tall brick chimneys. Willow had lost her virginity with Freddie Hunt in one of them. And her life had been chaos since.

"Yeah," she said. "I'm sure of it."

The car park was deserted except for a black Toyota Prius at the far end. A bank of clouds glowered on the horizon over the flat, moody ocean. Minutes passed. The clock on the dash clicked towards six am. They didn't speak. Willow cradled her forehead in the tips of her thumb and forefinger. She felt off-kilter, at odds with the world, the memory of her dream and the uncertainty of what she was about to walk into made her stomach quiver. Outside, there was no sign of anyone coming into or out of the car park.

"How long will you wait?" Ruby said. "If she doesn't show."

Willow turned to answer, but her phone rang. And at the same time, the lights of the Toyota flashed on. Heart in throat Willow snatched at the phone.

"Hello?"

"Is that you in the Fiat?"

She didn't recognise the voice. "Is that you in the Toyota?"

"Who's your friend, the blonde?"

"Ruby."

"She stays there."

"No," Willow said. "Whatever you've got to say to me, you say to her."

"Bye then."

"Wait!"

"I'm not playing."

"Neither am I."

"Look, I'm not waiting. If you want to hear what I've got to say, get over here now. Your friend stays where she is. You've got a minute to decide."

The phone went dead. Willow lowered it and peered at the handset.

"What was all that about?" Ruby asked.

Willow gazed from the Toyota to Ruby and back again. Daylight had crept across the car park. She could see the driver now, nothing recognisable, just a mop of wild curly hair and a flash of pale skin.

"She wants to talk to me alone."

"Better get your arse over there then," Ruby said.

Willow tried to swallow but she had no spit. "What if it's Raven?"

"You think it is?"

Willow stared at the Prius. Instinct said no, but instinct had also made her trust Goddard, so she didn't exactly trust herself right then.

"Look, you wanna know what happened to Ellie don't you?"

"I don't like the idea of getting in a car with someone I don't know."

"I'm here," Ruby said. "If I see anything I don't like, I'll be over there in a flash."

"What if she drives off?"

"There's like, one road out of here, and I'm closer to it than she is."

The Toyota shuddered as the engine gunned to life. The chance to find out the truth about Ellie was about to drive off. Panicked, decision made for her, Willow snatched at the handle and swung the door open.

"Good luck!" Ruby cried as Willow grabbed her bag from the back and ran for the Toyota, feet crunching on the gravel.

The driver leaned over, then the passenger door swung open as Willow approached. With a final glance at Ruby, peering straight at her, a frown carving her brow, Willow dropped into the passenger seat and turned to the driver.

Waves of frizzy brown hair bounced down either side of her oval face. Her skin looked dry and grey, and she had dark shadows around her eyes. She peered hard at Willow, her pale blue eyes watery, the whites stained pink like she hadn't been sleeping much. She wore a dark T-shirt, blue jeans and white pumps.

"So you're Megan then?" she said.

"Willow."

"Sorry?"

"That's my name now. Willow."

The woman frowned, then gave a shrug of the shoulders that said she didn't care what Willow called herself.

"You look like Ellie. Except the hair of course." She twisted her lips and looked away.

"And you are?"

The woman had a straight, thin nose and the glow of the early morning sunlight picked out the thin line of white-blonde hair on her top lip.

"Elizabeth," she said. "Elizabeth Steinberg."

*

Raven crouched behind a thicket that overlooked the car park and peered down.

The Fiat sat at one end of the car park. The only other car was a black Toyota. From where she crouched, she couldn't see anyone in either vehicle. She scanned the valley. There was no sign of Megan on the path or the bridge. She wasn't on the shingle or the rocks either. Could be in the engine houses or one of the caves. But why? What was she doing here?

Minutes passed. The sun rose, chasing away the last of the shadows. Raven crouched lower. The Toyota roared to life and the passenger door to the Fiat burst open. Megan leapt out and ran from the Fiat to the Toyota. Raven tried to snatch a glimpse of whoever was in the Toyota but could see nothing.

She looked for a better vantage point where she could see who was in the cars. There were thickets and hollows where she could have crouched, but little cover between them, and daylight would betray her if she made a bolt for them. Biting back the frustration, she peered at the Toyota. She got a glimpse of Megan's hair in the passenger seat. As she craned her neck to at least try to get a better view, her phone buzzed in her pocket. Keeping her gaze fixed on the Toyota, she dug it out.

"Wilkes?" she answered.

"The number you asked me to track."

"What of it?"

"It's a pay as you go," he said. "An unregistered SIM. Most likely a burner phone."

Raven lowered her head and swore into the grass. "Can you track any calls or messages it's sending?"

"Not without a warrant."

"So get a warrant then."

"Look, it's not that easy. I can't do that. I'm just a PC."

"Better get to Ann's emails before she does then," Raven said.

"It's too late."

Raven's head shot up. "What do you mean?"

"I told her. I told her everything."

Raven felt her stomach turn to ice. The breath caught in her throat and her blood froze in her veins.

"You fucking what?"

"The sergeant caught me trying to track the number. They nicked me. I told them everything."

"You're lying."

"They're coming for you, Raven. You've got no hold over me now. Ann knows everything. I'm on suspension. I'll lose my job. Maybe my wife. But at least I'm free of you."

Raven closed her eyes and swallowed. Her world tilted off-kilter, the ground beneath her plunged away.

Goddard would kill her now. No doubt about that. She knew him well enough to know he wouldn't let the police get that close.

She cut the call. Rising to her knees, she slid the back off of the phone. Took out the battery. Took out the SIM. She folded the SIM backwards and forwards until it cracked in half. Threw it in the bush in front of her. Then she rolled to her back, her sense of self-preservation still working to hide her from the people below. She threw the battery one way, the phone the other.

Then she peered back down at the cars below.

Part of her wanted to watch, to find out who was down there with Megan.

But another, far stronger part, no longer cared.

She had to get away. She had hours at most. Goddard already had people tailing her. They'd move as soon as he gave the word. She had to go now.

With a final glance at the car park, she leapt up and sprinted back up the hillside towards her hut.

35

Willow blinked and swallowed. Next to her, Elizabeth Steinberg sat still and silent, watching Willow's face.

"You're Eric's wife?"

Lizzie looked forward and nodded. "So you know something then." A silence thick with tension swelled around them.

She was sitting beside the wife of Ellie's lover.

The wife had sent the message that brought Willow home.

What was going on?

Willow stared ahead through the windscreen, at the stone bridge and the shale beach beyond. A kayak, paddling out from Trevaunace, emerged around the headland.

"I don't understand," she said.

"Understand what?"

Willow tried to figure which question she wanted to ask first.

"How did you know?" She gazed at Lizzie. "The code. Mine and Ellie's code. How did you know it?"

"So that's what it was. I did wonder." Lizzie blinked. "Ellie gave it to me."

"You spoke to each other?"

"A couple of times," Lizzie said. "After Eric died."

"Why did you speak to her though? I mean as far as you knew they were... he was..."

"Fucking your sister?"

Willow flushed. "Just for the record, I don't believe that."

"Oh they were, believe me. Your sister... she was very apologetic about it all." Lizzie shrugged.

Willow's heart jolted. She stared at Lizzie, looking for the lie, but she couldn't see it. She closed her eyes, wondered if she'd known Ellie at all.

"She turned up on the doorstep all tearful and begging for forgiveness," Lizzie went on. "Said she needed to talk to me."

"Talk about what?"

"What was going on."

"And what was going on?"

Lizzie sighed and shifted in her seat.

"Look...Willow... I can tell you what I know. But ask yourself this first. Do you really want to know?"

"Why wouldn't I?"

"Because two people have died already. My husband. Your sister. You sure you want to take that risk?"

"But you're husband... it was suicide."

"Was it though?" Lizzie's gaze flicked across Willow's face, her eyes cold and hard. The hint hung in the air between them. Willow looked away. Towards the path rising up the side of valley opposite. Towards the blue skies and the fluffy wisps of cloud tinged with pink and the promise of a gorgeous summers day. But the mood in the car felt dark.

"You're saying Eric was murdered too?" Willow said.

"Ellie said it. Not me."

"But... why? Because they were having an affair?"

Lizzie gave a hollow laugh. "God no."

"Then why?"

Lizzie peered at Willow, rapping her fingers on the steering wheel, a slight frown creasing her brow. Willow could see the grey roots in Lizzie's hair. The skin around her eyes looked almost bruised.

"Because they stumbled onto a conspiracy."

"A conspiracy?"

"Blackmail. But not for cash. For votes. Influence."

"Votes?"

"On the county council. You know what my husband did?"

"I read he was a property developer."

"And bloody successful too. Made a lot of money, and sold a lot of houses. But he upset the locals. Some thought he took too much money from the Cornish economy, that he priced the locals out of owning their own home. Didn't bother to think about the jobs he brought to the area."

Lizzie's lips twisted with bitterness.

"Not that it ever mattered what the locals thought," she went on. "The councils loved him because the rates they made on his property bought them a lot of cash.

"But about a year ago, maybe eighteen months, he started hitting problems. Paperwork was lost. His projects kept getting hit with unannounced inspections from the health and safety people which put him behind. Planning applications that had, in the past, been signed off without trouble were suddenly being rejected. He lost two or three big contracts. Then last winter he had to lay off a load of workers and his reputation took a hit.

"Then he told me he'd started hearing rumours. Putting two and two together, I think it was Ellie that told him. You know she worked in planning?"

Willow nodded. Lizzie continued.

"The paperwork wasn't being lost, just deleted or shredded. The health and safety inspections were more than just routine. He was being deliberately targeted. And the plans... well, whether they got signed off or not very much depended on who's desk they landed on. So he started digging. With Ellie's help."

"What did they find?" Willow said.

Lizzie sighed. "I don't know. Ellie wouldn't tell me anything except what I've told you already. That someone was blackmailing people of influence to vote a certain way or reject plans that would otherwise have been approved, or... I don't know, do surprise safety visits."

"And they did all of this just to get at your husband?"

"No, it's bigger than that. Eric wasn't the only one hit. He told me ages back that the offices of one of his rivals had been raided by the HMRC and the directors arrested on fraud charges. And there's been a spate of vandalism attacks on new builds that have been sold but are standing empty. Windows smashed, squatters getting in, driving down the prices."

"Yeah, but that happens everywhere. A house stands empty for too long, the squatters are always gonna find a way in."

"But there's a pattern. They only hit certain houses on certain estates. Estates owned by people like Eric. And when the police are called it's hit and miss whether they'll do anything. Again, it depends on who gets the call."

"Ellie told you all this?"

Lizzie shook her head. "Some of it. But the rest of it… Eric spent most of the last year bitching about these things. I thought he had a real victim complex brewing." Her face grew sad, and she gave a wistful smile.

"So what, Ellie comes to see you and she just happened to tell you about our code? Give you my number? Get you to send me a text? Ellie could've done all that herself." Willow turned to Lizzie, body taut, hands trembling with anger.

"The first time I saw her, she didn't mention you," Lizzie said. "She came to see me. Course, all I wanted to do was slap her in the face and kick her off my step, but she kept on pleading and begging for me to listen and when I calmed down I realised she was terrified."

"Of what?"

"Of whoever killed Eric. She was getting weird phone calls, people following her, someone had tried breaking into her flat. She thought they were after her now. She wanted to warn me to be careful."

Willow remembered the landlord, his comments about people trying to get in, and her own run-in with the biker.

"So why didn't Ellie just go to the police?" Willow said after a few minutes. "Why didn't she tell them about this conspiracy?"

"She said she couldn't trust them. It wasn't just councillors being blackmailed. It was coppers, and not just bobbies, but senior ones too."

"But... who's blackmailing them?"

"Ellie wouldn't say. She said it was better I didn't know." Lizzie rubbed her brow with her ring finger. Willow saw a pale patch of skin where the wedding band had been. "She... I think she just wanted to make amends. Or apologise at least. And when she left, I thought I'd never hear from her again.

"But she called two Fridays back. Said she'd sent me a package and asked me to follow the instructions inside."

"Did you get the package?"

"It came later that day."

"And what was in it?"

Lizzie rummaged into the side pocket of the car door.

"A mobile phone with a SIM. A piece of paper with a message and a number to send it to..." she pulled out a small, padded envelope and held it out to Willow. "And this."

Willow peered at the envelope. She felt her heart twist when she saw her name written on the front in her sister's elegant handwriting. She snatched it from Lizzie.

"And you didn't think to give this to me sooner?" Willow said, tearing at the envelope, glancing sidelong at Lizzie as she spoke.

"I didn't know how to find you."

"But I called. I called the number…shit, dozens of times. You could've answered. You could've called back."

"I wanted no part of this." Lizzie shook her head. "These people are dangerous. They already killed my husband. I've got a daughter to think about. I had to protect her. I couldn't put her at risk."

"So why now then? Why are we meeting?"

"Because Ellie is dead. And that changes things. I..." Lizzie dragged a hand through her thick curls. Her face had gone grey. She looked older all of a sudden. And tired. "I thought that you deserved to know why. I thought it might help."

"Could've helped if you answered my bloody calls," Willow said. She pinched the corners of the envelope and tipped it up.

"I'm sorry."

"Yeah, me too."

A USB drive made of clear dark plastic, the circuits visible inside, dropped into Willow's palm. Her heart jolted again. She glanced up at Lizzie, who was leaning forward to peer at the USB, then prised the envelope wide open. Inside, she saw a slip of paper. She pulled it out. Saw Ellie's handwriting again. The paper had one word on it.

"Breakfast?" Lizzie said. "What does that mean?"

Willow swallowed. She knew. And she had a pretty good idea why it was in with the USB too.

But she shook her head, unwilling to trust Lizzie with that information.

"And she said nothing else?" Willow said.

"I asked if she was ok. She said she was going away. That she might not be back for a while."

Willow looked at the USB. Was that the night she was supposed to run London?

"Did Ellie say where she was?"

"Some hostel or other."

Willow peered at the USB, then closed her fist around it. Around the last tangible link with Ellie.

"Why did she not call me herself?"

Lizzie shrugged. "I can't answer that?"

"Can't, or won't?"

"Sorry, but she never said."

Willow squeezed the USB in her palm. Was it fear for Willow's safety that made Ellie go through Lizzie?

Or was it a different fear?

The fear that if she tried to call, Willow would've ignored her.

"I've got to go," Willow said. She reached for the door handle.

"What are you going to do now?" Lizzie said.

Willow paused. "I need to see what's on this." She waved the USB.

"You should just leave. Head back to Oz. You know what's happened to Ellie, to Eric. They'll kill you too."

"I'm not running away anymore. I came back to find Ellie. Since I failed to do that, the least I can do is find out who's behind this." Willow pulled the handle and the door clunked open. She waved the USB again.

"Thanks for this." She stepped out of the car.

"Willow," Lizzie said.

She crouched to peer into the car.

"I'm sorry about Ellie."

Willow peered at her. "I'm sorry about Eric too."

Willow shut the door and ambled back to the Fiat.

36

The hut looked the same as when Raven had left it. The side door stood closed. The window at the back was still shut. No cars on the road below. No one watching from the drive opposite.

Raven rose from behind the wall where she'd crouched, leapt it in one bound then stalked to the door, scanning around her as she went. Without stopping, she yanked open the bolt, swung the door back, slipped inside and eased the door closed behind her. Back to the wood, she peered around, listening hard. Her heart throbbed in her ears and a bead of sweat trickled down her spine. The lamp still shone from the rafters. Had she turned it off though? Couldn't remember. But if the Chosen were waiting to jump her, surely they'd prefer the dark. She would.

She peered down the stairs to the darkness below. The thin shafts of light slicing through the gaps in the brickwork and wood did little to penetrate the dark corners down there. Anyone could be waiting in the shadows. Using the dark to hide. Waiting to pounce. But though the dark could cloak them, it couldn't hide their breathing, or the strange, almost electric hum that a hidden person seemed to give off. And she sensed none of those down there.

Satisfied she was alone, she pushed off and crossed to the mattress.

She grabbed the knife and tucked it into the belt of her black jeans at the small of her back. She peered around. Grabbed a dusty black hold-all from the far corner, unzipped it and stuffed half a dozen bricks of cash inside. She dragged off her coat and scarf, threw them in the bag on top of the cash, then pulled off her hoody and threw that in as well. She snatched up her leather bikers jacket, slipped into it. Then she grabbed her helmet, clasped it one hand and looked about her.

The hut wasn't much to get sentimental about. But she still felt a pang of regret that she had to leave. She'd been safe here. Cocooned from the outside world which saw her as a freak, a monster, a warped, scarred version of humanity. Now that safety had gone. She had no more time. She had to leave.

Leaving everything else behind, she snatched the bike keys from the floor by the mattress, crossed to the steps, took one final look around, then peered down into the darkness.

She listened hard for any breath, any movement, any whisper that would betray someone waiting down there. Still nothing. In those thin beams of light piercing the dark, she saw the bike in the far corner, the water glistening silver as it dripped from the tap, and the dust and debris on the flagstone floor. The smell of old dirt and hay seemed more vivid. The darkness between the shafts of light a black oblivion.

She crept down the stairs, cursing her decision to throw

away the phone. At least the damn thing had a torch. The wood creaked underfoot. A skittering came from the far corner, and several high pitched squeaks. Field mice maybe. Rats.

Barely breathing, she crept to the foot of the stairs. Then waited again.

Still no murmurs. Still no sign of anyone waiting. But the dripping tap sounded louder now, and the bird song outside seemed to have grown in volume too. From one of the nearby gardens, she could hear a dog barking.

She peered at the bike, standing idle in the far corner. A dozen steps, maybe less and she'd be on it. But the doors stood closed and they'd need to be opened first. With a final glance up at the light spilling down from the lamp up top and then around the darkness, she strode across to the door. It was locked from inside by a heavy wooden brace. She put the helmet on the floor.

Slipped her hands under the brace. The wood felt cracked and dry. She lifted.

She heard a whisper of movement behind her. Went to turn. Too late.

A metal bar cracked across the back of her skull. White pain burst like an explosion through her head. She cried out as she fell. A second blow whistled down. She had enough instinct left to cover her head. The blow glanced off her shoulder. Pain blossomed again. She grunted. Her body slumped on the flagstones. Hot blood oozed down the side of her face. She clawed the floor, her nails splitting. She slumped again.

The darkness swelled around her. The world spun. She heard footsteps. And a voice.

"Well, that wasn't so hard," Michael said.

One of them spat. It hit the flagstones with a wet slap. She felt a boot prodding her. Defiance flickered within her. She wanted to leap up, fight back. Make the bastards pay. But her limbs felt detached from her body. She couldn't move.

"Dead?" Michael again.

"Looks like it." A chuckle.

"Guess she won't be walking away this time."

The darkness took her, and she heard no more.

37

"I'll get the laptop," Ruby said, opening the front door to her apartment and striding upstairs.

Willow followed, a curious feeling tingling through her. She stared at the USB. Did it contain the information that Ellie had stolen from the council? Did it hold the answer to why Ellie had been killed?

She put her bag down by the bed and turned the USB in her fingers. It was a link to Ellie and she didn't want to let it go.

"You okay?" Ruby crouched by the bed and dug a laptop bag out from underneath. "You haven't said much."

Willow glanced at her. Didn't reply.

"You believe Steinberg's wife?" Ruby unzipped the bag, pulled out a MacBook, and took it to the table.

"Guess we'll find out in a minute."

Ruby unfolded the laptop, hit the power button then dragged a seat back. Her face glowed an eerie blue in the light from the screen. Willow sat next to her. She had butterflies in her stomach and her mouth had gone dry. Ruby reached out and took her hand. Squeezed her.

"You sure you wanna do this?"

Willow gave a tight nod. Pinched the USB. Then slipped it into the port. The stick flashed and a hard drive icon pinged up on the top right corner of the screen. Ruby slid the laptop in front of Willow.

"All yours," she said.

Willow peered at Ruby. Her throat felt blocked like she'd swallowed a golf ball, and spasms of cramp squeezed her stomach.

"I'll make coffee." Ruby slipped her hand onto Willow's shoulder and squeezed. Then she scraped the chair back and padded to the kitchen.

Willow took a deep breath, shifted her seat, then slid her fingers along the trackpad until the small arrow on the screen hovered over the drive. She clicked the icon.

A grey, rectangular box appeared. The USB was password protected and the box asked her to enter the password. Her fingers hovered over the keyboard. She remembered the message in the envelope. "Breakfast."

She typed 'Flake' into the grey box. A blue circle whirred.

Then the screen expanded out and she found herself staring at dozens of folders and files all arranged in a neat grid on a white background. Several of the folders had names; Council Minutes, Planning Applications, Health & Safety, Surveillance. Others were code, dates maybe. Most of the files looked like scanned copies of documents, but a few were Word documents.

One, in particular, caught Willow's eye.

The file had a one-word name.

Raven.

So the landlord had been right. There was a Raven involved. Question was, who?

Desperate for the answer, she went to click on it, but then another file grabbed her attention.

It was a video file with her name on it. The icon for the file showed a face. Half an inch high, maybe less. But Willow recognised Ellie straight away. She moved the mouse onto the video, clicked it, then held her breath.

A blue circle swirled. She heard footsteps behind her. Smelt coffee. Ruby put a mug down in front of her and touched her shoulder again, her fingers warm and smooth. She gave Willow a tight smile.

Then Ellie's voice filled the room.

"Hey, Flake. It's me."

Willow jumped, heart jitterbugging. She peered at her sisters face through a film of tears. Ellie looked thin. Pale and gaunt, her nostrils red and sore, like she'd had a cold. Or spent a lot of time crying. Her hair looked greasy and dull. And she couldn't look at the camera. Just kept glancing at it, then gazing around wherever she was, scratching her shoulder, her forearm, sweeping her hair back. Willow couldn't see much of the room she was filming in, but it looked sparse, with white walls and a fluorescent strip light overhead.

"I don't know if you'll ever see this. All depends on if Lizzie sends the text I suppose. And what you do afterwards. I'd have called you myself but if I do and they find out… if they think I've told you anything…"

She sighed, and dragged a hand through her hair.

"I'm in trouble, Megan. Things have got a bit fucked up. I got involved with some guy I shouldn't have, and I did stuff for him, and that stuff... I think it's got him killed and now there's people after me."

Ellie's voice broke here, and a tear trickled down her

cheek. She wiped it away. Her skin looked dry and chalky.

"I'm gonna try and make a break for it. Head to London if I can. But this is my insurance policy I guess. If something goes wrong, if I... if I don't make it, I hope you see this.

"This memory stick... the files on here are everything I've found for Eric. They show what he long suspected; that there's a conspiracy here. Someone is blackmailing people, influential people, to make life difficult for people like Eric, to drive away their business to ruin their reputations."

"She believes this," Ruby said.

Willow glanced at her, then back at the screen, at the face of her dead sister.

"But the files... I've also found something else. I think I know who's behind this. And I think I know how they've done it."

Now Ellie looked right at the camera.

"Look in the file named Raven. I know that name will mean something to you. And my guess is you'll think you know who Raven is. But it's not her.

"Zoe is dead."

Relief flooded through Willow, closely followed by confusion. If not Zoe, then who?

"But," video Ellie went on, "I don't think the name is a coincidence. I think I know who Raven is. And I think you'll make the same connection too. I just... don't know where he is." "Who's she talking about?" Ruby slipped into the seat next to Willow.

Willow didn't reply. Couldn't. She had a bitter taste in her throat. Of course. It had to be him.

"I don't know what you'll do with this," Ellie said. "Presuming you'll ever see it. But don't give it to the police. They're in on it too. This is big, Megan. And these people are dangerous."

Ellie went silent. She bit her lower lip and peered towards something off-screen. She sniffed once. Willow reached out and put her fingertips to Ellie's cheeks.

"I'm sorry," Ellie said, glancing at the screen. "For... everything."

Willow tried to swallow the lump in her throat.

"I love you, Flake. And..." Ellie sniffed and shook her head, "I miss you." She flicked her hair back and sucked in a breath.

Then she stared straight at the camera and for a second their eyes met. Willow's chest tightened. It felt like Ellie was peering out from the afterlife.

Then Ellie's gaze slipped away and the moment passed. On the screen, Ellie reached out, hooking her hair behind her ear with her free hand. The image froze and the video ended.

Willow stared at Ellie. Her cheeks felt warm and wet. She cuffed away the tears. Ruby squeezed her shoulder.

"You okay?"

Willow shrugged. "Not really."

She dragged a loose dreadlock back behind her ear, leant forward and put her elbows on the table. She moved the mouse across to the file named "Raven". Double clicked. The file expanded and filled the screen. It contained scans of a notebook with notes written in Ellie's hand.

Willow's gaze flicked across the writing.

"Raven? Deals. Threatens. Kills??? Rumours of it. No

proof???"

"Male? Female? Dealer not sure? Never saw their face. Always hidden. Thinks rides a bike? *Motorbike?"*

"Your biker friend?" Ruby said.

"I think so." Willow scrolled to the next screen.

"THE NAME COULD BE A COINCIDENCE??? Who knew though?"

"Harrison?? (Yeah, like he'd ever do anything more interesting than change a sparkplug!)" "Megan???"

"She thought it was you?" Ruby pointed at her name.

"Unlikely," Willow replied. There was no notes or comments against her name. Just a sad face that made her heart twist. "She knew where I was."

"Maybe she thought you'd come back?"

Willow half shrugged and kept reading.

"Zoe. Was Raven, but dead now. Eve knew but also dead."

"Freddie??? Not seen him in years. No-one has. Think he used to ride a bike too??? Unlikely but be good to find him though…"

Willow scrolled again. Ellie had listed half a dozen others, names she half recognised, but all eliminated for various reasons.

Then Freddie's name again.

"Can't find Freddie??? Not seen since Zoe's funeral. Rumours he left for London, but no leads there. Was a dealer though??? Zoe's BF so he'd know the name??? And he was cruel…Bodmin incident…"

"What's the Bodmin incident?" Ruby asked.

"We were hiking," Willow said. "Camping out. Harrison was sharing a tent with him. Harrison was getting undressed at the end of the day, and Freddie pushed him out of the tent butt naked. Blocked the flap and wouldn't let Harrison back in. We heard Harrison screaming and Freddie standing there, laughing and taking pictures on his mobile. We sorted everything out, but Freddie almost got expelled a month later cos he printed the pictures and put them on noticeboards around school."

"Charming," Ruby said.

Willow peered at Ellie's writing. At the line below.

"The Zoe - Megan thing..."

"And what's that mean?" Ruby pointed at the screen and peered at Willow. A sick feeling spread in Willow's gut and not because of the "Zoe - Megan" thing, shameful though that was.

Ellie was right. Freddie was cruel. He was a bully. He was manipulative. He would love nothing better than being a centre of a web of blackmail, lies and deceit.

Willow scraped the chair back. Peering at the screen, she stood, grabbed her bag, tugged on her boots and cardigan.

"Where are you going?" Ruby said.

Willow strode towards the stairs, looked back over her shoulder to Ruby sitting at the table. "To Freddie Hunt's house."

38

Goddard sat in the cafe that had once been the old St. Agnes post office, a cappuccino steaming in front of him, his phone next to it, screen black and silent. He wore dark glasses to mask the bruising around his eye from Willow's punch and sat in the alcove off to the side, peering out onto Churchtown. Beneath the table, his knee jerked as he bounced his heel.

In the main area, a group of mums sat around the large wooden table sharing baby stories and lattes. They were gentrified, like the old post office, given a modern, Shoreditch-chic makeover. All upper-middle-class accents, bright teeth, good skin, sparkling eyes. They radiated money. Wealth. Good fortune. And they flocked to trendy coffee shops like these, with its brick and metalwork interior and its industrial style lighting, to see and be seen, to show they were in the crowd, that they were discerning, cultured.

Goddard despised them.

They had no idea what lay beneath the surface of their safe, comfortable worlds. They'd never seen poverty. Desperation. The after-effects of their greed, lust, gluttony. They hadn't sat in a room with a grieving mother wondering why her baby had turned to drugs, why the child she'd struggled to love and raise and care for had ended up dead on a slab, another victim of the bad shit being peddled in the clubs and bars and backstreets.

And yet they talked like their problems mattered. Poor little Tarquin wasn't sleeping? The gardener had planted the wrong colours in the rose bed? Their gym membership hadn't been cancelled at the click of their well-manicured fingers? These weren't problems.

Goddard had seen problems. Real problems. He'd buried enough of them; the problem kids who'd never settled; those who'd turned to drugs to escape the mind-numbing tedium of winters spent in poverty and unemployment because the jobs had dried up with the last of the summer tourists; the strippers and the prostitutes whose only joy came from a line of coke or a shot of heroin.

They were his motivation. His driving force. The reason why he got into the dealing in the first place. And through that dealing, through his dealers and what they reported back, he'd found out enough about 'civilised' society and how base and corrupt it was. And he'd used that knowledge for his benefit.

Tonight, when he won the council vote, the plan he'd lain so carefully would come to fruition. The days of screaming at the world for change and getting only disdain back would be over. The whole Duchy would benefit.

There were too many of the Shoreditch set moving down here now, bringing their elitist, shallow London snobbery, buying second homes, driving up prices and leaving the locals, the ones who needed cheap homes, priced out and living in poverty.

Tonight, if the vote went his way that would all change.

And he would win the vote. The bill would be passed. Through dealing, he'd learned of the sins of the elite and used them against them, got them onside. That's where Raven had come in. She could persuade. Cajole. Threaten. And she could kill. Without regret. Without impunity.

She'd taught him the divine beauty of righteous purpose.

Was it a sin to murder when the murder was for the greater good? He had struggled with that dilemma for many nights after the first time. It had been one of the few times since graduating in Theology that he'd gone back to the Bible for guidance and in its pages, he'd found what he was looking for. Justification. Didn't God kill without mercy to protect His chosen people? When the Red Sea collapsed behind Moses, did it not destroy the enemies of God? Did God not ask Abraham to kill his son to prove his devotion to the Lord?

And was it not here, on the North Cornwall coast, with the arrival of St. Piran, that God returned to Britain after the pagan times? Were the Cornish not God's chosen people? He believed so. And like Moses leading the Israelites, was he not leading his people out of poverty and oppression?

Yes, in the dark with his thoughts and his demons for company, he doubted. But he had faith in the Divine. He felt sure of the righteousness of his purpose. He would free the Cornish from the yoke of the scum of London, the drug barons, the property moguls, the metrosexual elite. And if people had to die, well, they were a necessary sacrifice.

The phone in front of him buzzed loud and hard. He jolted, looked at the screen, and pursed his lips. It was Michael calling. Goddard snatched up the phone. One of the mothers looked over.

"What's up?"

"It's done," Michael said. "Raven is dead."

"You're sure?"

"She got hit twice round the back of the head with an iron bar. She ain't getting up from that."

"Well done," he muttered.

He killed the call and stared at the phone. He expected grief. Guilt. Maybe relief. But he felt nothing except the satisfaction of a job done. She was gone. Not even Gabriel and Michael knew how Ellie died. There was no one to link to him to her murder now. That problem was dealt with. Now there was the vote to win.

He glared at the yummy mummies.

In a few hours, everything they knew would change forever.

He drained his cappuccino and left the cafe, mind set upon the righteous victory ahead of him.

*

"So what was with the whole Megan-Zoe thing?" Ruby said.

Willow closed the passenger door of the Fiat. "It was nothing."

"So much of a nothing that Ellie put it in her

notebook?"

"Freddie's house is in Porthtowan," Willow said, ignoring the comment, reaching up and pulling the seatbelt down into the clasp. Ruby started the engine and backed out of the parking space, then turned and headed out onto Churchtown.

"The Megan-Zoe thing?" Ruby said again.

Willow sighed. "Is it important?"

"You tell me?"

Willow peered at Ruby, then at the road. "I'm not proud of it."

"Proud of what?"

Willow looked to her lap and began picking at her fingernails.

"We were going to Trevellas. Me, Zoe, Harrison and Freddie."

She stared ahead, remembering that day, a month after the incident in Harrison's shed, where she'd flashed her tits and terrified the life out of him.

"Zoe had been banging on for weeks about the things she'd been doing with Freddie. And Harrison..."

She sighed, closed her eyes, and rubbed her forehead.

"He was more interested in fixing engines than getting in my knickers and it was frustrating the hell out of me. But I had a plan."

She smiled at the memory, at how childish her plan seemed now.

"I was going to lure him up to the old mine workings, the engine houses or by the chimney stacks in the valley there. I thought that if I got him alone and out of his old man's shed he'd be more receptive. But he wasn't.

"Wouldn't take my hints, just wanted to lie on the shingle and read magazines. So I stormed off. And Freddie..."

Willow felt her face burning at the memory. The guilt.

"He followed me. Found me in the engine house. Started telling me that Harrison must be gay because if I was his bird he'd be all over me the second he had the chance.

"I pretty much pounced on him at that point." She cocked an eyebrow. "Not that he minded."

The memories came thick and fast, each one making Willow cringe a little bit harder... clashing teeth as they kissed... fumbling with each other's clothes... the awkward attempt to try and be sexy while putting a rubber on him, only for it to tangle and rip so he had to dig out another and tug that on as well and the time it took pretty much killed the moment, made her realise what she was about to do. She could've stopped. Should've stopped. But she'd gone ahead anyway, desperate to feel what Zoe had said she'd felt, even though she knew he was Zoe's and she was betraying her best friend.

"It was over in seconds, but he was still on top of me when Zoe walked in."

"Shit," Ruby said.

"Yeah," Willow swallowed, remembering the fight, Zoe and Freddie screaming at each other, Harrison in tears and her...

"I stayed in the engine room for hours after. Just crying. And when I got home..."

The memory stole her voice.

"What happened?"

"Zoe's parents had told my father what I'd done," Willow said. "I walked into a mouthful from Connie. We argued. I told her she had no say over me, that I wasn't her daughter. She went for me. Liked to get handy with her fists. But I was ready.

"I grabbed her shoulders, and threw her against the wall. I was about to swing for her, but my bastard father..."

Willow screwed her eyes shut. She wanted to stop talking, but the damn had burst. She'd never told anyone before. Not even Ellie. And now it had burst she couldn't block it again.

"He grabbed my hand, pulled me around. Then he slapped me." She felt the blow as if he'd just hit her.

"He hit you?" Ruby said.

Willow nodded. "Right across my cheek."

"Bastard."

"I fell into the wall." Willow went on. "Cracked my head. He... he tried to apologise. But I ran upstairs. Slammed the door shut. Barricaded myself in my room until Ellie got back.

"And that was it. That was the night Ellie and I decided to run. Or at least I decided to run and Ellie agreed to follow. So we woke up early the next day and left. I got away, but Ellie..."

The car had cleared St. Agnes and was weaving along the road that ran down into Porthtowan. Watery sunlight flickered through the trees.

"No wonder you ran," Ruby said.

"Thing is," Willow shifted in her seat, picking at her fingernails. "I can't help thinking that... if I'd have stayed... or if Ellie had come with me... none of this would be happening."

Ruby reached over and squeezed her knee. "It's not your fault." She peered at Willow. "You didn't cause this. In your shoes... I'd have run too."

Ruby looked ahead, through the windscreen.

"In fact," she said, "I ran for a damn sight less."

Willow peered at her. "Sorry?"

"I ran," Ruby said. "From my home. My family."

Willow blinked. "You too?"

Ruby nodded.

"Why?"

"Well, being gay isn't exactly easy when your parents are devout Catholics."

She tried to give Willow a cocky smile, but her lips quivered and tears sparkled in her gaze. The smile died and she looked straight ahead.

"And your sister?"

"She told them," Ruby said. "She caught me kissing my best mate."

Willow thought back to what Ruby had said a few days earlier. "This best mate, was she the one who got away?"

"Debs." Ruby nodded. "I'd fancied her for years. Came back from Uni and she asked me to go for a drink. On the walk home, she said she had something to tell me.

"Said she was gay and wanted to tell me face to face, cos she hoped we could still be friends."

"What did you do?"

"Pretty much leapt on her and snogged her face off. The only problem was my sister was watching from her room. And the next day, she tells my parents and it all just goes off. So I ran to Debs hoping we could be together, only she was already with another woman.

Practically ran in on them in bed. Never been so mortified in my life." Ruby sighed and dragged a hand through her hair.

"So, I kept on running. Ended up here."

"Have you spoke to any of them?"

Ruby shook her head. "They've called a few times. Texted. I just ignored it."

"You think you'll ever speak to them again?"

Ruby shrugged. "I've got nothing to say to them."

"That's what I thought about Ellie," Willow said, peering out of the passenger window. "But I'd give anything to speak to her just once more." She turned back to Ruby.

"You should call them."

Ruby glanced at her. "So where's this Freddie's place?"

Ruby's gaze was defiant again. And pleading for Willow not to press it. She knew that feeling. Knew it only too well.

"This way," Willow said, pointing to a road that led up the cliffs. Not much had changed in the years since she'd left. A couple of the houses had been done up. The road had been re-paved. But the views across Porthtowan were still the same and Willow couldn't look at them without remembering what she and Goddard had done on the sand the day before.

"There," Willow said, pointing to a white-walled house on the left. Ruby parked up outside.

"You really think Freddie could be this Raven?" Ruby shifted in the driver's seat to face Willow. They'd stopped outside a large, detached property with dirty cream walls and windowpanes that had once been pastel blue, but now looked chipped and salt scoured.

"You saw the file." Willow shrugged. "He's the only one who knew that name who Ellie couldn't eliminate."

The house had gables and chimneys at either end and a dilapidated porch at the front. In places, the grey slate roof tiles were missing and the bushes behind the low stone wall had grown tangled. There were no curtains in the windows.

"But.. if he is this Raven character he's a bloody psycho," Ruby said.

Willow ran through her childhood memories of Freddie Hunt. Dashing. Sporty. Smart. The catch of the school and Zoe caught him. Cruel on occasions. Selfish. A bully.

"He never cared about people," Willow said. "Just took what he wanted from them."

"And if he's in there? If he is this Raven character? What do we do then?"

Willow half smiled "How fast can you drive?"

"Look, just call the police. Tell them what you know."

"Raven has coppers in his pocket."

"So Lizzie says."

"So Ellie says. You've seen what I've seen. If even half of that is true, this Raven has his claws everywhere."

The house looked deserted. Empty. Inland, the skies looked heavy with rain. Thick grey clouds rolled across the horizon, and the wind kicked the ocean into peaks of white froth.

"You don't have to do this."

Willow tried to ignore the worm of fear squirming in her stomach. "I do."

"Why?"

"I abandoned Ellie once. Now she's dead. I'm not doing it again."

"That's guilt talking," Ruby said.

"Maybe," Willow replied. "But it's all I've got left."

She unclicked her seat belt, gave Ruby a tight smile, then opened the door. As she stepped out, the wind whipped through her dreadlocks, dragging them across her face. She jerked her head to get them out of the way, pulled her cardigan tight around her, then sucked in a deep breath and crossed the road to the gate.

Once outside, she peered back at Ruby. The worm of fear had begun turning somersaults in her belly. Seeing Ruby hunched over the steering wheel, engine running, chewing her lip, didn't make her feel better. She turned back to the house, reached out and lay her fingers on the gate. The white paint felt cracked and chipped. She nudged the gate towards her.

It squealed open and she watched the windows for any sign of life as she approached, twisting to avoid the snaring reach of the overhanging bushes. When she got to the step, Willow reached for the large iron knocker and hit it once. Flakes of faded turquoise paint fell to the cracked concrete.

She stepped away, glanced back at Ruby and gave her a reassuring smile. Ruby still had her hand over the steering wheel, chewing her lip. Willow heard movement behind her and turned back. The lock clicked, the door squealed open. Willow sucked a breath, heart fluttering.

A stooped woman with greying blonde hair and garish purple bags under her eyes clung to the door with both hands. A smell like stale urine wafted out. Willow stepped back. The woman had papery skin and thin red blood vessels across her nose and cheeks. Willow blinked. It took a second to place her.

"Mrs Hunt?" Willow said. "I'm an..."

"Megan?" Mrs Hunt's face softened and the ghost of a smile twitched the corners of her mouth. "Megan Rae? Is that you?"

Willow forced a grin. "Yes."

Freddie's mum stepped out, grasped Willow's arms in her thin, dry hands. The smell of urine grew stronger and it took all of Willow's willpower not to step away.

"You look different," she said. "How are you? How are your parents?"

"I'm fine," Willow said. "They're all...fine."

"And Ellie, how's she?"

The question brought tears to Willow's eyes and a lump to her throat. "She's er..."

What to say? The woman didn't know about Ellie. How to tell her? Willow settled for changing the subject.

"Mrs Hunt, is Freddie in?"

The woman winced as if the mention of his name physically hurt. Then her eyes fogged, her face brightened. She beamed.

"Of course," she said. "Come in, come in!!"

She turned and shuffled back down the hall. Grasped the bannisters and peered upstairs. "Freddie, hun. Megan's here." Then she trudged into the lounge.

A cold pit opened in Willow's stomach. She turned back to Ruby. If Freddie was Raven she didn't want to go inside alone.

She jerked her head towards the house and waved for Ruby to come in. Ruby cocked an eyebrow. Pointed at her chest and then at the house. Willow nodded.

"What's up?" Ruby said, closing the car door and hurrying up the path.

"His mum's invited us in."

"So, he is here then?"

Willow peered in, bending to look up the stairs. She couldn't hear anything. She turned back to Ruby.

"I'm not sure," she said. "But I guess there's only one way to find out." She turned and stepped into the morose hallway.

39

"Jesus, that smell!" Ruby said, closing the door, wrinkling her nose and putting her arm across her face.

Willow moved towards the living room.

"He lets her live like this?" Ruby said, stalking towards Willow.

"You want a cuppa love?" Mrs Hunt called from the lounge.

"I'm not drinking anything she gives us," Ruby hissed.

Willow looked up. Listened for any sign of movement from upstairs. Outside, the breeze had kicked up. The wind whistled through the letterbox and a broken windowpane. The smell of urine seemed to grow stronger as Willow stepped into the living room.

"I'm fine, thanks," Willow said.

Mrs Hunt sat in a frayed, grimy armchair. Dust clung to the mantelpiece over the fireplace. An old TV, boxy and out of date by at least ten years sat playing in the corner. Pictures of Freddie and his sister hung on the wall over the sofa.

"Freddie will be down in a mo," Mrs Hunt said, beaming. She still had a vacant, almost delirious look on her face. "Is that Ellie with you?"

Willow's heart jolted. She wondered if Mrs Hunt could see ghosts, if maybe those weird dreams had not been dreams at all, but when she turned, Willow realised the old woman meant Ruby, who had appeared in the doorway, her face full of disgust, trying not to touch anything.

"Er... no. This is Ruby. She's a friend of mine."

"Where's Freddie?" Ruby mouthed.

Willow gave a half shrug.

"Oh it's so good to see you, Megan," Mrs Hunt said. "I love what you've done to your hair. Who did that for you?"

"I did it myself," Willow said. "Is Freddie going to be long?"

"Not long love. Not long."

"Is he upstairs?"

Mrs Hunt blinked. "Yes, yes he is, m'duck. Yes."

Beside her, Ruby circled her finger around her temple and made goggle eyes.

"Can I go see him?"

"Hmm?" Mrs Hunt peered up at Willow.

"Freddie," Willow said. "Can I go and see him?"

"Er..."

"It's just I'm in a bit of rush."

"Meeting Zoe are you?"

Willow blinked back tears. "Something like that."

"Lovely girl she is. Lovely."

Ruby moved closer to Willow and squeezed her elbow. "Bat shit crazy," she crooned.

"So, can I go up then?" Willow said, ignoring Ruby.

"Well... I guess so... you know where his room is?"

"Think I can remember." Willow turned and headed

for the doorway. She heard Ruby following.

"The old girl's proper nuts," Ruby whispered.

"Yeah." Willow trudged up the stairs. Every footstep kicked up a puff of dust. The carpet smelt old and musty.

"You don't think Freddie's up here do you?"

Willow shook her head. "Wherever he is, I don't think he's been back here for a while. Strange that his sister isn't here though."

"Maybe she had enough of the old bird. I know I would."

Willow reached the landing and crossed to Freddie's door. It had an Exeter City F.C. plaque on, with his name spelt out in bold letter transfers under the badge. Pressing her ear against the wood, she listened for any sound from within. Unlikely though it seemed, Freddie could be in there, lying low and hiding behind his Raven persona. She listened for a long minute, heard nothing, then, with half a shrug at Ruby, she opened the door and stepped inside.

The bed lay unmade. The wardrobes had been flung open and clothes scattered across the carpet. The window opposite had been smashed.

A dirty boot had scuffed the windowsill, leaving a smudged print.

"Looks like someone made a run for it," Ruby said.

"I think they were coming in." Willow gazed around her feet, at the shards of glass in the worn pile of the blue carpet, at the papers scattered and tossed around the room. There were more boot prints on the bedclothes and half a brick against the wall.

"Who would break in here?" Ruby said. "Doesn't look like there's much to steal."

"Raven?" Willow said, turning to Ruby.

"What makes you say that?"

Willow nodded to the boot prints. "I can't be sure, but those prints look pretty similar to the ones on Ellie's door. And in my room at the Spars."

"Not exactly conclusive."

Willow shrugged. "We know this Raven was after Ellie."

"Why was he after Freddie though?"

"Maybe he weren't. Maybe Raven is Freddie and he came back to get something and didn't want to use the front door. Or maybe this Raven thought Freddie had what Ellie had taken."

Ruby peered around at the glass and the dirty bedsheets and the broken window. "You think Lady Gaga downstairs knows about this?" she said.

"Doubt it." Willow turned and headed for the door. "Come on, let's get out of here. Looks like Freddie's been gone a long time."

They trudged back downstairs, Ruby closing the door behind them. Willow walked into the lounge.

"Hello, love! Back so soon? Freddie will be here in a minute," Mrs Hunt said, rising as they entered.

"He's not here," Willow said. "We just went to see if he was in his room."

"He's not there?" Her face creased and her lip trembled. She looked ready to collapse into tears.

"Do you know where he's gone?" Ruby said.

Mrs Hunt peered at Ruby, her brow creased. Then she beamed and palmed her forehead, shaking her head.

"I'm so silly," she chuckled. "I forgot. He said he was going to see Eve."

Ruby frowned. "Eve?"

"You know Eve! Zoe's sister. Such a lovely girl Zoe. I hope Freddie does the right thing by her. Such a lovely girl. He'll be back soon. Did you want to wait for him?"

Willow peered at Ruby, who gave a terse shake of the head.

"We'd better get going," Willow said.

"Well, if you're sure dear." Mrs Hunt bustled them to the door. They left with promises to pop back and see Freddie again soon, then turned and walked back to the Fiat.

"Well, she'd leapt across the border, hadn't she?" Ruby said, slumping back into the driver's seat.

Willow reached for the passenger door, then stopped and looked back to the house. A thought nagged at the back of her mind. She chewed her lip, but the thought or the idea or whatever it was had slipped away like the memory of a dream.

"You getting in?" Ruby called out.

Willow sighed and pulled the passenger door open. She slipped into the seat.

"Poor cow. I wonder if anyone's looking after her."

"Didn't look like it." Ruby started the engine and drove up the road a little way. "I'd hate to end up like that."

"You think we should call someone?" Willow said as Ruby backed into a drive to turn around. "Like who?"

"The social?"

"Can do," Ruby said. "Doubt they'll do anything though."

Ruby steered back onto the road and headed back towards St. Agnes.

"So where now?"

Willow shrugged. Freddie hadn't been home for a good long while. But she had no idea where he was, or whether he was Raven or not. And if he wasn't Raven, who'd broken into his room? And why? And if not Freddie, then who was it? And had they killed Ellie? Questions. Too many questions. No answers.

"In all honesty," Willow said, "I haven't got the faintest idea."

*

"Guess she won't be walking away this time."

The words echoed in Raven's mind. She became aware of the darkness. Of the cold stone under her cheeks. Of the sticky warmth on the back of her head.

Her eyes snapped open. Through the thin shafts of light, she could see the dirt and hay and litter on the flagstones. Cold agony throbbed through her skull. Her arm had landed beneath her. Her fingers tingled.

She groaned. Tried to roll onto her back. As her head touched the stone, a cold pain flared around her scalp. She felt sick. She rolled to her stomach. Crawled to all fours. Breathed deep. The air rattled in her throat. The pain lanced down her neck. She dug her nails into the flagstones and grit her teeth.

She made it to her knees without throwing up or passing out. A small victory. Gingerly, she touched the back of her head, but the lightest brush of her fingertips triggered searing agony and she yanked her hands away. She breathed again. A tear escaped the corner of her eye and trickled down her scars.

The words played over again.

"Guess she won't be walking away this time…"

Which meant there'd been a time before. A time when they'd tried to kill her and she had walked away. She had to know when. She had to know how.

She eased herself upright, every move sending shards of agony through her shoulders, her neck, her scalp. The world swirled and tilted around her. Her stomach clenched with nausea. She glanced at the bike. Then at the doorway.

It stood open now. The beam had been thrown to the floor and a wedge of pale light spilt in. At least she wouldn't have to try and lift the beam out. The keys to the bike lay in the slither of light from the door. The helmet had rolled away into the darkness. Not that it mattered. The pain in her head meant she couldn't put the helmet on anyway.

She staggered to the bag that lay on the floor. Crouched then paused as the world swirled and nausea threatened to overpower her. The feeling passed. She undid the zip on the bag, then the zip on her biker's jacket. She threw the jacket to one side. Dug out the trench coat. Dragged it on. Then she picked up the mask. Tied it delicately behind her head. The movement made the hut shift and shimmy around her. Once tied, she touched her fingers to the flagstones until the room stopped spinning. Then she eased herself upright.

Something metallic and flat pressed against her back. She reached around. Felt the hilt of the knife sticking out of the belt of her jeans. All she would need. She lurched to the keys, picked them up, then swayed towards the bike.

She was in no fit state to ride. But she didn't care. She wouldn't be in a fit state to do anything soon. Grabbing the handlebars, she dragged one leg over the seat and then slumped forward. Every movement felt like a war against her own body.

She fumbled the keys into the ignition, fired up the bike. As the vibrations throbbed through her body, her fingers squeezed the handlebars. She eased onto the throttle. The bike rolled towards the light.

She knew where they lived. Gabriel was the closer of the two. She'd head that way first. Wincing against the daylight as she emerged from the hut, she turned the bike away from Trevellas and gunned the engine. The bike roared up the valley, breaking the silence and sending a murder of crows screeching into the sky.

Twenty minutes later, she stopped outside the semi-detached hovel on the outskirts of Perranporth that Gabriel shared with his mother. She peered up at the dirty, ripped net curtains, the warped and chipped paintwork on the window frames, the boarded-up window in the door. Two strips of concrete made a drive in the front garden. Weeds, old newspapers, chip wrappers and crushed cans of red bull littered the pebble beds around the concrete. She killed the engine.

Heavy bass throbbed from the upstairs fanlight window that had been propped open.

Gabriel was in at least. If his mother was home...

Raven slipped the knife from her waistband and stepped off of the bike. She limped to the door, breathing hard against the pain.

She was in no mood for mercy.

GARY KRUSE

40

Gabriel screamed behind the gag, the noise muffled by the thick fabric as Raven twisted the blade in the gash on his shoulder. The blood oozed and spurted over her gloves.

She'd found him naked on his bed when she kicked the door in. Smashed out of his face on dope or crack or some shit. Barely reacted when she tied his hands and feet to the bed. A couple of well-placed slashes with a knife had soon woken him up. And when he saw who stood over him he jerked and spasmed like she'd wired his balls to the electrics.

His screams died. Spittle dripped from his mouth. She put the blade to his face.

"I'll ask you once more," Raven hissed. "Then I'll cut your balls off. When was the first time?"

"It was Goddard!" he screamed.

"I know who it was," she said. "I'm not stupid."

"I didn't want to! Please!"

She dug the blade tip into his scrotum. "I want to know when the first time was?"

He tried to buck and writhe away but the rope around his wrists and ankles dug in tighter, chafing against his scabby pale skin. "Please...I don't want to die! Please!"

"Tell me what you know then."

"He'll kill me!"

"He's not the one standing here with a knife," Raven said.

"I can't."

She sighed. "Okay. Maybe this'll persuade you."

His cock had shrivelled and was all but lost in the untidy mound of pubic hair. But she found it, grabbed it and put the blade to his balls.

"No!" He bucked. "No!"

"Tell me, or I'll make you a woman."

"You wouldn't."

She slashed his scrotum. Blood welled from the gash. Seeped down the crack of his thin, bony arse and pooled on the mattress. He screamed. She clamped her hand over his mouth.

"That was a warning," she whispered in his ear. "Next time, I cut you properly."

He whimpered, tears spilling from his eyes, bloody snot bubbling from his nose.

"I want to know when you first tried to kill me."

He gasped and whined. But didn't answer.

"Ok," she said, grabbing his cock again.

"The fire!" He cried out.

She froze. "The fire?"

"The one that killed your family. Goddard... he told us, me and Michael... he told us to do it." She shook her head. Felt dizzy. Sick. And not because of the agony in her skull.

"You're lying."

He shook his head. "I'm not! Please! Your sister... she

knew everything... she went to the cops. But the cop she went to... they told Goddard. He told us to torch your place and make sure no one got out. Michael... he shat himself when the pigs showed up. We ran."

Her body went numb. Her scars seemed to ache. To burn. She closed her eyes. Heard her sisters dying screams as she pleaded with their parents to wake. Heard her own screams as she tried to reach her. Saw the flames again, felt them licking at her clothes, her flesh, remembered the burning agony before oblivion. Tears spilt down her cheeks but it wasn't sadness that made them fall.

It was rage.

"Please," Gabriel jerked at the ropes, "I'm sorry, please... don't hurt me... I was just doing what he said... I-"

Raven slashed the blade across his throat.

He died gurgling and choking on his blood as she sat on the end of the bed, remembering...

Goddard. He'd come to her afterwards. Used her. Slept with her. Desired her when she thought she'd never be desirable again. Made her believe in him, in the righteous purpose of his task. He'd organised the headstone. Hid her existence behind the tragic fanfare of her death.

She would get her revenge, Goddard had said. Revenge against the dealers who had set the fire because her sister owed them drug money. Revenge against the monsters and the users and the peddlers of filth that had stolen her family and her face.

"Every one of them you kill," he'd whispered as she lay in his arms, in his bed, six months after the fire, "is an act of divine retribution. The world lets these bastards live. They profit on addiction. Thrive. We have to make them pay." She'd bought it. Believed it. Lived it.

And all the time he'd been the one behind it all. He'd ordered her sister's death. He'd ordered the fire that had ruined her life.

He'd created Raven.

She rose to her feet, staggered from the room, stumbled down the stairs. Put a hand against the wall to stop from falling. Each step down brought a spasm of pain. She winced. Gasped. At the foot of the stairs, she stepped over the body of Gabriel's mum, the blood pooling from the gash in her throat. Then she shambled out of the doorway into the cool pastel light of dusk. She felt nothing except the rage burning inside of her.

Goddard had made her a monster.

Now the monster would come for him.

*

Except she couldn't.

By the time she reached St. Agnes again, Raven could feel herself fading. She didn't have long left. The world was swirling. Spinning. And the pain in her head...

She closed her eyes against the agony. Leant over the handlebars. The bike was parked outside the pub in Churchtown. She'd had to stop or she would have crashed. She clenched her jaw against the crescendo of pain, her fingers trembling. She could feel blood or fluid trickling from her nose, her ears. Her heart fluttered, making her breathe quicker, harder, even though she couldn't suck enough air. She'd never make it to Goddard's. And if she did, she wouldn't have the strength to hurt him now. It was all she could do to hold onto the handlebars.

She peered up at the flat above the supermarket. Ruby's flat. Once Raven's squat until Pete's property venture.

Ruby was friends with Willow.

Willow could still succeed where Raven had failed.

She felt cold now. Deathly cold.

And tired. She wanted to sleep. But if she slept she'd die. She killed the engine. Swung her legs off and went to step towards the flat, but her legs collapsed and she slumped to her knees. She vomited. Blood and bile hit the tarmac. Each spasm of her gut sent shards of pain through her. A couple approached, took one look at her, then scurried past. A few cars slowed.

No-one stopped. No one was going to help her.

She staggered to her feet, swaying and stumbling across the street, the world fading, then pitching and slanting, then zooming back into focus. She heard voices, muffled like she was underwater and people were trying to talk to her.

She reached the door. Put her hands against the wood. Sucked in a lungful of air and closed her eyes.

She was dying.

The realisation made her eyes snap open, and panic swept through her. What if Goddard was right? What if there was an afterlife? What if there was a hell?

A sudden fear of an eternity of hellfire swept through her. She could feel her body trembling, could feel tears burning her cheeks.

She wanted her mum.

But her mum was dead. And Goddard had killed her.

She had to hold on. She had to speak to Willow.

But everything was fading. Her legs collapsed and she fell against the door. And before the darkness took her again, she felt hands under her arms.

*

Goddard let the white water nudge the back of the board and rode it in, lying flat on his chest, resting on his elbows, saltwater dripping from his beard. Porthtowan was emptying as people packed up and headed home for the evening. The late afternoon sun glimmered on the waves. He heard the fins scrape into the sand, felt the drag on the board and then rose to his knees. He stepped off, into ankle-deep water, and swept his hair back with one hand as he snatched up the board with the other. He trudged back up to his gear which he'd left piled up by the rocks, nodded to a couple of old-timers he'd once known well as they jogged towards the surf with boards under their arms, then threw his board down and crouched, staring at the icy blue peaks rising and rolling into the sand.

He felt at peace, connected with the earth, in tune with her vibrations, her endless murmurs, the never-ending cycles of life and the seasons and the day and the night, cycles that stretched back to infinity, and would stretch out forever until the worlds ending, long after he was dead and gone. He said a quiet prayer, murmured it below his breath. A prayer of thanks. Of rejoicing in life's majesty. And it's divine cruelty.

He reached into his bag, dug out his phone, and his peaceful mood evaporated.

Missed calls. A blitz of texts. All from Michael.

He swore, then dialled and put the phone to his ear. When it connected, he could tell Michael was in a car.

"This better not be trouble," Goddard said.

"She survived," Michael said.

"Say that again."

"Raven. She survived."

"You told me she was dead."

"Gabriel done her skull in with an iron bar. She went down. She didn't get up. We thought she was dead."

Goddard heard voices, young and excitable close by. He looked up at the rocks and saw kids scampering over them. Turning his back, he walked away towards the surf. "So, what's changed your mind?"

A pause. And then...

"Gabriel is dead," Michael said.

Goddard's guts went cold.

"She trussed him up like a Christmas turkey. Cut his balls. Cut his throat."

"When?"

"Must've been this afternoon. I dropped him home. Left. Then went back cos I'd left my shit in his room. Door was open. Mum was dead. And Gabriel..."

Goddard grasped his temples between the middle finger and thumb of his free hand, and sucked in a deep breath through his nose.

"Where are you now?"

"I'm out of here, boss. I ain't hanging around for that bitch to kill me."

"Brave of you..."

"Never said I was brave, boss." Michael's voice began to break up. "If I was you, I'd do the same. Get out before she comes for you."

"What makes you think she will?"

"What makes you think she won't?"

Goddard wanted to argue, protest, but he couldn't. Raven wasn't stupid. She'd know who'd set them on her. And she'd be coming for revenge.

"You useless pair of-"

"Take care of yourself, boss," Michael said. "Maybe I'll see you around sometime."

The call cut. Goddard stared down at the handset. He clenched it in his fingers. Grit his teeth. Anger rose like hot pressure inside him, swelling, boiling, filling his chest, distorting his thoughts.

He surged up and roared, loud and bestial.

Goddard looked up. Three terrified children stared down at him.

"What?!" he roared.

They screamed as one, and scampered away. Sense returned.

He had to move. And quick. She could be anywhere. He needed to get home. Take out his... insurance policy. Get ready for her.

Not bothering to change, he threw his bag over his shoulder, tucked his surfboard under one arm, gripped his thongs in his other, then loped back up the beach towards his car.

41

"Well, that was an experience," Ruby said.

The Fiat swept around the bend and up the road out of Porthtowan. The shadows beneath the tunnel of trees deepened. Willow didn't reply. She peered out of the passenger window, and saw nothing, trying instead to focus on whatever it was that was nagging at the back of her mind. Every time she thought she had it, it slipped out of focus.

"You okay?"

Willow turned to Ruby. "Sorry?"

"I said it was an experience back there. And not a good one."

"No." Willow turned back to the passenger window, frowning.

"Willow? You okay?"

"Something wasn't right back there," Willow said.

"Something? The whole thing wasn't right."

"Yeah, but there was something she said that didn't add up... it's bugging me..." Willow rubbed her forehead. "But I can't for the life of me think what it is."

"Babe, the woman was a jam spread short of a Victoria Sponge. Nothing she said added up."

Willow half-smiled. "It keeps popping in my head then going again."

The car jolted through a pothole. Willow felt her stomach drop. The wheels clattered against the edge. The car settled.

"So, where do you think Freddie is then?" Ruby said.

"I dread to think," Willow replied.

"You don't think he's just upped and left for London or Bristol or someplace, do you?"

"Maybe. Him and Zoe used to talk about heading for the bright lights one day."

"So, he could've just decided to go it alone."

"Could've. I just wonder where his sister is? There was no sign of her."

The car hissed along the tarmac, past fields and farmhouses. Starlings burst from the hedgerows. Flew ahead of the car then banked out of sight. They turned onto Penwinnick Road and headed for St. Agnes.

"So, what are you going to do now?" Ruby said.

"Don't know. Guess I can't do anything until Freddie or his sister show up."

"You could tell the police what you know? Call that D.I. Pierce woman. She seemed trustworthy."

"Too risky," Willow said. "If what Ellie said about the police is right…"

The hedgerows became houses as they approached the village centre. They passed the museum. The graveyard… Zoe dead.

Ellie dead.

Harrison dead.

Freddie gone.

And still no closer to uncovering who Raven was, who

was behind the conspiracy that had killed Steinberg. That had killed Ellie.

No leads. No path to follow now. After everything she'd done, she'd ended up at a dead end.

"I'm tired, Ruby." She leant her elbow on the door and massaged her temples. "So bloody tired. I feel like... all I'm doing is chasing shadows."

Ruby squeezed her knee. "You'll get through this babe. I promise."

Willow smiled at her. "Thanks."

She turned back to the road. Ruby drove along Churchtown as Willow's thoughts dwelled on Ellie, Freddie, Zoe, Harrison, Eve, Goddard...

"Shit!" Ruby hissed, skidding to a halt a dozen yards from her flat. "Who is that?"

Willow glanced at Ruby, then followed her gaze. A figure in a long leather trenchcoat leaned against the door to Ruby's flat, short, slight, with closely cropped blonde hair on one side of their head and on the other... Willow swallowed.

The skin on the other half of their head looked as if it had melted and reset. Like it was scarred.

By fire.

And beyond the figure, a bike. A bike she'd seen before. Outside Ellie's flat in Perranporth. And the figure... she knew her...

"Zoe," Willow said.

"Zoe?" Ruby's head snapped round "Your Zoe?"

Willow was already out of the car and running for Zoe. She was slumping down now, leaving red smears of blood on the paintwork. Air howled in Willow's ears as she ran. Her mouth was dry. She could feel her pulse throbbing in her throat. A car door slammed behind her.

"Willow!" Ruby cried out.

But Willow ignored her. How had Zoe survived? Everyone thought she was dead.

She grabbed Zoe under her arms, eased her into a sitting position against the door, then peered hard at her. And then she realised she was wrong.

It wasn't Zoe.

"You," she said.

The girl opened her eyes. Willow knew those eyes. She went to speak but she heard Ruby approaching and glanced back. Ruby stopped and crouched next to her.

"What the hell has happened to her?" Ruby said.

Willow shook her head.

"You're Raven. Aren't you?" she said, turning back to the girl.

Raven nodded.

"But…" Ruby said, "you said Freddie was Raven."

"I was wrong."

"So who is she?"

Willow glared at Raven.

"You stole her name didn't you?" she said. "After she died."

"Seemed... fitting," Raven said. Her voice, thin and weak as it was, was as familiar to Willow as her own. "I wasn't me anymore. I needed a new name."

"You always wanted to be like her," Willow said. "I remember that."

Raven coughed. "I'm nothing like her."

"Who is she?" Ruby said.

Willow glanced at her, but she had more pressing questions of her own.

"If you survived, how comes your name is on that gravestone?"

"He got my name carved into it as cover," Raven said. "Made everyone think I was dead. So I could do his dirty work for him."

Ruby moved to stand beside Willow.

"He turned me into a killer," Raven went on. "An executioner. Then he tried to kill me."

Raven screwed her eyes shut. Her face twisted. She clenched her teeth and let out a low groan. Willow peered hard at the skeleton pattern on the face mask.

"Who is she?" Ruby said.

"Eve," Willow said. "Eve Everard. Zoe's sister."

Raven opened her eyes. "No-one's called me that for years."

She reached up and slipped the mask down. Then she turned to face them. Willow winced.

Half her face looked as Willow had remembered it: bright eyes, soft cheeks, playful. But the other half, the half that had been burned in the fire that had killed Zoe, it had melted, the features blurred and warped, the skin pink and rippled, like badly set blancmange. Black blood bubbled from her nose and stained her mouth. Her skin looked grey, ashen.

"Hiya, Megan."

Willow shook her head. "I'm Willow now."

"Funny. Raven and Willow. Together again."

"You're not Raven," Willow said. "Not my Raven."

Ruby stepped back, her fingers to her lips, her eyes wide with shock.

"I'll call an ambulance." She reached for her phone, dialled and walked away.

"Too late for an ambulance," Eve said.

"You're hurt," Willow said.

Eve chuckled. "I'm dying."

Tears welled in Willow's eyes.

"Guess the bastard got me after all," Eve said.

"Who?" Willow said. "Who are you talking about."

"Ambulance is on its way," Ruby said, coming back. "And the police."

Willow nodded her thanks at Ruby, then turned back to Eve. "Who got you?" she said.

Eve peered at her, then at Ruby.

"You might wanna record this," Eve grunted. "Seeing as its probably..." she gasped for air, and a strained wheeze escaped her lips, "...gonna be my... last will and testament."

Ruby looked to Willow, who nodded. Ruby unlocked her phone and switched on the camera, then flicked to video mode and gave Willow a nod back. She was recording.

"Who got you?" Willow said. "What did they do?"

"I thought he'd saved me," she said. "When I woke from the coma, when I found out Zoe... and my family were dead... I had nothing to live for. He... took my rage... gave me purpose..."

"Who?" Willow said. "Who did this?"

Eve gazed at Willow, her jaw clenched against the pain. Then she looked straight at the camera.

"I... worked for him... helped unload drugs on the beach at Trevaunance, run them up into the Driftwood Spars through the old wreckers tunnel... Pete... the landlord... he's in on it all. The entrance is... behind a fireplace... he lets us in, closes it...up... then lets us out again. He gets a cut ... keeps his mouth shut.

"And through the dope and the coke and the heroin, we found things out... things we used to blackmail people in power to do the things he wanted... and if... they thought complying wasn't in their best interests, we... made sure to... set them right."

She gasped, and her body spasmed. She gripped Willow's wrists. Her face was pale, waxy, and her lips had started to turn blue.

"I... I killed for him..." Eve said, and for the first time, Willow felt fear flickering in her stomach. "When people got too close, when we couldn't shut them up any longer, he'd come to me... tell me who to go for... and I did it... every single time.

"I killed... Eric Steinberg..."

Willow felt Ruby's gaze flick towards her but she kept staring at Eve, hoping she wouldn't say what Willow feared she would.

"...Wesley Peacock..." she went on. "Alan MacCallister... Harrison Gould...Freddie Hunt..."

Willow felt her heart jolt at Harrison's name, Freddie's. She screwed her face up in disgust, wanted to stand up, walk away and leave the bitch to die. But she clung to every word Eve said now, waiting for her to say the one name she couldn't bear to hear.

"Is that all?" Willow said when Eve fell silent.

Eve shook her head.

"Maybe you shouldn't hear this," Ruby said, touching Willow's shoulder.

Willow jerked her hand away, gripped Eve's shoulders. Eve grimaced.

"Say it," Willow hissed.

"Do I..." Eve stared hard at her... "need to?"

Willow glared at her. "I need to hear you say it."

Eve closed her eyes and nodded. "I killed her too." She sucked in a breath. "I killed Ellie."

The world seemed to fall away. To spin and swirl and plunge into nothingness. The sun went black. The voices and the music from the pub seemed to fall silent. Time froze.

Eve had done it. Eve had killed Ellie.

"It was quick," Eve said. "She didn't suffer."

Willow grabbed her shoulders and hauled her up. Eve cried out.

"Why?" Willow hissed.

Eve coughed. Blood splattered over her lips.

"For the same reason he killed my sister," she said. "They figured out what he was, what he did."

"Bitch!" Willow let her go, stood and stepped back. Eve hit the door with a thud and cried out.

Blood stained Eve's tongue and her lips, dazzlingly red against the paling skin.

"They figured out what who did?" Ruby said.

Eve stared at her.

"Was it the same person that attacked you?" Eve nodded.

Willow frowned at Ruby. Why was she asking? Why did it matter? Eve had killed Ellie. That was all that mattered. Then she saw the camera, still on Eve, and Eve staring right back at it.

"Who is it?" Ruby said. "Who's behind this all?"

Eve coughed, doubling up and rolling to her side. She gasped and rolled to her back, her eyes wide.

"I'd forgotten how blue the sky is," she muttered.

"Who?!" Willow screamed.

Eve closed her eyes.

"Goddard," she whispered. "The Reverend Richard Goddard."

42

"Liar!" Spit flew from Willow's mouth and flicked over Eve's face. Eve chuckled and broke down into a racking cough.

"Why would...I lie? Not like...I've got much to gain."

"He saved me! He saved us both, me and Ellie!"

"He saved me too. Now... look at me."

She broke down into coughs that made her body spasm, fold in on itself. She gave a pained gasp and closed her eyes.

"He did this..." she muttered, her voice barely a whisper now. "He did this to me."

"I don't believe you," Willow said. "He wouldn't!"

"Nothing... I can do about th... that. I've... I've..." Her eyes rolled into her head.

"Eve?" Ruby said.

A long rattling breath escaped her lips even as the sirens screamed down Churchtown.

"Eve!" Willow grabbed her shoulders.

Her head lolled to the side, hiding her scars and for a second Willow could believe she was looking at Eve again, young and vibrant and jealous of Zoe but innocent and carefree still. Not Raven. Not the monster she'd become.

"Eve?" Willow leaned closer. She looked too still. Almost empty.

"Shit," Ruby said, stopping the recording.

"You believe her?" Willow tore her gaze from Eve's body lying against the door and met Ruby's gaze.

"Well, there's definitely a wreckers tunnel behind the pub. There's a porthole looking into it in the music room."

Willow blinked and took in what Ruby had said. It didn't make her feel any better.

"I meant about Goddard."

Ruby flicked her hair behind her neck and turned to her. "Do you?" she said.

Willow stared at Eve. She'd been lying about Goddard. She had to have been. He was a reverend. A good person. He'd saved Ellie. He wasn't the kingpin of a criminal network.

And yet...and yet...

He'd lied before, about helping Ellie, about sleeping with Ellie. And the look on his face when Willow had confronted him, when he'd called her a selfish...

She remembered the name he'd called her, the venom behind it, the way he almost spat it at her, and the look in his eyes as he said it, the darkness blazing within...

But hadn't he saved her too, pulled her back from the cliff edge, kept her from falling, taken her home, looked after her, and comforted her?

Fucked her.

Lied to her.

The memory came with a pain, almost physical, that made her want to scream and run away.

She screwed her eyes shut, flinched, breathed deep and opened her eyes. She peered back at Eve.

He'd saved Eve too... so she said, and the fake grave... that had been his idea too... according to her. Why, when she was dying, would she lie? She'd admitted killing so many people. If she lived, she'd be in prison for the rest of her days anyway. Why admit all that, then lie about Goddard?

But then, if he was the kingpin, he was the spider at the centre of a sordid web. He was a monster.

He'd killed Ellie.

And Willow had slept with him. Her stomach flipped and it took all her resolve to stop herself spewing.

An ambulance screamed to a halt behind them. Ruby turned and ran to the first paramedic as he lumbered out of the passenger door. A police car skidded to a halt behind them. Ruby was talking to the paramedic as he lugged his gear out of the back of the ambulance. Willow looked back to Eve.

She had to know if she was telling the truth. She had to know if Goddard was the monster Eve made him out to be. She had to ask him, face to face. She wanted to see his eyes when she asked him. She wanted him to look in her eyes and know, KNOW that she knew exactly what he'd done.

To her. To her family. To all the families his little plan had ruined. To Harrison, Freddie, Zoe... even to Eve...

But most of all to Ellie.

She took a step back. Shifted her bag on her shoulders, tightening it as much as the weakened seams allowed her to. She gave Eve's corpse one final glare.

Then she turned and ran.

And behind her, Ruby screamed her name.

*

Goddard switched the shower off, let the last of the water run down his forehead, through his hair, down his back. He ran his hands back over his scalp, let the water run away, then stepped out of the shower. As he grabbed the towel from the rail and began to dry himself he glanced at the clock on the window ledge.

An hour and a half until the vote. An hour and a half until he took back control. Unless Raven found him first. His gaze slipped to the insurance policy sitting next to the clock.

Sleek lines. The bathroom spotlights gleaming off of the chrome barrel. The moulded rubber grip. Clip loaded. Ready to fire.

It had been a present from his main contact in Morocco. A reward for the steady supply of business over the past few years. At first, Goddard had refused, but the contact had persuaded him.

"A man like you, you make enemies," he'd said.

"I'm not in the business of shooting people," Goddard had replied.

"Your enemies will be."

Now, with Raven on her way, Goddard felt grateful he had it.

He wrapped the towel around his waist. Went to the vanity cupboard. Opened the door. Took out the beard oil, rubbed it on his hands, worked it through his beard, then combed it through. He ran a brush through his hair, cleaned his teeth, sprayed deodorant under his arms and eau du toilette around his neck. Then he pissed, flushed, washed his hands, grabbed the pistol from the window ledge and returned to the bedroom.

He placed the pistol on the bed, unwrapped the towel. Pulled out his Calvin Klein pants, slipped into them, then tugged on his socks, his best pair of jeans and a crisp white Hugo Boss shirt. As he buttoned up the cuffs, he peered out of the bedroom window.

No sign of Raven.

Maybe Michael has been wrong. Maybe she hadn't done Gabriel and his mother. Maybe it was someone else altogether. Which, in its own way was worrying, because it meant there was another threat out there. But that was a problem for tomorrow. The more immediate problem was, where was she?

He checked his watch. Nearly time to go. One more glance along the road. Still no sign of Raven. He turned from the window, crossed to the bed and peered down at the pistol.

At the council chambers, he'd be safe. She wouldn't make her move there. But on the way, he'd be vulnerable. She could be anywhere. Her normal style was to lure the victim to a remote spot where she could finish them without witnesses. But he knew that and she knew that he knew that. His guess was she'd go for ambush on the way to or from the car. Or on the route. He picked up the gun and tucked it down the back of his belt. He felt ridiculous but then remembered who was coming for him and didn't care how he felt. He needed an edge. The gun was it.

He grabbed his coat from the back of the door, threw it over his shoulders, picked up the frayed and faded leather pouch that contained his papers then grabbed his car keys from the side. Then he clicked the bathroom light off and trudged down the stairs.

*

Willow reached the end of Goddard's path as the bathroom light clicked off. She felt like she'd been split in two. At once nauseous, dizzy, her muscles aching like she had the worst flu ever, and at the same time trembling, boiling, burning, her jaw clenching hard enough to crack her teeth. Her mind whirled.

Eve had been telling the truth. Goddard was a monster.

Eve was a liar. Goddard was nothing more than a cheating bastard.

The world around her grew dark. Shadows lengthened. The sky burned purple, red, gold, pink. The bird song sounded shriller, almost hysterical. Goddard's front door appeared to shrink to the size of a postage stamp as the path stretched to infinity. Then it shifted and the door filled her vision like the path wasn't there at all.

She blinked. Tried to breathe. But she couldn't get the air down her throat.

The front door opened.

The world stopped.

Goddard stared at her. She stared at him. She could see the bruise under his eye. It felt good.

His hand drifted around his back. He stepped forward.

"Well," he said, closing the door behind him. "I didn't expect to see you so soon."

He sauntered forwards, lithe and slender, wrapped in a leather coat and tight jeans, a tatty folder in one hand.

The smell of his aftershave reached her as he got close. Brought memories of their sex. She stepped back.

"You gonna speak, or are you just here to see your..." his hand drifted to the bruise, "… handiwork."

Willow gazed at the dark pits of his eyes. In the gloom, in the shadows of dusk, they seemed deeper, blacker, like the eyes of the Devil himself. And she could see the monster within him.

Then the moment passed because he got closer and now she could see the softness there, the compassion and he seemed like the Archangel Gabriel instead.

She swallowed and remembered why she was there.

"Eve's dead," she said.

She saw his gaze widen, the shock flick across his face, followed by relief and then it was gone and he looked neutral again.

"Who?" he said. "Raven."

"Again... who?"

"She said you had Ellie killed," Willow said.

Goddard shrugged. "Sorry. I don't know any Eve. Or Raven."

"You know Eve. You buried her sister. Zoe. My best friend."

His face remained closed. "You mean Zoe Everard?"

"You know damn well I mean Zoe Everard."

"But... her sister is dead too. Whoever you saw, it wasn't Eve."

"I know who I saw. And it was definitely Eve."

"You're mistaken."

"Like fuck am I? She was burned. In the fire that killed Zoe. She said you saved her. Gave her purpose. Made her an assassin. Your..." she scrambled to remember the words Eve had used.

"...executioner."

"Christ, someone's turning your crank aren't they?"

Willow stepped forward. She peered hard into his face. "Did you do it? Did you tell her to kill Ellie?"

"Megan..."

"It's Willow." Her voice was steel.

He shrugged. "Look, I don't have time for this nonsense." He moved to pass her. She stepped in front of him.

"Answer me."

"Get out of my way." He moved to pass her again. She blocked him off.

"Say it," she said. "Say you didn't do it."

He peered down at her. The smell of him was stirring memories of his lean, muscular body beneath her hands, but she cast them away, remembered the lie he'd told, about never sleeping with Ellie.

"You're crazy," he said. "It's the grief. You need to see a shrink."

Willow peered hard into his gaze, but he couldn't look at her. He turned his head. Looked down the street. Over her. Away from her.

Anywhere but in her eyes.

The nausea, the dizziness, the fear in her guts passed.

And all that was left was rage.

Because she knew the truth.

She grit her teeth. Shoved him in the chest.

"You bastard," she hissed.

He staggered back. Looked startled.

The rage boiled up from her gut, through her chest, up her throat like lava, rising and rising, unstoppable, impossible to hold back. She pushed him again. And the rage burst out in a scream.

"YOU MURDERING FUCKING BASTARD!"

His hand went behind his back. Then whipped out. She went to scream again. But something hard and heavy struck her temple and the world went black.

43

Willow fell at Goddard's feet like a dead weight. She hadn't made a sound. The mist of anger dissipated. He peered down at her. Beneath the tangle of red dreadlocks, he could see blood oozing from her temple. Cold nausea spread inside him at the thought that maybe he'd killed her. He looked around.

No movement in the other houses. No one stepping out of their front door. No curtains twitching. Yet. But he swore he could feel eyes on him nonetheless.

Still checking around him, he tucked the gun in the back of his jeans. Unlocked the car. Still, no one appeared. Were they calling the police even now?

He had minutes at most. The vote didn't matter now. Raven was dead. One problem solved. The vote would be won or lost without him. He felt confident. He had enough councillors in his pocket now. But he had a problem at his feet that needed dealing with. Quickly. Quietly. He had to get out of here. And take Willow with him.

Still glancing around, he crouched down beside her. She lay face down, bag hanging off of one shoulder. Eyes closed. Blood trickling down her face. He could see her pulse fluttering in her neck. He felt a surge of relief.

Still alive then. Which meant she'd be trouble if she woke. He stood, crossed to the boot and popped it open. Then he walked back towards her, looking around, alert for the slightest hint that someone would intervene. The street remained quiet in the thickening night.

The car sat in a pool of shadow between two streetlamps. He crouched again. Slipped one arm under her chest, one under her legs, and pulled her towards him. Cradling her like a new-born, he stood and staggered towards the boot. Her bag swung from one arm, the strap trapped between her body and his. He reached the car and eased her onto the rough carpet inside. Straightening, he gripped the boot handle, then peered down at her and paused

Her eyes were still shut, but her airway was clear, and he could see the pulse in her neck. She looked soft, pretty. It was almost a shame that she'd have to go the same way as her sister. Then again, he'd only had Ellie done as a last resort, when she twigged who was controlling Raven.

Now Willow had done the same.

And sealed her fate.

He went to close the boot again, then a thought came to him. Glancing around, still keeping a watch out for any last-minute surprises, he checked the pockets of her cardigan. Empty. Then he reached over her, checked inside her bag. For one minute he thought about tugging it off, throwing it away, but the strap was pinned beneath her and besides, finding her bag around here would lead to a lot of awkward questions. Better it went with her. He rummaged through the bag until his hands closed over her phone.

He dragged it out and examined the screen. There was a single message. From Ruby.

"Where r u???!!!"

With the phone in one hand, he slammed the boot shut with the other. Then he stepped onto the pavement. He placed the phone on the concrete, with the screen facing up. He lifted his foot over it. Then he stomped down hard.

The screen shattered. He stomped again and again, until the case broke, until the circuits disintegrated and the phone was beyond repair. Then he kicked the pieces down the nearby drain and looked around. If anyone saw what he'd done, if they cared enough to intervene, they didn't show themselves. Unchallenged, he untucked the gun, placed it in the compartment in the driver's door, then slipped in the driver's seat. He fired the ignition and drove away.

Once he'd gotten clear of his road, as he joined the road out of St Agnes, he used the voice controls to call Pete.

"Driftwood Spars. Good evening," Pete answered.

"It's me."

"Aye?"

"I need a hand."

"Doin' what?"

"Got a... problem that needs dealing with..."

"This to do with your pet being found dead in the village? There's police swarming all over the place up there. 'S all over the local news, Facebook."

Goddard glanced in the rear-view mirror and the rapidly fading lights of St. Agnes.

"You could say that."

"What do you need?"

"I need the tunnel prepped and a boat waiting."

"Now?"

"No, after closing. I'll be there just after midnight."

"Going somewhere?"

"Think I need a break. And I hear Morocco is lovely this time of year."

Goddard rang off. He tapped the wheel, shifting his backside in the seat. He scanned the road ahead and the road behind for any sign of flashing blue lights. Nothing. But he had to know what they knew.

He reached forward. Tapped on the radio.

"And back to our main story. Police tonight are refusing to confirm reports on social media that the body found in Churchtown, St. Agnes is that of Eve Everard. Eve was declared dead after the fire that killed her sister and family two years ago. We go live to the scene..."

White lights glared in the rear-view. Goddard glanced up from the dark road ahead. The headlights sped up behind him. He reached for the gearstick and held his breath, waiting for the flash of blue lights and the scream of sirens, ready to take flight. The lights filled the rear window. His foot squeezed on the gas, and the engine growled in response. At the last minute, the car swerved onto the other side of the road and bombed past, the passengers, a group of young men, hollered out of the windows as the tyres screeched, the souped-up engine roaring as the car vanished into the distance. He breathed out through tightly pursed lips.

"... All we do know…" the voice on the radio was female now, and a heavy wind roared into her microphone, "...is that police were called earlier this evening to reports of a body found with head injuries outside a flat in Churchtown. They are refusing to name the victim or to confirm whether this is linked to any other deaths. The investigating officer, Detective Chief Inspector Anthony Harry had this to say moments ago.

"'All we can confirm at this stage is the victim is a white female, of approximately 18-25 years of age. Identification is still taking place.

"'We would, however, like to speak to a Reverend Richard Goddard, as a matter of urgency as we believe..'"

He stabbed off the radio. Swore. Then swore again. When that didn't relieve his anger, he punched the top of the steering wheel. They had his name now. He had to get away. He looked at his watch. A few minutes past nine. Night on the way. He had to avoid the police for a little over three hours then he'd get away from here.

Before he went though, he had one more problem to solve.

And he knew just the place to solve it.

*

The ground lurched beneath her, and Willow's eyes snapped open. Except maybe they didn't because the world remained dark. Panic flickered. She gasped. Threw her hands out. Rolled onto her back, but her bag got in the way and she couldn't get all the way over. She tried to straighten her legs. Her feet hit something solid. Her hands pressed against a flexible plastic above her.

Now she heard noises; the roar of an engine, the hiss of tyres on tarmac. She could feel movement. Jolts and bumps. She could smell the dirty carpet beneath her, and oil and exhaust fumes. She tasted copper in her mouth and on her lips. She could see light now, thin pale flickers of it, close to her face. There, then gone, then there again.

She was in a car boot. Either that or a carriage to hell.

Maybe they were the same thing.

Her head throbbed. The skin above her left eye felt swollen, sticky and tight.

But she could remember everything: screaming at Goddard, him lashing out, and a hard metal object striking her temple.

Then oblivion.

How long ago had that been? Where the hell was she now? And would she ever see Ruby again?

She shifted. The zips on the bag dug into her shoulders. An idea blossomed. Her phone was in her bag. If she could reach it.

She tried to shift the strap off of her shoulder, but couldn't twist enough. It snagged on her elbow, and her arm wouldn't bend anymore. She rolled forward, pressed her nose against the carpet, and held her breath against the smell. She kept her arm close to her body and managed to get the strap halfway down her bicep. To get it off completely she needed to extend her arm, but she had no space.

She swore, then lay still, fighting back the panic, listening, trying to figure out where she was, who was driving, if there were others in the car.

But it was pointless. She couldn't even tell how much time had passed since she woke. She felt every bend, every dip in the road. With every pothole, her hip jabbed into the floor of the boot. She winced and gasped, and tried to keep from screaming. Although she could feel the fear spreading in her stomach, though the boot seemed to close in around her, and the darkness grew and loomed and swallowed her up, she knew that if she screamed she'd lose the one advantage she had left.

Surprise.

Maybe Goddard, or whoever was driving, thought she was dead. Or at least unconscious. They wouldn't be expecting her to be awake when they opened the boot. Of course, if they had no intention of opening the boot, if they intended to set fire to the car, or push it into the sea, then they wouldn't care if she was awake or not. But she couldn't worry about that. She just had to hope that they had other plans. And that, when her moment came, she'd have the strength to act.

The car hit another pothole. It seemed like a crater to Willow. The wheels slammed into the edge, and she felt her body thrown up and back down onto the carpet. She hissed to stop from crying out.

She screwed her eyes shut. Swore. Angry tears burned her cheeks. She'd been a fool. A stupid bloody fool. Why had she gone to him? Why hadn't she let the police deal with him?

Because she'd needed to face him.

Because she couldn't believe what he was. No. Not couldn't believe it. She didn't want to believe it.

She didn't want to believe she'd slept with the man who'd killed her sister. And although that truth was too terrible to bear, she'd had to face it. She'd had to face him.

She needed to look him in the eye, she needed to see it

for herself, see the truth in his gaze. Whether he admitted it or not.

She'd seen the truth.

In the way he couldn't look at her. The way he couldn't meet her gaze.

And she'd felt it too, in the way he'd struck her.

Would she end up like Ellie? A corpse in the sea? Would anyone ever know what had happened to her? Or to Ellie?

He'd killed them all. Ellie. Zoe. Freddie. Harrison. He'd turned Eve, a sweet but jealous young woman into a vicious killer. And Willow would die next. She didn't doubt that.

But crying wouldn't help.

All she could do was wait. And if she got the chance, she'd mark that bastard one more time before her end came.

The car rolled on. And Willow's thoughts lingered on Ruby.

*

The car rolled to a stop. Goddard killed the lights, then the engine.

Darkness fell around him. The last light of dusk glimmered on the distant horizon. He could hear music thudding from the hostel behind him. The light spilt across the tarmac, even though the building itself was all but hidden behind the curve in the road. No prying eyes here.

He let out a deep breath. Checked the time.

Half ten. Almost high tide.

Perfect.

The rocks would hide her wounds and water would destroy any trace of him ever touching her. And after, he'd leave the car. Trek the coastal path back to Aggie, slip into the Spars, along the tunnel, into the boat and away before anyone knew she was even dead. He grabbed the pistol from the compartment in the driver's door. Tucked it into the back of his jeans and reached for the latch. Then paused and listened hard.

No sound from the back of the car.

She was still out of it.

Or faking.

Either way, he'd be ready.

He unlocked the door and stepped outside.

*

Willow lay still, hardly breathing. The silence roared in her ears. The darkness swelled around her. She bit her lip. Waited. Her desperate heart beat hard. Maybe Goddard could hear it.

Her stomach had turned to water. She clenched her fists. Tried to rise in a crouch, but the boot was too small and she had no spring. She only had one shot.

Fake being out of it?

Or fight straight away?

She heard the door slam, muffled footsteps on the tarmac moving around the car. Tried to think. Weigh the options. Plan. But her brain felt fuzzy. She could hear every whisper of the breeze, every spark plug settling, the petrol sloshing to rest in the tank, the exhaust cooling, but she couldn't think.

The smell of oil grew stronger. The dry blood on her lips tasted more coppery. The air in her lungs seemed thick as soup.

But she couldn't think.

Fake?

Or fight?

One shot.

She had to get it right. Or she was dead.

The footsteps stopped beside the boot. Her heart stopped. Her breath stopped. The world went still.

Fake?

Or fight?

She heard the lock unlatch.

And decided.

44

Goddard scanned the darkness around him as he walked around the back of the car. He could hear the thud of music from the hostel around the curve in the road, the ocean howling as it dashed itself on the rocks at the bottom of the cliffs. No sign of anyone. No-one watching.

He pulled out the pistol and reached down for the boot latch.

If she was faking, if she was readying to jump out at him, then it would happen as he opened the boot. He stared at the pistol.

It looked dark as iron and felt hard and metallic in his hands. He could feel his pulse throbbing in his palm around the grip, in the tip of his finger as it rested on the trigger. It smelled of oil, thick and cloying.

Could he do it? If it came to it, could he pull that trigger? Could he put a bullet in her head?

Would he become like Raven? A killer, with the blood on his hands now. Not murder by proxy this time.

Truth was, he had to do it, because there was no one else who could.

And Willow had to die.

He'd pop that boot and if she blinked the wrong way then he'd shoot. Not his preferred method of course. Too much mess and no chance of hiding the evidence of what he'd done.

But she had to die. And if that was what it took...

He sucked in a breath. Grit his teeth. Clicked the latch.

The boot popped up. He jabbed the barrel forward, expecting her to explode up in a mass of dreadlocks and rage.

But she lay still. Not exactly as he'd laid her, but close enough to suggest she hadn't woken yet. The blood had congealed around the wound in her temple, and dried into a dark brown crust down the side of her face. Her eyes remained closed. He couldn't see her pulse or hear her breath. Maybe she'd died in the boot.

She didn't stink dead. He knew what dead smelt like. Not that it mattered. She'd stink dead soon enough. He tucked the pistol into the back of his jeans. Glanced around again, in case he was being watched. He saw no one.

They were alone.

He leaned forward, slipped his hands under her legs and shoulders, and started to lift.

*

Willow waited until she felt his arms tense. Then she burst up at him. "BASTARD!" she screamed.

She grabbed his head and plunged her thumbs into his eyes, nails first. He screamed. She thrust him back, and he staggered away.

She swung her legs to the ground. The world swayed

as she staggered against the car boot. Her bag slammed into her lower back. Goddard was on his knees, clutching his eyes. She shook her head. Blinked. Rage swept over her.

She swung a boot at his face.

It caught him hard across the jaw. Snapped his neck back. Sent him sprawling backwards onto the tarmac. He cried out. Crawled away.

She ran. Away from the hostel, and his stooge Sheila. Towards the darkness of the coastal path and the cliff tops. The world seemed to pitch and move, like a crazy fairground ride. Her feet didn't land where she thought they should. She stumbled. Scuffed her knees, her wrists on the gravel path. She scrabbled up and lurched forward.

"Stop!"

She ignored him. Kept pounding up the path. In the darkness, the ocean roared against the foot of the cliffs.

"STOP!"

She ran harder.

An explosion burst in the dark. A bullet hissed past her ear. She dived forward, landed hard, the bag thudding into her back. She glared over her shoulder. Goddard staggered towards her, blood streaming from his nose.

Gun in his hand. Barrel pointing right at her.

"You move, and I'll send you to your fucking sister."

The mention of Ellie sent a reckless rage corkscrewing through Willow's veins. She glared at him.

"You will anyway," she said.

But she didn't back away. Instead, she rose and stepped towards him, closing the gap between them.

"I mean it!" He cocked the trigger.

She yanked open the cardigan, and tugged down her dress to reveal her ribs above her heart. "Do it then!"

"Stay there."

She kept walking. "I'm right here. Shoot," she said.

He grit his teeth. Gripped the gun in both hands. She could see the barrel waving crazily as she got closer.

"You're little killer ain't here to do it this time." He stepped backwards.

"You wanna kill me, you'll have to do it yourself."

Her gaze was fixed on the end of the gun. At any second he could fire. But right then, she didn't care. If he shot her dead, maybe she'd get lucky, find there was an afterlife, and have the chance to say to Ellie all the things she'd never said in life. And if not...

Well, it didn't matter anyway.

"Do it!" she hissed.

"I'll shoot!"

She stepped forward. The hard steel of the barrel pressed into her skin.

"I mean it," he said, looking in her eyes now.

"Do it then," she said, glaring at him. "I'm making it easy. You can't miss."

"Close your eyes."

She shook her head. "You want to kill me, you look in my eyes."

"CLOSE THEM!"

"Shoot me."

"CLOSE YOUR FUCKING EYES!"

"SHOOT ME!"

Time stopped. Nothing existed except her and him. In the dark. Face to face. An arm's length between them. He couldn't miss. One jolt. One twitch. One wrong move and he'd put a hole in her chest and that would be it. His eyes looked like dark pits now. His jaw was a demonic mess of blood. No beauty there anymore.

Just a beast. A beast who had her life in his hands.

A tear trickled down her cheek. She thought of Ellie.

"Do it," she whispered.

He screwed his eyes shut. His finger tensed. Now she closed her eyes.

I'm coming for you Ellie, she thought. I'm coming.

She heard a high pitched squeal. It grew in volume, filled her senses, got louder, more drawn out until it was a bestial howl. The cold steel of the barrel tip vanished from her chest. The howl became a scream of anguish.

She opened her eyes. Goddard had dropped to his knees. Cast the gun aside. Tears streamed down his face.

"I... I... can't..."

He looked up at her.

Willow shook her head in disbelief. "Now you get a conscience."

"I never wanted Ellie to die. She didn't have to die. She just had to..."

"Let you get away with murder."

He looked to the ground.

"You may have fucked us both. But you don't know us at all," Willow said, staring down at the pathetic figure weeping before her. The cause of all chaos. All the death. "You're going down. Reverend."

"I'm s-" He went to speak.

"NO!" Willow jabbed a finger at him. "Don't you say you're sorry. Don't you fucking dare."

She turned and began to trudge away back down the path, towards the lights and the road that led to town.

"Megan," he said.

Willow stopped.

"She suffered." His voice drifted from the darkness. "Ellie. She suffered when she died."

Willow grit her teeth. Swallowed down the anger. He was goading her. Wanting her to react.

She wouldn't. She *wouldn't*.

"Fuck you," she said. "You're pathetic."

She walked away. To her left, the land plunged away to blackness. She could hear the ocean beating at the rocks. The distant thud of music. Her breath in the warm night air. And then a scream.

"BITCH!"

She spun.

Goddard ran for her. He dived forwards. Arms outstretched. Fingers like claws. Eyes wide. Teeth bared. Blood staining his beard.

He barrelled into her. Knocked her back. They tumbled together. Over and over. Across the grit and onto the grass. Towards the edge. He grabbed her. Wouldn't let go.

They plunged over the cliff edge. Oblivion roared beneath them.

She screamed.

Threw out a hand. Her nails dug into the rock. She felt them split and break, firing white agony through her fingers, her wrists.

Still, she clung on. His momentum carried him down. His hands scrabbled in vain to grab her hair, her neck, anything.

He caught the straps of her bag.

She felt it dig into her shoulders as he tugged it and her

down. Pain lanced up her fingers again.

Together, she and Goddard swung above the roaring ocean, the rocks digging into her knees, her skin, her arms. She could feel the rock she held slipping.

She reached up with her free hand and grabbed another rock. Larger, more secure.

"Hang on!" she screamed.

Then she felt him. Trying to clamber up her. Trying to push her down.

"No!"

Her fingers slipped. She squirrelled down the cliff edge. Scrabbled for hold. Found it in a deep fissure in the granite. Her arm locked straight. Forearm, biceps, triceps straining. Her shoulders burning. She swung one-handed over the sea.

She felt Goddard slip. Fall. He snatched for the bag again. Grabbed one strap. It tugged her shoulders. His weight dragged her back.

The weakened seams of the strap began to tear and pop.

Like a zip coming undone.

The bag jolted loose.

The weight vanished from her back.

She looked down.

The bag, straps flailing, tumbled into the dark.

And Goddard tumbled with it.

Silent at first.

And then with a blood-curdling scream. Filling the night. His body smashed into the rocks. His scream cut off. The swell crashed down on him.

Then he was gone.

Hanging in the dark by her split and bleeding

fingernails, she peered at the spot where he'd vanished. "For Ellie," she whispered. "For Ellie."

45

The wake had begun to break up. Willow's relatives drifted away back to their homes, their lives, their futures. Empty beer bottles and half-drunk flutes of wine littered the dining table, the windowsill, the gleaming white island unit in the centre of the kitchen. Beyond the glass sliding door, a striped lawn stretched away to the brown river, where a sleek white motor cruiser drifted past, the guy at the wheel glancing at the black-clad mourners dotted around the garden. Uneaten food sat on greasy paper plates laid out on the glass patio table as overhead the late July sun burned white in a clear blue sky.

Inside, Willow stood staring out of the window, her back to the room. She wore a high collared black dress and both halves of the 'Sisters' pendant. She'd tied her dreadlocks behind her neck and sipped the beer in her hand, tasting nothing.

Two weeks passed since Goddard had plunged into the Atlantic. His body had never been recovered. Pete and his sons had been arrested, Ruby had been promoted to Acting Bar Manager, and the Devon and Cornwall Police had arrested many high profile members on the County

Council, the Police Force and in the media.

Sheila at the hostel had been amongst the arrests and had filled in the blanks in the puzzle of Ellie's last days; how Goddard had told Ellie to go back to the hostel, how he'd spent several weeks popping in to see her, and then how, on the night of the 29th, he'd told her she had to move on and someone would pick her up.

That someone had been Raven.

After Goddard's plunge into the water, Willow had spent the night in hospital, under observation for concussion.

When she was released the next day, it was Ruby who picked her up.

In the weeks since the bruise on her forehead from where Goddard had hit her with the gun had faded to little more than a yellowish blemish, and her split nails had almost grown out. The physical pain had all but gone.

Maybe now, after Ellie's funeral, the emotional pain would start to heal too.

In the garden, she saw her father talking to a stranger. He kept stealing glances towards her mother, playing the graceful hostess in a sleek black dress, adorned with neat silver jewellery and smiling and chatting and gliding around the garden like it was a society dinner party and not the funeral of her daughter. Anger flickered in Willow's stomach. She swallowed the last of her beer, crushed the can and threw it at the bin. It hit the edge, bounced away and clattered across the floor.

"Something wrong?"

Willow turned as Ruby strode back in, her heels clicking on the glossy white tiles, dressed in a black trouser suit, white shirt and black tie. She had dark Wayfarers tucked into her bob of sandy blonde hair, and the faintest smudge of pink lipstick on her mouth. As she approached Willow, she tucked her phone into her back pocket.

"You wouldn't think it's Ellie's wake, the way my mother's carrying on," Willow said.

"Don't let her bother you." Ruby squeezed her wrist and kissed her forehead.

Willow closed her eyes, relishing the warmth of Ruby's lips, the floral smell of her perfume and the faint tang of clean sweat underneath. Ruby pulled away. Willow peered at her.

"So, did you do it?" she said.

Ruby nodded.

"You spoke to your mother?" "Yeah," Ruby replied.

"And?"

"She wants me to meet them. At home. This evening."

"And what did you say?"

Ruby shrugged. She hooked her thumb over the back pocket of her trousers. "I said I'd let her know."

"Tell her yes," Willow said.

"I don't know." Ruby crossed to one of the stools by the island unit. It had metal legs and a black leather seat. She slipped onto the seat and knitted her fingers in her lap.

"What have you got to lose?"

"It just seems a bit quick. I'm not sure I'm ready."

"Why not?"

"I just don't know if I can be in the same room with them," Ruby said. "It's been so long."

"You'll have to do it sometime."

"Does it have to be today?"

"If not now, when?"

"It'll take a good few hours to get to Bristol from here," Ruby said. "I don't know if I can get there in time."

"Don't make the same mistake I did, Ruby," Willow said, reaching out and squeezing her shoulder. "You've got a chance to start again. I never did."

Ruby glanced at Willow then peered out towards the garden.

"You won't have to go alone," Willow said, "I'll come with you."

"You don't want to stay here?"

Willow glared at her parents, now standing hand in hand, her mother's head resting on her father's shoulder, like the past few weeks, the last six years, the decade or more since they'd split had never happened. She shook her head.

"There's nothing here for me."

Ruby squeezed her hand. "Thank you."

"What for?"

"Making me call home."

She kissed Willow. Her lips tasted soft, warm and tacky with lipstick.

"Come on," Willow said, jerking her head towards the kitchen door. "Let's get you to your parents."

They left the kitchen and Ruby had opened the front door when Willow heard a voice behind her.

"Running again?"

She looked back. Her father stood inside the patio doors, his face ruddy from the sun, or the amount of alcohol he'd knocked back.

"Going home actually," Willow said.

"Without saying goodbye?"

"You looked..." She flicked her gaze towards her mother, still holding court on the patio. "Busy."

She felt Ruby squeeze her hand.

"I'll go get the car," Ruby said.

Ruby's fingers slipped out of her grasp and Willow folded her arms as she faced her father.

"You never could face up to life could you, Megan?" he said.

"What do you want?" Willow said.

He licked his lips. Lowered his gaze. Lifted the toe of his black shoe as if to inspect it.

"I thought you'd be happy," he said.

Willow frowned. "About what?"

"Your mum and me. But you've not said a word to us."

Willow rolled her eyes. "Are you serious?"

"You always said you wanted this. Me and your mum back together. A family again." She snorted, and it became a bitter chuckle.

"It's a bit late for that."

She turned and pulled the door open. Ruby had pulled the Fiat up outside and was standing against the driver's door, her hands in her pockets.

"Wait!"

She sighed and glanced back.

"That night," he said, stepping towards her. "The night you ran."

"Is this going somewhere?"

"Please." He had a panicked look in his eye now. "Just... hear me out."

She sighed. Her hand slipped off the door handle. "Well?"

He came close to her. She could smell his aftershave. And the alcohol on his breath. He reached to touch her face, but she backed away.

"I... I'm sorry." He lowered his gaze. "I never meant to hit you. It just happened. And I've regretted it ever since."

He gripped her hand and squeezed.

"I am so sorry."

The anger bubbled inside her, and her gaze flicked across his face. A face she'd adored once. The face of a man who she thought strong, a father who would always look out for his daughters. Once, in the days and weeks and months after she ran, she'd wanted his apology.

Now though, she realised that sorry meant nothing. It would never make up for the nights spent terrified in the dark, hearing her parents fight, or waiting for Connie to storm in and start the beating. It would never change the fact that he'd chosen Connie over them and then chosen to run back to their mother while Ellie was missing.

It would never bring Ellie back.

"Yeah." She dragged her hand out of his. "You should be."

She strode out of the front door and down the steps. Her black dress sucked in the sun's heat and sweat prickled on her lower back.

"You can't run forever, Megan."

"Who's running?" she called back.

Ruby cocked an eyebrow. Willow smiled and winked. Ruby smiled back and slipped into the driver's seat as Willow walked around to the passenger side.

"Megan!" Her father ran out onto the step. "Come back here! Megan!"

"I told you." She glared at him over the top of the Fiat. "My name is Willow." She slipped into the passenger seat and shut the door.

"So are you?" Ruby said.

"Am I what?" Willow reached up and untied her dreadlocks.

"Running?"

Willow stared forward, went to speak then stopped as a needle of cold pain lanced behind her eyes. She scanned around.

On the road outside, a raven pecked at the mangled mess of a dead animal. And behind it, in the trees…

Maybe it was a trick of the sunlight.

She only saw it for a second.

It made her heart swell, brought tears to her eyes anyway.

And for the rest of her life, she was sure it was them.

Freddie. Harrison. Zoe.

Ellie.

Standing together.

Watching her walk away.

Then a warm breeze kicked up and the moment passed. The needle of cold pain vanished. The raven cawed and took flight.

Her sister and friends were gone.

She had nothing to stay here for now.

"Maybe." She reached out and squeezed Ruby's leg. "But only if you're running with me."

"Sounds like a plan," Ruby said, grinning.

She put the car into first and floored the accelerator. The car lurched forward, spitting out gravel and dust from the rear wheels, growled through the open gate and onto the road.

Her mother's house receded behind them. Willow never looked back.

THE END

Read on for bonus content including 3 deleted scenes.

Acknowledgements

Badlands started life as a note on my phone on 28th August 2017. The first edition was published on the 21st January 2022. Following the closure of the original publisher, the book was republished on 7th August 2024, before falling out of print again in December 2024.

So here we are, the third version.

If this was you're first time visiting the Badlands, I hope you enjoyed the story. If you're a returning reader, you may have noticed a few little changes throughout the text. Nothing major, but I've just tidied things up and added a few extra details.

Plus, given that this is the third edition, it felt right to do an extended edition, with some bonus materials, including a few deleted scenes that flesh out the back story of one of the minor characters, Detective Inspector Robyn Pierce. Originally, Pierce played a much larger role in the story, but her back story was cut for pacing. But, it's still canon, so I hope you enjoy this foray into what might have been. And what yet may be…

I said this in the first edition and it's equally true now, but it's been a long road to get here, and it couldn't have happened without the support, help and advice of a whole raft of people.

Firstly, thanks to Laurence and Stephanie at darkstroke for taking a chance on Badlands in the first place. You started me off on this wonderfully wild journey and I'm forever grateful, not only for the opportunity you gave me, but also for everything I've learned in the years since.

Thanks also to the wonderful community of former darkstroke authors who welcomed me with open arms and continue to support me on social media. You're all sorts of awesome and I'm humbled to find myself amongst such a talented bunch of authors. Whilst darkstroke may be gone, the darkstroke family lives on.

To my Mum, Denise, Glenn, Harriet and Felicity, thanks for your support and also thanks to all my wife's family for the fun and madness. I'd name you all but I'm on a word limit here!

To my wife Nicole, and my sons Ewan and Alex and my baby daughter Jaida, I love you all. This is for you.

Finally, to you dear Reader, thanks so much for taking the time to read Badlands. Whatever your thoughts on the story, please don't forget to leave a review once you've finished. They really are the lifeblood of indie-publishing. And if you want to know more about my other books and upcoming releases, check out my website, https://garykruse.com/.

And while you're there, sign up to my mailing list to receive a Badlands bonus chapter.

DELETED SCENES

Detective Inspector Robyn Pierce, of the Devon and Cornwall Police Serious Crime Unit, glanced down at her watch. Three thirty in the morning. The first birdsong of the day trilled in the hedgerow beside her black Ford Focus. In the rearview mirror, dawn approached, turning the eastern horizon into a band of brilliant white-yellow.

"'You're sure they're in there?" Detective Sergeant James Tate said.

Pierce glanced at Tate, slouched in the passenger seat, clad in a dark hoody and dark jeans, his square jaw clenched, the fringe of his chestnut brown hair curling over his forehead.

"As sure as I can be," Robyn replied. She wore a leather coat over a black hoody which hid the body armour covering her chest and abdoment. "The informant is pretty reliable."

Stifling a yawn, she scratched an itch on her neck, her fingers working beneath her bob of glossy black hair. The smell of coffee drifted from the two empty coffee cups in the holders between the front seats.

"So far." Tate pursed his lips and nodded.

In the lap of her black jeans, her radio crackled to life. "Alpha team in position."

She glanced up, saw a van swing into a lay-by ahead. She lifted the radio to her lips. "Copy."

The plan was simple. A dawn raid. Two teams. The target was the house a hundred yards down the road, sitting on the crest of a shallow hill just off of the main road between Perranporth and St. Agnes. The house overlooked fields and farm land. Alpha team would go in through the front. Beta team the back. Pierce and Tate would follow Beta team in while D.S. Jane McClellan would follow Alpha team with a van of Uniform. Forensics would follow once the site was secure.

"How many, you reckon?" Tate said.

"At least three," Robyn said. "Could be up to five or six though, maybe more."

Goddard had been vague about that. He'd been vague about the day too. All he knew for certain was that two girls were going to be dispatched from Plaistow in East London in a hire car early one morning and would arrive at the house sometime in the evening, with a not insubstantial haul of coke and heroin in their boot. They'd be met by a handler there, a local contact with links to their gang bosses in London. And there may well be others too.

As a tip off it had been precise enough to get her interested but vague enough to be frustrating too. She'd had to put in a bit of leg work herself. A call to the Met had yielded interest from their end, but no support. She couldn't give names, and while they knew the County Lines gangs were operating across the capital, they had nothing specific for Plaistow, just a few leads that they were chasing. And some of those leads were a lot more promising than vague hints from a rural D.I.

So she'd put the house under surveillance and then squeezed a few local snouts for more info. Finally, after several days chasing ghosts, a breakthrough.

Not from a snout. An anonymous phone call in the

middle of the night from an unrecognised number to her personal mobile. Which struck her as strange until she heard what they were saying. The caller had been female. The message short and sweet.

"The gear is on the move," the caller had said.

"Sorry, what?" Pierce had said, groggy from being dragged from sleep.

"The girls are leaving Plaistow early tomorrow. Be at the safe house by that night. Overnight stay then they're turning around. They're in a black Mercedes A Class."

"Who is this?" Pierce stammered, but the call had cut off. When she tried to call the number back, she got a message saying it was out of service. Which was strange, but she had bigger fish to fry right then.

She'd sprung into action. Called D.C.I. Anthony Harry at home immediately. Requested warrants for a dawn raid the following morning. Plus two armed units and a van of plonks for crowd control if needed. Harry had rung off and called back an hour later. She had the green light.

As a final move, she talked a couple of guys from the traffic department who were angling for promotion to Serious Crime into staking out the road into Exeter Services to keep a look out for them. The second move was a gamble, because the chances of spotting anyone at Exeter were always remote considering the amount of traffic that poured in an out daily.

But the traffic grunts were desperate to move up in the force and their desire to impress had struck gold. Two girls had stopped at Exeter around mid-afternoon in a black Mercedes registered to a hire car firm in Seven Kings in the East End.

The car had left Exeter and become a baton in a game of car relay. The traffic guys, patrolling in an unmarked car from Serious Crime, had followed them out, tracked them all the way to Bodmin, when another unit took over. The second unit had followed them to Newquay, then passed them over to a third unit who tracked them to the house, and then left them for the surveillance team.

As of midnight, the surveillance team, stashed in an old barn set on a high ridge of land in a field across over the road, had reported the Merc was still there. Further, at least four suitcases had been unloaded from the boot and back seat by the girls and their handler. There may have been another one, possibly two guys inside, but surveillance had only caught brief glimpses of movement through the windows so couldn't be sure.

Pierce had led the briefing ten minutes later, had been in her car twenty minutes after that finished, persuaded the hippy in the garage at A30 junction to open up so they could get coffee (a cop I.D. worked better than any master key in her experience) and then driven into position.

She glanced down at her watch. Three forty am. Ten minutes to go. Beta team would drive into the fields at the last possible minute.

"This informant," Tate said.

Robyn turned to Tate.

"What about him?"

"Where does he get this intel?" he rubbed his nose with his finger. It made a fleshy, popping sound as he pushed it up and then it flopped back into place. "I mean, he's got a pretty good hit rate. If this comes off it's three for three."

"He's in with all the surf crews," she said. "And some of those guys have... bad contacts and big mouths, shall we say?"

The radio in Pierce's lap crackled again.

"Beta team, ETA 5 mins."

"Copy," She replied.

Silence fell in the car again. A light came on behind a frosted glass window on the upper floor of the house. The occupants were stirring, the girls getting ready to head out again.

"You trust him?" Tate said.

Robyn glanced at him again. "Of course. Why?"

"Cos we're about to storm a drug den and dealers aren't always afraid to shoot people bursting through their doors. He could be setting us up."

She gave him a tight smile. "It'll be fine." She stared at the house, tried to still the worm of fear squirming in her belly. The light went off. Darkness fell again. The first light of day had stretched halfway across the sky now, the stars retreating, the eastern horizon glowing pale pink and yellow as the sun raced towards them. She glanced at her watch. Two minutes to go. Robyn's heart quickened, punching at her ribs. Her stomach fluttered. She breathed deep, fingers tapping the arm rest. Thirty seconds to go. A black van, no lights, running lights disabled, raced up the road towards them. Beta team.

"Ready?" she said, unlatching the handle.

"No," Tate replied, unlocking his door.

She gave a grim smile. A gust of wind shook the car, the blowback from the van as it flashed past. It braked, then swung off of the road and into a gap in the hedges, then lurched to a stop.

"Beta team in position."

"This is Pierce. All units go. Go. Go." She leapt out of the car, sprinted towards the black van. It's door slid open and then heavily armed, black clad figures sprung out and over the fence, tracking behind a colleague with a heavy black battering ram. Up ahead, Alpha team's van screeched to life, ploughing down the road and skidding to a halt at the front. Doors swung open. McClellan leapt out behind a unit of Uniformed officers in riot gear and another half a dozen armed officers.

For a moment all was silent. Just birdsong and the breeze rustling the hedges.

Then the night exploded into noise. The ram struck. Metal striking wood. Deep concussive thuds. The front door went first. Wood splintered with a sharp crack, followed by a loud bang. Voices roared in the night.

"Armed Police! Stay where you are!"

The back door caved in. Beta team piled through.

"Armed Police! Raise you hands!"

Screams. Shouts. A gun shot from the front. Pierce threw herself flat against the wall, shoulders pressed against the rough bricks. Her heart jumped into her throat. She glanced at Tate. He cocked an eyebrow.

Heavy footsteps on the stairs. Lights being thrown on. Girls screaming.

"Get down! Down!"

"Hands behind your back."

"On your knees."

"Drop the weapon! Drop it! We'll shoot."

Another gun shot. Pierce flinched. Tate closed his eyes. Put his head against the brick. Silence. Then anguished cries. High pitched and almost inhuman.

The radio crackled to life.

"This is Alpha leader. All clear."

Seconds later. "Beta leader. All clear."

Pierce and Tate slipped inside, stepping over broken wood and shattered glass. McClellan piled in with the team of Uniform. Sturdy and squat, with close cropped white blonde hair and bags underneath eyes, she gave Pierce a nod.

In the hallway, five prisoners sat on their knees, hands on their heads, guarded by members of Alpha team. The uniformed officers started cuffing them while Tate and McClellan read their rights. Three men. The two girls. The Londoners, Pierce reckoned.

From upstairs came a high pitched wail. Members of Beta team lined the steps. She moved up. Found a sixth gang member, a white male in his mid fifties, laying on his back with his hands over his eyes, one knee raised, the other leg flat out and held by a member of Alpha team. He'd been shot in the thigh, the fabric of his grey joggers torn and blood stained.

Pierce lifted the radio to her lips, a sick feeling in her stomach. "Tate."

"Go ahead."

"Call an ambulance and the IPCC. Prisoner injured."

"Copy."

An investigation into her raid. Not ideal. But a semi-automatic lay underfoot of one of the members of Alpha team. She shared a few words with Alpha team. The guy had come out of a back room, pointing the semi at them. They'd followed procedure. Warned him. Fired only when he went to fire at them. The gun had jammed though. Lucky them.

Lucky her.

"You er... might want to check in there," Alpha one said, nodding to the bedroom behind him. Only his eyes were visible beneath the balaclava and the tactical helmet, but there was a glimmer in his eye and he gave her a wink.

She cocked an eyebrow, stepped inside.

The room was full of suitcases stuffed with bricks of white powder, syringes, condoms, cash... and guns; semi- automatics, pistols, sawn-offs. There were other weapons too; long katana blades, wickedly curved and serrated hunting knives and small flick knives. Her heart lifted.

This was big. Absolutely huge.

Career changing huge.

"Tate," she said into the radio. "I think we've just struck gold."

Eyes gritty, limbs heavy, and the beginnings of a headache gnawing at the back of her neck, all Robyn Pierce wanted was to crawl indoors and sleep for a few hours before she had to head back to start questioning the suspects all over again.

Stonewallers, the lot of them, exercising their right to silence, encouraged by their briefs and experienced enough to see through the bluffs and bluster that Pierce has tried to put on them.

But it didn't matter. The evidence spoke for itself... the haul of coke, the weapons, the hire car with traces of drugs in the back, the cache of mobile phones that had been found in the living room, the DNA everywhere in the house, the vehicles...

When all the forensics came back, when the phone records had been pulled, when the evidence gathered, it would be an open and shut case, notwithstanding the independent investigation into the discharge of police firearms. The victim would live. And Pierce felt sure the body cam evidence, along with statements from his colleagues, would exonerate the shooter. And besides, there was a bigger picture here.

There were links to London, a major County Lines supply network intercepted. The quantity of drugs and weapons seized told her that. And with a bit of luck, the trail would lead back to a big fish this time. Right now though, all that could wait. Her body ached for sleep after almost thirty hours awake. And with the suspects stonewalling, and the forensics still being gathered, Pierce had decided to cadge a lift back to home to Redruth off of a uniform patrol.

Her house sat at the low end of a terrace of old miners

cottages, a hodgepodge mix of unevenly sized bricks, some red, some black, some the size of letter box, others the size of a breezeblock. It had a slate roof, and the previous owner had replaced the original windows with double glazing and a bay window downstairs. She'd staggered up the path, weaving between the overgrown bushes of the small front garden, towards her front door, dragging her key from the pocket of her black leather jacket.

But as she went to put the key in, she noticed the door open a crack, and all the tiredness fell away.

Her pulse throbbed in her ears. Her mouth went dry as sand. She peered over her shoulder at the street around her. Opposite, the low white bungalows looked empty. No cars on the drive. No sign of life in the windows. She looked up the shallow incline, then down. The street looked deserted, the tarmac, the slate roofs wet in the mizzle. No strange cars. No sign of forced entry in the lock. Which meant whoever it was had a key.

She smiled.

Eased open the door, then turned the latch, eased the door into place, then let the latch fall silently back. She glanced up the stairs. She'd ripped out the carpet a year ago when she moved in, and left the wood exposed, just running a coat of varnish over it. Now she could see wet trainer prints leading up the steps.

She shrugged off her coat. Hung it on the rail. Slipped her handcuffs out of the pocket and crept upstairs. Soft singing, a male voice, drifted from the bathroom. She smiled. Unlatched the cuffs.

Sleep could wait.

The shower clunked off. Pierce slipped into the spare

room opposite the bathroom. A minute passed. Two. The bathroom latch clicked open. The door squealed as it swung back. She peered round the chipped white paintwork of the doorframe.

Tall and lean, he walked half naked back to her room, a towel wrapped around his waist.

In three steps she caught him. Grabbed his right arm. Yanked it up behind his back. He screamed. She grabbed his other arm, tugged it down to his backside. Used her weight to force him forward onto bed.

She snapped a cuff around his wrist, put her weight on his back.

"You're nicked," she whispered. Her breath moved the sandy curls around his ears. She saw him smile.

"I'll come quietly Officer," he said.

'Oh no.' She raised her weight from his back, rolled him over and dragged his hand up to the metal bars of the headboard. Hooked the cuffs through the bars, lashed the free one to his other wrist, then tossed the key onto the carpet. She tugged off his towel, then grabbed the hem of her black t-shirt, lifted it over her head and then reached back and unclasped her bra. She threw the bra and the t-shirt on the floor. Leant in close and kissed him hard on the mouth, then put her lips to his ear again. "I want you to scream."

Her hand snaked between his legs and rubbed him. She slid down his body, biting his nipples, kissing the soft curls of his chest, running her tongue down his lean hard abs.

As she slipped the tip of his cock into her mouth, the Reverend Richard Goddard closed his eyes and let out a low soft moan.

*

D.I. Robyn Pierce sat back from the screen and rubbed dry eyes with drier hands. The fluorescent lightbulb overhead buzzed and flickered. In the open plan office beyond, most of the lights were off, but Tate was still at his desk, his fingers rattling across the keys of his computer. She took a sip of lukewarm mud that was supposed to be coffee, winced and push it away. Then sighed and returned her attention to the screen.

The preliminary lab reports had confirmed that the gear seized was indeed cocaine, and was indeed worth well over a million pounds. Initial forensics had identified several different DNA profiles from the house. Swabs had been taken from the suspects. And the stash of weapons was worth a pretty penny too. The cash was building nicely, but the IPCC were sniffing, as were a few major news channels and the suspects in the cells had spent another day perfecting the art of silent stonewalling. A good day, but not the open and shut, quickly tied up case Pierce would've liked, but she couldn't do anything else that night. The case could wait until morning.

She reached out, switched off the PC, then grabbed her leather coat from the back of her chair. She stood, went to hit the lights. Then the phone rang on the desk.

She contemplated ignoring it, but Tate had glanced up, and her professional curiosity got the better of her. Plus Goddard wouldn't be at hers tonight and she didn't really fancy going back to a cold empty bed just yet.

"D.I. Pierce," she said into the handset.

"Good, you're still there." The voice on the other end

sounded deep and smooth.

Pierce cursed silently. Detective Chief Inspector Anthony Harry. Head of Serious Crime and her personal champion. He'd spotted her potential in uniform, promoted her to Detective Constable and then Detective Inspector.

"I was just leaving," she said, hoping he'd take the hint.

"Is Tate with you?" Harry said.

Pierce glanced up. Tate had swung back his chair and strolled towards her, his brows knitted, carrying his metal coffee mug in his hand. Unlike Pierce, Tate always made sure he had a steady supply of proper coffee.

"Yeah, why?"

"Coastguard have dragged a body out of the caves near Hanover Cove. They thought it was just a drowning at first glance. But when they got it up on the cliffs, they realised otherwise."

A sinking feeling settled in her stomach. She glanced at Tate and rolled her eyes. He sighed, returned to his desk and swung on his jacket.

"What did they find?"

"A substantial wound to the throat."

Pierce swore mentally.

"I know you've had a lot on with the drugs bust. Good job by the way."

"Thank you, sir."

"But McClellan and I are dealing with another body, possible homicide, that washed up near Newquay and I need you two there right away."

"We'll be thirty minutes." Pierce said, then hung up.

"Well?" Tate had returned and was leaning on the

doorframe to her office.

"Coastguard have dragged a body out the water near Hanover Cove. Looks like its throat was cut."

"Fuck," Tate said.

"Yeah."

"Well." He sighed and followed Pierce out. She shut off her office light and locked the door. "It wasn't like I had anything to go home to anyway."

"No," Pierce replied, silently cursing Goddard. "Me neither."

The journey took a bit longer than thirty minutes, and by the time Pierce and Tate had trudged up the path, forensics had a tent up around the body and had floodlights running. Blue lights from the half a dozen cars and vans dotted around the area flashed in the clear night sky. Pierce pulled up next to a police van and stepped out.

A uniformed sergeant scurried over.

"Body's over there, ma'am," he said, pointing to the forensic tent. "The coastguard and the poor sod who found her are in the van."

"Her?" Pierce glanced at the sergeant.

"Body's female ma'am."

Pierce nodded. "Okay, take statements from the coast guards and the guy who found her. Tate and I are going to look at the body, then we'll come and have a chat with them. Anyone else hanging around?"

"No-one."

Pierce nodded and the sergeant scurried off to round up a couple of Uniforms to take the statements, while she and Tate trudged over to the forensics vans and suited up. As they trudged back to the tent, Pierce tugged at the sleeves and mask.

"Do they put itching powder in these things?" She muttered.

"Only in yours." Tate flashed a grin.

The door to the tent opened and a petite figure in a white forensics suit and mask stepped out to greet them.

"Evening Robyn," Priya Agrawal said. At thirty two, Priya was the rising star of forensic pathology in the South West. She'd trained in London, worked with the Met for a year, then took a position with the Devon and Cornwall Police about a year ago, around the time Pierce was made D.I. "Thought I heard you grumbling."

"These suits are a bloody nightmare."

"They're not made for comfort," Priya said, stepping back and holding open the tent flap. "Care to join the party?"

Pierce and Tate ducked inside. The smell of decay punched the back of Pierce's throat. The first time she'd seen a body, she'd been too morbidly absorbed by the carnage in front of her to notice the smell. It was only later, when the initial shock had passed that it hit her. Some days it felt like it had never really gone since. She knelt down and peered at the body.

Clearly female, it had been laid out on a coastguard stretcher, arms strapped to its side, head supported in a brace. The skin looked pale in the floodlight, swollen and waxy. What was left of its clothing- a torn t-shirt and underwear- looked sodden and coated in sand.

"Coastguards left the body as they had transported it as soon as they saw the wound." Priya said, her voice partially muffled by her face mask. "I've got a few guys probing the cave where she was found, but I doubt there'll be much there. She's been in the water, and I'd guess she was carried there by the tide."

"That what made them call us?" Tate nodded to the blue-ish gaping wound in the throat. It almost looked like a bruise.

"Five inch gash across the throat," Priya said. "Can't tell you much more at the minute."

"But it's what killed her though?" Pierce said.

"Can't even tell you that for sure." Priya moved around the body to face them. "It could be, or it could be that she was alive still when she went in the water."

"And you're sure she went in the water? Couldn't have been killed down in the cave?'"

"Unlikely. The body seems quite swollen for one, which suggests some significant submersion. Plus, there's some significant loss of tissue suggesting that she's been on the menu for all manner of sea-life." She pointed to the fingers, the thighs, the tip of the nose, the ears. "And then there's this."

Priya pointed to the left leg of the corpse. Pierce peered closer. With the body in the stretcher she'd taken it for a tattoo at first, but now she saw it was a length of rope, looped around the ankle and trailing a foot long length that ended in a frayed edge.

"Looks like she was tied down, but something or someone has cut her loose."

Pierce swallowed and glanced at Tate, who looked grey and stood rubbing the back of his neck.

"What do we know about her?"

"She's about five five, probably between twenty and thirty five years old, blonde hair, slim, no visible distinguishing marks at this point. And that's about it. I'll know more when I get back to the lab. May get some more info from toxicology, and if I'm really lucky she's got a record and she's in the database so we may get an I.D. But otherwise, very little at this stage."

Pierce nodded. "Ok, let's go speak to our witnesses."

She rose and left the tent. Tate followed. The sea air tasted clean and fresh as Pierce crossed to the cliff edge and peered down into the swirling foam crashing into the cove below.

"Poor cow," Tate said.

'Yeah.' The water smashed into the rocks, a maelstrom of writhing foam that roiled and whirled between the granite stacks, then fell back only to swell up and crash into the jagged granite again.

"Come on," she said.

As they trudged towards the van, a heavy fear settled over her shoulders; the fear that the girl would never get the justice she deserved, that Pierce would fail her. She glanced back to the tent and clenched her jaw.

She'd do her best. That was all she could ever do.

It was just that sometimes, their best wasn't enough. And it was those cases that haunted her the most.

About the Author

Gary Kruse began writing after seeing The Craft in the cinema and wondering who would win in a supernatural royal rumble; the girls from The Craft or those terrors of Santa Carla, the Lost Boys.

All these years later, he's still writing about outsiders, broken and found families and coming to terms with who you are.

Living in Hornchurch, Essex with his wife and three children, Gary writes around his day job in membership. His short fiction has been published in print anthologies and on-line, and his story, Hope in the Dark, won the Writers' Forum magazine story competition for the November 2021 issue.

His dark suspense novel Badlands was inspired by the wild North Cornwall coast around St. Agnes.

Printed in Dunstable, United Kingdom